Shadow

Wolves of the Forest

Book 1

ISBN 978-1-63972-514-4

Contents

To my loving parents,
who never gave up on me or my writing and inspired so much in me.
I can never thank you enough.

Chapter One

Shadow squirmed, listening to her mother's heartbeat as she lay in the soft curve of her belly. Her brother, Kele, grunted as she moved, pushing a paw in her face as if telling her to stop. She growled, pushing his paw away and opening her eyes to the dimly lit cave. Sunlight shone through a small crack in the dirt roof, barely allowing her to see.

Looking around, she saw Heather lying on a pile of leaves. Miku and Breeze, her pups, were curled up under her. All three of them were sleeping. Heather was a beautiful wolf, with sleek, creamy brown fur and a white chest. Her pups, Miku and Breeze, were both males. Although they were two weeks older than Shadow and her brother, they still played together. Miku had dark, grayish-brown fur, and Breeze's was long and black.

Their den, the Newborns' den, was a large hole dug out from under a giant oak tree. It was supported on all sides by large rocks and tree roots, and the inside was dark and cozy. Shadow and Kele's mother, Storm, was sleeping on a pile of leaves and ferns for comfort. The Newborns' den fit all six of the wolves just fine now, but Storm thought that when the pups got bigger, it would be pretty crowded.

Shadow yawned and sat up to look at her brother. Kele was large for his age and had sand-colored fur and a long tail. He was curled up beside Storm, his flank rising and falling softly as he slept. Her mother was sleeping too, her smoky gray tail wrapped protectively around her pups. Shadow twitched an ear then stood to stretch, feeling her muscles relax as she did so. She had pitch black fur and was told that her eyes were a piercing blue, a color that she got from her mother. She was only about two months old, and Storm had finally just shown her and her brother the world beyond their den site. He and Shadow had been introduced to the rest of the pack a couple of weeks ago when they were given their names by Oak, their father, the Alpha. Oak was a large, muscular, tawny brown wolf with large, rounded ears and a battle scar running across his face. He was stern, yet kind and compassionate. He occasionally stopped by the Newborns' den to check on the pups and talk with Storm.

After peeking her head out of the den, Shadow blinked furiously to adjust her eyes to the light. Some of her packmates were sitting lazily around the clearing, their movements slow. Oak was lying atop the Alpha stone, his muscular body outlined against the pale blue sky. He was watching the pack, his eyes half-closed.

The Alpha stone was a large boulder that sat at the edge of the clearing. The Alphas of the pack, Oak and Storm, stood on the rock to assert their dominance. Usually, when Oak would speak to the whole of the pack, he stood on top of the stone. This helped his voice be heard above any other chatter and told the wolves that he was in charge and needed to speak.

Shadow also recognized Luna sitting in a patch of morning sunlight. Luna was the pack's Healer. She had beautiful black fur and yellowish-gray eyes. Once, Shadow stepped on a thorn while playing with Kele. Luna cared for her and was quite nice and very comforting.

Shadow noticed that some wolves were missing from the clearing and guessed that the pack's Beta had sent them out to hunt or check the territory for predators. After taking a few more deep breaths of fresh air, Shadow turned back into the den and trotted over to Kele to shake his shoulder with a paw.

"Wake up, sleepyhead!" she growled playfully, jumping on him as if he were a piece of prey. He let out a yelp of indignation, squirming away from her and burying his face in Storm's belly fur.

"Leave me alone," he growled, his voice muffled. Shadow rolled her eyes, then gripped his scruff and pulled him away from their mother. Kele whimpered in protest before craning his neck and nipping at her ear. She dodged his teeth and dragged him out of Storm's reach into the uninhabited area of the den, where the light from the entrance made it bright enough for them to see each other.

"You have to get up," Shadow growled before letting go of his scruff, dropping him, and grinning. He scrambled to his paws, facing her with his teeth bared.

"Leave me alone," he growled again, flattening his ears and sitting down, his eyes still bleary with sleep. Shadow huffed, nudging his flank playfully. He shrugged her off, turning his back to her with a growl. She sighed before trotting over to Storm, who was now awake.

"Good morning!" Shadow exclaimed, jumping on her mother's tail with a grin. Storm smiled slightly and watched her with sleepy eyes.

"Good morning," her mother replied, shaking Shadow off her tail. Shadow yelped as she fell, tumbling onto her back. She quickly stood and jumped on her mother's flank, clambering onto her spine. Storm stood up, causing Shadow to slide off. She fell to the ground with a *thud,* her paws flailing. She wagged her tail, standing and balancing on her hind paws, landing on her mother's tail again. Storm growled, shaking her off and trotting away. Shadow frowned and watched as her mother left the den. Kele glanced at Shadow before following their mother, his tail tip pointed up. Shadow waited for a few heartbeats before following them, sliding out of the den with a bright expression.

Shadow could hear birds chirping overhead and felt a soft breeze blow through her fur. She tilted her head, listening to the wind blow through the leaves. A little sunlight filtered through the oak and maple trees that loomed overhead, but most was hidden by their branches. Storm trotted over to Oak, who was still lying on the Alpha stone. Scout was talking with Mako in front of the Tracker's den, while Max and Amber spoke beside the entrance to the Beta's den. The Tracker's den was dug underneath the roots of a small maple, while the Beta's den was dug under an uprooted oak. Ferns hid the entrance to the den, making it private and cool inside.

Mako was an uncommonly large male with light gray fur and a battle-scarred pelt. Shadow was told the story of how Mako had been blinded in one eye during a battle with a lynx. His milky white eye was accompanied by a long scar and an underbite. Shadow was sometimes frightened by his appearance. She was also told that he is an outstanding Fighter and has won many of the pack's battles. Scout was a small male with large ears and short brown fur. As the Tracker of the pack, his job was to go with the Hunters and track down whatever they were trying to find. To acquire such a high rank, one must have a great nose, above-average hearing, and sharp eyesight. For that, Scout was highly respected.

Amber was the pack's beloved Beta. Her fur and eyes were both a lovely shade of amber, and she was known to be very caring and selfless. Max was the pack's Guard. His job was to watch over the pack while they slept. He had brown and black fur with warm amber eyes. He always sat beside the entrance of the clearing, where he was able to see everything. He was normally nocturnal and slept during the day in the Guard's den, which was dug underneath a birch tree.

Shadow looked out past the den site and into the deep forest beyond, where mostly maple, birch, and oak trees grew tall, shading the ground below. When Shadow had explored with her mother outside of their clearing, she had seen many things—different types of bugs, plants, bushes, trees, and animals. The thing that she had liked the most was a very large oak tree, not far from the wolves' den site. It had been somehow uprooted and fallen onto its side, where it now lay. Creatures of all kinds made their homes within its rotting wood. Shadow had liked it because she had been able to climb on top and see the world from a higher point of view. Being up there, she was able to see above the bushes and ferns that were taller than she was. She felt powerful and thought that was how Oak and Storm must feel when they were on top of the Alpha stone.

The wolves' dens were built around a large opening where no trees were growing. Storm explained once that their clearing had once held a small pond. She said that was why no trees were growing in it, and why the clearing was filled with sand and rocks instead of grass. She also told of how beavers dammed up the stream, and that was the reason there was no more water.

A thick wall of buckthorn surrounded the den site, making the clearing hard to see and easy to defend. Shadow looked beyond their clearing into the immense forest that surrounded their home. She breathed the cool, crisp air of the forest, and watched the oak branches sway above her head. She looked down from her surroundings, glancing playfully at Kele. He was watching her with a smile on his face. It looked as though he had forgotten any quarrel they had earlier.

Shadow broke the silence. "I bet you can't catch me!" she challenged, going down into a playful bow. She laughed as Kele accepted the challenge, lunging forward and cuffing her ears. Shadow flattened her ears gleefully, pulling away from his paw as he aimed another blow. She turned and bolted away from him, dodging around her packmates and sidestepping to throw her brother off course. She could hear his paws pounding the ground behind her and feel his warm breath blowing on her tail. She ran harder, listening with satisfaction as his paw steps died away. She came to a stop at the entrance of the Newborns' den, looking over her shoulder to see where her brother had disappeared to. He was sitting halfway across the clearing, his tongue lolling as he panted for breath. She glanced triumphantly at him. That was one of the pros of being smaller. She was faster and more agile. She grinned and trotted over to him, tail tipped to the sky. "Ha! I knew I'd win. I guess I'm just too fast for you," she joked, panting from her run around the clearing.

"Yeah right! I would have won if you didn't *cheat!* You got a head start!" he argued between breaths. Shadow rolled her eyes, cuffing him lightly over the ears.

"Stop being such a sore loser and just admit that I'm faster than you."

Shooting forward and closing his jaws around her snout, he smirked as he shoved her to the ground. She responded with a whimper, flattening her ears. She tried to pull away, shoving a paw in his face and pushing him off.

"Get off me! What are you doing?" she snarled. Kele had a satisfied look on his face as he pulled away.

"See? You may be fast, but I'm strong," he tittered, though Shadow was too mad to take any notice of him. Her fur spiked on her shoulders as she glared at him through narrowed eyes. "Stop acting like you're so much better than me! You're such a sore loser, why can't you just let *me* win for once?" she growled, pouting.

Kele growled. "Well, at least I'm not a wimp. Maybe you should grow up and learn that life isn't fair," Kele countered sharply.

Shadow winced, but her hurt was replaced by hostility. "Oh yeah? I'll show you who's a wimp!" she snarled, leaping at him and knocking him off his paws. He growled, quickly jumping up and lunging at her. They tussled for a while before Kele eventually gained the upper hand

and pinned her, hard, against the ground. Shadow growled but tucked her tail in between her legs. She knew that she had lost.

Kele eventually climbed off her, a smug expression on his face. He walked over to the Newborns' den and laid down to lick his paws, his fur disheveled from their scuffle. Shadow sat up, panting. Taking a few deep breaths, she fought down her anger and then went to sit alone under the shade of a clump of ferns. The bright morning sun had warmed her black pelt.

After sitting for a while, she noticed that most of the pack was either out hunting or marking the borders of their territory. She laid down and rested her head on her paws, heaving a sigh as she did so. Her tail patted the ground as she thought of what she would do.

I wish I could leave, she thought to herself, tilting her head skyward. She looked around and noticed that no wolf was watching her. With a small grin stretching across her face she slowly stood up and stalked backward out of the clearing, watching to make sure that no wolf saw her. She winced as the buckthorn branches rubbed her fur backward. *I'll just take a look around and be back before any wolf notices,* she thought, turning and trotting away from the voices of her packmates. Mist hung in the air and trailed on the ground, filling her nostrils with an earthy smell. Dew still clung to the leaves on the ground, soaking her paws as she walked around and gazed at her surroundings with astonishment.

All around her, what she saw was beautiful. The leaves on the oak and maple trees were shiny with dew, reflecting the light of the sun and lighting up what would normally be dark. The oak trees swayed as a breeze blew against their leafy tops, and she could hear the soothing calls of birds as they flew above her. The crunch of leaves and twigs under her paws made her smile, and the early morning air filled her lungs.

Suddenly feeling a surge of energy, she reared up and stretched her paws to the sky before slamming them to the ground and springing through the forest. Her tail streamed behind her as she bolted around the trees and ducked under branches. She ran through bramble bushes and the thorns slid past her fur. Growing tired quickly, she soon realized that her paws had led her to the oak tree that she had seen when she was out with her mother. With a squeak of joy, she bunched her muscles and pounced on the tree trunk, eyes shining. She crawled up on the large trunk and looked out at the still, quiet forest, her heart racing. She looked up and saw how the clouds swirled around above her head. She let out a short howl of happiness and was delighted when a group of birds were startled and took off to the sky.

Just as she was about to head back, a harsh male voice sounded from behind her. "What do you think you're doing?" the voice barked. Shadow whirled around; her joy instantly replaced with fear. Scout, his face creased into an angry frown, stood in front of her. "Shadow! What are you doing out here?" Scout growled. His ears were raised with surprise to see such a young pup away from her mother. Flanking him were Sparrow and Amber. Shadow guessed the three had been hunting and heard her howl. Shadow crouched down with submission.

"I, uh, was just… exploring," she tried to say, her paws trembling with fright.

"Get back to the den site," Scout commanded, raising his tail. Shadow whined, sliding off the trunk and landing on the ground with a *thud*. Head low and tail between her legs, she slowly began walking back to the den site. She heard Scout tell Sparrow and Amber to continue hunting while he escorted Shadow back home. When they got back to the clearing, Scout told Oak what happened.

"Shadow, why were you out in the forest? You know it's against the rules to leave the clearing without your mother," Oak growled.

Storm, her eyes betraying a mixture of anger and worry, stood beside him on the stone. Shadow shrugged, shuffling her paws anxiously. She *had* known that she would get in trouble if she was caught. *I should have been more careful,* she thought, angry at herself.

"I guess I just wanted to see what was out there," she muttered, her gaze locked on her paws.

"That's not allowed, and you know it. As punishment, you will be confined to the den site for a full day. If you leave, I will double your time. Do you understand?" Oak growled in a deep voice.

Shadow nodded, curling her tail between her legs at her father's angry stare. Her packmates were all surrounding her, looking stern yet sympathetic at the same time. With an annoyed movement of her ears, Storm trotted over to Shadow and herded her to the Newborns' den. Shadow looked up into her mother's angry eyes.

"I am *very* disappointed in you," Storm growled, slipping into the den without another word. Shadow looked at Kele, who had been following Storm. He gave her a half sympathetic, half annoyed look, then followed Storm into the darkness. Shadow whined with regret before following her brother.

"I'm sorry, Storm. I-" she was cut off as Storm raised her tail for silence.

"And I *also* heard that you and Kele were fighting earlier today and disrupted Luna's concentration! What was that about?" Storm demanded with a growl. Shadow shifted her paws uncomfortably, shooting a glance at Kele. She hadn't known that they had been disrupting the Healer's work.

"We were just playing," Kele piped up, his tail low. "Don't just blame it all on Shadow. *I* was the one who pinned her first, and *I* was the one who made her run off into the forest," Kele growled, shooting a sympathetic glance at Shadow. She gave him a look of gratitude, flattening her ears. Storm stood up and walked over to Kele, grabbing his scruff and dragging him over to Shadow. She then plopped him next to her before walking back over to her bed without a word. Storm could now face them both, her fur bushed on her scruff.

"I don't care if you started it, Kele, because I'm going to finish it. What if a fox found you? Or you got lost? What then, Shadow?" Storm accused. Shadow bowed her head in silence. "This is not acceptable. If I ever catch you sneaking away again, you'll be confined to this den for a week. Do you understand?" Storm growled. Shadow nodded sullenly, her eyes closed. Storm gave a huff of acknowledgment before beckoning the pups closer with a nod of her head. Shadow crept forward, head down, and curled up beside her mother. Kele sat down with a sigh.

"I don't want to sit in here and do nothing," he complained, and Storm sighed in annoyance.

"Well, that's just too bad. You have both misbehaved today, so you are going to sit in here and think about your actions. I'm going hunting with Oak. If I come back and Max tells me that you've left this den, you are going to be in big trouble," Storm spoke. She then stood and trotted over to the den entrance, slipping out of sight. Shadow exchanged bored glances with Kele. She looked hopefully over to where Heather and her pups had been earlier but sighed in frustration when she saw that all three of them were gone. They must have been playing outside, and Shadow hadn't noticed. Sighing, she rested her head on her paws, figuring the only thing to do now is sleep.

Chapter Two

"Kele, get off of me!" Shadow yelped in protest as her brother pinned her down. He gave her a smug grin as if saying, 'I won!'

It was mid-afternoon, and most of the pack was back from the morning hunt. The only wolves that hadn't yet returned were Heather, Sparrow, and Scout, who had been sent out to track an injured deer that had wandered away from its herd. Shadow and Kele had been playing together outside the Newborns' den all day. Max was keeping an eye on Miku and Breeze, who would be otherwise unwatched.

Shadow squirmed under Kele's grip, whining in annoyance. "Get off!" she growled again, nipping at his ear. She was finally able to grasp his scruff in her jaws and shook him until he let go.

"Hey, no fair!" he complained as he was thrown aside. Shadow gave him a cross glare, her tail held high.

"It is fair! You were pinning me down!" she protested, getting to her paws and shaking out her dust-covered pelt. Kele glared at her, his ears flattened to his head. He growled and bit down on her tail. Shadow yelped as she turned and clamped his scruff in her jaws, throwing him aside and forcing him to give up his grip. He quickly regained balance and crashed into her flank, sending them both tumbling into Storm.

"Sorry, Storm," Shadow apologized, scrambling to her paws and dipping her head apologetically.

"Kele!" Storm growled at him, fixing him with a stare. "Calm down a bit. You or your sister might get hurt," she scolded. Kele huffed and sat down beside Shadow. "*She* started it," he mumbled, staring down at his paws. Storm shook her head, her bushy tail brushing the ground.

"I'm not blind, I saw you provoking your sister." Storm tilted her head, giving him a dubious stare. Kele glanced guiltily up at Storm before turning to Shadow and growling softly at her. Opening her jaws in an enormous yawn, Storm stood up and stretched. "Okay, now tell your sister you're sorry," she ordered him, lying back down and curling her tail around her flank.

Kele scrunched up his nose before muttering, "Sorry," to Shadow, his fur bristling with irritation. With her ears flattened, Shadow shot him a glare.

Storm fixed them both with a weary look before asking, "Who's hungry?" Shadow instantly sat upright, eyes shining.

"Me," Kele said not very enthusiastically.

"I am!" Shadow added, wagging her tail.

"Alright." Storm nodded, standing and beginning to walk over to the prey pile. "I'll go get you some food. Now stay here and *no fighting,*" she growled, then turned and walked over to the pile without waiting for their answer. Kele stood and moodily walked over to a spot in the shade. She ignored him and looked around the clearing. She spotted Miku playing with Breeze a few feet away from her, their fur merging as they tumbled with each other, growling and snarling.

They suddenly began to tumble toward where Shadow was sitting, swiping at each other's faces and biting each other's tails. They didn't seem to notice Shadow until it was too late. Breeze gave Miku a kick that sent him flying into Shadow, knocking her off her feet.

"Ouch!" feeling a sharp pain shoot up her hind leg as Miku landed on top of it, Shadow yelped. He quickly got up, his fur ruffled and breath coming in quick gasps.

"Sorry Shadow! Are you okay?" Miku asked quickly, his eyes rounded with concern.

"Yeah, I'm fine," she replied with a thin smile, shaking her leg to get the feeling back into it. Miku looked unsure, tilting his head to the side to look at her leg.

"Are you sure? It looks like you got hurt," he said. She shook her head, standing up and putting her weight on her leg to show that it was fine.

"See? I'm okay." He nodded, relaxing a bit.

"That's good."

Shadow looked over Miku's shoulder at Breeze, watching as he slowly stalked forward. In the blink of an eye, Breeze was shoving Miku from behind, and Shadow narrowly avoided being crushed again. She watched as Miku pinned Breeze to the ground, then watched Breeze wriggle out of his clumsy grip. They wrestled in the dirt until Max, his fur bushed with alarm, trotted over to them.

"You two were supposed to stay by me," he growled, leaning over to Breeze and gripping him by his scruff. He dragged Breeze back over to where he had been sitting while Miku trailed behind. Shadow let out an amused snort before turning back to Kele, who was still facing away from her, pouting. She sat behind him, her belly rumbling as she waited calmly for Storm to return. When she looked over at the prey pile, she saw Storm talking with Oak. There was a big, plump rabbit at her feet. Finally, the two nudged each other and Storm picked up the rabbit before trotting over to Kele and Shadow and dropping it at their feet.

"Sorry, pups. That took longer than anticipated," she apologized, sighing with a small grin. "Your father had to talk to me," she explained, lying down next to Shadow and nudging her toward the rabbit. "Go ahead," she urged with a nod. Shadow lunged forward, biting down and tearing off a mouthful. She smiled as the delicious flavors reached her tongue and quickly filled her stomach. When she was done, she looked back at Storm, who was watching them from the entrance of the Newborns' den.

Shadow tilted her head before picking up the remains of the prey and dropping it in front of Storm, leaving it for her to finish. She then shook out her pelt, shooting a weary glance at Kele. To her surprise, he smiled at her.

"I'm full," he told her, lying down on his stomach and lolling out his tongue. She smiled, doing the same.

"Me too," she replied.

"I'm glad you're getting along again," Storm mused. Shadow observed she had begun to eat the rest of the rabbit. Shadow let out a bark, shoving Kele with a paw. He turned on her, bowling into her side and sending them both tumbling. Shadow yelped, attempting to shake him off, but Kele was bigger and stronger, making it hard to escape his grip.

She growled, nipping his ear and squirming onto her back, kicking his underbelly with her hind paws. He eventually got off, whimpering but baring his teeth playfully. Shadow scrambled to her paws and leaped at him, sending him flying into the dirt. She then growled in victory, shaking the dust from her pelt and licking her nose.

"Shadow, be nice to your brother," Storm spoke, though she sounded amused. Shadow smiled, sitting back on her haunches.

Suddenly, the scent of blood filled Shadow's nose. She looked to the entrance of the clearing and saw Sparrow, Heather, and Scout dragging a large doe through the bushes. The wolves around her gave howls and yips of excitement as the hunters dragged it to the center of the clearing, their eyes lit with triumph.

Shadow knew that Sparrow and Heather were the Hunters of the pack, which meant they were mostly responsible for gathering food.

Sparrow was the most skilled Hunter, and almost always brought back food for the pack. He was a big wolf with a mixture of light and dark brown fur. He was also very hard-working and respected. Oak trotted over to the three hunters, his eyes bright.

"It's a beautiful deer. Thank you," he said, and beckoned Storm with his tail. Storm left Shadow and Kele, going to eat beside her mate. Shadow, still full from eating the rabbit, sat and watched with the scent of blood in her nose. Kele went to sit behind Storm and wait his turn to eat, his tail patting the ground with excitement.

When the Alphas had their fill, Amber, the Beta, ate with Luna. After that, Kele, Miku, and Breeze ate alongside Scout, Heather, and Sparrow. Finally, Mako, Lynx, and Max finished the rest.

"Was it good?" Shadow asked Kele as he walked over to her. Kele nodded.

"It was even better than rabbit," he replied, and Shadow's eyes widened.

"Better than rabbit? Wow! I'll have to try it next time," Shadow said as Storm led them into the Newborns' den. Their mother sat down in her bed, licking the deer blood from her lips.

"I'm going hunting with your father tonight, so I need you to get to sleep," Storm said. Shadow frowned. "Sleep already? This day went by fast," she said with a sigh.

"But I wanted to play more!" Kele whined as he slumped down.

"Will you two stop complaining if I tell you a story?" Storm asked, rolling her eyes. They both nodded excitedly. Storm smiled, and as she did, Heather led Miku and Breeze into the den, looking tired from the long hunt. She led them over to their bed and curled up with them, looking at Storm. "I was just going to tell Shadow and Kele a story. Do you want to join us?" Storm asked Heather's pups, and they both perked up. Storm looked at Heather for approval, and the she-wolf nodded with gratitude, nudging them both forward with her nose.

"Yes!" Breeze exclaimed as they both scrambled to sit in front of Storm. Miku sat beside Shadow. His tail was wagging in excitement.

"Now listen well," Storm began. "Once long ago, before the humans walked the earth, there lived two wolves, Life and Death. They were brothers and shared the same world while keeping the earth in balance. Life was made of everything good in the world, such as happiness, love, friendship, and forgiveness. Death was the opposite. He was everything cruel in the world, things like hatred, fear, greed, and war. Life was given the job to create good things in our world, like animals, plants, lakes, and rivers. Death was given the job to create everything else, like fire, predators, and hatred that corrupts this earth."

Shadow shuddered, listening attentively as Storm continued. "So, they created us. Life gave us happiness and love, while Death gave us the desire for war and spite. When they finished creating us and they had told the animals what they had done, all animals favored Life over Death. They despised Death, casting him away and making Life their king. This caused Death to turn cold, despising Life and everything that he created. Death recruited wolves that were just as cold-hearted as he was to join his pack. He named them the Dark Pack. Life was then forced to create a pack, too, to try and keep the peace. His pack was named the Light Pack. It was made up of all of the most caring and selfless wolves in the world," Storm continued. "It is said that the two packs have been fighting ever since. Life fighting for peace and Death fighting for vengeance." Storm said with a serious look in her eyes. "Death captures the souls of those who are weak and corrupt and drags them down to where he lives in the underworld. Life gets the rest, bringing them up to live with him in the stars," Storm concluded, eyes shining.

Shadow widened her eyes, flattening her ears. "That sounds scary!" she exclaimed. Storm nodded, her eyes sad.

"Yes, it is scary, but that doesn't mean you need to be afraid. Everyone dies eventually, no matter how selfless or caring you are. All you can do is what you think is right and judging by the decisions you make during your time on this earth, either Life or Death will claim your soul," She replied, looking into Shadow's eyes. Shadow frowned, twitching an ear.

"What does Death look like?" Miku asked from beside her. Storm took a moment to think before replying,

"He is a pitch-black wolf with blood-red eyes and long silver claws. He has power over earth and fire, earning him a pair of fire wings and stone horns. Some wolves call him the devil because he rules the death place, the underworld. Life, however, is the opposite. He is a snow-white wolf with ice blue eyes and a long bushy tail. He rules over water and ice, earning him a pair of white feathered wings and horns of shattered ice. His symbol is a dove, while Death's symbol is a blood moon," Storm explained carefully. Imagining what the two brothers could have looked like, Shadow closed her eyes.

"And, it is told that each blood moon, Death is summoned to earth. Legend tells that he lurks through the darkness, dragging souls back to the death place with him, even if they aren't ready to be taken," Storm added dramatically. Shadow gasped, wondering when the next blood moon was. "That's all for tonight. It's time for you four to close your eyes and get some rest," Storm grunted, nudging Shadow and Kele into their bed. Shadow frowned, her ears still pinned to her head. "I don't think I'll be able to sleep tonight," Shadow whispered to Kele. Across the den, Miku and Breeze said their goodnights and went back over to Heather to sleep.

"Have you ever seen the Death Wolf?" Shadow asked her mother, burying her face in Storm's warm fur. Storm smiled softly, licking her forehead.

"No, and don't worry, you and I never will," She promised, wrapping her tail around Shadow's small figure. Shadow sighed in relief, curling up and resting her head on her paws. Her eyelids suddenly became heavy, so she let them drop. Kele curled up next to Shadow, his warm breath blowing on her face. She listened to her mother's steady heartbeat until she was eventually lulled to sleep.

Chapter Three

Shadow peeked her head out of the Newborns' den, scanning the clearing for her mother. It had been nearly a full month since she had snuck out of the clearing. At this point, Storm had begun to take Shadow and Kele farther out into the territory, allowing them to try and catch mice if they could find them. She also let them mark the territory, which was fun. She said that when they were made Learners they would need to know how to do the basic things, like how to stalk a mouse or mark a border.

Storm was now lying next to the Alpha stone, the sun shining on her smoky gray fur. Shadow narrowed her eyes and slid out of the den and into the shadows of the bushes surrounding the clearing. She stalked quietly along the side of the clearing until she locked eyes on Storm's unsuspecting tail. She then scrambled forward quietly until she was within jumping range of her mother's hind legs. She skidded to a stop and clumsily leaped onto her Storm's tail, gripping it in her teeth and batting at the fur with her paws.

"I've got you!" she exclaimed, her head raised in triumph.

"Ah!" Storm yelped, jumping up and pulling her tail away from Shadow. "You win! Great job. I didn't suspect a thing," she laughed, lying back down. Shadow yipped in triumph, grinning.

"I finally win! I got her tail first!" she snickered, her tail patting the dirt. Suddenly she was flung to the ground, her paws thrashing in the air. She yelped in surprise as Kele pinned her shoulders to the ground, his nose inches from her own.

"*You* lose, *I* win," he corrected, nipping her ear.

"Get off!" She growled, squirming until he moved away. He snickered. She curled her lip at him before flattening her ears and walking away. The sun shone brightly above the trees, lighting the clearing and warming her fur. She twitched an ear and tilted her head skyward, watching as a pair of birds fluttered around the trees.

"Shadow," a voice sounded abruptly behind her. She turned around to face Oak, who was sitting at the edge of the clearing watching her sternly. She trotted over to him, her ears quivering nervously.

"Yes, Oak?" she replied with a dip of her head. He dipped his head slightly in return then stood up and lifted his tail.

"I think you are ready to become a Learner," he said. Shadow widened her eyes with excitement, a smile creeping onto her face.

"Really?" she gasped, standing taller. He nodded, and she wagged her tail in delight. Oak dipped his head and trotted over to Storm, exchanging a few words with her and Kele. Kele looked with wide eyes at Shadow as Oak finished talking to them. Shadow trotted over to her brother, excitement making her paws shake.

"We're going to be Learners!" Shadow exclaimed happily, and Kele joined her with his excitement.

"I can't wait! I wonder who my Basic Trainer will be?" Kele spoke, looking around at the wolves in the clearing. Shadow watched as Oak strode over to Heather, Breeze, and Miku, who were all sitting together, sharing a squirrel. Oak spoke to them, and Breeze and Miku jumped up in excitement, their tails wagging uncontrollably. Shadow guessed they were all being made Learners together. Oak then trotted over to the Alpha stone and jumped on top of it, his eyes shining as he looked out at the wolves in front of him.

"Aspen pack," he called out. "Gather around me, for I have an announcement to make." Shadow smiled brightly, clearing her throat before trotting forward and sitting down beside the Newborns' den. Storm sat beside her, while Kele sat on Storm's other side, his tail wagging happily. Shadow shot him a smile, staring up at the Alpha stone as she waited for her packmates to gather. This didn't take long, since most of them were already in the clearing. Luna emerged from her den smelling of plants, while Max came closer to Oak so that he could hear better. Shadow wagged her tail happily, her paws tingling with excitement.

When every wolf was seated near the Alpha stone, Oak began to speak. "Today is a good day for all wolves. We have four young pups who need Trainers, and are on their way to becoming full members of our pack." Oak suddenly beckoned Shadow forward with his tail, his eyes warm and full of pride. Shadow stood and walked forward, struggling to keep calm as she approached the Alpha stone and stood in front of her father. Kele walked behind her, coming to stand beside her as Oak jumped down from the rock and stood in front of them.

"You have both reached the right age to become Learners," he said, his bushy tail swaying behind him, "and now, a Basic Trainer must be selected to teach you what you need to know about hunting and fighting. Shadow, you have grown big enough to endure the difficult training, so I expect you to try your hardest in becoming a complete member of our pack." Oak shifted his gaze from her eyes to a wolf sitting within the crowd. "Lynx, please step forward," he barked, twitching an ear. Shadow craned her neck, looking over her shoulder to see Lynx emerging from the crowd and striding forward toward Shadow. The beautiful she-wolf bowed her head to Oak, her brown and black spotted fur shining in the sunlight. Lynx was a skilled Fighter and a respected wolf of the pack. "Lynx, as Shadow's Basic Trainer, I trust that you will teach Shadow all you know about fighting and hunting," Oak said as he dipped his head, his eyes shining.

"Of course," Lynx replied, turning to Shadow and leaning forward to touch noses with her. Shadow quickly leaned forward, touching noses with her new Trainer and wagging her tail happily. When they finished, she stepped back into the crowd, sitting down next to Storm, her mind buzzing with anticipation to start learning.

She watched as Oak turned to Kele and spoke the words, "Kele, you have grown big enough to endure the difficult training, so I expect you to try your hardest in becoming a complete member of our pack." Kele dipped his head and Oak again turned to the crowd, this time his gaze resting on a wolf sitting behind Shadow. "Mako, please come forward," he barked, his tail waving slowly behind him. Shadow was surprised to hear Mako's name be called. She turned her head, again looking over her shoulder to see Mako pushing through the crowd, his expression unreadable. Shadow moved aside, letting him pass as he shouldered his way past her packmates. When he reached Oak, he bowed his head with respect, his scarred gray pelt glistening in the light. "Mako, I trust that you will teach Kele all you know about fighting and hunting." Oak dipped his head as he spoke, his facial expression calm.

"Of course," Mako replied, reluctantly turning to touch noses with Kele. They hesitantly touched noses before backing into the crowd, Kele coming to sit next to Shadow. Oak then beckoned Miku and Breeze forward with his tail. He repeated the same words for them, making Heather Breeze's Trainer and giving the job of training Miku to Sparrow. The pack broke up at the ending signal from Oak and spread out around the clearing. Shadow turned to Kele, noticing he looked agitated. "I'm sure you'll be fine," she whispered, shooting a glance at Mako. Kele shrugged her off, standing up and walking over to his new Trainer. Shadow's gaze followed him, a frown rested upon her face. Mako was a very strong wolf, and would probably make a good Trainer, but he was also feared by some of the wolves in the pack. He was known to be mean, and not very tolerant to pups. Shadow had once been scolded by him when she had accidentally run into him while playing with Kele. He had snarled at her, nearly biting her ear if Storm hadn't interfered, chasing him off. It had frightened Shadow badly, and she and Kele never liked him after that.

Shadow went to stand next to Lynx, looking up at her with a smile. "Hi!" Shadow yipped, wagging her tail in anticipation. Lynx looked down at her with a smile, her tail waving.

"Hello," Lynx replied, dipping her head slightly. "I suppose I should take you out for a tour of the territory," Lynx said, her amber eyes shining. Shadow jumped up in excitement, spinning around in circles happily.

"Great!" she exclaimed, looking up at Lynx with excitement in her eyes. Lynx smiled and began to trot lightly out of the den site. Shadow followed, her tail streaming behind her as she ran to catch up with her Trainer. She exited the clearing into the forest.

Oak trees towered above her head, their branches swaying in the wind. A sweet, sappy odor filled the air and Shadow recalled when she had snuck out of the clearing, and how she had climbed onto that oak log and was then caught by Scout. She snickered, also recalling how small she had been at the time. *I'm much bigger and smarter now!* she mused to herself, running to catch up with her Trainer.

"Today we will be checking the territory for predators and marking the borders," Lynx told her. "I will teach you about the different kinds of prey and about the resources we have within our land." Lynx trotted on with Shadow trotting beside her. Lynx led the way along a long game trail that ended at a stream. "This stream marks the border between Aspen Pack territory and Cedar pack territory," Lynx explained as she left her scent.

The Cedar pack was the Aspen pack's rival. The two had never gotten along, making them both wary of each other. Shadow watched the stream and listened to the calm sounds of the forest. Birds chirped overhead and the buzzing of bumblebees hummed in her ears as they gathered pollen from the flowers surrounding her. She heard a waterfall rumble in the distance, while the rustle of scuffling prey sounded from beneath the ferns. Soft sunlight shone from above the tips of the spruce trees while the wind rattled the branches of the birches and blew through the reeds and brambles, creating a soft whispering noise. Shadow looked up at the sky, her ears strained to hear even the slightest noise.

"Well, come on!" Lynx spoke in an amused tone, snapping Shadow back to reality. Shadow shook her head and trotted to catch up with a look of awe on her face. They continued along the stream, stopping occasionally to leave their scent and check to make sure that the borders hadn't been invaded.

"So, why would the Cedar pack want to come into our territory anyway? Storm told me that they used to try and steal our territory a lot," Shadow asked with a frown, trotting beside her Trainer. Lynx shook her head with a look of confusion on her face.

"I don't know," she confessed, "but I have a feeling that we might find out soon enough," she growled, looking down at Shadow with a mixture of foreboding and bewilderment. Shadow frowned slightly, looking down at her paws as they trotted along the bank of the stream.

"Do you think that they might be in trouble? I mean, if they are trying to steal our land, then they might be running out of food in their own territory," Shadow suggested, jumping nimbly over a fallen log.

Lynx was silent for a moment before answering. "That's a thought. I don't think we would go so far as to give them our prey though."

Shadow frowned, twitching her ears. "Why not? I think we have enough to share," she protested, looking up into Lynx´s eyes. Lynx's amber eyes looked bothered as if she didn't know what to say.

"Well, it's up to Oak," Lynx said after a moment of silence. "If he chooses to help them, then we will help them. But, otherwise, keep to yourself, and don't get any ideas." With that, Lynx huffed before picking up speed as an end to the conversation. Shadow followed with a frown.

Lynx left her scent on a birch tree as they passed, Shadow following close behind. "Make sure to leave your scent, Shadow," Lynx reminded her as they neared the territory line. Shadow marked a bush, then ran to catch up.

"How big is our territory?" Shadow asked, looking up at Lynx as she caught up again.

"The stream falls into a tunnel about half a day's trot up ahead. After that, the territory stretches into a field of tall brown grass. The line then curves until it gets to the lake, then stretches up to the river. We will follow the whole border line until we reach the den site," Lynx replied.

Shadow nodded, trying to imagine what that would look like. "Now, let's keep going. We have a *long* way to go," Lynx spoke as she trotted forward with Shadow following, her tail wagging slowly. They continued along the stream, listening to the wind rattle the branches above their heads.

"Here, Shadow. Come and look at this," Lynx directed from ahead. Shadow tilted her head to the side before joining Lynx and looking where her paw was placed on the ground. A small hole was dug into the dirt, tunneling for what looked to be a long way down. "This is what we call a squirrel hut. Ground squirrels burrow all over in this area," Lynx explained, pointing out several places where holes were dug. Shadow looked down into the hole, her eyes wide.

"Wow! They must be small to fit in that little hole," she commented, attempting to stick her paw inside.

"Yes, they *are* pretty small, but they still make a good meal and are easy to catch. So, if you ever want to catch some quick prey, come here. You'll surely catch something if the weather is right. They hibernate, though, which means that they sleep all through winter. Oh, look over there, next to that spruce tree," Lynx said indicating a small brown animal with dark stripes scurrying about the pine needles. "That's a ground squirrel." Shadow watched it, her fur bristling with excitement.

"How do you catch them?" she asked, looking up at her Trainer. Lynx turned and trotted away from the animal, twitching an ear signaling Shadow to follow.

"I'll teach you when it's time," Lynx replied. After watching the ground squirrel for a minute longer, Shadow followed, running to catch up.

Shadow and Lynx continued trotting along the bank of the stream. It wasn't long before Shadow spotted yet another small creature scurrying out from under some fallen leaves. "Lynx, look over there. What's that creature called?" Shadow asked, pointing with her snout at the small brown creature.

"Ah, that one is called a vole," Lynx mused, lowering her head as if to not be seen by the animal. "Voles usually live in the fields, but some are brave enough to come and try to survive in the forest. We don't usually prey on voles, considering their small size, and because they are so hard to catch. If food is scarce, they do make a good snack for a pup. If you ever want to try and catch one, they usually burrow near trees and around moist areas, like creeks or streams. They also live out in dense grassy areas, but it's not unusual to see one in the forest, too." Lynx watched as the vole scurried along the grass and disappeared under a pine tree. "Let's keep going," Lynx said as she jumped up and padded along the shore, leaping over another fallen oak tree. Shadow hurried after her, leaping over the log and catching up with a few quick strides.

Lynx and Shadow trotted along the trail until they came to the end of the stream. By now, the sun was at its highest point, and they had been trotting for a long time. The water tumbled down a small waterfall into a pond, creating a loud splashing sound that echoed along the edge of the cliffs surrounding the pond on three sides. "So, is this the corner of the territory?" Shadow asked. Lynx shook her head, trotted over to a stone ledge, and beckoned Shadow with her tail.

"No, not yet. Follow me," she said. Lynx jumped down the cliff side, moving quickly and gracefully from one stone ledge to the next. She stopped when she reached the bottom. She then backed to the edge of the pond, which was a few yards from the base of the rock wall. Shadow trotted over to the ledge and looked down shakily. It was nearly a thirty-foot drop.

Lynx looked expectantly up at Shadow, a hint of amusement in her eyes. "Well, what are you waiting for?" she asked as Shadow stood there, staring down with wide, nervous eyes. Shadow shook her head, as if clearing the fear from her mind, and gulped, building enough courage to jump down onto the first ledge. The rock felt smooth under her paw as she skidded to a halt, narrowly avoiding slipping off the side and falling to the rocks below. She glanced at the next ledge, bunching her muscles before hesitantly making the next jump. She landed with a grunt, one of her paws slipping on the wet stone. Shadow thought she might slide right off the edge, but she quickly regained her balance, her heart racing in her chest. Taking a deep breath, she leaped onto the next ledge. Thankfully, the stone was covered in roots, making it easier for her to get a good paw hold. Three more to go. She quickly went to the next one, then the next one, until she finally reached the sandy ground.

"Good job," Lynx praised before turning to the pond that was formed by the stream. Shadow twitched her tail and went to sit beside the she-wolf. Lynx bent down over the water and lapped up a few drops, her fur glistening as the spray from the waterfall clung to it. Shadow looked around the pond before bending over for a drink.

"I've always loved this place," Lynx said softly, her tail wrapping around her paws. Shadow nodded in agreement, looking at her reflection in the still pond. "Yes, it is beautiful," she agreed, looking into the crystal-clear water. There she saw small fish darting in and out from among the rocks, their scales flashing as they jerked from side to side. Ripples passed through the water as droplets escaped the waterfall and fell to the pond. Shadow again bent over and lapped up another drink.

"Well, we had better keep going," Lynx said as she stood and then walked around the edge of the pond to where the cliff face had fallen away. She leaped up the fallen rocks in three or four bounds and then disappeared into a thick stand of bushes at the top. Shadow jumped up after her, sticking out her tongue. She had to flatten her ears to squeeze through the bushes. On the other side, she opened her eyes to see an open field that stretched as far as she could see. The field was surrounded by a thick hedge of underbrush, and then a dense forest of oak and aspen trees. The only break in the hedge was a dirt path, almost like a hunting trail, but much wider. Shadow guessed that humans had made that path. Her mouth gaped open, and Lynx glanced at her, amused.

"Our territory stretches around this field and leads to the lake," Lynx said. "We come here to catch groundhogs, turkeys, skunks, gophers, and anything else we can find." Shadow followed Lynx along the edge of the field staying close to the forest and watching the crop stalks sway in the wind. They created a soft whispering sound as they rubbed together.

They trotted along the forest edge, keeping an ear out for any unwanted visitors. After half an hour of walking, Shadow stopped and sniffed the air, picking up a strange scent. "Lynx, what is that scent? It's not a squirrel or a vole. Is it a mouse? I remember eating one of those a while ago." Lynx trotted over to her, sniffing the ground in front of her.

"Yes, that's a mouse," Lynx confirmed with a nod. "We'll leave it for now. We need to keep moving." Shadow shrugged, wagged her tail, and followed Lynx as they continued trotting along the hedge.

They kept up the pace for another hour until they reached the lake. The water was surrounded by a sandy shore with reeds and cattails growing from the edges of the waterline. Shadow saw ducks swimming in the greenish water, and the nose-tips of turtles and frogs sticking out of the surface.

Lynx continued on, her tail waving calmly. "We are nearing a coyote den, so be alert. I don't want to get into a fight with any hungry scavengers." Lynx led Shadow to a large pile of rocks. She explained how the humans moved the rocks off the field and piled them along the edge of the forest. She told Shadow how foxes, coyotes, badgers, and other animals burrowed under rock piles like this to make dens. Shadow twitched her tail in acknowledgment. She knew what a fox looked like from the stories that her mother had told her as a newborn – and she had no desire to meet one.

When they reached the rock pile Lynx lowered her head and signaled for Shadow to stay behind a bush. "I'm going to check if the den is empty," Lynx said as she turned and trotted over to the rock pile. Shadow crouched down and watched as Lynx slowly approached the rock pile, peeked around a boulder, and disappeared into the darkness of a cave beneath it. After a few heartbeats of waiting in silence, Shadow heard a twig crack behind her. She whirled around, scanning the forest with wide eyes. The bushes seemed to dance as a large figure moved about inside of them.

"Who's there?" she called, her voice shaking. There was no answer, but as she watched, a large red-furred creature emerged from the brush and into the sunlight. Its pelt gleamed and its muscles rippled under its skin as it stared menacingly at her from only a few yards away. Its mouth foamed as it took a step toward her and a low growl came from deep within its chest. Shadow jumped back, yelping in surprise at seeing a fox so close. She backed further away as the growl grew louder, and the fox inched ever closer. She quickly whirled around to try and run, only to see another fox was cornering her from behind. Surprised, Shadow jumped, falling backward and scrambling against the oak tree she was cornered against.

The foxes let out savage growls as they continued to creep toward her. Shadow attempted to let out a growl, but it came out as a pitiful squeak. This seemed to set off the foxes, who both lunged forward, their teeth bared as they let out a snarl of fury. Shadow howled in fright and curled into a ball, closing her eyes and preparing herself to feel teeth tear into her pelt and claw her apart.

But nothing happened. Instead, she heard the loud, furious sounds of a vicious fight going on in front of her. She dared open her eyes, her legs shaking with dismay. Lynx was there, battling both foxes, her teeth bared and her fur bushed as she fought fearlessly against her two attackers. The larger fox lunged at Lynx and bit down on her neck, while the smaller fox bit down on her paw, causing her to fall. Shadow barked in surprise, feeling rage bubble up inside of her. She lunged forward with a snarl, feeling her teeth sink into the flesh of the smaller fox's hind leg. She bit down until she felt the skin break and tasted the fox's blood as it ran into her mouth and down her chin.

The fox let go of Lynx and turned on her, lips drawn back to reveal blood-stained teeth. Shadow jumped back with surprise, letting go of her hold on the fox's leg and crawling backward, her tail between her legs. The fox advanced on her, bloody saliva dripping from the tips of its teeth. It snarled, lunging for Shadow's neck, quick as a flash. Shadow quickly dodged to the side, instinctively lashing out a paw and raking her claws across the fox's nose. Now, without thinking she bared her teeth in a snarl and bit down on the fox's ear shaking her head and tearing a piece of the ear clean away. The fox reeled back, squealing, blood pouring from the wound and covering its face. Shadow spit out the ear-chunk and bared her teeth, her eyes wide with fear of what the fox might do next.

The fox advanced again, rearing up on its hind paws and standing to its full height. Blood dripped from its chin and into Shadow's eyes. The fox lunged again, its bared fangs aiming for her face. Shadow ducked aside as the fox came crashing down and missed her by a hair. She lashed out another paw and swept the fox's front paws out from under it. She grabbed a paw in her teeth, biting down and jerking her head from side to side. The fox yelped as it fell to the ground, its paws flailing and its blood-soaked face thrashing from side to side. The fox ripped its paw from her jaws and lashed out at her with a snap of its teeth. Shadow howled in pain as the fox's canines dug into her flank and she was thrown to the ground. She closed her eyes as she was picked up again and thrown to the side, her leg hitting a rock as she came crashing into a tree stump. She then watched in horror as the bloodied fox advanced on her once more, teeth bared and aiming for her exposed throat.

Just as the fox was about to lunge Lynx stepped in between them and crouched in front of the fox, blocking its view from Shadow. Shadow then watched as Lynx jumped toward the fox and dug her teeth deep into its neck, a loud cracking noise echoing throughout the clearing. The fox let out a deep gurgling noise before going limp, its legs twitching vigorously. Lynx then dropped its limp body, her ears flattened. Shadow stared wide-eyed at the dead fox, her body shaking as she crouched low against the bush. Her heart pounded in her ears and her breathing was fast and shallow.

"Shadow," Lynx said after a moment of silence, turning to face her. Shadow looked up and saw Lynx was injured with a steady stream of blood oozing from a bite on her forehead. Lynx looked at Shadow, her eyes showing concern. "Are you all right?" Lynx asked in a shaky voice. Shadow could say nothing. She just buried her face in Lynx's chest fur and whimpered. Lynx nestled closer and licked Shadow's wounds. After a few moments, Lynx pulled away, her eyes fixed with determination.

"Shadow, are you alright to walk?" Lynx asked. Shadow looked at her Trainer's face, trying to read the expression to figure out what she was thinking. *Was she mad?* Shadow wondered. *Why would she be mad?* Shadow lowered her head, wiping the blood on her face away with a paw. *I must look pathetic right now*, she thought. "Yeah," Shadow said, "I think I'm okay to walk." Her legs ached for her to stop, and her wounds burned with pain, but she was determined to keep going and show her Trainer that she was strong.

Shadow stood up, testing her leg to make sure it would carry her weight. She grimaced as pain shot up her leg but said nothing. "Good," Lynx replied, shuffling over to Shadow to lick the bite wounds on her flank. Shadow whimpered in pain as Lynx cleaned the wound, licking the blood and grit out of her fur. When she finished with Shadow, she moved on to clean her own wounds. Shadow understood – they were going to continue marking the territory. As loyal wolves to their pack, they had a duty to protect the territory line to the best of their ability, even if they were injured. Shadow sat down and continued cleaning the bites on her leg. When they had finished licking their wounds Shadow stood up, ignoring her pain. Lynx stood, too, her face lined with pride.

"We should continue," she said. Lynx's voice was confident but uneasy. Shadow gave a weary nod of her head and looked back at the dead fox. Blood was pooled around its neck where Lynx had seized it. "What should we do about the fox? We shouldn't just leave it here," she said. She was mostly too weak and tired to worry about it, but it didn't feel right just leaving its dead body where it laid. Lynx shook her head.

"When we get back to the pack, we can tell them what happened. Others will come and bury it." Without looking back Lynx began to walk along the border once more. Shadow stood watching Lynx walk away, shooting one last glance at the dead fox before turning to follow.

Chapter Four

When Shadow and Lynx finally reached the den site, they went straight to the Healer's den. They had completed marking the borders but were now completely exhausted. From where they fought the foxes their territory stretched for about another four miles until it came to the corner at the Winding River. From there they traveled through the gorse and swamps until they reached a beaver dam. While they rested there, Lynx explained to Shadow how a stream had once run into the river. Beavers had moved in a long time ago and dammed it up. Lynx told her it was now the best place to catch beavers, otters, and muskrats.

Wolves were lying around the clearing lazily as they ate their evening meal. Shadow's legs just about buckled under her as she limped through the entrance, but she made it to the Healer's den and laid down in one of Luna's beds of moss, wrapping her tail around her small figure. She heard Lynx drop down beside her.

"Lynx, what happened to you?" Luna asked, concern edging her voice. Lynx lifted her head and looked wearily up at the Healer.

"We were patrolling the territory and came across a couple of angry foxes," Lynx replied, laying her head on her paws. Luna sighed and began to check their wounds more closely.

"Where does it hurt most?" Luna asked Lynx. Lynx pointed with her tail to the bites on her head, paw, and chest. Luna thoroughly cleaned the wounds with her tongue before retrieving some tree roots from a hole in the ground. She chewed the roots and then applied the poultice to

Lynx's deepest punctures. "This is willow root," Luna told both of them. "It helps with the pain and keeps out infection." After the willow root was applied, Luna retrieved some moss from a herb hole and pressed the moss onto Lynx's wounds. "Shadow, where are you hurt most?" Luna asked when she was done, her face creased with concentration. Shadow stretched out her leg and showed her flank, where four deep puncture wounds lay. Luna cleaned the wounds, as she had done for Lynx, and then chewed the willow root and pressed it into her punctures. She then added moss. "Moss protects the wounds from infection and keeps them clean until they begin to heal," Luna explained.

"Alright, you're done, Shadow," Luna said. "Now go to your den and sleep. Stay still and come back in the morning so I can make sure that your wounds aren't infected." Shadow nodded her head obediently and glanced at Lynx. Her eyes were closed as if she were sleeping. Shadow took one last look around the den before turning to leave. The Healer's den was a cave cut into the face of a rock wall and was the largest den in the clearing. The main area of the den was dedicated to treating wolves' wounds, the herbs sorted into holes in the ground. Although the mouth of the cave was wide, it was nearly impossible to see inside because of the thick bushes and ivy vines that hung from the roof. The entrance sloped down into the main area, and then a tunnel led to a smaller portion of the den where sick wolves could rest without being bothered. Shadow saw all this as she made her way outside, her tail dragging wearily on the ground. As she squeezed herself out of the den, she was greeted by a group of her packmates, all asking questions at once.

"Shadow!" Miku was the first one to appear in front of her. "Miku!" She exclaimed, an unexplained feeling of happiness washing over her at the sight of him. He covered her face with licks before pulling away, not knowing how she would react. "Sorry," he said, tucking his tail under his legs and backing away into the crowd that surrounded her.

"Wait!" she tried calling, but he was already out of sight. Shadow frowned, her tail drooping.

"Shadow, what happened?" Amber asked, standing in front of her, eyes wide. Heather stood at the Beta's side, with Storm at her other side. Shadow flattened her ears at all the attention, backing away.

"All right, everyone, give her some space!" Oak growled above the rest. Amber backed away, followed by the rest of the pack. "Shadow, see me in my den and bring Lynx with you. You can talk to me before you tell the pack," he said before turning and trotting over to his den. Shadow watched, turning as Lynx emerged from the den.

"Oak wants to see us in his den," Shadow said, shooting a glance at her packmates. They had slightly disappointed looks on their faces but otherwise looked satisfied that they would receive *some* news on what happened. Shadow then trotted over to Oak's den, followed by Lynx. The Alphas' den was a deep cave carved into the side of the same rock wall as the Healer's den. Shadow guessed that it had been formed by water a long time ago. It was the second-largest den next to the Healer's den. At the mouth of the cave, there was a large hazelnut bush that hid the entrance and the darkness inside. The only way to get in was through a small hole in the center of the thick bush. Shadow peeked inside, flattening her ears. She slipped through the branches, Lynx on her tail.

"Oak?" Lynx called into the dimly lit cave. Shadow heard light paw steps coming from deep inside the cave.

"Come in, Lynx," Oak responded. Shadow shuffled forward, her eyes wide to see through the dark. She soon came to see a faint light showing through a crack in the roof straight ahead and she walked forward more confidently, Lynx right behind her. Shadow came to a stop when she saw Oak, who was sitting on a deer hide a few steps in front of her. Shadow knew that the Alphas of the pack took the deer hides and used them to sleep on, though she couldn't imagine sleeping on top of something that had once been alive.

"Sit down," he told them. Shadow sat next to Lynx, straining her eyes as she looked around the den. The cave walls stretched high above her head, and the width of the room was very large. Shadow took a deep breath of the cool, misty air, appreciating the cold stone under her paws. "Tell me everything that happened. Why are you two injured?" Oak asked, twitching an ear.

"We were marking the west border line, near the coyote den," Lynx reported. "I told Shadow to wait behind a bush while I checked to see if the coyotes were there. I did not see any coyotes, so I returned to get Shadow. She was cornered against a tree with two foxes advancing on her. I fought off the biggest one while Shadow took the smaller one. We ended up killing the second one, my mistake," Lynx explained. Oak frowned at their words, standing up.

"Alright, I'll send a group to take care of the body," he said. "Is there anything else I need to know?" He looked at Lynx, and then Shadow. Shadow shook her head. "There is one thing," Lynx added. "Shadow fought very bravely today. When both of the foxes had me pinned, she got the smaller one off of me so I could chase off the bigger one. I'm proud of her." Oak dipped his head, smiling pridefully at Shadow. "Good job, and thank you. Would you like me to tell the pack?" he asked cordially. Shadow nodded gratefully, sighing. Her ears felt warm at the older wolves' praises. Lynx gave a small smile.

"Sure, thank you, Oak," Lynx replied before politely dipping her head and standing up, motioning for Shadow to do the same. Shadow stood and followed Lynx out of the den and into the warm evening sunlight once more. Shadow shook her paws to relieve the numbness from the cold stone floor, smiling slightly as the sun shone on her face. Clouds were beginning to build overhead so she soaked in the last of the daily warmth before the sun disappeared behind a large dark cloud. She walked with Lynx to the Learners' den, a hole dug out from under an uprooted birch tree. Shadow couldn't see very far into the den since the sun had disappeared, but she assumed that it was big and deep enough to fit four wolves.

"You'll need your rest if we're going to start training tomorrow, though I don't know if you'll be quite ready yet." Lynx glanced at Shadow, twitching an ear. Shadow dipped her head.

"I think I'll be fine, but I might have to check with Luna about my wounds. I'll see you tomorrow!" Shadow smiled and turned to the den to get some badly needed rest. Lynx padded away, waving her tail in goodbye.

When her eyes had adjusted to the light of the cave, she looked around, taking note of her surroundings. The entrance sloped down into a large hole that looked to be dug out many years before she had been born. The roof hung low and her ear tips brushed against the ceiling as she slowly walked around the den. It was empty, she realized, with no sleeping holes. "I guess I can make one," she said to herself, shrugging. She trotted over to a corner of the cave and dug her claws into the dirt. After scooping out a few pawfuls she spread the dirt out around her and curled up, the dirt strangely warm and comfortable. It was not as comfortable as the moss and ferns she had slept on in the Newborns' den, but it was nice enough. Shadow noticed that the walls were damp as her fur brushed against them. She huffed, curling her tail around her body and laying her head on her paws.

Shadow's fur prickled as she lay there. She felt eerily alone. She lifted her head, knowing that sleep wouldn't come anytime soon. Shadow sighed, stood up and shook out her pelt. She walked over to the entrance, wincing at her injured leg. She poked her head out of the den and saw that the clearing was empty. A light rain was falling, small droplets leaving marks on the ground as they landed. One drop plopped on her nose as she stared up at the clouds in wonder. Shadow quickly pulled back inside, shaking her head as she walked back over to her sleeping spot.

Shadow lay there in silence until a soft scuffling noise jolted her from her drowsiness. She looked up at the entrance to the den as Kele entered, his pelt dripping with water. "Hey, Shadow," he said after first shaking the water droplets from his fur.

"Hey, Kele. What took you so long to finally get in here?" she asked him, gesturing for him to lay next to her with a wave of her tail. He dug a shallow hole and curled up next to her, twitching water from his ears.

"Miku, Breeze, and I had to go with Sparrow and Mako to help bury the fox that Lynx killed. It was quite unpleasant. Miku and Breeze should be here any moment," he said, resting his head on his paws. Shadow yawned, stretching her paws. A few seconds later, Miku entered the den, panting, Breeze right behind him.

"Get out of the way, it's raining out here!" Breeze growled, shouldering his way past his brother to get inside. Miku growled but said nothing before shaking out his pelt all over Breeze. Shadow snorted with amusement as Breeze turned on Miku, eyes wide and fur dripping. "Gross! You got all your wet fur all over me," Breeze snarled, and Miku snickered, scampering away before Breeze could shake the water back onto him. Miku quickly dug a sleeping hole beside Shadow, Breeze digging his last, after he finished shaking the water from his long fur.

"You three stink," Shadow said, wrinkling her nose at their wet, musky odor. Kele shrugged, and Breeze scoffed.

"You would stink, too, if you just spent an hour burying a dead fox," Breeze replied, twitching a wet ear. Shadow grinned the faint light that came from the entrance lighting up Breeze's eyes.

"I know that you and Lynx were the ones who had trouble with those foxes. What happened?" Miku asked, looking at Shadow. Shadow nodded, twitching an ear as all their eyes focused on her.

"Lynx and I were checking on the coyote den, and a couple of foxes cornered me. We fought them off, but not before they could get a few bites out of us. The one that Lynx killed was the smaller one," Shadow spoke, and Miku's eyes widened.

"Small? That fox looked pretty big to me," he commented, and Shadow shrugged. Changing the subject, Shadow brought up Kele's Trainer, Mako.

"How did it go today? Did you two explore the territory?" Shadow asked, and Kele nodded. "Yeah, we did. Mako is nice as a Trainer. He's very knowledgeable," Kele said, and Shadow nodded, smiling slightly.

"That's good. Lynx is a good Trainer, too. Without her, those foxes could have killed me," Shadow spoke, and a brief silence filled the den before Shadow finally broke it. "I mean, probably not – one of them *was* pretty big, though." Kele nodded, and Miku wrapped his tail around himself.

"I'm glad you're okay," Miku said and nudged Shadow on the shoulder. She felt her pelt grow warm at the brief contact.

"All right, well, we should probably get some sleep," Breeze said, tucking his face under his paws. Shadow nodded and curled up beside Kele where she quickly fell asleep to the soft sound of the rain pattering against the roof of the den.

"Shadow, wake up," a soft voice called to her from above her head. She opened her eyes and lifted her head, startled from her sleep. She couldn't see anyone, but she could smell a strong, acrid odor. She was lying on a bed of moss, with ferns and oak trees surrounding her. Confusion clouded her mind as she slowly stood up and looked around, breathing the strange air. The wind had a strange, putrid smell and it was burning her eyes and throat as she breathed. Shadow coughed, wrinkling her nose.

The smell was getting stronger as if it were coming straight toward her. She looked up and saw that it was night. Thousands of glittery stars shined against the pitch-black sky. She again looked around, noticing that some sort of fog was swirling in the air and through the trees surrounding her. She angled her ears behind her as she heard the loud crackle of what sounded like a branch breaking. Shadow whirled around and was startled to see bright orange and yellow flames licking at the leaves of the trees just a yard from where she stood. She yelped in surprise, stumbling backward. The flames blazed before her, clogging her senses with the unbearable scent of smoke. She staggered back, wide-eyed, blood pounding in her ears.

She howled, horrified. "Fire!" Her mother had told stories about how these hot ribbons of light and heat had destroyed the homes of many of their ancestors. The flames seemed to thicken with rage as she backed away. The bright red and orange flames spread around her, instantly embracing the ferns and setting them to ash. The trees surrounding her shook as they crackled and burst before they came crashing down, shaking the ground with the impact.

Shadow yelped, turning tail to flee, eyes watering and cloudy because of the smoke that stung her senses. She jumped over the burning-red coals, feeling the heat pass under her and singe her belly fur. Nostrils flaring, she sprinted through the forest, away from the flames that seemed to trail right behind her. Half blinded by the smoke, she ran, dodging the burning trees and flames that ate at her surroundings. She came to a frantic stop when she reached a tall, broad dogwood bush. She looked back at the flames, horrified to see they were only a few yards away from her shaking body. She yelped in fear, closing her eyes and plunging into the brambles. She grimaced as the sharp thorns pierced through her skin and fur.

Shadow kept running, feeling the heat on her tail. She finally broke free of the brambles, gasping for air. The smoke clogged her throat and burned her eyes and nose. She coughed, feeling her legs begin to weaken. Her whole body throbbed with pain as she limped forward. Shadow realized with a jolt that she was now in the clearing of her own home. She watched as her packmates ran, terrified, around her, howling with fear and pain. Shadow comprehended with horror that they were all slowly fading away as if turning to ash. She yelped in fear and surprise, spotting Kele through the chaos.

"Kele!" She howled, but he didn't seem to hear. He was sitting across the clearing, head down, pelt slowly burning away. She tried to get to him, but her packmates were swarming around her, faces twisted in pain and apprehension, flames licking up their pelts and sizzling their skin. She saw her mother's face twisted into a crooked mask of anguish and her father's face was broken and coated with dust and ash. Her packmates pushed her and clawed her pelt, their shrieks of pain echoing in Shadow's ears.

Shadow closed her eyes, covering her ears and letting out a howl as she tried to block out their heart-wrenching cries. She suddenly fell back, but instead of landing on the hard ground, she fell into empty darkness, her paws flailing helplessly. She yelped loudly as she fell, the wind being knocked straight out of her chest as she abruptly crashed into a body of warm liquid.

She snapped her jaws shut as she was twirled and thrashed about by the churning current. She finally gathered what was left of her strength and began paddling upward, her lungs burning and screaming for air. She tasted the metallic liquid as it filled her mouth. Her eyes stung as she finally broke to the surface, filling her lungs with much-needed air. She gasped for breath as she frantically began paddling for shore, eyes locked shut against the smoke that still clouded the air. Finally reaching shore, she weakly pulled herself onto solid ground before collapsing on a bed of grass.

Shadow gasped for air, exhausted, her body shaking. She slowly blinked her eyes open and looked back at the thick, ash-covered liquid that she had landed in. *I landed in the Winding River*, she thought, recognizing the steppingstones to get to the other side downstream. *But that doesn't explain why the water tasted like...* Her breath caught in her throat as she realized that instead of water, the river was running red with blood. Her stomach churned with unease as she realized how much of the crimson liquid she had swallowed.

Shadow scrambled weakly away, eyes wide with horror, her pelt growing hot. She looked behind her and saw fire licking at the ground just a footstep from her tail. She whimpered in desperation, now noticing how the crimson river was growing larger, eating its way up the sandy banks toward her broken body. Shadow felt helpless as if she was stuck to the ground. She whimpered as the warm liquid made its way to her chest and she could feel the current tugging at her paws. She realized that it was no use trying to escape. She took one last look at the angry flames before letting her mind go blank as she was swept away by the current of the churning river.

Chapter Five

Shadow jumped up with a yelp, hitting her head on the roof of the cave. She frantically looked around the darkened den, her claws scraping against the cave floor and her heart racing in her chest. With relief, she realized that she was back in the Learners' den, and there was no sign of any fire or bloody river. Her mind was fuzzy and her eyes a-blur as she sat down to try and calm her sailing heart.

"A dream. It was just a dream," she whispered, panting, eyes wide against the dark cave. She rubbed the tender bump on her head, wincing as she did so. She noticed that Miku, Breeze, and Kele had all left. She stood up and shook out her pelt, her legs stiff from lying on the bare, cold floor. The scratches from the fight with the foxes burned and her eyes stung as if she had been squirming around in her sleep. Shadow stretched before trotting over to the entrance of the den and peeking outside.

Some of her packmates were gathered in small groups, chattering among themselves. Storm, Oak, Amber, and Luna were huddled together near the Alpha stone, their heads close as if deep in conversation. Sparrow, Scout, and Max were chatting near the entrance to the clearing, heads down. The rest of the pack was probably either still sleeping or hunting, Shadow thought. She slipped out of the den and into the sunlit clearing, her black pelt absorbing the warmth. She smiled, looking up at the sky. The early morning sun shone just above the treetops, sending splotches of bright yellow light to shine on their home. The cool dewy air filled her lungs and seemed to soak into her parched tongue. Birds chirped from the trees around her, their calls filling her ears and echoing around the clearing. The clear sky promised a beautiful day. She trotted over to the Fighters' den and peeked inside, finding the den to be empty. Shadow then looked around the clearing. She spotted Luna walking toward her, her black pelt glistening in the sunlight.

"Shadow, come see me in my den – I need to check your wounds," Luna said, and Shadow nodded before following Luna into the Healer's den. The den was dark and musty and smelled of fresh leaves and herbs. Shadow slid down the steep entrance and farther into the cave, her eyes wide to adjust to the light. "All right, I'm just going to have to take off the moss," Luna muttered as she leaned toward Shadow and nipped at the dressing on her flank. Shadow winced as Luna peeled the moss and let air soak into the wound. Shadow looked down at the punctures, seeing they looked clean and were scabbing already. Luna sniffed it and sat back with satisfaction. "The punctures look clean and smell like they are healing. You'll be able to begin training again tomorrow if Lynx feels up to it. She went to stretch her legs earlier, so she should be back soon," Luna commented, turning to her herb holes to re-dress Shadow's wounds. The Healer cleaned the dried blood out of the wounds before pressing on more moss.

"Ouch!" Shadow yelped in pain as pressure was applied.

"Hold still," Luna spoke as Shadow attempted to scoot away. "The wound needs to be kept uninfected," Luna explained, pressing harder. Shadow gritted her teeth, letting out a low whimper. She relaxed as Luna sat back, a look of satisfaction on her face. "Alright, now let me see your other wounds."

When Luna finished dressing Shadow's scratches she told her to rest. "Take the rest of the day to recover your strength," she said. Shadow scoffed. *Yeah right*, she thought as she exited the den. She then trotting painfully over to where Lynx now sat at the other end of the clearing.

"Hey, Lynx! Are we going training today?" Shadow called. Lynx pricked her ears toward Shadow, smiling.

"Hey, Shadow. I don't know if you're healed enough yet. What did Luna say?" she queried, tilting her head to the side. Shadow cleared her throat to stall time, sitting beside her Trainer with a weary smile. Lynx stared at her skeptically, a spark of amusement in her eyes. "Well?" Her Trainer pressed.

Shadow sighed heavily. "She told me to stay near the den site," she mumbled, looking at her paws. Lynx dipped her head.

"Thank you for telling me. You should stay here and help Amber with anything she needs. Mako, Kele, and I are going out to mark the territory. I'll be back soon," Lynx promised as she stood and stretched. Shadow's mouth dropped in open disappointment. "Why does Kele get to go and I don't?" she said crossly. Lynx cast her a pitiful glance.

"Because Kele wasn't attacked by foxes yesterday!" She said. Then, sympathetically, she added, "we can start training again tomorrow." Shadow sat for a moment, pouting, before turning to where Amber sat at the other end of the clearing. The Beta was giving orders to a group of wolves surrounding her. *I should make use of myself,* Shadow thought as she trotted over to the Beta. "Hello Amber," she addressed the she-wolf, dipping her head respectfully. Amber twitched an ear, signaling for Shadow to sit down. Shadow sat between Sparrow and Scout.

"Scout; take Heather, Breeze, and Sparrow to hunt," Amber said, giving Scout a nod as if to say 'get going.' Scout dipped his head, gathered Heather, Breeze, and Sparrow with his tail, and led them out of the clearing. Amber then turned to Shadow, a pitiful, yet amused look on her face. "I sent Lynx, Kele, and Mako to check the territory already. Luna told me you needed to stay near the den site. Sorry,"

Amber said, dipping her head slightly. Shadow hid her disappointment with a smile.

"It's all right. I'll just help with anything that needs to be done around here," she said, tilting her head as if waiting to be told what she could do. Amber nodded.

"Well, we can start with covering the top of the Hunters' den with moss. Heather and Sparrow have been complaining about the wind for days," Amber mused. "Follow me," she said, turning and trotting over to the exit. Shadow trailed behind, sulking with the duty of gathering moss. Amber led Shadow to a giant uprooted oak tree. Moss had grown underneath the tree and coated the tree's bark. "Scrape the moss off this tree and roll it into a ball. Carry as much as you can back to the den site and lay it outside of the Hunters' den. I'll take it from there," Amber instructed. Shadow nodded gloomily and watched as Amber trotted back in the direction of the den site.

Shadow began scraping moss off the fallen tree with her front paws and piling it next to a branch. When she felt the pile was big enough she rolled it into a tight ball and picked it up, her head drooping with the weight. She trudged back to the den site and dropped it outside of the Hunters' den, her tongue lolling out. Just then, Amber appeared behind her and began to examine her moss. While Amber was occupied, Shadow looked at the Hunters' den.

The Hunters' den was a deep hole dug under the roots of a huge maple tree. Peering inside, Shadow saw that it was bigger and deeper than it looked on the outside. Roots from the tree were holding the dirt in place on the ceiling, while small boulders kept the dirt compact in the walls of the den. The entrance was surrounded by clumps of ferns, making it hard to see the hole without looking closely. The tree stood taller than any maple Shadow had ever seen. She looked closely at the dirt that formed the roof, noticing now how some rocks had been knocked out, possibly by the wind or rain. Otherwise, the den looked cozy, and could easily fit four wolves. Next to the Hunters' den was the Fighters' den, which was dug out from under a large flat boulder. The dens were so close together that they were touching. On the other side of the Fighters' den was the rock wall, where the Healer's and Alphas' dens were. Shadow dragged her gaze away from the clearing and watched as Amber took the moss and began shoving it in the holes in the Hunters' den's roof, blocking off ways for the wind to get inside.

"Good job, Shadow. You got just enough to fill in the gaps here," Amber praised her as she finished. Shadow smiled gratefully, sitting back on her haunches.

"What should we do now?" Shadow asked, her tail twitching as she waited eagerly for something else to do.

Amber looked around at the dens before answering, "We could help Luna with any herbs she needs to collect." Shadow nodded and whirled around to trot over to Luna's den. She slipped inside and let her eyes adjust to the light before making her way farther into the cave.

"Luna?" she called quietly, not wanting to make her angry if she was deep in concentration.

"Shadow, is that you?" Luna called back, peeking from around the corner that led to the smaller section of the den.

"Yes," Shadow replied.

"Good. Have you come to have your wounds checked again?" Luna asked, and Shadow shook her head, watching as Luna emerged from around the corner, her black pelt shining in the light that shone from the entrance of the cave.

"No, I came to see if you need Amber and me to collect any herbs for you," Shadow replied, and Luna nodded.

"Okay. I'm running low on willow root, tormentil, honey, and moss. Just tell Amber what I need – she knows what they all look like," Luna said, and Shadow dipped her head, turning and exiting the den.

Amber was waiting outside the den, her amber fur glinting in the afternoon sunlight. "What does she need?" Amber asked, and Shadow repeated the names of the four herbs. "Let's get going then," Amber said as she stood to slip through the ferns and out of the clearing. Shadow followed, glad she could do something important, even if it wasn't training.

"Is this tormentil?" Shadow called over to Amber, who was sniffing at a bee's nest. Amber trotted over to Shadow and sniffed at the white-colored flowers. Amber had explained that tormentil was a plant with long stems and lots of white petals and that the whole plant was used, even the roots. The roots were best for keeping out infection, but the petals and stems worked well, too.

"Yes, that's it. For this particular plant, you have to dig the roots out, like this," Amber said, digging her claws into the dirt and tearing out the shallow roots. Shadow followed Amber's demonstration, gently tearing the roots from the ground and putting the plants in a pile. When she gathered enough, she trotted over to Amber and helped her get some honey from the bee's nest. She used a wad of moss and quickly covered it in honey before the bees could realize what she was doing. Once they collected enough honey and flowers they brought them back to the den site and gave them to Luna. Amber then led Shadow back out to gather willow roots and moss.

"Okay, now use the hooks of your claws to rip out the willow roots," Amber instructed. Shadow dug her claws into the soft soil and tore the roots out of the ground with a grunt. Ignoring the pain in the wounds on her flank and leg, she then leaned down and grabbed the root in her teeth, ripping it free. She then turned to Amber and dropped it at the she-wolf's paws. "Good. I'll go collect the moss – stay here," Amber said as she turned and slipped out of sight through the ferns. Shadow turned back to the willow tree and began tearing more roots from the ground. Her muscles were beginning to ache when Amber returned carrying a large ball of moss.

"Okay, Shadow, I think we have enough roots now," Amber said, glancing at the heaping pile of roots that Shadow made.

"Good," Shadow panted, picking up the chunks of root and carrying them back to the den site with Amber on her tail. After dropping the herbs at the Healer's den Shadow looked up at the sky, noticing that the sun had gone down while she and Amber had been collecting. It was nearing the end of the day, the sun barely resting above the treetops. The pack had returned from hunting or marking the borders and were now sitting lazily around the clearing, eating or simply talking. Shadow looked across the clearing and saw Lynx sharing a large piece of prey with Max, Sparrow, and Heather, their eyes shining. Shadow trotted over to them, asking Sparrow what the animal was called.

"It's called a raccoon. Heather caught it," Sparrow replied, shooting a fond look at his mate, Heather. She smiled, glancing at Shadow. "Do you want to try a bite?" Heather offered, and Shadow nodded. She took a bite out of the flank of the furry animal, the musky flavors bathing her tongue. "It's really good," she commented after swallowing, and Heather smiled with gratitude.

"What did you do with Amber today?" Lynx asked, and Shadow told her how she had patched the holes on top of the Hunters' den and helped collect Luna's herbs. The she-wolf nodded with approval.

"Good job keeping busy," Lynx praised before taking another bite of the flavorful prey. Shadow gave a nod before turning and trotting over to the prey pile, taking a squirrel for herself. She then went to sit next to Kele, who was licking his lips as he finished a rabbit.

"How was it?" Shadow asked, smiling as she seated herself at his side. He grinned, swallowing the last bit that was stuck in his mouth.

"It was good. Sorry, I didn't save any for you," he apologized, dipping his head slightly. Shadow scoffed in mock disappointment.

"Oh, it's alright. I've got a squirrel. How was the patrol?" She asked, intent on telling her brother how she helped Luna with gathering herbs.

"It was great. I caught a rabbit today! You should have seen it. Lynx chased it right into my paws. I almost missed it, but I didn't," Kele told her, pride shining in his eyes. Shadow smiled, hiding her envy. She was happy for her brother but also felt a prick of jealousy. *I should have been the one to catch that rabbit,* she couldn't help thinking to herself. She shook the thought out of her head and joined her brother in his pride.

"Good job! Rabbits are hard to catch," she exclaimed, a grin stretched across her face. He smiled widely, clearly happy with impressing her. "Guess what I did today," Shadow blurted, her eyes alight. Kele shrugged. "Well, first I collected moss for the Hunters' den and helped apply it to the roof, and then I helped Luna with collecting her herbs," she told her brother brightly, her chin high. Kele grinned.

"That's great, Shadow!" He exclaimed through a yawn, his eyelids suddenly looking heavier.

"You must be tired," Shadow said, nudging his shoulder. He nodded and stood up, smiling wearily. "Yes, I am. I'll see you in the morning." He strode off to the Learners' den and disappeared through the entrance. Shadow stared after him, sighing. She then quickly ate the squirrel, glad that it filled her belly. When she finished, she shook out her pelt and ran across the clearing to the entrance, glancing around to make sure that nobody was looking. Oak and Storm were talking to each other near the Alpha stone, so involved in their discussion that she didn't think they would notice if she slipped out. Lynx and Max were sitting beside each other, facing away from her, cleaning each other's fur as they spoke quietly. The only other wolves in the clearing were Sparrow and Heather, who were sharing what was left of the raccoon. None of them was paying attention to her, so she quickly slipped out of the clearing and into the forest.

It was a cool night, with the sun dropping below the treetops and the stars beginning to show in the cloudless sky. She padded nimbly through the woods, stepping softly between logs and underbrush. She smiled at the colors of the night, enjoying the way the wind buffeted her pelt. Her injury was long forgotten, she began to run, picking up speed as she went. Her paws pounded against the ground as she skimmed a grove of birch trees and swerved around a berry bush, veering off the trail. She cleared a fallen pine without breaking stride, her eyes watering as the wind blew in her face. She panted heavily as she leaped over a marshy area, her ears pinned and eyes wide. The trees flew past her as she seemed to fly over the ground. She tested her speed, racing her shadow as she bunched and stretched her muscles swiftly. Shadow hurled over a bush, feeling the thorns skim her underbelly as she soared past. Her throat burned and her paws stung every time they touched the ground. She didn't stop until she reached a small ditch filled with water. She skidded to a stop and bent over, her breath coming in ragged gasps. She felt a bit dizzy from the running, but otherwise was fine, her injuries barely noticeable.

Regaining her breath, she lapped from the earthy water, cherishing its touch to her dry tongue. When she was satisfied, she looked up at the sky, noticing that the moon was now starting to rise over the horizon. It looked to be almost full. She sat down next to the water, her tongue lolling out and tail patting against the leaves and twigs that littered the ground. She was happy to finally be out of the clearing on her own but was now half-regretting leaving. She realized that with the moon up it would be harder to get back to her home, with shadows reflecting off every tree trunk and wind rattling the branches overhead. She shook her head and stood up, suddenly daunted by the wide forest in front of her. She began wearily trotting forward, adrenaline coursing through her veins, blood pounding in her ears. She kept her senses alert for signs of other animals around, her fur on end.

She was half-way home by the time the moon was high above her head and the wind was raking through her fur. She shivered and hurried along, trying to remember the way she had come. *Maybe if I wasn't so intent on running away I would have thought about how I would get back,* she thought crossly to herself. A gust of wind buffeted her fur. It was strange, she thought, that there was a wind on such a clear, cloudless night. She abandoned the thought and continued on, eyes wide. After a few heartbeats of silence, she heard a twig crack behind her.

Shadow whirled around, teeth bared in surprise and ears flattened to her head. The bushes rattled in front of her. Her hackles raised defensively as she bowed her head and lowered herself to the ground, teeth bared in a snarl. Suddenly, a shadow emerged from the bushes. Just as it stepped into the light of the moon, Shadow let out a sigh of relief. "Kele!" She exclaimed, surprised. She stood up and let her fur drop, her paws tingling with happiness to see him.

"Shadow, what are you doing out here?" Kele asked her in a voice tinged with fear. Shadow walked toward him and nudged him happily.

"I'm glad it's just you. I was just out here to stretch my legs." Shadow told him, frowning as he whirled around with a huff and disappeared into the bushes he had come from. Shadow followed him, and they trudged silently through the forest. Kele seemed to be upset.

When they finally made it back to the den site, they entered quietly through the side of the clearing, glancing warily around for Max. He was at his post beside the entrance, his eyes half-closed.

Shadow and Kele slipped through the shadows until they got to their den, entering quietly and going to lay in their sleeping holes. They were careful not to wake Breeze or Miku, who were sleeping soundly. Shadow curled up between Kele and Miku, anxious to talk with Kele about why he was out there. "Why were you out there? I thought you were going to sleep," Shadow whispered, looking at him. He had bis back to her.

"I was looking for you, of course! I expected you to come straight in here after me, but when you didn't come for half an hour, I knew something was wrong. So, I tracked your scent and found you going the wrong way. You would most likely still be out there if it wasn't for me," he replied, not looking at her. Shadow felt her face warm with embarrassment.

"I'm sorry I was going the wrong way, but you don't need to be so angry about it," Shadow whispered, sounding hurt. At that, Kele turned to face her, his face softening slightly.

"I know, but do you know how annoying it is, having to track down your sibling after they leave without saying a thing? You have only been around the territory once. It was a dumb idea to leave the hunting path," he whispered. Shadow sighed, giving a small smile.

"I guess I don't know how annoying it is. Thank you," she said, and he gave a small smile in return.

"Yeah, okay. Just don't do it again," he said, and Shadow bit her tongue to keep from laughing. She then yawned and closed her eyes, glad that she was able to make amends with her brother.

Shadow sat at the edge of the clearing, waiting for her Trainer to return. Lynx had gone out early with Mako, Kele, and Sparrow to mark the territory, leaving Shadow behind. She had been waiting for a while now, busying herself with cleaning out her fur and eating her breakfast. The sun was now up, and Shadow was growing impatient.

Eventually, at the entrance of the clearing, she heard a rustling noise and thought Lynx had finally come for her, but instead she saw Amber pushing her way into the clearing. Breeze was at her heels. Behind them trailed Miku and Scout, their expressions equally severe. They were talking quietly, Breeze carrying a shriveled bird in his jaws. Shadow trotted over to Miku, hoping he was up to talk. "Hey Miku," she called, moving up to walk beside him. "Hello Shadow," Miku replied, giving a slight smile. Amber looked at Shadow, twitching an ear in hello. The Beta then dipped her head and strode over to where Oak was sitting at the foot of the Alpha stone, his head held high as he talked to Storm. Oak looked expectantly at Amber as she approached. She whispered something to him and his expression changed from happy to concerned in an instant. Oak, Amber, and Storm began conferring with each other, their heads close together. Shadow dragged her gaze over to Breeze, who was dropping the bird onto the prey pile, his expression blank.

"What happened out there? Why is every wolf looking so serious?" Shadow asked Miku, confusion edging her voice. Miku sat down heavily in the shade. Breeze quickly joined them and sat beside him. Shadow sat in front of them, ears pricked to hear what Miku would say.

"Breeze, Scout, Amber, and I didn't see a living thing in the forest today, besides Breeze's bird," Miku told her with a troubled frown. Shadow was taken aback as she sat beside him, her ears pricked.

"Really?" She asked. "That's hard to imagine." Breeze nodded, looking up at her from where he lay.

"Everything else we saw was either dead or dying," Miku added, his voice lowering into a growl. Shadow sat back on her haunches, confused, her face creased with worry.

"What?" she whispered disbelievingly. Miku nodded matter-of-factly, a mixture of fear and bewilderment showing in his eyes.

"Poison," Breeze said. "Poison tainted the water in the stream, killing everything that drank from it. Birds, squirrels, you name it. Everything we saw was dead." Breeze looked at her darkly. Shadow gasped, eyes wide with disbelief.

"Everything?" She breathed, staring at him. He nodded, a weary look in his eyes. "How will we get enough prey if everything is dead with poison?" Shadow worried, eyes wide.

"All I know is that we can't trust anything anymore. This must have been the work of humans, those terrible creatures who destroy anything and everything that doesn't match their expectations," Miku spat, growling. Shadow didn't say anything. She just stared at the ground, her mind whirling. She pricked her ears but didn't look up as the bushes swayed and Lynx emerged into the clearing, Kele, Sparrow, and Mako at her heels. The three were dead silent as they walked over to Oak and reported what they had found. Judging from their blank expressions and heavy paw steps, Shadow guessed they found exactly what Breeze had just explained. Kele walked over to her and sat at her other side, his expression hiding nothing.

"What did you find?" Breeze asked with hope dwindling. Kele turned to him, his eyes clouded.

"We found…" he began, but was cut off as Oak jumped onto the Alpha stone and gathered the pack with a howl.

"Aspen pack, gather around me. I have an announcement to make!" His voice broke the quiet noises of her packmate's whispers. Tension filled the air as Shadow and her pack gathered around the Alpha Stone. Oak raised his tail to silence the whispers, his expression grim. After a moment of silence, he began. "As most of you may already know, the stream that separates our territory from the Cedar packs has been poisoned," Oak began. Anxious whispers burst out among the crowd, crackling in the air. "We don't know if the humans have poisoned it, or if it if something worse than that," he added over the voices of her packmates, his tail raised for silence. "What we do know is that anything that drinks from the stream will die. Half of the prey in our forest has already been killed by this poison. We may go hungry until this problem is solved. We will have to drink from the lake until our stream runs clean again. Amber, Scout, Luna, and I will deliver this news to the Cedar pack, for they share the same stream as us." Oak sat and waved his tail in dismissal.

Shadow watched as Amber, Scout, Luna, and Oak huddled together. Oak led them out of the clearing, his head held high. After sitting for a while and wondering what to do, Shadow turned and walked over to the prey pile, snatching the bird in her jaws. She then trotted up to her mother, who was sitting beside the Alpha stone, her eyes clouded with worry. Shadow dropped the bird in front of her and sat at her side, nudging her toward the kill. "It's not much, but I can tell you're hungry. I can see your bones through your fur," Shadow fretted, licking her mother's cheek. Storm smiled a bit as she bent down to eat the bird.

"Thank you, Shadow, but you mustn't worry. I'm fine," Storm said as she chewed on the prey. Shadow's gaze softened when she looked at her mother. Thoughts whirled in her mind and her packmate's whispers filled the air and she watched them huddle around each other, sharing rumors. "Is something troubling you?" Storm asked, her wise eyes missing nothing. Shadow shuffled her paws, wondering whether she should share her dream or not. After a few moments of silence, Shadow answered.

"Well, I suppose I'm just worried. What if some wolf accidentally drinks from the water, or steps in the water and licks its paws? My pack is my family and I don't want anything to hurt them. It would hurt me, too," Shadow spoke quietly, looking up at her mother. Storm was nodding thoughtfully, understanding in her eyes. Shadow squirmed, wrapping her tail over her paws. "And what if we starve? With not enough prey in the forest, every wolf will need to be hunting. And if the Cedar pack attacks us, we will be in no state to fight them off. They might steal our territory, and then what would we do? Wolves would die, pups would starve, and our pack would…" Shadow stopped with a glance from her mother.

"Shadow, you need not worry. Just help your pack in every way you can. Train hard, understand what you're facing, and you will find that this challenge is nothing more than a minor setback to what will come. This has happened before, and it will happen again. Soon, the humans will move on, and the stream will run clear again," Storm told her, her eyes shining. Shadow dipped her head politely.

"Thank you for sharing your wisdom with me, mother," Shadow thanked her quietly, looking up at Storm thoughtfully. The pretty she-wolf smiled down at Shadow, giving a nod as a signal for her to go.

Shadow stood and trotted over to where her fellow Learners were seated near the prey pile. As she neared them, Miku called a greeting.

"Hey, Shadow! We were just talking about going…" He beckoned her closer with his tail and continued, "On a secret hunting trip," he finished with a whisper, glancing around to make sure no other wolf had heard. Shadow tipped her head to the side and glanced at her three friends, confusion and excitement lighting her gaze.

"A secret hunting trip?" she queried, smiling.

"Yes. We would go out in the night, once every wolf is asleep. It will be easy since we all share the same den," Kele explained, grinning.

"We would hunt for our pack. They need us," Breeze added, leaning forward. Shadow smiled widely, her tail skimming the ground.

"That's a great idea! But what about Max? He will be guarding the entrance," Shadow whispered, looking across the clearing at Max, who was sleeping in the sunlight on a pile of moss, Lynx beside him.

"We would leave one at a time and tell Max that we either need a drink of water, that we need to make dirt, or that we can't sleep and want to go on a walk. Those are reasons that always get wolves away from the den site," Miku said thoughtfully, glancing at Shadow. Shadow nodded, finding it might work.

"All right. So, we wait until the wolves go to sleep, and then we…" she was cut off as Oak burst into the clearing, followed by Amber, Scout, and Luna. They were all bristling, their eyes filled with anger. Shadow pricked her ears with interest as Oak leaped onto the Alpha stone and called a meeting. Most of the wolves were already in the clearing but just needed to center themselves in front of the stone. Shadow slid in between Lynx and Mako, who were whispering urgently to each other. They cut off abruptly as Shadow slipped between them. Lynx shot a glance at Shadow, a bit of frustration sparking in her eyes. Shadow lowered her head at her Trainer, embarrassment heating her ear tips. She looked up as Oak quickly motioned with his tail for the wolves to settle down.

"As you all know, Luna, Amber, Scout, and I traveled to warn the Cedar pack about what had happened to our stream," Oak began. Shadow noticed there was blood shining on her father's shoulder and muzzle, as well as his ear. Shadow realized with a jolt that all four of them reeked of blood. She stared up at him as he continued, her eyes wide. "Instead of thanking us for warning them, they decided to challenge us for our land! We barely made it out. Their Healer, Echo, decided to help us. She got us away. But, that does not forgive what the Cedar pack has done to us. We must attack at once! To drive them away from our land!" Oak howled, his eyes cold. Shadow watched in horror as her packmates erupted in agreement around her. She turned to see that Kele shared her same horrified expression, his eyes wide and tail between his legs.

Miku and Breeze shared frightened expressions, their ears pinned to their heads. Shadow stood up and made her way through her packmates, her expression grim. She knew that she must get to her father, to stop this madness. Storm was already at his side, attempting to talk him out of it. Shadow bunched her muscles and leaped up to stand beside Storm, eyes wide. "We cannot do this! The pack is in no state to be fighting right now and we need to be united. The Learners have barely started training!" Storm was arguing with him, shooting a glance at Shadow. Shadow dipped her head, staring pleadingly at her father.

"Oak, you can't do this. Your pack needs you to be strong. And sometimes, being strong means letting things go, and listening to what your packmates have to say!" Shadow told him, pleading in her voice. Oak stared at his mate and daughter, an angry expression on his face.

"Are you both blind? The Cedar pack attacked me! I could have died, along with some of the highest-ranking wolves in this pack! The Cedar pack would have killed us, and for what, a scrap of land? They cannot be trusted. They need to be driven away!" Oak snarled, his tail raised in authority. Shadow winced as if she had been hit, while Storm stood tall, refusing to give in.

"Oak, you must see reason. We are in no state to fight. I'm sure there is a way to solve this peacefully. Fighting is not the answer! Blood will be spilled, and that blood will pour at your feet. Is that really what you want?" Storm growled.

"You are a great leader, Oak. I know you know what is best for your wolves. Do you really want to do this?" Shadow queried, standing tall beside her mother. She was a little over half her size, but she knew she was doing the right thing by standing up for the starving pack.

"We have enough problems to worry about without a battle raging out in front of us," Storm said, her tail tucked between her legs. Oak stared at them both, his eyes deciding. He reluctantly gave a heavy sigh, though he still looked angry.

"You may be right, Storm. Maybe we don't need this battle. I'm sorry for being so selfish. It was wrong of me. Thank you for helping me to see reason," Oak spoke, turning back to the wolves before him, who had quieted down. Shadow sighed in relief and jumped back down to join her brother, her legs shaking.

"My pack, I am sorry, for I have made a mistake. We will not harm a Cedar pack wolf today. My mate and daughter have helped me to see reason and there is no good outcome from starting a war. You may go back to your dens. No wolf will leave tonight," Oak finished, waving his tail in dismissal. Shadow sighed deeply with alleviation.

"Well, it is too bad we can't go hunting," Kele whispered in her ear as he stood to retreat to the Learners' den. Shadow followed him, glancing at Breeze and Miku as they came to walk beside her.

"Well, I guess we're just going to have to plan for a different night," Miku said as they all entered their den and curled up in their sleeping places.

"Shouldn't we be doing something other than sleeping? It's not even sundown yet," Shadow complained, sitting down in her hole. Kele shook his head, sitting next to her.

"What the Alpha says, goes," he told her, curling up to sleep. Shadow huffed, then curled up and wrapped her tail over her nose, listening to the steady breathing of her brother beside her. After a while, she felt herself grow tired. She was eventually lulled into a deep, calm sleep.

Chapter Six

Shadow dropped her head and slowly crept forward; her eyes locked on the leaf laid out in front of her. Lynx had been training her all afternoon, testing her knowledge, and teaching her new hunting moves. It had been weeks since they had reported the water problem, and her pack was coping well. Because the lake was so far away, Oak had sent out wolves to find closer sources of water, and Scout had found a small pond near their den site. Shadow found that prey was a lot easier to come by on the side of the forest opposite from the stream. She and her packmates sometimes journeyed outside of the territory to find more prey.

Shadow strode forward silently until she was directly behind the leaf. She remembered what Lynx had told her, making sure to be downwind from her prey. She suddenly shot forward and snapped her jaws around the leaf's stem, tearing it clean off. Lynx had told her to practice the killing bite, and she had been doing it all afternoon. Her Trainer had then left her and returned to the den site, letting her practice by herself. She focused on a stick a few yards away, lowering herself and creeping up behind it, making sure to stay downwind. She studied it for weaknesses, focusing on a thin part where it was broken off. When the time was right, and the wind moved the trees above her, she shot forward and clamped her jaws shut around the weak area, her paws silent, her aim precise. She then spit out the splinters and moved on to another target, this time finding a large fallen branch. She repeated the steps and then shot forward, this time from a bit of a distance away. She silently snapped its 'neck' and sat back, panting.

Shadow pricked her ears as something moved out in front of her. She instinctively dropped down and hid behind some bushes, her senses alert. The scent of hare filled her nose just before she spotted the creature. A large, fat hare emerged from between two thorn bushes, grabbing at some clover with its little paws and beginning to nibble at the leaves. The shadows danced along its milky brown pelt, and its ears were laid back. Shadow's heart raced as she stared at the creature, unsure of what to do. *Lynx would want me to kill it, right?* she thought, twitching an ear. She crept through the shadows, stopping about ten feet behind it. There, she waited for a gust of wind to blow the treetops, sure the hare would hear her pounding heart. She studied the animal for weaknesses, remembering what Lynx had told her. *Hares are vulnerable without their legs, so they can't spring away,* Shadow recalled, her muscles tense. Suddenly, a gust of wind rattled the branches around her, changing direction. She realized with a jolt that it was sending her scent straight toward her prey! She instantly shot forward, advancing on the hare. But, it was too late. It had already caught her scent and was bounding away.

Shadow raced after it, her eyes locked on its hips. She put on a burst of speed and caught up with it, snapping her jaws around its hind leg just as it was about to disappear down a hole. She lifted it, surprised at its weight. The hare pounded her in the nose with its other leg, jabbing her eyes. She kept her teeth wrapped around it, unsure of what to do next. Thinking quickly, she slammed her paw down on its neck, pinning its head to the ground. She let go of its leg and could taste blood on her tongue. Shadow sunk her teeth into its neck and heard its spine break. The hare instantly went limp at her feet, its injured leg twitching. Shadow let go, wincing at a cut on her forehead. She sat back to admire her catch, her tongue lolling out. Then, she stood, snatching her kill off the ground, and returned to where she was practicing in the clearing.

It was now later in the day, after Lynx had come back to check on Shadow. Her Trainer had taken the hare back to the den site while Shadow stayed in a small clearing practicing swiping at enemies with her front paws. She stood on her haunches and swiped with both her forepaws, lashing out at the birch tree that stood in front of her and sending shavings of bark flying through the air. Shadow dropped back onto four paws and looked up at the next tree that she would practice on. She caught her breath and trotted over to the tree, heaving herself onto her hind legs, and swiping at the tree with a growl.

When she finished marking the trees surrounding her clearing she sat down to rest. It was a beautiful day. The sun was shining through the oak and maple leaves, sending shadows dancing throughout the grass-filled clearing. Birds chirped all around her and flowers were blooming in the crevices of the tree roots. A small breeze blew through the forest occasionally, drifting under Shadow's fur and cooling her warm skin. She licked one of her sore pads and then stood up, wondering what to do next. Suddenly, she smelled Lynx's scent. Shadow turned around and followed the scent until she reached the edge of the clearing, where she peeked out, looking for the familiar patterns of Lynx's pelt. She spotted no movement, so she dropped her tail and stalked forward, her ears angled forward. *You will usually hear or smell your prey before you see them,* Lynx's words rang in her ears. She made sure to keep quiet, her head low. Shadow stopped, listening to the faint noise that came from ahead of her. She found the scent trail, following it at a trot until she finally found her Trainer.

Lynx was sitting under a fern, her pelt barely visible in the shadows. Suddenly, Lynx shot out from underneath the ferns, her teeth bared, aiming at Shadow's neck. Shadow jumped, snarling, and instinctively nipped at her Trainer's ear. Lynx sat back with a satisfied look, a drop of blood running down her cheek.

"Good. I'm glad you've been listening to me. Always be ready. I was wondering how long it would take you to find out I was here," Lynx said humorously, standing and heading back up the trail Shadow had been following. Shadow followed with her tail held high.

"Well, I've been training, as you told me," Shadow said, her eyes light. Lynx nodded, not taking her eyes off the trail ahead of her.

"I know, I've been watching. You didn't really think that I would leave you alone, did you?" Lynx chuckled as they entered the training grounds. "No, I know how hard you have been working. And Oak does, too," Lynx told her, an amused expression on her face. As she spoke, Oak emerged from the bushes on the other end of the clearing, his head held high. Shadow looked at him with surprise and gently dipped her head in respect. Oak twitched his tail in dismissal, his eyes bright.

"I, too, have been watching your progress Shadow. It's amazing how fast you learn! Lynx and I think that you are ready to go on your first real hunt," Oak told her, excitement glowing in his eyes. Shadow's ears perked up at the sound of that.

"Really? You think I'm ready?" she asked them both, her tail skimming the ground. Only the best hunters, along with the highest-ranking wolves, were chosen to go on actual deer hunts. Lynx and Oak both nodded, Oak's eyes glowing with pride. Shadow raised her head proudly, happiness warming her from her ears to her tail. "When will we be leaving?" she asked them, glancing at Oak.

"As soon as we can. Sparrow, Heather, Scout, Lynx, Storm, and I will be going, as well," Oak said, glancing at Lynx. Shadow sighed in relief knowing that her Trainer was coming.

"We must be getting back to the den site, then," Lynx piped up, smiling. Shadow gave a nod, barely containing her excitement and pride to be chosen for such an important thing.

"We will set out toward the lake. There have been reported deer sightings around the area, and I want to see if we can bring back something good for the pack," Oak told them from where he stood on the Alpha stone. Storm stood at his side, her eyes flitting to each wolf in the clearing. Shadow sat with Miku and Kele at the edge of the crowd, murmuring eagerly to each of them.

"I was chosen for the hunt! I wonder if I'll be a Hunter or a Fighter when I get older," Shadow whispered to Miku. He looked back at her, amusement in his gaze.

"I think I might be a Hunter. I kind of like hunting. Sparrow says I'm good at it," Miku whispered back, staring up at Oak. Kele huffed, clearly jealous.

Shadow nodded back, whispering, "Yeah, me too. I still can't believe that Oak was impressed enough to let me join this hunt!"

"Well, I'm really bad at hunting," Kele whispered ruefully, twitching an ear. Shadow felt a twinge of pity for him. It must be hard, having such a strict Trainer. She was thankful that Lynx was so laid-back. *At least we haven't started battle training yet,* she thought, sighing.

Oak was now naming off the wolves who would join the hunt. "Sparrow, Heather, Scout, Amber, Shadow, Lynx, and Miku will follow me to the hunting grounds. Storm will stay behind and watch over the clearing," Oak called before jumping down from the stone with a flick of his tail. Shadow brightened with excitement when she heard her name called along with Miku's.

"You're coming, too?" She asked him happily, her eyes wide. Miku stared at Oak, his mouth gaping.

"Me? Really? I can't believe it! Nobody even told me," he said, his eyes bright. Shadow grinned, glancing over at Kele. He was walking away toward the Learners' den, his tail drooped. She rolled her eyes and turned back to Miku, her heart warming. "Well, we better go and join the group," Miku said, glancing at the group that was forming of the wolves chosen for the hunt.

"I wonder why Breeze isn't coming," Shadow said, glancing at Miku. Breeze was slumped on the ground outside of the Learners' den, his ears flat.

"Oh," Miku answered, amusement shining in his eyes. "He was confined to the den site for half a day because he was caught trying to sneak out during the night. It was hilarious," Miku chuckled, hurrying to join the others as Oak led them out of the clearing. Shadow followed him, shaking her head and smiling.

They moved as a group through the forest, stopping only to taste the air and listen for deer. They had almost reached the lake as the sun was setting, casting shadows over the group as they veered along the hunting trail. Shadow trotted alongside Miku, Lynx ahead of her. "We should split up, but stay in earshot," Oak told them, signaling with his tail. Shadow nodded and went off with Miku toward a big oak tree, her ears flattened, eyes wide. She spotted some hoofed tracks in the dirt and bent over to sniff them. *Get a whiff of the scent so you can track it to where it lies,* Lynx had told her. Shadow beckoned Miku with a wave of her tail and followed the scent with her head low and ears angled forward to catch any sounds of her prey. She moved quietly through the brush, sniffing the air as she went. At the edge of a small clearing Shadow crouched down and peeked through the ferns, her eyes widening. There, in the clearing, stood three deer. The biggest stood in the middle of the clearing, its giant, vicious-looking antlers planted on the top of its head. Shadow felt a jolt run through her when she thought of attacking that animal, fearful of what could happen if those long and deadly points contacted her body.

The buck stood tall and proud, its jaw moving rhythmically as it chewed on the tall grass that filled the clearing. The muscle rippled under its skin as it took a step forward, unaware of Shadow and Miku's presence. Miku crouched tensely beside her. Shadow's heart pounded in her ears, its vibrations thrumming through her body. The big deer's fur was lighted by the fading sun, giving it a sort of eerie brown glow. Two smaller deer flanked him, their heads bare of antlers. They stood quietly, chewing, unaware of the attack that was coming.

Suddenly, one of Shadow's packmates appeared beside her. *Lynx!* Shadow breathed a silent sigh of happiness at the sight of her Trainer. Lynx crouched, muscles tense, waiting for the right time to attack. Shadow's packmates filed in around her – first Oak, then Amber, then the rest of the group. At a wave of Oak's tail, they would all spring into action. But Oak was playing something different this time. He stepped out of the bushes with his lips drawn back in a snarl, ears pinned to his head, and fur fluffed up to make him look bigger than usual. The smallest deer took one look and bounded away, its eyes fearful. Shadow had to stop herself from chasing, remembering the rules. *The Alpha always makes the first move on a hunt. Only attack when he or she gives the signal,* Lynx had explained on the way here. Lynx gave her a warning look as if reminding her to stay put. Shadow sat still, watching her father as he slowly advanced on the giant buck, his snarl echoing through the trees.

The buck suddenly reared up on its hind legs and let out a snort, its giant hooves waving in the air. Oak let out a yelp and jumped back out of range as the deer came crashing down, its sharp hooves piercing the ground Oak had just left. Shadow's packmates shot forward and advanced on the deer, leaving Shadow and Miku in the bushes. The two deer turned tail and ran, now being chased by a pack of hungry wolves. Shadow bounded after them, Miku on her tail. They ran through the forest, chasing the deer, snarling, and nipping at their legs. Shadow tried to find a way to help, watching as Lynx and Sparrow left the group and raced ahead on one side. Heather and Amber did the same on the other side. Thinking fast, Shadow followed her Trainer, her paws pounding against the ground. Her breath came ragged in her throat as she ran faster and faster, racing ahead of the deer. Shadow jumped onto a ledge of dirt and ran above the deer and her packmates.

The deer were being chased into a corner, she realized. Up ahead was a dead end, where the ledge wrapped around and connected with a rock wall running along the other side, providing a large open space surrounded on three sides. It was a perfect place to finish the hunt. Shadow pulled ahead, her paws skimming the ground as she stopped to watch what would happen next. Her packmates chased the deer into the corner where the big animals whirled around, surrounded by bared teeth and sharp claws. The wolves advanced on the deer, Oak in the front, flanked by Amber and Scout. Oak shot forward and sunk his teeth into the buck's exposed throat, snarling. The buck reared, snorting in pain, and kicked Oak away with his front hoof. Oak pulled back, the deer's blood dripping from his chin. Crimson liquid poured out of the wound, staining the deer's fur and filling the air with its sweet metallic smell. The doe reared up and stomped down, missing Sparrow by a hair. The buck swayed on its feet as if he were about to fall, but then reared up and turned to escape.

The buck placed its giant hooves on the crumbling ledge and hauled himself up, his breath heaving with effort. He crawled to the top where Shadow stood, his eyes wide and crazed with desperation to escape. Shadow's packmates watched, horrified, as the buck escaped their trap and turned his attention to Shadow. Shadow yelped in surprise as the deer turned to her, head down, ready to charge. Instinct took over and Shadow dove to the side, snarling. The deer turned, confused, and took a step back toward the ledge, its hoof slipping in the crumbling soil. Shadow shot forward, driving it back, letting her teeth dig into its neck. The buck stepped back and tried to rear up but the dirt at the edge of the ledge crumbled under its weight. Shadow let go as the buck fell tail first back into the hole, hitting the ground with a massive thud and a sickening crunch.

Shadow looked over the edge. The buck lay on the ground below her, its hind leg broken. The buck made a horrible gurgling noise and attempted to stand, but the leg gushed blood and he crumbled back to the floor. Shadow's packmates advanced, Amber taking hold of its injured leg and Sparrow biting into its flank. Oak lunged forward and bit into its neck once more, this time not letting go. Shadow heard a crunch as its windpipe was crushed, and then the deer went limp, its foreleg twitching violently. The doe let out a bleat of despair and then began frantically trying to escape, rushing at the wolves and attempting to jump over them. But the wolves were too fast, and its efforts were wasted. The doe went down within seconds, its eyes still opened. Shadow jumped down from the ledge and watched the deer bleed out onto the sandy floor.

Shadow was the last to slip through the entrance into the den site, her head high. Her packmates were dragging the deer in front of her, laying them out in the center of the clearing. The rest of the pack filed in around them, drawn by the scent of blood. Their eyes widened at the sight of the deer, and they began to whisper excitedly. Shadow looked at her packmates, ears perked. Oak stood on the Alpha stone, the moonlight glowing on his pelt and lighting his eyes. "We will feast tonight!" he called to the surrounding wolves.

Shadow's packmates cheered, eyes locked on the deer. Oak jumped down from the Alpha stone and stood beside Storm. Together, they began to eat. When they finished eating the best part of the deer, Oak waved his tail, signaling for the rest of the pack to eat. Shadow sat back, waiting her turn. Kele appeared beside her, eyes bright. "What a feast! I haven't seen a deer that big in my whole life," Kele said. Shadow smiled.

"Yes, great job, Shadow," Miku's voice sounded from beside her. She turned to look at him, her ears hot.

"Thanks, but I didn't deliver the killing bite," Shadow explained, shuffling her paws.

"Well, you sure didn't just stand there and do nothing! You trapped that deer back in the hole. If you weren't there, we would have lost the deer," Miku told her, half talking to Kele. Shadow suddenly found her paws very interesting and stared down at them, her face hot as she smiled.

"Well, that was just luck," She explained, thankful as it was her turn to eat. Oak and Storm backed away, followed by Amber and Luna. Shadow took Storm's place, tearing off a mouthful of warm meat. The delicious flavors spilled out on her tongue, warming her body. The smell of blood and fresh meat filled her nose and lungs. She hungrily tore off another piece and chewed quickly, noticing how fast the flesh was disappearing. When the meat on the hind quarters was gone she moved on to one of the front shoulders, gnawing on the flesh and stripping the bone clean. When her belly was full, she pulled away, her eyes drooping. Miku was finished, too, and he stood beside her, blood dripping from his chin. He looked happier with a full stomach, and Shadow felt happier. She licked the blood out of her fur and sat back on her haunches, satisfied.

Her packmates were slowly backing away from the deer, most of the bones licked clean. There was enough food for maybe one more good meal, Shadow thought. The wolves around her were disappearing into their dens, feet dragging on the ground, ears twitching, obviously satisfied. Shadow and Miku helped Oak and Amber drag the leftover deer to a sheltered place under the buckthorn, protected from other animals like foxes, coyotes, or bears. Then, Oak sent Shadow and Miku to bed, thanking them for their help. Shadow curled up in her sleeping place between Kele and Miku. She longed for Miku's warmth but was unsure if he felt the same way. She wrapped her tail over her nose and quickly fell asleep, her belly full and pelt warm from the wolves surrounding her.

Shadow opened her eyes not to the Learners' den, but instead to a wide, open forest surrounding her. She prepared herself for another dream, standing and taking in her surroundings. Large, tall oaks stretched to the sky around her. Shadow trotted through the forest, seeking the purpose of her dream. Like before, the scent of smoke filled her nose and lungs. "What are you telling me?" she asked her dream, coughing. The smoke stung her eyes and throat, filling her lungs painfully. She held her breath, the thick air pressing down on her and seeming to wrap its arms around her throat. She gagged on the stench, unable to hold her breath any longer. *This is worse than before*, she realized. She scrambled through the forest, frantically looking for a way away from the acrid smoke. Suddenly, a fire was blazing in front of her, burning everything in its path. It moved quickly through the trees, destroying everything it touched. Trees crashed to the ground all around her, shaking her paws. She pressed herself against the ground, tears streaming from her eyes and blurring her vision. Animals scurried away from the flames but were soon turned to ash, the hot red flames burning through their fur and destroying them right before her eyes.

Knowing there was no escape, Shadow pressed herself to the ground, the sound of the flames burning the forest around her filling her ears and thrumming against her eardrums. Just when she thought she would be consumed by fire, the ground caved beneath her and she fell through the darkness into what seemed like an endless black hole. She howled, eyes screwed shut, paws flailing in the empty air. Suddenly, she crashed to the ground, the sound of wolves howling in pain filling the air. She blinked the smoke out of her eyes and looked up, horrified by what she saw. Humans were invading the territory, towering over her packmates. She watched helplessly as they speared her packmates with the flames, turning them to dust. She would never forget the horrified expressions on their faces as they slowly perished, disappearing into the air and leaving nothing behind but the echoes of their howls.

Suddenly, she was all alone. There was no one left. Dark shadows spilled out around her, filling the clearing. Humans towered over her, their eyes red. Crimson blood dripped from their mouths and noses. They grew taller, laughing maniacally, their gruesome shadows casting over the forest. Shadow stared, horrified, willing the dream to end. Again, the scene changed. The humans morphed into pine and spruce trees, the scent of sap filling her nose. She was in a different clearing now, somewhere new. Her packmates were sitting in a group in the center of the clearing, unaware of her presence. They were all looking up at a dark wolf standing on top of a fallen aspen trunk. Shadow could sense something different about them, though. Lynx was sitting next to Max, her head rested on his shoulder. She was watching four pups that were sitting side-by-side at the front of the group, looking excitedly up at the dark wolf. Shadow didn't recognize the pups, but one of them had the same fur patterns as Lynx.

Shadow couldn't see Oak or Storm among the wolves, and when she looked closer she realized she couldn't see Amber, either. Puzzled, she looked up. The sun was beginning to disappear behind the horizon, letting off an eerie red glow that lit the sky. The shadow of the dark wolf stretched out over the pack and instantly Shadow realized that must be the Alpha. Then, as quickly as it had started, the dream faded, and Shadow opened her eyes to the darkness of the Learners' den.

Shadow waited outside the Healer's den, listening to the quiet shuffling that came from inside. She was worried. Oak had been injured on the hunt, and now Luna was tending to his injuries. *"I think he might have a broken rib,"* Luna had told her. *"If he doesn't recover soon, he might be too weak to lead the pack."* Luna's words echoed in Shadow's ears. Some of her packmates were surrounding her, waiting for news from Luna. It was a cool morning, with birds chirping overhead and the sun shining lightly on their pelts. A low breeze stirred the trees and ruffled their fur, disturbing the still, silent air. Suddenly, the Healer emerged, relief and weariness lining her face. "He will recover. His injuries are under control and his breathing is normal. I will allow one visitor at a time to accompany him while he is healing," Luna told the crowd before disappearing back into the den.

Shadow hesitated, watching as Storm stood to enter the den. "Storm," Shadow stopped her, an apologetic look in her eyes. "I must speak with him. I promise I will let you know when I am done." Storm was reluctant to step back.

"Very well, Shadow," she agreed, turning and walking over to the Alpha stone and then jumping on top. The crowd dispersed, merging into small groups that spread across the clearing. Amber barked an order, calling everyone to be sent hunting or marking the territory. Shadow disappeared through the bushes into the Healer's den and padded up to her father, who lay sprawled out in a bed of moss, his eyes filled with pain.

"Oak," Shadow whispered, dipping her head.

"Shadow?" He called back, his voice raspy. Shadow pressed her muzzle against his, listening to his breathing and allowing him to smell her scent.

"Oak, why didn't you tell us that you were hurt?" Shadow asked softly, settling herself beside him. He sighed, wincing.

"I thought I was fine, and I am," he told her briskly, ears pinned. Shadow dipped her head, checking to make sure that Luna wasn't within earshot. She was sorting herbs on the opposite side of the den, paying no attention to their conversation. Shadow looked back at Oak and sighed. "Well, what is it Shadow? I know you didn't just come here to keep me company," Oak said, looking up into her eyes. After a silent moment, Shadow began to explain her dream from the night before and the dream that she had suffered previously. Oak looked nervous yet understanding. "Thank you for sharing this with me, Shadow. These are indeed strange dreams and may have great meaning. I will tell Amber to watch for signs of humans that may invade our territory." Shadow dipped her head in return and pushed past the bushes to leave the den, finding Storm still on the Alpha stone. Shadow gave a nod and Storm jumped down, slipping into the Healer's den as Shadow padded away.

Shadow walked toward Amber, who was sitting at the base of the Alpha stone talking to Heather. "Amber," Shadow said, dipping her head. Amber gave a nod, signaling for Shadow to speak. "You may want to visit Oak sometime today. I think he wants to talk to you." Amber nodded in acknowledgment and then went back to Heather, continuing their conversation. Shadow sighed, feeling as though a huge weight had been lifted off her chest, and looked around the clearing for something to do. She spotted Lynx and Max talking near the entrance, looking as though they were about to leave. Shadow hurried after them, wondering if she could join, wherever they were going.

"Shadow, what are you doing?" Lynx asked as Shadow was coming up behind Max.

"May I come with you? I have nothing to do," Shadow asked her Trainer. Lynx shook her head.

"No, Shadow. Max and I are going to mark near the coyote den. You should not come with us. I don't want you to get hurt again." Lynx said. "Sorry."

"Maybe you could ask Sparrow if you can go with him and Miku. I heard they were going out to train earlier, but I don't know if they've left yet," Max added, and Shadow perked up. "

Yes, good idea, Max," Lynx said, casting him a fond look. With that, Lynx and Max exited the clearing, their tails whisking away. Shadow turned back to the clearing where she saw Mako, Amber, Breeze, Miku, Kele, and Sparrow sitting in a group on the far end. Shadow went to join them, her head high.

"Shadow! Are you going to come with us?" Kele asked, going out to greet her. The group locked eyes with her. Miku looked at her hopefully. "Sure!" She replied.

"Where's Lynx?" Sparrow asked, looking at her.

"She just left with Max to check the coyote den," Shadow explained, padding along with the group as they left the den site. "So, where are we going?" Shadow asked Miku, padding alongside him. The group ducked under a fallen tree and continued along one of the many trails.

"We're going to a hunting clearing where we're going to practice fighting. I guess we need to learn to fight in case the Cedar pack attacks us, or something like that. I'm pretty sure that Amber is leading the training," Miku told her, looking over the heads of their packmates to spot Amber, who was in the lead. Shadow nodded, beginning to walk faster to keep up with her packmates as they increased their pace. They finally reached a huge hunting clearing, with tall standing trees and bramble thickets surrounding them. The morning sun shone down on them, heating their pelts, while a cool scented breeze blew through the woods and cooled their skin. Birds chirped overhead, accompanied by the soft sound of the leaves shifting in the wind. Leaves and pine needles littered the clearing, providing comfortable fighting ground.

"Here we are," Amber addressed the group, turning to stand in the center of the clearing. "Today, you will begin to learn how to defend yourself in a fight. You may need to fight off bears, coyotes, foxes, wolverines, bobcats, cougars, and maybe even other wolves. Later, we will teach you more offensive tricks and tips, moves, and strategies. Now watch," Amber told them, standing on her hind legs. "If something ever attacks you from above, what do you do?" Amber asked them, dropping back onto all fours.

"Move out of range?" Shadow asked, remembering what happened on the hunt.

"Correct, Shadow. Good," Amber praised. Shadow hid her delight with a twitch of her ear. "Now, I want you all to practice on a partner. Shadow and Miku, you practice over there," Amber told them, pointing with her tail toward the far side of the clearing. Shadow beckoned Miku with her tail and raced over to the edge, her tail sticking straight out.

"Okay, so who should rear up?" Shadow asked when Miku reached her.

"I'll do it," Miku volunteered, backing up. Suddenly, he heaved himself up and stood tall on his hind legs. He towered over her, his tail sticking out for balance as he tried to crush her with his forepaws. At the last second, Shadow dove to the side and he missed her by a whole foot.

"Missed me," Shadow laughed, facing him. "Okay, my turn," Shadow said, rearing up on her hind legs and throwing herself forward. Just as she was about to crash into Miku's nose he dove aside and she missed by a hair. "Nice move, Miku! You fooled me," Shadow told him as he stood and walked back over to her.

"Thanks!" Miku replied, grinning.

"Again," Amber commanded from where she sat in the center of the clearing. Shadow was training with Breeze now. Miku, Kele, Mako, and Sparrow were out hunting, while Shadow, Amber, and Breeze continued training.

"We'll be back soon," Miku had told her, but that was some time ago. The sun was now high in the sky, already past its peak, and beginning to make its way back to the horizon. Shadow and Breeze had been training for what seemed like hours, perfecting the moves and learning different tactics. Amber was an outstanding fighter. She could easily beat Shadow and Breeze's efforts combined. Shadow obediently crouched down and then leaped over Breeze, landing behind him. Breeze whirled around, but it was too late. Shadow had already "bit down" into his flank and was now pushing him down to the ground. In reality, she had only nipped him, but if it were a real battle he would be running home badly injured. Shadow then let him go, glancing at Amber for approval. They had been practicing that same move for half an hour, and Shadow felt it was her best one.

"Alright, I would like Breeze to do it one more time, then we can be done with this move," Amber said, satisfaction in her voice. Shadow sighed quietly, willing Breeze to get it right. Suddenly, Breeze leaped over Shadow and landed behind her, nipping her flank. She tried to spin around, but he was already pressing her to the ground. Her legs collapsed from under her. Breeze had won. "Very quick, Breeze. Well done," Amber praised him. Shadow groaned with relief and stood up, panting. The hot sun was baking her, and she could tell Breeze felt the same way. "All right, we can take a break," Amber told them, leading to a small puddle formed from the last rain. They drank the warm water until their bellies were full, then began cleaning the sweat and grit out of their paws.

When they were cooled down they returned to the clearing and continued where they left off. Amber showed them a new technique, and they practiced, understanding it almost at once. When they finished, Amber had them sit on opposite ends of the clearing with their backs turned to each other. "Now, when I say go you will turn and practice your new moves on each other. You are well-matched. I hope to see a clean fight. Try to keep your claws to yourself, and bite only to give a warning. I don't want to see any blood or Luna will have my tail," Amber mused, sitting in the center, out of range. Shadow breathed to calm her racing heart. She wanted to impress Amber but didn't know if she was strong enough to take on Breeze. He was taller and stronger. *But maybe I can outsmart him,* she thought, shuffling her paws, her ears flattened to her head. She was barely listening to Amber, her head swirling. "Shadow!" Amber barked, throwing Shadow back into reality. "Go!" Amber repeated.

Shadow stood and whirled around, eyes wide, to see Breeze rushing at her, his teeth bared. Shadow yelped and sidestepped, watching him whoosh past her in a blur of fur and dust. He quickly skidded to a stop and turned on her, rearing up, his eyes half-closed, as if he were scared. Shadow reared to meet his attack, her hind legs shaking, pelt hot with embarrassment. She growled deep in her throat, ears pinned to her head, as she matched him blow for blow. Just as he was about to bite her muzzle, she ducked out of the way, and he snapped at empty air. Breeze immediately dropped down to his paws and swiped at her again, this time also lunging at her nose. Shadow dodged his blows, snarling, smacking him with her paw. He flinched away, eyes closed. Shadow thought quickly and rushed at him, staring at his forehead so that he would think to duck. But, just as he ducked down to avoid where she was looking, Shadow swiped at his face and sidestepped out of reach, panting.

This was all going in slow motion in Shadow's head. She rushed him again, this time nipping at his flank, pulling him to the ground with her forepaws. She then jumped on top of him and pinned his head and legs to the ground, keeping him in place. Knowing that he could easily get out of her grip, she leaped over his head, snapping at his ears as she did so. Suddenly, the scent of blood filled her nose. Breeze had retaliated, nipping at her leg. Blood was welling at the tiny cut, a small drop beginning to run down her leg. Shadow quickly licked the scratch and turned back to Breeze, seeing he was rushing her. She yelped as he leaped into the air and landed on her back, flattening her in an instant. He pressed her snout into the dirt as she struggled to get away. After a few moments, Shadow gave up.

Shadow knew Breeze had won but she wasn't very disappointed about it. At least their training session was over, and she could go do what she was good at – hunting. "Great job, Breeze," Shadow said. "Now we can hunt, I think." Shadow saw that Miku, Kele, Mako, and Sparrow had returned during the fight. Miku held a big bird, Kele a lizard, Sparrow two rabbits, and Mako a squirrel.

"That was good. I saw exceptional skills in both of you. Now, we can take our turn to hunt. Mako, Sparrow, make sure that Miku and Kele get enough training. When we finish hunting, we will return to the den site," Amber told them with a flick of her tail. Mako and Sparrow dipped their heads to Amber before leading their Learners into the center of the clearing. Shadow turned back to Breeze and Amber, her eyes bright. "Shadow, you're bleeding," Amber said, pointing out the scratch on her hind leg. Shadow licked the blood and dirt off the cut and shrugged.

"It's fine," Shadow replied to the Beta, following her into the trees. Shadow kept her senses alert for signs of prey. Every few yards she stopped to sniff the air, listen for prey, and look around to take in her surroundings.

"Okay. Split up," Amber directed Shadow and Breeze. Shadow nodded and then signaled for Breeze to go toward a large clump of ferns, turning herself toward a stand of birch trees. Amber went straight ahead, her head low. Shadow stalked quietly forward, listening, smelling the air, ready for anything. It wasn't long before she spotted a hare sitting under an oak tree nibbling on an acorn. Shadow lowered her head and crept closer, unaware of the twig that was under one of her paws. Shifting her weight, the twig cracked, giving away her position. The hare perked its ears and shot away, its fuzzy tail bouncing between its legs. Shadow growled under her breath and bolted after it. She didn't think of saving her stamina but ran full speed behind the hare, her lips drawn back in a snarl. Just as she was about to bite its leg, the hare sidestepped out of reach, swerving around a tree. Shadow, too focused on trying to bite the animal, ran straight into the tree. Pain shot through her face and forepaws, blinding her. A horrible burning sensation traveled from her eye to her nose, back to her eye again, spreading through her face. Not only did she lose the hare, but something had been lodged in her eye, too. A piece of bark, she guessed. Shadow whined in pain, unaware of where she was, half of her body burning with pain. She tried to open her eyes, but one of them seemed to be sealed shut. She lifted a paw to her face, feeling gingerly around the injured places. Blood ran from a scratch on her forehead and dripped from her nose, minimizing her ability to smell what was around her.

Shadow stood, looking down at her paws. One of the claws had been torn from her front left paw, and the other was dampened with blood from a scratch on her leg. She suddenly felt a presence behind her. Breeze had appeared, a worried look on his face. "Shadow, what happened?" Breeze asked. Shadow ignored the question, her pelt hot with embarrassment. "How did you get hurt?" Breeze repeated, and it was clear that he would not give up. Shadow sighed.

"I was chasing a hare and I…I ran into a tree," she admitted, studying her paws with one eye. Breeze hurried to her side and nudged her forward, noticing how she was limping from her torn claw.

"How did that happen?" Breeze asked, pointing at her paw with his nose. Shadow huffed.

"I don't know! Can't you just leave me alone," she snapped? Breeze winced, frowning. Shadow immediately regretted being so harsh. "I'm sorry, Breeze, I..." Shadow tried. Breeze flicked an ear in acknowledgment, hurrying forward. Shadow limped after him, grimacing with every step. Amber emerged from the bushes, a squirrel in her jaws. She dropped her prey and hurried to Shadow when she spotted her swollen face.

"What happened?" Amber demanded, glancing from Shadow to Breeze and back to Shadow again. They both exchanged weary glances before Shadow replied.

"I was chasing a hare and ran into a tree," she admitted, flattening her ears. Amber stepped forward and began licking the blood out of her eyes. Shadow winced at the tender wound on her eye. "It stings!" she yelped, stepping out of reach of Amber's tongue. Amber looked around and Shadow guessed she was finding how much daylight was left.

"It's getting late, but we still have a few hours before dark," Amber said. "We should get back to the den site. We can hunt again later," Amber said, whisking her tail. Shadow followed close behind Breeze, sad that she was the reason they had to go home. *I'll make up for it,* Shadow thought, her tail curled between her legs.

"Hold still, Shadow, I need to get this piece of bark out!" Luna scolded, flattening her ears. Shadow held her breath as Luna pulled the piece out of her eye, barely biting back a howl of pain. She and Luna were inside the Healer's den, Luna treating Shadow's wounds. Luna went over to the holes filled with herbs and came back with a piece of moss soaked with water. "This is water that has been tinged with a lily petal poultice. It will help soothe your eye and clear infection," Luna told her, the moss dripping from where she held it in her mouth. Shadow opened her eyes widely as Luna leaned over her and let a few drops wash the bits of remaining bark out of her eye. The Healer then placed her paw over Shadow's eye to keep the medicine from draining out. Shadow felt a burning sensation under her eyelid, but kept it to herself, not wanting to disturb Luna's concentration.

As Luna worked on Shadow's wounds, Shadow glanced at her father. He was sleeping peacefully in a bed on the other side of the den, his flanks rising and falling while he slept. Storm was sitting beside him, gently stroking his spine with her tail, her eyelids drooping. Shadow felt her heart soften for them both. Pity washed over her at the sight of her father, in pain, unable to lead his pack. *He's a strong wolf, and he will make it through his,* she assured herself, wincing as Luna applied some sort of herb to her torn claw. "My eye will be okay, right, Luna?" Shadow asked softly, trying to blink open her eye. It seemed to be swollen shut.

"Yes," Luna replied, not looking up from her herbs. Shadow sighed with relief as she waited for Luna to finish, trying to be patient.

When the Healer finished, Shadow thanked her and hurried out of the den and into the cool, fresh air. Dark blue clouds swarmed above them, stretching as far as the eye could see. Rain scented the breeze. Shadow frowned. *This means I won't be able to go hunting tonight,* she realized, growling quietly to herself. Shadow shook off her worries and turned back to look at the pack. Lynx had returned with Max and they were sitting together, eating the leftover deer with Amber, Scout, and Heather. It seemed all the wolves were back in the clearing, except Miku, Mako, Kele, and Sparrow. Shadow sighed. Breeze was sitting outside the Learners' den, looking lonely. Shadow strode over to him and sat beside him. He glanced at her and then went back to fiddling with a feather.

"Look, Breeze, I'm sorry for before. I was just in a lot of pain, and I wasn't thinking straight. I shouldn't have snapped at you," she apologized again, dipping her head. He accepted her apology with a dip of his head, then stood and went off to the prey pile. A squirrel, a pigeon, and a rabbit were the only things left from the daily hunts. Shadow hurried after him, grabbing the squirrel.

"I'm going to bring this to Luna," she told him, hurrying off to the Healer's den. She gave Luna the squirrel, then exited the den quickly, hating to see Oak in so much pain. The clouds were growing darker by the minute, the air thick with the smell of rain. Shadow was just about to join Lynx, Max, Heather, Scout, and Amber to finish the deer when a bolt of lightning lit up the sky, followed by an enormous boom of thunder. She yelped, her ears ringing, the ground shaking under her paw. She crouched down, eyes wide, as a giant drop of water landed on her nose. Suddenly, without warning, rain began pouring from the sky, almost instantly soaking the clearing and splattering at her paws. Buckets upon buckets of water seemed to pour on Shadow's fur, chilling her to the bone. The wolves around her yelped, scurrying into the shelter of their dens. Another blinding bolt of lightning flashed across the sky, shining bright in Shadow's eyes. She blinked furiously, jumping as another boom of thunder shook the world around her, ringing in her ears. She yelped in pain as small pellets of hail shot from the sky and raked through her pelt. Thousands of the tiny ice pellets bombarded her as she backed away into the Learners' den, whining in pain.

"Ouch, that hurt!" she exclaimed, peering farther into the den. Breeze was huddled in a corner, muttering to himself, while Miku and Kele stood there watching her from the center of the den. Miku's head was tipped to the side and his fur was matted from the rain.

"That was crazy!" Miku exclaimed, touching his nose to Shadow's cheek.

"When did you get back?" Shadow asked Miku and Kele.

"Just a few seconds ago, right before the rain started," Miku replied. "What happened to your face? Did a fox get you?" he added, surveying the injuries on Shadow's face and legs. Shadow, her face hot with embarrassment, told him and Kele about how she had run into the tree while chasing the hare. Miku licked her sympathetically while Kele snickered, curling up in his sleeping place and wrapping his tail around his lean figure.

"Oh, stop it, Kele," Shadow growled, her ears flattened. She then walked over to her sleeping place and curled up, weariness dragging at her paws.

"I'm sorry that happened, Shadow," Miku spoke, walking over to her sleeping place and licking one of her ears. Shadow smiled up at him, and he turned to curl in his own sleeping hole.

"I wish I could have eaten before the rain started. I'm hungry," Kele spoke softly from his bed before drifting off to sleep. When she finished cleaning the dirt and water from her fur, Shadow, too, was feeling drowsy. She watched Miku lay down in his hole and lick his paws, obviously annoyed the rain had soaked his thick fur. Shadow stood and quietly, not wanting to wake Kele or Breeze, walked over to him and dug out a new sleeping hole right next to him.

"Let me help you with that," she said as she began licking the water out of his fur to help warm him up. He smiled gratefully at her and then began cleaning the water out of her scruff, his breath warm on her neck. She licked his chest and then rested her head on her paws, comforted by his warmth, and soon drifted off to sweet, dreamless sleep.

Chapter Seven

Shadow woke the next morning with Miku still sleeping peacefully beside her, his head resting on his paws. Shadow felt her heart swell as she looked at him. The scratches on her face were already healing, and she was feeling better. She blinked open her injured eye, sighing in relief when she realized she could see fine. She then stood and stretched, shaking out her pelt. Shadow glanced at her brother, Kele, who was sleeping, paws in the air, head tipped back, snoring lightly. Breeze, too, was still asleep, his eyelids fluttering nervously as he slept, as if he was having a bad dream. Bright sunlight was shining through the entrance of the den, making Shadow wince, as her eyes were not adjusted to the light. She slipped out of the den and into the damp morning air. Large puddles of water from last night's storm littered the clearing. The damp earth stuck slightly to her paws and underbelly as she trotted over to her Trainer, who was sitting drowsily beside Max, letting him lick her scruff. Birds chirped in the trees around them, the leaves on the buckthorn that surrounded the clearing sparkling with dew in the sunlight. Shadow admired them, pricking her ears. It would be a good day for hunting, she thought, smiling. Lynx sat up as Shadow approached her, her ears twitching.

"Good morning, Lynx!" Shadow exclaimed, rushing to her Trainer. Lynx dipped her head.

"Good morning, Shadow," Lynx replied slowly, sitting back on her haunches.

"What are we doing today? Hunting? Training? It would be a good day for either," Shadow said, tipping her head to the side.

"Actually, Shadow," Lynx replied, "I was thinking, today, we go to the lake and hunt. I can show you different kinds of fish, and maybe we will see an otter or two. If we do, I can show you how to catch those, as well," Lynx told her, standing up. Shadow jumped up.

"Really?" She breathed excitedly. Lynx nodded, beginning to pad out of the den site. Shadow followed, beaming.

When they reached the lake, Shadow, again, was awestruck by its beauty. The bright morning sun shone across the ripples and lit the water. Nearing the shoreline, Shadow noticed that she could see right to the bottom. Weeds and cattails surrounded the outer edge of the lake, giving shelter to fish and otters, and other animals. Lynx led her to a clump of cattails and sat down, motioning to them with a paw.

"Do you see these? These cattails give shelter to fish. If you can get close enough to the water, you can scoop the fish out with your teeth. Watch," Lynx instructed, bending forward. "Make sure your breath doesn't send ripples through the water, or the fish will see you. And try to keep your shadow out of the water, or they get spooked and swim away," Lynx told her, still staring at the water. In a flash, she shot forward, her face going under. A moment later, she resurfaced with a big fish in her teeth. Lynx threw it to the ground and bit down hard on its neck, water dripping from her chin. "Your turn," she said, motioning Shadow forward with her tail.

Shadow walked to a clump of lily pads a few yards farther up the shore and peered through their petals. She spotted a small, shiny fish, its tiny fins allowing it to dart from side to side. Shadow plunged her face into the water, clamping her jaws around something small and slimy. When she lifted her head and looked down at her catch she realized she had captured a small clump of weeds. The fish had gotten away. Shadow huffed and spit out the weeds. She wasn't giving up that easily! She shifted to a different spot and bent carefully over the water, her eyes darting at every sign of movement. From the corner of her eye, she saw a huge large-mouthed fish emerge slowly from a clump of cattails. She sat perfectly still as the fish swam toward her. Shadow braced herself and, when the time was perfect, shot forward and clamped her jaws around the wriggly, slimy fish. She hauled it out of the water, surprised at its weight, and hurled it onto the ground, just as Lynx had done. Then, she grabbed it behind its head and snapped its spine. Lynx gave her an approving nod before picking up her fish and trotting away. Carrying her first catch, Shadow hurried behind, once again beaming.

Shadow, so focused on her first fish, didn't notice the otter swimming in the water until Lynx pointed it out. She widened her eyes and watched the creature as it swam so easily. Lynx silently set her fish on the ground, then signaled for Shadow to watch from behind a bush. Lynx began walking toward the animal, her head down, limbs moving rhythmically. Shadow watched carefully, studying her movements and techniques. When Lynx was close enough to the otter, she shot forward, plowing through the water until she reached the otter, who was now frantically attempting to escape.

Lynx bit into the furry creature's scruff and hauled it back to shore, the animal squealing and wriggling frantically, trying to get out of Lynx's grip. Lynx dropped it on the ground next to Shadow and held it down with her paw. "Take a good look at it, Shadow," Lynx said. Shadow looked closely at the otter, noticing it looked sort of like a really big weasel. She drank in its scent, remembering it, storing it, recalling it. Wriggling and thrashing, the slippery otter managed to escape the wolves' grip. The animal scurried away, almost reaching the water before Lynx shot forward again, racing down the shoreline and sinking her teeth into its neck. Shadow heard a loud crack, and the otter went limp. Shadow carried both the fish while Lynx carried the otter as they made their way back to the den site.

Back at the clearing, the wolves were out and about, talking, getting ready to leave for a hunt. Shadow noticed the deer bones were gone, guessing that her pack had eaten the rest of it while they were gone. Shadow dropped her fish on the prey pile. "Lynx, can we patrol the territory today?" Shadow asked, glancing at Lynx. "Maybe hunt along the trail, too? I want to learn more about the prey, and what other things we can catch." Lynx thought for a moment before nodding.

"But first, let me take this fish to Oak and Storm. I'm sure they're famished unless they helped eat the rest of that deer this morning," Lynx said, picking up her fish and trotting over to the Healer's Alphas' den.

"Hey, Shadow!" a wolf exclaimed from behind her. She turned around, spotting Miku as he walked over to her.

"Hey, Miku," Shadow replied happily, smiling. He grinned, gazing at her.

"Where are you going today?" he asked, glancing at Lynx, who was returning to Shadow's side.

"We're going out for a patrol of the territory," Shadow replied, motioning toward Lynx. "Want to come?"

"Sure! Just let me make sure it's okay with Sparrow," he replied, hurrying to check in with his father. Sparrow nodded his approval and looked at Lynx who nodded back in agreement. Sparrow then dipped his head to Miku and headed off to join Heather at the entrance of the den site. Miku hurried to join Shadow as she and Lynx exited the clearing.

Shadow was exhausted when they finally returned from their patrol. Lynx had shown them how to catch birds and snakes, and they had marked the whole territory. Shadow and Miku stumbled over to the prey pile and sunk down, their paws throbbing. "That was a long trot," Shadow huffed, glancing at the sky. It was already darkening, she noticed. The sun was slipping under the treetops, giving an eerie orange glow. All they caught was a small pigeon, which for now was the only thing on the prey pile.

"Ugh, I could just curl up in my bed and sleep for a month," Miku said. Shadow scoffed, standing up. There was still daylight, and she didn't want to waste any of it.

"Come on, Miku, let's go do some training. I'm sure our Trainers would be fine with it," Shadow told him, beginning to exit the clearing. "Come *on,* Miku!" Shadow prodded, just loud enough for him to hear. He groaned and hauled himself to his feet before following her out of the clearing.

"I don't see why we have to do this. We can just practice tomorrow," he yawned. Shadow ignored him, emerging into a small training clearing. She crouched, waiting for him to be ready. "You know, we could just talk, and not have to train," Miku told her, sitting down. Shadow sighed, sitting down as well. Maybe he was right. Her paws throbbed, and her face stung. She trotted over to him and sat down beside him, glancing up at his face. He looked somewhat relieved, she noticed.

"Have you seen those strange creatures that moved onto the fields? I think they're called humans, but I don't really know. Heather told me about them once, but I guess I never thought I'd actually see one," Miku said, lying down. Shadow laid down next to him, pressing against his flank.

"No, I haven't seen them. We didn't go near the fields today on the patrol," Shadow said, tipping her head to the side. The humans she saw in her dreams were incredibly scary, she thought.

"Well, I think they're building some sort of den site. There are a bunch of walls and stuff," Miku said, twitching an ear. Shadow thought of what he was saying, her eyelids beginning to droop.

"Hmm…" She replied, resting her head on his shoulder and letting her eyes close. Miku whispered something in her ear, but she couldn't hear it. She was already drifting off into sleep.

Shadow woke the next morning with a start. Realizing she had fallen asleep away from her packmates, she slowly stood up and stretched. Miku was awake, too, blinking open his eyes and yawning. "Miku, we should get back to the den site. They might be wondering where we are," Shadow told him, beckoning him up with a wave of her tail. Miku slowly stood up and shook out his pelt, his eyes bleary.

"I'm sure they just think we've been out early hunting," Miku assured her, glancing up at the morning sky. It was a bright and early morning, with the dew still clinging firmly to the grass and leaves that weren't covered by the shelter of the trees. Shadow shook the frost from her fur and looked up at the sun. It was still behind the treetops, she noticed, sighing with relief. Her packmates would still be sleeping.

"Come on, Miku. The pack is still sleeping, but not for long now," Shadow said, beginning to walk back to the den site. She looked back to make sure he was following, happy when she saw that he was trailing after her, looking somewhat annoyed. Shadow turned and led him back to the pack, becoming more and more worried that her packmates would wake up to see her gone. By the time they got to the den site, Shadow had sped up to a trot. "Finally, back," She muttered to herself as she pushed herself through the entrance and into the clearing. Thankfully, there were no wolves in the clearing except for Oak, who was sitting on the Alpha stone, his eyes closed. Shadow and Miku slipped silently into the Learners' den, sitting down in their beds. Shadow curled up, feeling tired again. She rested her head on her paws and fell back asleep, her tail curled around her flank.

It seemed she had only just fallen back asleep when she woke again, her Trainer standing above her and prodding her with a paw.

"Shadow, wake up," Lynx huffed, clearly annoyed. "It's almost past sunhigh! Usually, you are up early," Lynx growled, turning and exiting the den. Shadow quickly scrambled to her paws and followed after her Trainer. She trotted over to Lynx, who was sitting with a mouse between her paws. "Eat this, and then we are going to train with Kele and Mako," Lynx told her, shoving the mouse closer to Shadow. Shadow ate the tiny scrap in a single bite, frowning at the stringy, dry taste. *How long ago had this been caught?* she thought, swallowing. Shadow then stood and shook out her pelt, watching as Kele and Mako came to join her and her Lynx.

"Greetings, Mako," Lynx said, standing. Shadow met Kele, grinning.

"I guess we're training together," Kele exclaimed, smiling. Shadow nodded, following the Trainers out of the den site. They walked mostly in silence, stopping only to point out prey or talk about where to go. They arrived at the training clearing with a squirrel and two ravens. *Only enough to feed two wolves*, Shadow thought. At first, Lynx and Mako had Shadow and her brother practice old moves, but as the day progressed, they began teaching more complicated tricks of battle. They showed Shadow and Kele how to swerve around their opponent and attack from behind, and to rear up on their hind paws and attack from above.

It was nearing evening when they finished training and they decided to do some hunting on the way back to the den site. Shadow and Kele broke off from their Trainers and hunted together, talking quietly. Shadow searched for signs of prey, pricking her ears as she heard the sound of shifting leaves. Crouching low, she scanned the area, alert for the slightest signs of movement as a snake emerged from a small patch of grass. Shadow, eyes wide, wondered whether she should attack it. She heard stories about how snakes had poisoned wolves and killed them.

Pushing her fears away, she shot out of the underbrush, snapping the head of the snake off the body. She then spat out the head and snatched the body off the ground, beaming. She found Kele, noticing that he had caught a fat rabbit. They returned to their Trainers, who were talking rather than hunting.

Shadow and Kele were congratulated on their hunt and the group returned to the den site, the sun still high enough in the sky to warm their pelts. When they returned and had added their prey to the prey pile Shadow and Kele went to sit near the edge of the clearing, in the shade and out of the heat. "We should go out and train this evening. I'll be bored here," he said. Shadow was only half listening. She was staring at Storm, who was sitting on the Alpha Stone, watching the clearing through narrowed eyes. Shadow wondered if Oak had taken Shadow seriously about her dreams. What if she was right and humans were going to take over the forest? Shadow shook her head and looked around the clearing, watching her packmates. Lynx and Mako were sitting in the sun next to the entrance of the Fighters' den and speaking quietly to each other.

Shadow caught movement out of the corner of her eye that pulled her gaze to the prey pile. The movement was slight, but Shadow thought she saw something sitting in the bushes. Kele had stopped talking and was following her gaze, squinting through the sun. Suddenly, there was a flash of red and white, and a fox shot from the bushes, grabbing a rabbit from the prey pile and disappearing back into the buckthorn. It had all happened quickly, but Shadow reacted immediately, jumping to her paws and racing across the clearing, her paws flying over the sandy ground. She growled, furious, as she spotted the fox weaving its way through the bushes, escaping. Shadow raced after it, pushing herself through the buckthorn and sprinting to catch the animal, fury heating her pelt. She advanced on it quickly. *It must be running slow because of the weight of the rabbit,* she thought subconsciously. She was panting as she bunched and stretched her muscles, intent on catching the animal and getting the wolves' prey back.

With a final lunge, Shadow caught up with the foul-smelling fox. She snarled and bit into its tail, yanking it back to stop it. The fox yowled and dropped the rabbit before racing away through the bushes, its tail dripping blood. Shadow stood panting, watching it go before picking up the rabbit and trotting back to the den site.

Shadow was greeted by Kele and Storm, both standing near the prey pile waiting for Shadow to return. "What happened?" Storm asked as Shadow dropped the rabbit back on the pile.

"A fox tried to steal our prey. I chased it off," Shadow replied, watching as Lynx trotted over, curious about what had happened.

"I didn't even see it until it was too late," Kele added, twitching an ear. Shadow sat down beside the pile, glancing at Storm. She noticed that her mother looked impressed.

"Good job, Shadow," she praised before turning and trotting back over to the Alpha stone.

Lynx dipped her head at Shadow, as if in agreement with Storm, and then trotted across the clearing to sit in the shade. Kele left and slipped into the Learners' den. Shadow sat down in the sun and spotted Miku across the clearing. He was talking to Sparrow, obviously annoyed. Miku noticed Shadow and his gaze softened. He walked across the clearing and sat down beside her, huffing. "What's wrong?" Shadow asked, shifting to give him room to sit.

"Sparrow said I'm to train to become a Fighter, but I want to be a Hunter. Doesn't my opinion count?" He growled, his ears flattened.

"Well, it matters what your Trainer thinks will be best for you. You're obviously the fighting type," Shadow told him, flicking him with her tail, smiling.

He shrugged. "I guess so, but I still think I would make a better Hunter," he said, giving her a sideways glance.

"Well, you shouldn't be worried about that when we have a whole pack to watch over. You will be helping the pack either way, no matter what you become. The pack needs protection just as much as it needs food," Shadow reminded him.

Miku nodded. "Yeah, I guess you're right," he sighed.

"Which reminds me, I should get out hunting!" Shadow exclaimed, sitting up.

"Shouldn't we rest first? I didn't sleep very well last night," Miku said, tilting his head to the side.

Shadow shrugged. "You can do what you want, but I'm going hunting," Shadow replied, making her way out of the clearing. As she was leaving, Max, Mako, and Heather burst into the clearing, their flanks heaving as they fought for air. It looked like they had been running for a long time.

"Storm!" Max snarled, bounding across the clearing until he was right below the Alpha stone. Storm stood up, looking down at him with confusion filling her eyes.

"What is it, Max? What's happened?" Storm asked, waving her tail for silence as the wolves gathered around them, mumbling to each other.

"It's the Cedar pack. We spotted a large group of them deep inside our territory. They seemed to be hunting, or possibly building dens. I don't know. We didn't stay long enough to find out. We came back here so that we could tell you what happened," Max growled, trembling with rage. Storm's face was grim as she waved her tail for silence and jumped down from the stone. "I will inform Oak," she said as she ran over to the Healer's den and pushed past Luna, who was standing at the entrance, her eyes wide and ears flattened at the news. The pack broke into conversation as Storm disappeared inside.

"We should tear them to shreds!"

"I wonder what they want?"

"We have to get them off our land!"

Shadow heard all these things as she looked around, her tail tucked between her legs. A few moments later, Oak emerged from the Healer's den, his eyes burning with anger as he limped over to the Alpha stone and climbed on top of it. Storm followed him, her eyes grim.

"We will send a group to chase them off at once! Max, you will lead a group of Storm, Amber, Mako, Kele, Shadow, Miku, Breeze, and Lynx. Don't come back until the Cedar pack is off our land!" Oak growled, and the pack erupted into a chorus of agreement and excitement. Shadow couldn't help but feel excited. *My first battle!* she thought before standing to follow Miku in joining the chosen wolves. Max gathered the group together with a wave of his tail before ducking out of the clearing, the group following. Shadow was one of the last to leave, her heart pounding in her chest. She was scared, yet excited. *What if I get hurt? Or one of my packmates get hurt?* Shadow fretted, taking a shaky breath. She swallowed her worries as the group swerved around a fallen tree, trotting now. Shadow guessed they would soon be running. As they cleared a patch of ivy, Shadow wondered if the Cedar pack had been driven off their own territory. *Maybe the humans took over? Or a sickness spread, and they had to leave? Or the prey died like it did in our territory?* Shadow thought, recalling how hungry they all were.

Shadow pushed the thoughts away as they neared the place where Max had seen the Cedar pack. The ferns and brambles were trampled and reeked of Cedar pack scent. Shadow lifted her head, standing tall to see over the heads of her packmates, and spotted a group of wolves within a large clearing. They were huddled together, tearing into a small deer they had brought down. Their bones jutted out from under their skin and their breath came in ragged gasps, loud enough for Shadow to hear from where she hid. They ate hungrily, quickly ripping the flesh apart as the deer disappeared. They growled and nipped at each other, trying to get more, as the deer wasn't enough to fill all their empty bellies. As Shadow and her packmates slowly surrounded them, the Cedar pack, no longer crazed by hunger, became more aware of the danger they may be in. The Alpha stood tall, staring into the shadows of the trees, watching for movement. Remembering what Lynx told her, Shadow lowered her head and stood completely still, her eyes trained on her target until Storm emerged from the shadows, growling, tail raised with anger.

"What are you doing on our territory?" she snarled, staring at Slate, the Cedar pack Alpha, with fury burning in her eyes. Slate was a huge dark-gray male with scars covering his body. Shadow couldn't help staring at his blind eye. She thought it looked intimidating, all white and gray. Shadow heard stories about Slate, how he was always picking fights with the Aspen pack, and how he always wanted their territory. Storm's muscles rippled powerfully under her pelt as she took a slow step forward, showing power. She lifted her head and growled deeply, her hackles raised. Slate took a step forward to match her pace, his lips drawn back in a snarl.

"We need food. The prey on our territory has become harder and harder to catch, so we figured it would be okay to stay with you for a while. You can share, can't you?" The Alpha snarled, baring his teeth.

Storm let out an enraged howl. "Are you out of your *mind?*" she snapped, ears pinned to her head. "When have the packs *ever* joined together? Get back on your own territory *now,* stay *off* our land, and find a way to catch *your own* prey!" Storm snarled, waving her tail as the signal. Shadow and her pack instinctively shot out of the underbrush and advanced on their targets. Shadow leaped on top of a skinny she-wolf, knocking her off her paws. She then bit down hard on her scruff, throwing her aside. The she-wolf went stumbling to the ground, her eyes wild with fear. Shadow chased after her as she tried to escape. Jumping nimbly over a fallen branch, Shadow caught her easily. The she-wolf tripped over a tree root and was now lying on the ground, writhing in agony. Shadow advanced.

"Don't hurt me! It wasn't my idea!" the she-wolf begged, still writhing on the ground. Shadow hesitated. *She's already in so much pain, it would be cruel to hurt her more,* she thought.

"Go! Get off our territory," Shadow growled menacingly, jumping forward to scare her off. The she-wolf jumped to her feet and ran off, lifting her injured leg off the ground as she stumbled through the underbrush, back toward her own land. Shadow then whirled around and returned to the fight, pleased to see that the Cedar pack wolves had been driven back to their own land. Her pack was returning together, sharing only a few small scratches and shallow bites.

"We must return and tell Oak what happened," Amber spoke, raising her tail. The pack followed her home, silent except for a few shared words of relief or satisfaction. When they returned they told the pack everything. Shadow didn't join in on the gossip but sat down next to Miku, an unreadable look on her face.

"Is something wrong?" Miku asked, breaking the silence between them. Shadow sighed.

"Well, I've been thinking, and I have some concerns," Shadow confessed. "Did you see how skinny the Cedar pack wolves were? I just can't help but feel bad for them. Especially that she-wolf that I chased away. She looked so scared," Shadow explained, sighing. "I don't know. Fighting. I guess it's just not my thing, if it means hurting others," Shadow declared, shuffling her paws.

Miku nodded. "I understand," he said, "but I think fighting might be what I am meant to do. If it's what is best for the pack, then I'll do it." Shadow nodded, then left to join Luna, who was sitting outside her den looking at the moon. Luna's eyes gleamed in the moonlight and her fur stood on end as a large cloud moved to cover the moon, blocking her view. A cold breeze blew through the clearing. Luna looked at Shadow in surprise.

"A shadow that covered the moon," Luna whispered to herself.

"Luna, is something wrong?" Shadow asked, tilting her head at the Healer as she drew near. Luna stared at her, wide-eyed for a few moments before shaking her head and standing up, snapping herself out of the vision that she seemed to be having.

"No, nothing is wrong," Luna answered, standing up and facing Shadow. "Is something wrong with you? Are you hurt? Why have you come to see me? The moon is already rising," Luna huffed, holding her tail to the side.

"Well, no, nothing is wrong with me, but I was wondering how my father is doing. Will he be fully recovered soon?" Shadow asked the Healer, worry glinting in her eyes. Luna nodded, though she didn't look too confident in what she was saying.

"Oak is doing well. He is healing quickly. I'm…not sure of what might have happened to him, though. Maybe he had a bruised bone of some sort. I don't know," Luna whispered. Shadow pricked her ears, frustration pricking her paws.

"You're the Healer. You are supposed to know! He could be hurt, and you wouldn't even know?" Shadow demanded, growling. Luna looked unfazed by her words as if she had been asked the same questions many times before.

"Although I am the Healer of this pack, I still do not know everything. I have learned many things over the years, and I'm still learning today. You, along with any other wolf, cannot expect me to know everything," Luna replied calmly.

Shadow sighed. "I guess that is so, but that doesn't explain why you don't know what happened to my father," Shadow replied stubbornly.

Luna shook her head. "I can only hope that he regains his strength soon. We need him now more than ever."

Chapter Eight

Shadow crouched and leaped at Miku, toppling him over, but being careful not to hurt him. He easily kicked her away, pinning her shoulders to the ground. She growled and tried to kick him away, but he outmatched her in weight and size. She growled and gave up, pushing him off. "For the last time, Shadow, if you are attacking an enemy, you can't be worried about hurting them!" Lynx growled, padding out from the underbrush from where she had been watching. Shadow ducked her head.

"I'm sorry," Shadow said, "It's just that whenever I try to attack someone, even in training, the face of that she-wolf flashes into my mind. Remember, from the battle with Cedar pack?" Shadow sighed and shuffled her paws anxiously. It had already been a week since the battle and Shadow was still seeing that scared she-wolf in her dreams. Lynx glanced at her, her gaze softening.

"It's okay, Shadow, I understand how you feel," Lynx said, nodding. Miku gave her an understanding look and Shadow dipped her head in response. "Well, we can work on strategy, then," Lynx said. "Shadow, you stand over there, and Miku, you stand over there." Shadow moved to stand where Lynx had indicated, her ears pricked, and muscles tense. "If we were in battle right now, and I was the opponent, which strategy do you think you would use?" Lynx asked, looking from Shadow to Miku, a questioning look in her eyes.

Shadow assessed the situation. Miku and Shadow were both smaller than Lynx and had less experience in fighting. It seemed that Lynx would have the advantage.

"One of us could distract, while the other attacks from behind," Shadow suggested.

"Good suggestion. Try that out," Lynx replied, waving her tail. Miku instantly shot forward, baring his teeth and swiping at Lynx's face, rearing up. Of course, Lynx reared up to match him, and Shadow slipped behind her, biting down on her leg and pulling it out from under her. Lynx wobbled and then fell to the ground, exhaling sharply. Miku and Shadow pinned her, Shadow pinning her hind legs while Miku pinned her shoulders. But Lynx was too strong. She wiggled out of their grips, standing and baring her teeth. "Not the best choice if your opponent is bigger than you," Lynx pointed out, licking her paw. Shadow sighed.

"We could try jabbing from behind, and use our speed to our advantage," Miku suggested. Lynx dipped her head, and Shadow and Miku returned to their places, attacking at the wave of Lynx's tail. Shadow was the first to reach the she-wolf. She nipped her flank before jumping out of range as Lynx turned on her. Miku nipped the other side, and then Shadow bit her tail, pulling before letting go as Lynx snapped at her. Miku landed a bite on her shoulder, while Shadow managed to leap over her flank and nip her scruff. They continued this tactic for a few minutes until Lynx finally collapsed, her flanks heaving as she gasped for air.

"Great job, you two, great job!" She huffed between breaths, standing up. "That was a good idea, Miku," Lynx praised, dipping her head. Miku shrugged, dipping his head in return. "Well," Lynx said, shaking out her pelt, "we should move on to the next lesson then." They practiced battle strategies all afternoon until Lynx finally decided it was time to go home and rest for a while. Shadow collapsed in the shade beside the prey pile, sighing. Her legs and shoulders were sore from training, and her pads felt like they were on fire. She lay there, cooling down, panting heavily.

The sun was high in the sky, shining brightly down on the forest and heating the air. It was humid, too. It had been this way for the past few days and the forest was beginning to dry up, along with the prey. They had found quite a few animals that had been killed by the heat. Shadow sighed, her tongue lolled out, dry as a bone. She soaked in the cool air while she could. "Shadow," Lynx abruptly said from behind her. Shadow stood and turned, waving her tail in greeting. "I need to speak with you," Lynx said, leading her out of the den site. Shadow followed close behind, curious about what her Trainer had to say. She was led through the ferns until they reached a small clearing, where Lynx sat down on a small, round boulder.

"Oak and I have been talking," Lynx started. "We think it might be time for you to receive your Advanced Trainer," Lynx said, smiling. Shadow gasped.

"Really? I mean, are you sure? I feel like, well, like I might need more training," Shadow said. Lynx silenced her.

"I know, and that's why I'm telling you now. I wanted to ask you what would you like to become when you are made a full member of the pack? This decision will shape your life, and you will stay in this position until you are too old or weak to carry on with your duties. Unless you are chosen for the special role as Alpha or Beta, this will be the role that you play within the pack," Lynx warned, twitching an ear, lying down on the rock. Shadow stared at her Trainer, barely believing her ears.

"I mean…" Shadow tried, but she was at a loss for words. Shadow sat, pondering this most important decision. *Of course, I want to be a Hunter… But is that the best choice?* Shadow pondered.

I could be a Tracker...or a Guard... No, there's only one Guard... And besides, I wouldn't want to do that. I've been training so hard for this moment... Shadow thought, her mind whirling. "I- I would like to be a Hunter," Shadow asserted, standing up, her fur bristling with excitement. *A full member of the pack! Kele will be so proud,* Shadow thought, beaming, her paws shaking with anticipation for what her Trainer would say.

"Very well. That is the best choice, and I am proud of you for how far you have come. I believe that you will make an excellent Hunter," Lynx told her, jumping down from the rock, smiling proudly. Shadow dipped her head in return before rushing forward and placing her head on Lynx's shoulder, her heart swelling.

"I couldn't have done it without you, Lynx. Thank you for all you've done for me," Shadow said, her nose buried in Lynx's fur. Lynx pulled back, smiling, her eyes shining as she led Shadow back to the den site.

"There's just one more thing I have to tell you. Oak and I thought that Sparrow would be a good choice of a Trainer for you," Lynx said, glancing at Shadow. Shadow didn't respond but just kept walking, and thinking. *It's either Heather or Sparrow. Heather is nice, but Sparrow seems to have more experience,* Shadow thought to herself, nodding.

"Yes, Sparrow would be a good Trainer for me, I think," Shadow replied. Lynx was nodding, her eyes on the path ahead.

"Your training will begin tomorrow at sunrise and continue until Sparrow thinks that you are ready to become a full member of the pack," Lynx told her as they reached the den site. They slipped through the entrance into the clearing, where the pack was lounging in the shade. Shadow dipped her head to her Trainer and ran off to join Miku, Kele, and Breeze, who were all sitting together in a small patch of shade under a spruce tree, talking and laughing quietly.

"Guess what!" Shadow exclaimed, running up to them and skidding to a stop between Miku and Kele.

"What is it?" Kele asked, turning his head to look at her. Shadow sat down next to him, beaming.

"Lynx just told me that I'm ready to start my Advanced Training!" she exclaimed. Kele jumped up, grinning from ear to ear.

"Really? Shadow, that's great!" he exclaimed, jumping on top of her and toppling her over. Shadow and Kele burst out laughing, tails wagging and ears pointed up with excitement.

"Shadow!" Miku exclaimed, jumping over Kele and rolling over next to Shadow, so he was next to her. "That's so great!" he exclaimed. "I'm so happy for you! I know you'll do great," he exclaimed, wagging his tail.

"You'll be right after me!" Shadow exclaimed in response, a smile plastered across her face.

"Great job, Shadow! Are you going to be a Hunter, Tracker, or Fighter?" Breeze asked, standing over her, wagging his tail.

"I'm going to be a Hunter," Shadow replied, smiling.

"You'll make a great Hunter!" Breeze exclaimed, grinning.

"Thanks, everyone! You're the best friends I could ever have," Shadow exclaimed, smiling, her heart swelling with love and appreciation for her friends' support. Shadow then stood up and shook out her pelt, still smiling. "I'm going to talk with Lynx again, to get any more information," Shadow told them, dipping her head before going to speak with Lynx.

Lynx was smiling, watching Shadow with warm eyes. "You have some good friends, Shadow." Shadow smiled, nodding.

"Can we hunt, Lynx?" Shadow asked, still smiling.

"Of course. You should go with Sparrow, though," Lynx replied, pointing her tail to where Sparrow was sitting with Heather, eating a rabbit. Shadow's smile faded. She stared at Sparrow, swallowing her nervousness and twitching an ear of acknowledgment to Lynx. Sparrow was one of the most experienced and respected wolves of the pack. She then lifted her head and trotted over to Sparrow, smiling.

"Greetings, Sparrow," Shadow said politely, dipping her head.

"Hello, Shadow," he replied, dipping his head as well. "Here, sit down so we can talk," he told her, motioning for her to sit at his side. "So, I hear you want to become a Hunter?" Sparrow said, chewing a bite of the prey. Shadow nodded in confirmation, smiling a bit. "That's good," he replied, dipping his head and standing up. "You can finish this, Heather, I'm taking Shadow out for a hunt." Sparrow nodded to his mate, smiled, and then exited the clearing. Shadow trotted after him, glancing at Miku as she passed. Miku was watching, and smiled when their eyes made contact. Shadow smiled back, following her new Trainer out of the clearing. She knew Sparrow was Miku's father. "Now, do you think you are good at hunting?" Sparrow asked, looking down at her.

"Yes, Lynx taught me well," Shadow replied, her tail swaying as they walked along a trail that led through the forest.

"Well, she is a Fighter, not a Hunter. You will learn more about hunting with me," he replied, his eyes ahead.

"What exactly am I going to be learning?" Shadow asked.

"I will be teaching you what you will need to know about advanced hunting. Different types of skills and tactics to killing each animal. Take a rabbit, for example. You want to approach a rabbit head-on. That is where their blind spot is. You will need to step lightly and keep downwind, or else they will know you are there. A rabbit can hear better than it can smell, so if you want to catch it easily, you must stay as quiet as possible. Keep your weight on your hind legs, so you can spring farther and quicker. They have extremely sharp senses. They are better to hunt in packs, so one wolf can chase them into the other's teeth,"

Sparrow explained. Shadow nodded. *That's a lot to know about catching a rabbit*, she thought. They continued walking, Sparrow explaining in detail what they would be doing. "Okay. Now, I want you to hunt for something. I will be watching, though you won't know I'm there," Sparrow told her, sending her off with a wave of his tail. Shadow dipped her head and slipped into the underbrush, walking slowly, careful not to step on anything that may make noise. She stepped nimbly over a twig, her ears pricked, and jaws parted to catch any faint scents.

The familiar, musky scents of the forest filled her nose, while the soft noise of the leaves shaking around her filled her ears. She suddenly stopped, closed her eyes, and breathed deeply. Ears strained she caught the faint sound of a scurrying animal to her left. Opening her eyes and lowering her head, she veered off the path and toward the noise. Her eyes narrowed. She heard the bird before she saw it. A large, fat blackbird sat on the ground, pecking at a bush covered with berries. Its shiny black feathers glinted in the sunlight, and its beady black eyes shone against the leafy background. Shadow slowly stalked forward, tense, wondering if Sparrow was watching. Shadow reared up, shooting forward and attacking from above, blocking its only way to escape. She sunk her teeth into its fleshy body and pulled it to the ground, shoving its head into a rock. It let out an abruptly cut-off call of alarm before going limp, its wing twitching. Shadow looked up, licking the blood off her lips as Sparrow emerged from a shaded place in the bushes, looking impressed.

"That was quite good, Shadow. I see you already know some of the tactics of catching a blackbird – attack from above, quick and sharp," Sparrow praised, smiling. Shadow dipped her head, taking the praise.

"Thank you," she said. "What shall we do now?"

"We should head back to the den site. I just wanted to see your skill level," Sparrow told her as he turned to trot back to the den site.

Shadow followed him, carrying the prey. When they returned, Shadow gave the blackbird to Oak and Storm before going to sit outside of her den and watch the sunset. The sun glowed orange as it began fading behind the horizon, sending a beautiful purplish color across the sky. Shadow stared at the slowly appearing stars, eyes wide with awe. Her gaze shifted back to Miku as he padded up to her, his fur glistening in the fading sunlight. Shadow smiled at him, scooting to give him more room.

"A beautiful night," he said, sitting beside her and looking up at the sky. Shadow nodded, her gaze darting to a shooting star.

"Oh, look!" she pointed with her snout, but it was already gone. "Oh," she said quietly after that.

"What was it?" Miku asked, looking up at the stars and twitching an ear.

"I saw a shooting star," Shadow said softly, looking up at him.

"I'm sorry I missed it," Miku replied, standing and stretching. "Well, I think I'm going to turn in," Miku yawned, whisking his tail as he slipped into the den. Shadow stayed outside for a few final moments before following him in and curling up in her sleeping place beside his. Resting her head on her paws, she quickly fell asleep, listening to the slow, steady sound of Miku's breathing beside her.

Shadow woke early the next morning, standing to stretch before exiting the den. Looking around, she spotted Sparrow and Lynx talking at the entrance of the Hunters' den, drowsily stretching and yawning as they spoke. Shadow went to the prey pile and picked out a squirrel, settling down to eat it. She ate slowly, enjoying the dewy morning air and the scent that still clung to her nostrils. As she finished, she stood and stretched, looking up at the sky. The sun still hadn't risen, giving them plenty of time to hunt. Shadow trotted over to Sparrow, who was now sitting down, his eyes closed.

"Hey, Sparrow, let's get going!" Shadow exclaimed, realizing after she had spoken that she had just told her Trainer what to do. "Well, I mean, can we hunt soon?" Shadow said quickly after a nervous laugh. Sparrow looked at her, slightly amused.

"Yes, we can hunt soon. I'm glad to see you're eager to learn," Sparrow replied, dipping his head as he stood up.

"Great!" Shadow exclaimed, giving a little bounce. Sparrow grinned. He then proceeded to lead her out of the clearing, yawning. After a few minutes of walking, Shadow asked, "So, what about Miku? Does he get a different Trainer while you're with me?"

"No, I am still his Trainer, too, until he is ready to be given an Advanced Trainer," Sparrow explained, still walking, eyes forward.

Shadow nodded and looked up at Sparrow. "So, where are we going now?" she asked.

"You are going to hunt something for me," Sparrow replied, speeding up to a trot as they continued along the hunting trail. They stopped in a little clearing filled with small holes. Shadow guessed they had been dug by some sort of animal, like a mole or a ground squirrel. "Now, Shadow, I want you to catch a specific animal for me," Sparrow started. Shadow looked at him, head tilted to the side. She had never been told to hunt a specific animal before. "I would like you to catch me a rabbit, using the instructions I gave you yesterday," Sparrow said. Shadow looked at him for a few seconds before dipping her head and turning to slip out of the clearing. She ducked under an ivy vine and slipped through the brush, ears pricked. When she had reached a safe, calm place in the ferns, she closed her eyes and drank in the scent and sounds of the forest. Calming herself, holding her body completely still, she allowed herself to blend with the environment around her. Feeling her paws on the ground and her tail brushing against the ferns, she felt the forest around her.

Shadow opened her eyes, knowing where a rabbit might be. Whipping around, she ran noiselessly through the forest until she spotted a small, fuzzy creature hiding between the bushes and nibbling noiselessly on some raspberries. Shadow got closer, placing her paws carefully between twigs, careful to step just as the wind blew, to mask any faint noise she should make. She kept her weight on her haunches as she slowly came within attacking range, making sure to come in at its blind spot and to stay downwind. Shooting forward, quick and soundless, she grabbed it by its neck, killing it. She smiled through the fur, beaming as Sparrow slipped through the bushes, eyes wide.

"Perfect," he said, "and on your first try. I'm impressed!" Sparrow took the rabbit from her jaws. Shadow grinned.

"Thanks, Sparrow!" She replied. She was nervous, but the praise sounded good. Sparrow dipped his head and turned back toward the forest.

"Now, we shall patrol the territory, and you will learn every hunting trail, hidden path, or place to hunt. You will learn the best spots to hunt certain animals, and where to look for certain plants that the animals eat," Sparrow told her, padding forward. Shadow followed with excitement throbbing in her paws. They made their way through the forest, Sparrow telling her where the prey burrows, what they do during the winter, and how to catch them. Shadow listened intently, noting his words and paying close attention.

They soon made it to the other side of the territory, where he explained in more detail how to catch fish or water animals. She listened, watching him demonstrate how to catch beavers and otters in the water. They then moved on while Sparrow continued to explain the things they saw, such as the best paths to follow for hunting. Shadow carried the rabbit and listened happily, her paws aching as they made their way through the territory. While checking the coyote den, Sparrow had caught a raccoon. When they had done a full patrol of the territory, Sparrow veered away from the riverbank and back in the direction of the den site. "Time to head home," he said. "You've learned enough for today."

Back at the den site, Shadow dropped her rabbit on the prey pile, took a quail for herself, and retreated to her sleeping place, exhausted. Panting, she collapsed in her den, tucking her legs under her and eating quickly, her paws throbbing and legs aching. The sun was retreating below the treetops, sending shadows to cover their clearing. Most of the wolves were returning from their daily hunting or border-checking, chatting in the clearing, or sharing prey. Shadow hastily finished her bird then closed her eyes and fell asleep, thankful for the quiet den.

Shadow woke to the steady stream of sunlight beaming in from the entrance of her den. Wolves were beginning to move around the clearing, sending shadows cutting through the sunlight and flashing in Shadow's face. Growling, she stood up and shook the sleepiness from her mind. With bleary eyes she made her way outside to see Sparrow standing at the foot of her den, looking annoyed. "Come on, Shadow, we don't have all day! We're wasting daylight. Hurry up!" Sparrow snapped, staring her down. "Why are you sleeping so late? I thought you wanted to be a Hunter," he growled, ears pinned to his head.

"I- well, we've-" Shadow started, tail between her legs. Sparrow sighed and raised his tail for silence, beginning to make his way out of the clearing, beckoning for Shadow to follow him. Following shamefully, Shadow looked around. The sun shone bright and the wolves around her scurried around normally, talking to each other or getting ready to leave for the day. Shadow quickly made her way out into the forest, silently promising Sparrow that she would work extra hard today to make up for sleeping in. It had been about two weeks since Shadow had started training with Sparrow and she learned something new every day. They usually stayed out for most of the day, practicing hunting certain animals or tracking deer. It seemed, however, there was less and less prey every time they went out. Breeze was also training to become a Hunter and he noticed the same thing.

The days were long and tiring and the heat pushed down on them harder every day. Shadow wondered if the summers were always this hot. Water became harder and harder to come by. It got to the point where they had to travel all the way to the lake just to get a drink during the day. Shadow followed her Trainer through the woods, her tongue lolling out, head low and tail between her legs.

Hoping Sparrow's mood was better she ran to catch up with him, walking at his flank. They walked in silence until they came to a large, fern-filled hunting clearing. Various bushes and plants grew on the outside, while the ferns in the center of the clearing were shriveling. Sparrow sat down and faced Shadow, wrapping his tail around his paws. "Okay Shadow, I want you to catch something in this clearing. You need to learn how to catch food with the space you have," Sparrow told her, lying down in the shade, his eyes narrowed. "I'll watch you from here," he said, twitching an ear.

Shadow dipped her head and stalked off into the ferns, scouting out the area. She looked for possible homes for prey, or signs that they have been scurrying about. She spotted a berry bush. It was withering from the sun and the hard, dry berries had fallen to cover the ground. She moved toward it, looking around, but staying hidden in the shadows. She spotted a small burrow beneath the bush. It looked as if there was a small body scurrying around inside. Creeping forward, she remembered to distribute her weight evenly. Shooting forward, she launched herself into the air, barreling down on the hole with her two front paws. Ripping the dirt away from the hole, she quickly snatched the small body that lay, horrified, in its home. Shadow plucked it from the hole, noticing how scrawny and gamey it felt between her teeth. *This would hardly make a meal for a pup!* She thought. Frowning, she returned to Sparrow, finding him looking somewhat impressed. "Well, it's not much," he said, "but at least it's something."

Relieved that he had forgiven her for sleeping so late, Shadow sat down. "I suppose," she replied, dropping the scrawny mouse at his paws. He looked at it, frowning.

"You're a good hunter, Shadow. It's not your fault the prey is going away. We've never had a summer this hot before," He told her, staring out into the dried-up forest. "It can only get better from here," Sparrow huffed. Shadow wished she could believe him. It seemed like it would never get better. Standing up, Shadow returned to hunting, a new determination filling her mind and giving her strength. They hunted for a while longer, catching nothing but a whiff of a rabbit. They returned with only the mouse, giving it to Luna.

Shadow was glad to see that her father was getting better. He was now leading hunting groups or checking the territory markings, regaining his strength, and showing the rest of the pack that he was still strong. Shadow went to sit next to Kele and Breeze, who were talking lazily in the shade.

"Hey, guys," she greeted, and they twitched their ears in acknowledgment, shifting to give her room to sit. "What're you talking about?" she then asked, leaning into their conversation.

"We were talking about the prey," Kele answered, sighing.

"Oh," Shadow answered, sitting back.

"I hope that this summer heat breaks and the prey comes back soon," Breeze said, shuffling his paws anxiously.

"The pack can't function properly without water and prey," Kele agreed.

"Yes," Shadow answered, but in her mind she was worried. It had been a long time since it rained, and prey was becoming more and more scarce. She looked up as Lynx pushed herself out of the Healer's den, looking shocked but happy. Her tail was raised and her paws were shaking, while her eyes were filled with emotion. Shadow jumped up and raced over to her, eyes wide. "Lynx, is something wrong? What happened?" Shadow asked the she-wolf, her tone edged with curiosity.

"I- I…" Lynx started, stopping as Max appeared at Shadow's side, his gaze filled with concern.

"Lynx, what is it?" he asked, and Luna appeared behind Lynx, her eyes warm.

"I'm going to have pups!" Lynx exclaimed, her eyes wide and filled with elation. Max gasped with delight and rushed to Lynx's side, smiling as he pressed his flank against her.

"Lynx, that's wonderful!" he exclaimed, too filled with emotion to say anything else. Shadow stared at her former Trainer delightfully, beaming happily for the she-wolf.

"Congratulations! You'll make a great mother, Lynx!" Shadow exclaimed, resting her chin on Lynx's shoulder, her tail wagging wildly. Lynx looked to be overjoyed, her paws shaking, and ears pinned with excitement. Shadow grinned as wolves surrounded them, excited by the news. Oak and Storm were on the Alpha stone talking with smiles on their faces, while the rest of the pack were breaking into groups, chattering excitedly. New pups in the pack! This was good news to all. Shadow stayed at her former Trainer's side as she made her way around the den site sharing the good news. Shadow noticed for the first time that Lynx's belly was beginning to swell. Once the pack had settled down, Lynx sat down by the Hunters' den, panting in the sunlight.

"You might want to move into the Newborns' den, Lynx," Luna spoke as she padded up to sit beside them.

"Already? But, shouldn't I have a little more time?" Lynx replied, twitching an ear.

"Well, you should get a comfortable place in the den, to be ready. You want to stay as comfortable as possible until you have your pups, or there could be complications," Luna told her, dipping her head.

"All right," Lynx replied, standing up and walking over to the Newborns' den, pushing her way inside. Shadow remembered when she was a pup, and she slept in that den. Smiling, she stood and dipped her head to the Healer before padding over to Miku, who was sitting in the shade of a pine tree, his eyes closed.

"Hey, Miku," Shadow greeted as she sat down beside him. "Did you hear the news?" Shadow asked.

"Yes. Every wolf in the pack knows, now. Lynx looked pretty excited, and I'm happy for her," Miku replied, nodding. Shadow nodded in agreement, smiling at the thought of pups running around the clearing, clambering on top of the Alpha stone, or running under the feet of the adults. Smiling, she turned back to Miku, sighing.

"So, how's training going?" Miku asked her, licking his paws.

"It's fine," she replied, "although the prey is disappearing, I still learn something new every day. Sparrow is a good Trainer. How about you? How's your training coming along?"

"Oh, it's fine. Mako is a good Trainer, too, and a very talented Fighter. I wonder how Kele is going to finish his training, with Lynx out with the pups?" Miku answered, looking at her.

"Well, I'm sure he'll find a way. Maybe Mako will take him to train with you," Shadow replied. Miku nodded.

"Should we hunt tonight, when the pack goes to sleep?" Miku then asked, looking at her. "The prey might come out at night, when it's cooler," he added.

Shadow nodded. "Great idea! Then we can get more food for the pack!" Miku nodded in agreement and sat up.

"Should we tell Breeze and Kele, too?" Miku then asked, looking at her. "They might want to join us."

"Sure, why not. More teeth mean more prey," Shadow replied. Miku dipped his head, standing up.

"I'll go talk to them, then," he replied. Miku trotted over to the Learners' den to find Breeze and Kele. Shadow scratched a spot behind her ear, looking around the clearing. Amber was sitting outside of the Beta's den, talking to Max, while Lynx, Heather, and Storm spoke together in front of the Newborns' den. *Lynx is probably getting some pup-rearing advice,* she thought. Shadow sat in the shade, looking up as Sparrow approached her.

"Greetings," she said to him, smiling. He dipped his head, then sat down next to her.

"Heather, Amber, Oak, Scout, and I are going hunting. I was wondering if you wanted to come, to show off your skills," Sparrow told her, shoving her teasingly with his shoulder.

Shadow looked up at him, beaming. "When are we leaving?" she asked, wagging her tail.

"Now," Sparrow replied, standing up and trotting over to the group that was already walking out the entrance of the clearing, led by Oak. Shadow followed him, smiling, excitement shining in her eyes.

The group made its way through the dense underbrush, senses alert, ready for anything. They veered off the main trail and made their way to the end of the territory well away from the tainted water. They stretched a little way out of the territory, stopping to smell for prey or to tell the others of signs of prey. Although it was dry and the sun had shriveled the ferns, some prey still found a place to live and have shelter. They stopped in a large clearing filled with shriveling ferns and surrounded by tall, strong-looking oak trees. The group split up, each wolf going in a different direction. They agreed to come back to the clearing once they caught something.

Shadow went deeper into the unknown forest, head low and ears strained to collect any sounds that came from the prey. She heard a faint shuffling noise coming from ahead of her and stopped. In a small clearing, she spotted a raccoon eating some dried-up seeds, its bushy tail curled around its body. *It hasn't scented me yet,* she realized, shifting so that she was downwind. Peeking through the bushes, she saw that she was now directly behind the animal. Tensing her muscles, she sprang forward, snapping at its neck, but missing. The raccoon squealed and shot forward, out of reach. Shadow growled and leaped quickly after it. She jumped nimbly over a branch as she chased the animal, aiming for its hind legs.

Propelling herself forward in a massive burst of speed, she closed her jaws around its hind leg, pulling it back toward her. It squealed in fright, scratching at her face and scrambling to get away. Shadow let go, wincing as its claws pierced her skin. It was trying frantically to escape, screaming in pain and dragging its broken leg, its eyes filled with agony. Shadow felt pity pierce her heart. Lunging forward, she bit down hard on its neck, killing it. *I need to feed the pack,* she reminded herself as she stared at her kill. She wiped the blood off a scratch above her eye, picked up the raccoon, and returned to the clearing, finding that she was the first one back. Sparrow appeared only a moment later carrying two large crows. Oak and Amber arrived soon after, each carrying a mouse in their jaws. And, finally, Scout and Heather joined them, Scout carrying a hare and Heather a squirrel.

They returned to the den site and dropped their prey on the prey pile. Shadow took a small mouse for herself and ate it in a single bite. Her belly growled for more, but she refused to eat anything else. Her packmates needed food more than she did. She gave Lynx the other mouse and then went to the Learners' den to lay down, ignoring the sound of her stomach growling for more food. Miku appeared a moment later at the entrance of the den, carrying a rabbit.

"Here, I caught this today for you," Miku told her, setting the prey at her side.

"For me?" She asked, lifting her head. "Are you sure? I mean, aren't you hungry? What about your brother?" Shadow asked, tilting her head to the side.

"No, Kele, Breeze, and I shared a rabbit while you were gone," Miku replied, twitching an ear as he sat in his sleeping place beside her.

"Oh. Well, thank you," Shadow replied, dipping her head gratefully. She finished the rabbit quickly, her stomach now full. She licked her lips, satisfied, and rested her head on her paws, thanking Miku again. Just as she was about to fall asleep, Kele and Breeze entered the den, settling down in their holes, chattering like blackbirds.

"Hush! Some wolves are trying to sleep here," Miku snapped, quieting them both down. Shadow rested her head on his paws, closing her eyes to sleep as Miku rested his head on her neck. She quickly dozed off, listening to the soft, rhythmic sound of his heartbeat. She woke later that night to Miku prodding her on the shoulder with a paw.

"Come on, let's go," he whispered, just loud enough for her to hear it. She stood up and stretched, excitement flooding her mind. They woke Kele and Breeze, then together they snuck past Max through a weak spot in the buckthorn, leaving the clearing silently. Anxious for the hunt, Shadow's heart was beating quickly. They walked quietly, Shadow at Miku's side, their pelts brushing. She hoped he didn't mind. They walked along a rarely used hunting trail, ears pricked and alert for prey. "I sure hope we catch something," Miku whispered.

"Me, too. I hope we aren't tired tomorrow," she whispered back, shrugging.

"Yeah, but what's life without a little fun, eh?" Kele replied, twitching an ear with a grin.

At that, Shadow raced ahead, laughing, challenging Miku to a race with a lash of her tail. He followed, laughing, and they raced along the trail, Breeze, and Kele following. Miku took the lead, his legs being longer than Shadow's. She raced after him, not a worry in her mind. Together, their paws thrummed against the ground, probably scaring off any prey that was nearby. They ran a long way, Shadow getting slowly closer and closer until she finally caught him and jumped on him to get him to stop. They went tumbling through the underbrush, laughing, until their momentum stopped. Shadow ended up on top of him, her ears buzzing and her head spinning.

"Whoa!" Miku exclaimed, his chest shaking as he exploded into laughter. Shadow joined in, her paws throbbing. She then stood, letting him up.

"Well, that was fun, but we probably scared off all of the prey in the territory by now," Shadow exclaimed, still laughing. A moment later, Kele and Breeze appeared through the ferns, amusement glinting in both of their eyes.

"You two are loud," Breeze commented, and Kele nodded in agreement.

"It was worth it. We would never able to do that around our Trainers," Miku said, smiling and wagging his tail. Shadow nodded in agreement and looked around. They were now a quarter of the way into their territory.

"Well, we should probably keep going. The prey in this area must be scared off," Shadow said, still smiling. Miku nodded, and they trotted through the forest along a dense hunting trail. The four hunters swerved around a newly fallen tree and jumped over a thorn bush. Shadow yelped as a thorn ripped at her soft underbelly, the pain causing her to come crashing to the ground, wrenching her paw on a tree root. She whined in pain, licking the few drops of blood that had welled up on the thorn scratch in her belly. She then looked down at her paw, raising it and placing it carefully on the ground. She stood up, sighing with relief when she realized that it would be fine. Miku, Breeze, and Kele trotted over to her, Kele helping her to walk until she was sure that she could do it on her own.

They continued along the trail, Miku in the lead. Shadow hoped some prey would turn up soon. The moon shone brightly in the sky, and she noticed it was nearly full. They kept moving until they got to the field on the opposite end of the territory.

Shadow looked up at the hedge that separated the field from the forest. It looked shorter than she had remembered. Berries grew on the dense branches that were weaved together tightly.

"Okay, let's get to the other side," Shadow exclaimed, bunching her muscles and leaping over the bush, landing easily on the other side. Her friends followed her, looking around as she was. The moonlight shone on the huge field, giving the stalks a goldish brown color. The wheat swayed and shifted in the wind, creating a cool, hissing noise. Shadow breathed deeply. The dust in the air made it taste like chalk.

"Look over there," Miku whispered, and Shadow was jolted from the grace of the calm, whispering crops. She followed Miku's gaze until her eyes rested on a far-off light. A tall wooden structure stood towering above the wheat, dull against the beauty of the moon. A smaller, darker structure stood beside that one, smoke and ashes streaming out of a hole in the top.

"Is that the thing we saw some time ago, where the humans seemed to be building their den?" Shadow asked in a hushed voice. Miku and Kele both nodded.

"I think so," Miku answered.

"Let's go closer," Breeze suggested. Not waiting for an answer, he trotted forward warily, his head down. Shadow followed, Miku and Kele right behind her. As they neared, she noticed small, square holes in the sides of the smaller structure. She could see right through them, though they were glinting with the shine of the moon. Shadow saw two humans, or at least she thought they were humans. They were hiding under a cover, so she couldn't really tell. They were laying on a large square of strange material, seemingly sleeping.

Moving closer she saw the den was made mostly of long, square-shaped logs and strange-looking flakes of bark. The bigger den was colored red and had a dark top. Huge, dark blocks of wood seemed to block the entrance. Ears pricked she heard sounds of other animals coming from inside the den. Peeking under the blocks of wood she could see small orange feet moving around and the strange cluck-cluck noise of the prey that was being kept within.

Moving away from the strange-smelling place Shadow walked back toward the human-filled den. Miku was behind her, sniffing everything. She guessed he was just as curious about this as she was.

"What is all this?" Kele asked, as if in awe. Breeze was standing beside him, staring at the humans through the clear square hole in the side of the wall.

"I don't know," Shadow whispered back, eyes wide. Shadow looked around, still taking in their surroundings. Large piles of brush lay beside the red den, heaped almost to the top. Shadow looked back to the small den. Looking inside she spotted the humans again and farther inside the warm, dimly lit den she saw two dogs lying peacefully on the ground, sleeping next to the humans. One was large, with big, strong muscles and a mean-looking pelt, while the other was smaller, but still just as mean-looking. Their teeth jutted out from under their lips, while drool dripped down from their chins. They twitched in their dreams but did not wake up.

"Do you see those two dogs? I bet the humans command them," Shadow whispered to Miku, who was looking inside the den, too. He nodded, eyes wide. Shadow continued surveying the area. Piles of rubbish and debris littered the den, causing the whole place to stink. She wondered how those dogs could possibly live in there! Sticking out her tongue and wrinkling her nose against the foul smells, she turned and padded silently away from the opening in the wall. She trotted around the corner of the den to look behind on the other side. A circle of tall wooden poles enclosed a large area. No wheat stalks were growing in the enclosed area. Only grass. Long, flat pieces of wood connected the poles, two for each gap, one high and one lower. Looking closer, Shadow saw several very large, fat animals inside this enclosure, standing peacefully out in the open. They had white fur with large black splotches.

"Whoa! One of those could feed the whole pack for a month!" Breeze exclaimed, staring at the large animals.

"We have to tell Oak!" Shadow replied, her tail wagging. Breeze nodded and slipped under the wooden plank. Shadow followed, head low, Miku and Kele close behind. The first thing she noticed was the stench. She had smelled it before, by the human dens, but it hadn't been nearly this bad and she hadn't paid much attention to it. Now, it was overwhelming, pressing in around her and burning her eyes. When she got a closer look at the prey she realized they were larger and fatter than any deer she had seen before. They had pink noses and loud mouths. They seemed to be always chewing. Maybe they ate the dry grass that the human kept beside that huge den? Shadow saw large, square blocks of dry grass beside a wooden box filled with water. The wooden poles that surrounded the area apparently were intended to keep the prey in one place. The large animals stunk worse than anything she had ever smelled before. They seemed to make dirt wherever they went. They seemed to *live* in it. Waste filled the whole area, stinking up the air and clogging Shadow's nose. The animals were filthy themselves, too. Waste stuck to their hooves and the backs of their legs, down their tails, and under their bellies. Shadow couldn't imagine living in there. She gagged just walking on the waste that the filthy animals had created. Her paws sunk into the ground, making it hard for her to move. She could hardly wait to reenter the forest where she could breathe in the sweet, calming scents of their home without this stench filling her nose.

The prey seemed unbothered as Breeze, Miku, Kele, and Shadow quietly neared them. Shadow knew they had to get more information about these animals so they could have a chance at attacking them. She didn't see any small or weak ones within the cluster. She thought there might be about a hundred animals in this group. Wincing again at the smell, Shadow suddenly had enough. "Alright, let's get out of here and hunt a bit," Shadow told the others, beginning to make her way away from the humans and back to the forest. Finally making it out of that wretched, smelly place they headed straight for the lake to wash the horrible scent off their paws. She gratefully washed her paws, hoping that she never had to do that again. She dunked her head underwater to get the scent out of her nose before sitting back, breathing the cool, gentle air of the forest. It was very hot during the day, but during the night it was cool and perfect for roaming about the forest. After they washed, they began making their way back to the den site, hunting along the way.

By the time they reached their clearing the stench was nearly gone from her mind. Now, the only thing she was thinking about was what they were going to do about the humans. Max was still sitting at the mouth of his den beside the clearing's entrance. He didn't know they had left, not to mention that they were out alone, without their Trainers, in the middle of the night. Shadow pushed through the buckthorn, eyes widening when she saw him, sitting at the other end of the clearing, eyes narrowed as he watched her. He did not approach Shadow or her den mates as they dropped their prey on the pile—a small mouse and a shrew—and returned to their den silently. Shadow glanced at Miku, adrenaline coursing through her veins.

"Well, Max saw us," Shadow said. "Why didn't he confront us?"

"I don't know, but he'll probably tell Oak, or at least our Trainers," Kele replied quietly.

"Maybe he thinks it doesn't matter that we were out alone. After all, it is a full moon in a couple of days and it is bright enough to see," Shadow said, shrugging, lying down in her sleeping hole.

"Hopefully," Breeze replied, shrugging and laying down as well. Shadow quickly fell asleep, realizing how weary she was.

Chapter Nine

The sound of rain pouring down on top of her den woke Shadow from a deep sleep. "Finally," she muttered quietly. "We need this rain." Opening her eyes, she looked around. The den was empty. She stood up, smiling at the scent of rain. This would put the forest back on its feet. She scrambled up to the entrance of the den, peering outside. The clearing was empty. She pushed herself out, going over to the Hunters' den and looking inside, hoping to find Sparrow, or some wolf to tell her where her fellow Learners had gone. The den was empty. She flattened her ears in confusion, looking up at the sky, rain pouring down into her face and streaming through her fur. The clouds were cold and dark, promising more life-giving rain. Still confused, she went over to the Beta's den and looked inside. It was empty, as well. She checked the other dens, too. They were all empty. She was panicking now, confused and a bit scared. "Where is everyone?" she asked herself, twirling around the clearing, looking for signs of where they could be.

Shadow rushed out of the clearing, her vision blurry with the rain. She raced through the forest, calling her packmates' names, eyes wide with fear. *Did they go somewhere and leave me behind? What if I never find them again?* she thought, horrified. Shadow continued swerving through the forest, checking popular hunting places, and looking for scents. When she stopped, her breath was ragged in her throat. The rain seemed to be pouring down harder. She sat under a tree, tears welling up in her eyes. Where was everyone? She looked around, hoping to see or hear the sound of a wolf nearby. Nothing. She panted, wondering what to do. She stood up again and raced back into the rain, calling her packmates' names again. She felt dizzy, her mind whirling, her fur sticking to her skin and weighing her down as the rain pelted against her. She looked hopelessly around as she ran, howling now, eyes wild with fear. Not looking where she was running she suddenly crashed into something hard, knocking the breath from her chest.

Looking up Shadow saw two red eyes staring down at her from over her head. Yelping in fear, she backed away, growling, accidentally cornering herself against a tree. It was a human and it was coming right toward her, holding a long, shiny steel stick in its pink, fleshy paws. It raised the stick and pointed it at her head, eyes glowing red, a long smile spreading across its face. Shadow stared in horror at its eyes. She was frozen to the spot, her legs shaking madly with fear. She saw the stick had two holes in the tip. Suddenly, the human jerked its paw and there was a loud bang. Then her mind went dark.

Shadow woke in the Learners' den, her paws throbbing and her ears pinned to her head in fear. She looked frantically around the den, letting out a sigh of relief as she spotted her three packmates, all still sleeping peacefully around her. She took a moment to calm herself, her heart still beating so hard she thought it would explode. When she had caught her breath and calmed her heart she opened her eyes and looked around the den. She wondered if that dream would come true. Shuddering, she looked outside. The sun was bright, even though it was very early in the morning. No rain. She sighed again, extremely thankful that it was only a dream. *It felt so real,* she thought, shuddering again.

Shadow stood and walked over to the entrance of the den before slipping into the misty morning air. Only a few wolves were in the clearing. She guessed most of them were still sleeping. It was quite early, after all. She sat beside the prey pile, yawning. She realized that her paws felt heavier than usual. *This is going to be a long day,* she thought, knowing she didn't get enough sleep last night. She yawned again, looking around. She spotted Max talking to Oak, who was looking at Shadow. A feeling of dread filled her stomach. Max was telling Oak! She tried to think of an explanation as Oak walked over to her, a frown of confusion on his face.

"Hello, Oak," Shadow greeted, dipping her head, trying to sound casual.

"Shadow, why were you out with the other Learners last night, after dark?" Oak asked, anger edging his tone.

"Um, well," Shadow started, shifting her paws. "We couldn't sleep, so we decided to hunt," Shadow lied, twitching an ear. She winced, knowing that she had said it in a way that seemed less believable. She was horrible at lying.

"Tell the truth, Shadow, I won't be upset. I think you're old enough to go out alone, but I want to know why you left. Did something happen?" Oak asked, his gaze softening. Shadow took in a breath and told him the truth. Max was standing behind Oak as she told her story. She told how they saw the human's den, and the big, smelly prey, and how they traveled the territory alone in the dark. He just stared at her, curiosity filling his eyes at the mention of the prey.

"Thank you for telling me, Shadow. I will send out a hunting party to try and catch one of these...animals," Oak said.

"Wait, Oak. Maybe it would be a good idea to find out more about these animals before we blindly attack. The humans own some vicious-looking dogs, too, and probably have some other weapons. We don't know. Maybe we should be cautious and send a group to get more information," Shadow warned, suddenly remembering her dream. Confronting this human might not be the best idea. Oak looked thoughtful for a few moments.

"You're right, Shadow. I will send a group to try and find out more about these animals and how to kill them. You will lead the group and will take Miku, Sparrow, Amber, and Scout. Please be careful. I will make an announcement to the pack. Until then, get some rest and think of how we could capture this prey," Oak told her, dipping his head. She dipped her head in return, going back to her den and curling up in her sleeping place, sighing.

Shadow was troubled. *Maybe we should just leave these humans alone and not provoke them,* she thought. *I don't have a very good feeling about it. But then, the pack could starve without this prey. Our prey is disappearing more and more every day, and there is nowhere else that we can hunt, except outside our territory. But, what if my dreams were somehow real? What if they come true if we provoke these humans? Then, it would be my fault. If I had these dreams for a reason, then maybe I should take them more seriously. Then again, they might just be normal, useless dreams that have nothing to do with the future.* Shadow buried her nose deep in her tail fur. Lost in her thoughts, she hadn't realized that Sparrow was standing outside of her den, calling her name. It was only when Sparrow entered the den that she snapped out of her daydream. "Oh, hello Sparrow," Shadow greeted him, nose still in her fur.

"Shadow, come with me. It's time to hunt," Sparrow said, twitching an ear.

Shadow looked up at him through blurry eyes. "But Sparrow, Oak told me to rest. He said I'm going to lead a group later," Shadow replied.

She heard Sparrow sigh. "Very well, but when this whole conundrum is over, you'll be hunting extra," Sparrow told her, exiting the den. Shadow seeped deeper into her hole and fell back asleep, enjoying the company of Miku as he slept next to her.

Shadow woke to Oak prodding her with a paw, his gaze sharp. "Wake up, Shadow," he told her, sitting back on his haunches.

"The sun is already starting to fall," Oak said. "It's time to go."

Shadow jumped to her paws, sleepiness gone from her mind. She slipped past Oak and out of the den, looking around. He was right. The sun was starting to slip behind the tops of the trees, its amber glow shining through the clearing and lighting the wolves' fur. The rest of the group she was intended to lead was sitting in the center of the clearing, talking quietly. Oak appeared behind her. "I let you sleep," he said, sitting down. "You needed it. I already told the pack the news."

Shadow looked at him and dipped her head. "I'm sorry, I didn't mean to sleep…" She started.

"I said it's fine, Shadow. Now go and help your pack." Shadow dipped her head to her father and raced over to the group, nervous excitement filling her mind. They greeted her and she made her way to the front, her paws itching to get going. She exited the clearing into the forest. Shadow enjoyed the fading sun's warmth on her back as she led her packmates through the underbrush toward the humans' dens. They spoke only quietly to each other, the air static with excitement as the wind slowed to a stop. Shadow led them along the path that she and the rest of the Learners had followed the night before. Miku was talking quietly to Shadow.

"How far along are you in your training with Sparrow? I think I might almost be done with mine," Miku told her in a hushed whisper.

"Me, too. I think that Sparrow knows I'm learning fast," Shadow replied, twitching an ear. They walked in silence the rest of the way. The sun was now almost down, casting shadows along their path and cooling their pelts. Shadow's heart caught in her throat when she spotted the fence that circled the humans' animals. She led the group to the hedge, jumping over and waiting silently for the rest of her group to follow. They formed a single-file line behind her, and she led them along the wall of bushes to a small, enclosed area where the hedge had broken off. They crouched in the shadows where they could see the humans' dens and everything around them. Her pelt tingled with unease when she spotted one of the humans sitting drowsily next to the small den.

"Is that a human den?" Sparrow asked quietly, tilting his head to the side. Miku nodded. A small gust of wind picked up, blowing from the area where Shadow and Mako saw the large prey. The horrible stench filled her nose once more, making her wrinkle her nose. The wolves beside her let out yelps of surprise at the sudden change of scent.

"How did we not scent this back at our den site? It's horrible!" Scout exclaimed, bristling.

"I know, but that's not the point. The scent is probably so strong, it will cover our scent! The human will never smell us coming," Miku pointed out, and the wolves let out murmurs of agreement.

"That is true," Sparrow said with approval.

"We'll attack downwind. The dark will cover us," Amber spoke to herself as if taking notes.

"Wait, we're attacking *today?* I thought we were just checking to see how we should do it," Shadow exclaimed, eyes widening. She was *not* ready for that.

"No, no, of course not. We're just figuring out what to do when we *do* attack," Scout told her, nodding.

"Okay, good," Shadow replied, her pelt burning with embarrassment for making assumptions. She shook out her fur and looked back at the wooden poles, thinking.

"If we duck under those sticks we could get one of the animals away from the rest. Then we could easily kill it," Amber continued speaking, eyes narrowed.

"Yes, but how would we get the animal out of the trapped area? That thing looks *big*," Sparrow queried, half to himself.

"Well, we would have to corner it, then kill it, and then try to dig under the sticks so we could pull it out," Amber spoke, glancing at Sparrow.

"But, wouldn't the humans hear us? I'm sure those things could make quite a bit of noise," Scout spoke, frowning.

"Well, we would have to end its life quickly, then," Amber said. Shadow listened to them talking, her ears pricked. She was staring at the human, hoping it couldn't see them. Suddenly, Sparrow let out a yelp as he stepped on a thorn from a bush behind him. Shadow stared at him as Amber and Scout asked loudly if he was okay.

"Hush!" Shadow exclaimed in a whisper as the human's eyes met hers. It stood up, yowling something she couldn't understand. Then it picked something up in its pink, fleshy paws. Strangely, it was an exact replica of the stick that the human had held in her dream. She realized with a jolt that it must be a weapon of some kind. Shadow looked at her packmates, eyes wide with horror. "Get down!" Shadow howled, throwing herself on top of them as a loud bang echoed across the forest. Quickly scrambling to her paws, she shoved her packmates deeper into the forest, out of sight of the human's strange and terrifying contraption. "Run!" she exclaimed as she heard another loud bang, her heart pounding so hard she thought it might burst out of her chest. Her packmates ran, even Sparrow with the thorn in his paw until they reached safety. Then, they sat down, panting, fear showing in their eyes.

"What just happened?" Amber asked when they had regained their breath.

"That thing. The thing the human was carrying. I saw that in a dream. I think it is some sort of weapon," Shadow explained.

"And...you just saved us?" Sparrow asked, eyes wide. Shadow shrugged.

"I guess. That is if 'saved' is what you would call it," she answered, shuffling her paws.

"Thank you, Shadow, that was a very brave thing for you to do," Amber spoke, dipping her head. The rest of the wolves dipped their heads, too. Even Miku crouched down, his head bent in respect.

"It was nothing. Really. You would have done the same thing," Shadow said, her face hot with embarrassment. Her packmates raised their heads, eyes warm.

"Well, now that we know what to do, I think we should go report to Oak. He needs to know about this," Scout said, jumping to his paws. Shadow dipped her head, glancing at Miku. He was looking at her. Dropping her gaze, her ear-tips warm, she began heading back to the den site, her ears held high. When they returned, they reported to Oak. He looked impressed when he had heard how Shadow had saved them. She blinked, twitching an ear.

"We should send out a group to try and kill one of these animals, but not now. Now, you all must sleep, for you have made a long journey. You must be exhausted. While you were away, I sent the remaining wolves to hunt. There should be enough for everyone, though we didn't catch very much," Oak told them, dipping his head to Amber. She nodded gratefully and led the group to the prey pile, where they each picked something out to eat. Shadow took the smallest piece, knowing the prey could be better used elsewhere. She ate silently beside Miku, chewing slowly. It took the edge off her hunger, though it didn't fill her belly. Miku was still eating when she finished. He was enjoying a small rabbit.

"Here, Shadow, have a bite," he offered. She refused. He pushed it closer. "Come on, I won't be able to finish it alone," Miku told her. She eyed the prey, her mouth-watering. "Fine, *one* bite," she told herself, taking a bite, glancing thankfully at Miku. He smiled, taking another bite for himself. "One more," Miku told her, pushing it farther toward her as she finished swallowing. She sighed.

"If it makes you leave me alone," she joked, taking another, smaller bite. He dipped his head.

"Alright, but I won't stop bothering you," he teased, nudging her with his nose. She swallowed her bite, twitching an ear.

"Thanks, I'm full. The moon is up, and I think I'm going to turn in," she said, nudging him as she turned back toward their den. Shadow curled up in her sleeping place, glancing at Kele and Breeze, who were already sleeping. Miku came in shortly after, curling up beside Shadow and quickly closing his eyes. Shadow tossed and turned in her sleeping place for a while, becoming more and more annoyed as the moon rose higher, shining through the entrance of the den.

Shadow sighed, finally sitting up and looking out of the den. She saw Max guarding the entrance as usual, but otherwise, the clearing was empty. A slow, steady breeze traveled through the oak trees that surrounded the den site, creating a soft rustling sound as the leaves and branches rubbed together. Shadow stood and spilled out of the den, going to talk to Max. He eyed her wearily as she approached him. "Hello, Max. I want to go out for a walk. I can't seem to fall asleep," she said. He looked at her, then at the moon.

"Alright, but I expect you back by the time the moon reaches the highest point. If you're not here by then, I'm coming after you," Max told her, shuffling his paws to let her pass. Shadow slipped through the ferns and out into the still air. The moon was shining brightly through the treetops, casting shadows along her path as she made her way along a hunting trail. She walked aimlessly for a while before her eyelids began to grow sleepy. She turned around to go back, but as she did, she heard a soft-moving noise coming from behind a wall of brambles. Shadow lowered her head, watching where she stepped and peeked out into a small clearing. In the clearing sat three rabbits, all sitting together nibbling on some grass. Shadow's eyes widened at the sight of *three* animals. Her heart racing, Shadow made sure that she was downwind.

Without warning, one of the rabbits stuck its ears up and angled them right at Shadow, thumping its hind foot loudly. The other two rabbits pricked their ears and looked at Shadow, but it was already too late. Shadow lunged from the bushes and bit into one of the rabbit's necks, killing it instantly. She then turned to one of the other rabbits, which was now starting to hop away. Shadow snarled, attacking it quickly and killing it. She then spun around and ran back to the small clearing to track the last rabbit. She found it almost immediately hiding under a fern, trembling with fear. Shadow let out a low growl and shot forward, cutting off its scream with a swift bite to the neck. Shadow then dragged all three of the rabbits to one spot and picked them all up by their ears, hauling them back to the den site.

When Shadow returned, she dropped her prey on the prey pile, glancing at Max, who was watching her with an impressed expression. She dipped her head wordlessly to him and returned to her den, curling up in her sleeping hole, glad that she was now tired. It would be much easier to sleep now. She quickly drifted off, letting her mind wander as her body went still.

The next morning, Shadow woke to the sun shining through the entrance of the den onto her face. She squinted as she opened her eyes and raised her head. It was early, she realized, smiling at the coolness of the morning. She stood up and stretched before slipping out of the den, breathing the fresh, dewy air. She looked around. The buckthorn leaves were lined with dew, a good sign. Shadow trotted over to the nearest bush and bent down to lap up a few of the cool, beautiful drops of water.

She felt bad ruining something so pretty, but her parched tongue got the better of her. She lapped up the few, cool drops, relishing the way they seeped into her tongue and cooled her throat. When she was done she yawned and looked around once more. She was glad to see that she was one of the first wolves awake. Lynx was lying outside of the Newborns' den, her eyes half-closed, soaking in the sun that shone on her swollen belly. Shadow felt a surge of affection for her former Trainer. Trotting over to Lynx, she glanced at her belly, smiling. "Hello, Lynx," Shadow greeted the pretty she-wolf. Lynx opened her eyes, smiling when she saw Shadow.

"Shadow! Great to see you," Lynx exclaimed, licking Shadow's shoulder. "How is training going? Is Sparrow a good Trainer?" Lynx asked her.

"I've learned a lot so far! I think I'm going to finish soon," Shadow replied, beaming. "And yes, Sparrow is an excellent Trainer," she replied, holding her breath. "He's not better than you, though," she added in a whisper, smiling. Lynx grinned, shoving Shadow lightly with a paw.

"Well, thank you. You were my first Learner, you know," Lynx told her, smiling. Shadow twitched an ear.

"You did a very good job," Shadow told her, eyes light. Lynx laughed.

"I did my best, though there are always some things that I can't prepare you for," Lynx said, glancing at her. Shadow shrugged.

"There are things we will never understand," she replied with a smile. "How are you? Are you hungry? I caught a few rabbits last night, you could have one," Shadow asked.

"Oh, yes, I'm fine. And no, I already ate, but thank you Shadow," Lynx replied, smiling down at her unborn pups. Shadow smiled, too, glancing at Lynx's facial expression. She looked delighted, but Shadow could detect a hint of nervousness in Lynx's eyes.

"You'll be a great mother, Lynx," Shadow told her, smiling as Lynx looked up at her, eyes wide.

"I know, but...I'm just afraid for them. I don't want them to be born during a drought like this. It would be hard, for them, and me," Lynx told her, frowning down at her paws. Shadow wished she knew what to say to reassure the she-wolf, but she didn't want to make any false promises. What if the drought never ended? She looked up at the sky, frowning at the sun.

Shadow smiled. "It will all work out in the end, Lynx," she said.

Lynx looked at her, affection filling her eyes. "Thank you, Shadow."

"Of course. Just tell me if you ever need anything. I'd be happy to help," Shadow told her, dipping her head and standing as Sparrow emerged from his den, yawning. Shadow said goodbye to Lynx and trotted happily over to her Advanced Trainer, the trees shifting in the wind around them. "Hello, Sparrow! What shall we do today?" she asked excitedly, a bit of a bounce in her step.

"Today, you will be assessed to see if you are ready to become a full member of the pack, along with Miku, Kele, and Breeze, if they ever wake up," he said, letting out a little growl at the end. Shadow was caught off guard.

"Today? Already? Are you sure I'm ready? You didn't prepare me for this!" Shadow exclaimed, excitement and fear crowding her mind.

"What do you think I've been doing for the past months? Training you! You have been ready for this almost ever since we began. You have hunting in your blood. You'll do fine, Shadow," Sparrow soothed her, yawning again. Shadow shook her head as if clearing the fear from her mind.

"You're right. Thank you, Sparrow," she said dipping her head. Even though she knew all she had to do was try her best she couldn't ignore the tiny voice in the back of her head telling her she might not make it. She sat down, eyes wide as wolves emerged from their dens. Mako, Amber, and Heather went to retrieve their Learners from their den, tails high. Before they reached the den, Miku emerged, yawning. Kele and Breeze followed him out as if they were woken by the excitement that now hung around the clearing. Wolves were excited to hear that there may be new Hunters and Fighters in the pack. Shadow jumped a little as Miku trotted over to her, with his eyes glazed by sleep.

"What's going on?" he asked, yawning again.

"We might finish our training today!" Shadow exclaimed as Breeze and Kele drew near with Heather, Mako, and Amber following them. Their gazes instantly lightened, sleep gone from their eyes.

"Really?" Miku exclaimed, eyes wide, ears pricked.

"Already?" Kele gasped, glancing at his Trainer, Mako. Mako nodded, twitching an ear. The four Learners shared excited words until Amber silenced them, beckoning Miku, her Learner, with a twitch of her ear.

"We will split up. Shadow and Breeze will go toward the lake, where they can hunt, while Miku and Kele can stay closer to the den site, and show their Fighting skills," Amber said to the Trainers. They all nodded simultaneously.

"Alright, let's go," Mako said while heading toward the exit. Sparrow followed, and Shadow stayed at his side as they slipped out of the clearing. The group split up, Breeze and Heather going toward the shore of the lake while Shadow and Sparrow went deeper into the forest. They walked silently through the underbrush for a while before finally stopping.

"Okay, Shadow. Now, I want you to catch as much prey as you can before your time is up. I'll tell you when you have to stop hunting," Sparrow told her, sitting down. "I will be watching you the whole time.

Try to hunt away from the lake," Sparrow told her, dipping his head. "Good luck."

Shadow walked slowly through the forest, ears pricked and senses on high alert for any sign of prey. She stopped when she heard a slight noise coming from behind a berry bush. Lowering her head, she slowly stalked forward, making sure not to step on anything while walking and only placing her paws down when the wind blew. Being careful to always walk into the wind, she finally spotted the animal. She saw a fat, furry creature sitting in a small, sunlit clearing nibbling on a berry it had plucked from the berry bush. Shadow squared her shoulders to the squirrel and shot forward, careful to make no sound. She ended its life with a swift bite to the back of its neck. She then hid her prey under some ferns, saving it to collect later. She continued along a rarely used hunting trail, wondering if Sparrow was truly watching her. She looked around, but couldn't see him among the shadows. *Perhaps he climbed a tree,* she thought, chuckling to herself.

Shadow trudged on, finding it harder and harder to continue as the sun grew hot. She pricked her ears as she heard the faint, unnatural rustle of pine needles on the ground. Holding her breath, Shadow had to try extra hard to be quiet as she scented hare. She slowly made her way toward the sound with her ears pricked. She spotted the small, scrawny hare, thankful to see that she was downwind of the animal. Stalking up behind it, she winced as the wind shifted, and her scent was carried toward the animal. Thankfully, Shadow had been ready for this. She bunched her muscles, shooting forward just as the hare was about to bound off into the bushes. She sunk her teeth into the hare's neck and threw it to the ground. She then reared up and slammed her paws down on its spine, killing it. She hid it under the bushes, her heart slamming in her chest. She then got to her paws and continued along the trail, glad that she had chosen one that seemed to have some prey.

A rustling noise from the deep underbrush caught Shadow's attention. Lowering her head, she slowly stalked forward, eyes wide looking for prey. She sensed a sharp movement out of the corner of her eye. Her gaze shot toward the movement and landed on a large mouse. Rearranging her body so that her shoulders were squared to the prey, she got ready to shoot forward. Just as she was about to spring Sparrow emerged from the bushes looking smug. The mouse raced off, diving through the underbrush. Shadow growled at Sparrow, ears pinned to her head.

"I would have gotten that!" she snarled, confused at why he would willingly scare away prey.

"Yes, and if you weren't so busy howling at me, you would have noticed that the mouse had just appeared right behind you, and you had just scared it away again," Sparrow told her, sniffing. Shadow whirled around, spotting the mouse's tail disappearing into the bushes. She lunged forward, snapping her jaws at its tail. She was surprised to realize that she caught it, and it was now squealing in pain. She plucked it from the bushes and threw it at the ground with such force that it stopped moving, its tiny paw twitching vigorously. She nipped its neck, just to be sure it was dead. She then stood up, glancing at Sparrow. He was watching her, amused.

"I'm impressed, Shadow. I didn't think you would catch that," he told her.

Shadow sighed. "Well, I didn't think you would barge right in, scaring away a perfect kill that I would have made."

"I guess we surprised each other," Sparrow scoffed, twitching an ear.

"I suppose so," Shadow replied, grabbing her prey. She didn't dare ask if she had done well.

"Your time is up, Shadow, in case you hadn't noticed," Sparrow told her, following her back into the forest.

"Yes, I know," She answered through the mouthful of fur. "I'm just going to retrieve my other prey."

Sparrow nodded. "Of course," he answered, following her. They walked quietly until she reached her rabbit. "I'm proud of you, Shadow. You will make a good Hunter," he told her, dipping his head. Shadow looked up at him, the prey falling from her mouth, her jaws wide open.

"Thank you," she stuttered, looking up at him, warmth and disbelief filling her eyes, her voice thick with emotion. She had always dreamed of this day, though she never imagined it happening so soon. Sparrow nodded, his eyes filled with pride and happiness for her. "Thank you, again, Sparrow! I couldn't have done it without you!" she exclaimed, spinning around in circles happily. She then realized that this wasn't something fully grown wolves would do. Stopping, she laughed nervously, going up to Sparrow and resting her head on his shoulder, thanking him silently. She then backed up and dipped her head in the most respect possible. She couldn't help her tail from wagging, though. Sparrow didn't seem to mind. He just moved to collect the prey that she had dropped. He grabbed the mouse by its tail and the rabbit by its leg, dragging its head on the ground as he led her back to the den site.

Shadow followed, a bit of a bounce in her step. When they returned and Sparrow had collected her squirrel, Shadow saw her den mates were sitting clustered together, talking excitedly. When they spotted Shadow, they all ran toward her, each sharing the same excited expressions. "Shadow, I made it!" Kele exclaimed, jumping on her. She wrapped her paws around him happily.

"Me, too!" she exclaimed. Breeze and Miku toppled over them, too, laughing, exclaiming that they had passed, too. "We did it!" Shadow exclaimed, laughing.

"I can't believe we all passed, and on the same day!" Miku exclaimed, equally happy. They just sat in an excited circle, laughing, until Shadow squeezed herself out, a smile plastered across her face. She looked up as Oak walked over, his eyes lit with amusement. Shadow shoved a paw at Miku, motioning with her head toward Oak. He quickly scrambled to his paws, followed by Kele and Breeze, their eyes lit with joy. Shadow sat with them in a line, watching as Oak nodded to them before turning to jump up on the Alpha stone. Shadow noticed his muscles rippling powerfully under his pelt.

"Miku, Shadow, Kele, and Breeze," he said, beckoning them forward with his tail. All the wolves were already in the clearing, forming a ragged circle around where the four Learners sat. Shadow tried to control her tail, which was wagging uncontrollably, skimming the dirt. "Shadow, please come forward," Oak said, jumping down from the Alpha stone so that he was standing right in front of her. She took a step forward, eyes wide. "Sparrow tells me you have trained hard in the ways of a wolf, and that you are now ready to become a Hunter. Is this what you wish?" Oak asked, his voice filled with pride.

"Yes," Shadow replied, twitching an ear.

"Then, from this moment on, you will hunt for your pack. You will keep them well fed, for you are now a Hunter, and a full member of this pack," Oak said loudly, his voice ringing in Shadow's ears. She then dipped her head deeply, turning back to the pack. They were howling. She raised her head proudly, her heart warm when she spotted Lynx and Sparrow among the crowd, heads tipped back as they let out light, happy howls. Storm sat right in the middle, her call long and beautiful. Shadow went to sit next to her mother as the howls faded away. She buried her nose deep into her mother's fur, joy making her heart race. Her mother sat with her, her pelt warm.

"I'm so proud of you, Shadow," Storm told her, smiling warmly. Shadow didn't reply, only buried her nose deeper into her mother's fur, drinking in her sweet, warm scent. Miku was next, being named a Fighter. Shadow howled long and deep, warmth filling her gaze as he came to sit next to her, eyes wide and shining with excitement. Shadow laughed and buried her nose in his fur, affection filling her body from ears to tail tip. Kele was next, earning his name as a Fighter, too. He went to sit next to Mako, his eyes glinting in the sunlight. Breeze earned his name last, becoming a Hunter, like Shadow. He came to sit next to Miku to share the moment with his brother, and Kele joined them soon after, smiling. They talked excitedly to each other for a few moments before splitting up, going to talk to other wolves around the clearing. Oak had ended the meeting with a wave of his tail and was now sitting happily on the Alpha stone with Storm at his side. Shadow went up to Lynx, a smile plastered across her face. Lynx looked equally happy, her eyes glinting with pride, mixed with joy and love.

"Shadow, I'm so proud of you! I know you'll do great things someday," Lynx exclaimed emotionally. Her face was stretched in a wide smile as nudged Shadow's shoulder. Shadow beamed, licking her former Trainer's cheek.

"I'll make you proud, Lynx," Shadow exclaimed, her voice thick with emotion.

"You already have," Lynx replied, sitting down, her voice filled with affection. Shadow turned as Miku prodded her on the shoulder with a paw, his gaze lit with joy.

"Shadow! I can't believe we made it together!" He exclaimed, his tail wagging uncontrollably.

"Neither can I!" She exclaimed, laughing, jumping on top of him.

"Anyway, Breeze and Kele went to make their new sleeping holes in their new dens. Should we?" Miku asked her, still smiling.

Shadow nodded. "Sure!" she exclaimed, her tail thumping against the ground.

The Hunters' den was a deep, dark hole dug under the strong roots of a maple tree. Shadow pushed her way inside, thankful to see that there was quite a lot of space, more than she thought there would be. Looking more deeply into the den she saw a hole through one of the walls. It looked like it had been dug out long ago. Peering through, she saw Miku and Kele chattering excitedly as they dug their sleeping holes. Mako was there, too, watching them silently.

Shadow pressed through the hole, realizing that she was now standing in the Fighters' den. The Fighters' den was a deep hole dug out from under a large, flat rock. The top reached about an inch above her ear tips, lower than her own den. Even though the roof was lower than in the Hunters' den, the Fighters' den had more space, with walls stretched out and rocks shoved inside the walls holding the dirt firmly in place. "Wow!" Shadow exclaimed, drawing the three wolves' attention.

"Shadow! Did you come in from the Hunters' den? I didn't know that opening was even there! I mean, I knew the dens were close together, but I didn't know that they were connected," Miku exclaimed, trotting up to her, small chunks of dirt sticking to his pelt.

"Yes, I like how they are connected. And your den is big! Come and see mine when you're ready," Shadow exclaimed, smiling and slipping back into her own den, looking around for a place to dig her sleeping place. Breeze was digging his own sleeping place next to Sparrow, his father. Shadow watched him briefly before starting to dig, hooking the dirt with her claws and forming a hole. When she finished she went to sit outside of her den, tail wrapped around her dirty paws.

Oak was sitting on top of the Alpha stone watching the clearing thoughtfully, while Storm slipped out of the den they shared, eyes warm with affection as she went to sit next to her mate.

Shadow continued looking about the clearing, spotting Lynx lounging outside the Newborns' den, her eyes half-closed. No other wolves were in the clearing, and Shadow guessed that Amber was leading some wolves on a hunt. They would want the pack to eat well and celebrate the new members of the pack. Shadow then went to sit by the prey pile breathing the hot, humid summer air. White, wispy clouds floated above, almost close enough to touch the tops of the trees. Shadow sat for a moment drinking in the warm afternoon sunlight before she stood up and started toward the exit. She planned on hunting. She slipped out of the clearing and into the hot, windless forest, her tail swaying behind her as she walked.

She followed a small, sparse hunting trail, her head low and ears pricked for signs of prey. She twitched her ears when she heard the soft, quiet sound of shuffling leaves coming from behind a bush. She veered off course to follow the sound, being careful where to put her paws. Soon, she spotted a raccoon. It looked fairly well-fed, with long black-and-gray fur and a big belly. Shadow prepared herself to attack, tensing her muscles.

Shadow stopped when she heard a new sound coming from the other side of the raccoon. She backed further into the shadows when she spotted another wolf, its eyes savaged with hunger and foam spilling from its mouth. Its leap from the bushes was barely fast enough to catch the raccoon. The strange wolf brought it down with a single bite and then began tearing hungrily into its flesh. Shadow watched, horrified, her nostrils flaring at the wolf's horrible smell. Its ribs jutted painfully out of its chest, and it breathed heavily as it tore into the prey. She held her breath as two more wolves appeared behind it, growling savagely. They lunged forward, trying to take the remains of the animal from the still-hungry wolf that had made the catch. Shadow realized with a jolt that they were Cedar pack wolves, fighting savagely over the prey they had taken on *Aspen pack* territory. The three wolves all had the same body shape and size, with bones jutting out of their flanks and breath coming raspy in their throat. Shadow watched as one of the wolves bit the other one, drawing blood. The wolf who had caught the prey drew back, blood welling from a wound on her scruff.

"It's mine! I caught it!" the she-wolf snarled, the remains of the raccoon in her jaws. The two male wolves, one white with large claws and raging amber eyes and the other black with long fur and long, skinny legs, stood next to each other, hunger driving them on.

"Come on, Echo, we just want some food," the white one growled in a deep, menacing voice.

"Catch your own food, Bone!" Echo shot back, her milky gray fur bristling, and ears pinned to her head in defiance. The black wolf shuffled his paws, the menace gone from his face.

"You're right, Echo, we're sorry. Come on, Bone, I'm sure we can catch our own food. Let's just leave her alone, and hope no Aspen pack wolves catch us," he growled, turning to leave Echo alone.

"Fog, wait. We should get some of her food," Bone growled, turning back to Echo. Shadow had to stop herself from shooting out of the bushes and defending the poor she-wolf. But she knew they were rivals and she couldn't do that without likely being attacked. Echo just stared at Bone menacingly, her head lowered and tail raised in the air. Bone stared at her for a moment longer before growling and turning to follow Fog, who had disappeared into the brush. Shadow watched Echo tear into the rest of the raccoon hungrily, until nothing was left but the bones. Shadow wondered what to do. *Should I go warn the others?* she wondered. *I can't fight them off on my own. But then, if I leave them they might wander off and we won't be able to find them!* Shadow was indecisive but finally decided to go back and report to Oak. He would send out the Fighters, and the wolves would be pushed off their territory in no time. She slipped silently through the underbrush and raced back home, hoping that the Cedar pack wolves didn't leave that spot.

Shadow burst into the clearing breathing heavily, eyes darting around the clearing looking for Oak. She found him sitting on the Alpha stone, eyes alert, watching her, curiosity edging his voice as he spoke. "Shadow, what's wrong? What happened?" Oak asked, jumping down and walking toward her, his head tilted to the side.

"Cedar pack wolves! On our territory!" Shadow exclaimed, getting the attention of most of the wolves in the clearing. She noticed Amber and the Hunters had returned. Oak raced over to her, anger sparking in his gaze.

"Where? What were they doing?" Oak asked her, rage edging his voice.

"They were deep within the territory, hunting. I only saw three, so I don't know if there were any more than that," Shadow replied.

"Okay, Shadow. You will need to lead us to where you found them. Mako, Miku, Max, and Amber, come with us." Oak finished with a growl and pushed his way through the exit. Shadow followed him, hearing the four wolves' paw steps thumping against the ground behind her. Shadow pushed past Oak and took the lead, now going at a quick pace. They were full-on running through the forest when Shadow finally stopped where she had seen the three Cedar pack wolves. Silently telling the others to keep quiet, she slowly stalked forward, eyes wide for signs of movement. She smelled them before she saw them. They were all sitting in a small, sunlit clearing, Bone and Fog tearing into a bird that they must have caught. Echo was sitting in a patch of sunlight, her limbs stretched out, the remains of a mouse at her front paws. They had stolen more prey! Shadow felt anger spark in the air as her packmates saw what had happened. Miku appeared next to her, looking at her from the corner of his eye.

Suddenly, Oak exploded from the bushes, growling and snapping his jaws angrily. The three wolves stood up, Bone holding the rest of the bird in his jaws. He looked defiant as he took a step back, holding the bird protectively. "What are you doing on our territory?" Oak demanded, fur standing straight up, his eyes glowing with hatred.

"Eating. Why?" Bone replied with a snarl.

"Does your Alpha know about this?" Oak snarled, taking a menacing step forward, lowering his head. The three wolves exchanged uncertain glances, Echo looking the most frightened.

"We came looking for food. Our pack is starving," Fog replied, taking a step forward and bowing his head, his pelt reeking of Cedar pack stench.

"That gives you no right to be on our territory!" Oak snarled loudly, causing all three of the wolves to take a step back, eyes wide. Even Bone looked unsure of himself. Suddenly, Echo turned tail and ran, followed by Fog, and then Bone. Miku, Amber, Mako, Max, and Oak shot after them, leaving Shadow behind. Shadow emerged from the bushes with a sigh, listening to the chase fade away as her packmates drove the rival wolves off their land. Shadow hid the bones of the mouse under a bush, twitching an ear as Oak returned with the rest of the group following.

"They went running with their tails between their legs," Miku exclaimed, bouncing a little. Oak gave an unsatisfied look in the direction the Cedar pack wolves had disappeared.

"Let's go back," he said roughly, leading them back to the den site. They trotted silently along the trail that led back to their home, tension still high in the air. Miku was trotting happily beside her. *They looked so skinny... We have to do something,* Shadow thought, raising her head with determination. They arrived back at the den site and Oak went directly to the Alpha stone. He surveyed the clearing with narrowed eyes before speaking. "My pack, gather around me for I have an announcement to make." The wolves who weren't already in the clearing emerged from their dens and sat before Oak, who stood over them, the sun shining over his back, sending his shadow to cover the wolves that sat in front of him, below the rock. Shadow sat beside Miku and Kele, their eyes wide with excitement. "Our group just returned from chasing a group of three Cedar pack wolves out of our territory!" he snarled with rage in his eyes. "They have stolen our prey and eaten it for themselves!" The wolves in the clearing erupted into outrageous howls. Shadow was the only one to stand.

"They are starving and weak!" she howled above the noise, quieting down the wolves. "They are dying, Oak, driven by hunger. They have it worse in their territory. The poisoned stream stretches almost around their whole territory. They have had more prey loss than us. Did you not see how starved they all looked? Will you show no mercy?" she demanded, turning her gaze to Oak. She saw he looked just as angry, with no pity in his eyes.

"They crept onto our land and stole our prey!" he snarled, his muscles rippling underneath his pelt. "They deserve to be chased away!" Shadow ignored the feeling of her packmates' eyes raking down on her pelt and continued.

"They need help, Oak. They need help from the strong, optimistic leader that I know you to be! We are Aspen pack, not some revenge-driven bunch of loners who just live off other wolves' mistakes! What does that make us, if we just decide to drive a whole pack out of their home because of something *three* wolves did?" Shadow demanded in a growl, looking around at her packmates challengingly. She knew that this was not the way to talk to the Alpha of her pack, but she could not stop. Wolves were starving and if she didn't step up a whole pack would be driven from their home.

Oak looked hesitant for a moment, his eyes flashing with indecisiveness. Shadow took a step forward, pressing him. He finally seemed to come to a decision. Standing tall, he stared down at Shadow, his tail raised. "I am the Alpha of this pack, Shadow," he stated with a snarl. "I will do what I think is best!" Oak growled, scraping his claws on the stone. "And that is…" He tried to speak, but stopped as Miku stood up.

"You may lead this pack to fight a battle that we've already won, Oak. But I will not come with you," Miku stated with a defiant growl. Oak looked taken aback as if he had not expected to be confronted like this.

"Neither will I," Sparrow growled, standing up, defending his son and former Learner. Shadow shot him a grateful glance.

"Nor will I," Heather spoke with a nod to Sparrow. Most of the pack eventually added their chorus of agreement, though some looked more reluctant than others. Mako was the only one who stayed seated, glaring at the wolves around him.

Oak looked enraged. "What is the meaning of this! I am the Alpha of this pack. You will come with me or suffer the consequences!" The wolves who had spoken stayed standing, looking defiantly up at him.

"We cannot fight wolves that have only done what they needed to survive," Shadow spoke, quieter now, her head low.

"Oak," Shadow heard Storm speak from Oak's flank as she hauled herself on top of the rock, her gaze soft. She talked quietly to him for a few moments before, stepping back, dipping her head. Oak then faced the rest of the pack, his eyes weary, but muscles still tensed.

"A leader is nothing without their pack," he growled, dipping his head. "I will respect your wishes. But, if the Cedar pack puts one paw out of line I will do what I think is best," Oak spoke loudly and strongly, eyes rigid. Shadow, along with the rest of the pack, dipped their heads and began to spread out around the clearing as Oak signaled that the announcement was over. Shadow's paws tingled and ears twitched at the thought of speaking out in such a way at a pack gathering. She walked slowly over to her den and stood outside, thinking. Miku walked up from behind her and stood at her side.

"Thanks for speaking up for me, Miku," Shadow said, nudging his neck fur affectionately.

"It was nothing. I was standing for what I believe in, and I believe in *you*," Miku told her, returning the sign of affection. Shadow smiled gratefully at him before he turned and slipped into the Fighters' den. Shadow slipped under the roots of the maple tree into the Hunters' den and made her way over to her sleeping place, glancing at her den mates, who were already in their sleeping places. Sparrow was watching her carefully as if he was thinking about what she had done. Shadow wondered if he was mad or glad that she had stood up for the Cedar pack wolves, even though they had stolen prey from Aspen pack territory. Shadow curled up in her hole, facing away from the others, and slowly fell asleep, listening to the slight, gentle sounds of her packmates stirring around her.

Shadow trotted along the long, narrow path with Miku and Scout following. She had been chosen by Amber to lead a group to check on the scent line with the Cedar pack. It had been almost three weeks since she had been made a Hunter, and since then not much had happened. Small groups had been sent out every day to try and learn more about the human and how to catch its prey. The human seemed oblivious to the fact that the wolves were gathering more information every day. Prey continued to disappear, causing both packs to go hungry, while the stream still reeked with the scent of poison. Shadow walked beside the stream now as she led her group to check on the border line. They hadn't scented anything unusual, other than the unnatural tang of the poisoned water.

The light morning sun shone on their backs as they made their way through a small clearing, senses alert and paws moving silently over the forest floor. Humidity hung in the air along with the promise of yet another hot, windless day. Shadow sighed. The heat hadn't let up since she was named a Hunter, and not a whiff of rain had been scented from the clouds that hung in the sky. This heat and lack of rain forced the pack to hunt in the mornings and nights rather than during the day. After the morning dew disappeared there was just no scent left in the dry underbrush. Shadow tried hunting anyway but found it harder and harder to catch anything while the sun shone from the sky.

Shadow listened to the soft crunch of her paws as they landed on the leaf-covered ground, wondering if it would ever rain again and bring life back into their forest. She glanced at her wavy reflection in the stream as they walked along its bank, seeing past the surface and staring down at the bottom. Not a fish in sight. She tore her gaze from the stream as she heard scuffling on the floor up ahead. Shadow signaled with her tail for her packmates to be quiet then silently crept forward, ears laid back. Looking through the brush Shadow saw a flash of fiery orange moving along the trail, the shadows from the trees dancing along its pelt. A fox, she thought, letting out a low growl. She was bigger than a fox and fluffed her fur to look even larger.

The fox jerked its head toward her, its beady black eyes glinting in the sunlight, its nose twitching vigorously as it tried to pick up her scent. She was downwind, thankfully. Its ears twitched with agitation. It hadn't spotted her yet. She knew that her fur blended well with the shadows surrounding her. Shadow let out another menacing growl and shot out of the bushes, snarling, her piercing blue eyes reflected in the fox's own. It let out a yelp of fear and turned tail to run, its black paws and white tail tip disappearing into the undergrowth. Shadow watched it go, letting out a sniff of contempt. She felt Miku and Scout appear behind her, emerging from the bushes. "Was that a fox? I thought I smelled it," Miku growled, eyes darting around the clearing.

"Yes. I chased it away," Shadow told him with a nod, glancing down at the ground. The fox had taken down a rabbit and was just about to eat it when Shadow caught sight of it.

"We should take that," Scout said, nodding at the rabbit.

Shadow nodded. "Yes," she said, slipping out of the clearing and back onto the trail. Miku emerged next, followed by Scout, who was now carrying the rabbit. Shadow dipped her head to them and then continued along the trail, eyes narrowed.

The group returned to the den site after a long, hot trek along the border. The sun was now beginning to lower in the sky, burning down on the forest. They had found nothing to report aside from the fox, and that Shadow was grateful for. She trotted over to the prey pile where Scout was dropping the rabbit. Shadow dipped her head to him and sat down in the shade, stretching out. Her paws ached, and her pelt stung from scraping through a bramble thicket to chase after a mouse. It had gotten away, and all she had caught was a pelt full of thorns. *I think I've gotten most of them out, but I can't be sure,* Shadow thought. *I should probably go talk to Luna.* She strode over to the Healer's den and pushed through the bushes to enter the cave, her paws cooling as they touched the cold, smooth stone floor. She padded along through the dark until she finally spotted Luna sitting in her bed of moss. Shadow called Luna's name quietly as she neared. Luna quickly opened her eyes and looked up at Shadow with a twitch of her ear.

"Shadow! I didn't hear you enter the den," Luna said, dipping her head as she stood up. Shadow dipped her head in return and smiled.

"Hey, Luna. Sorry if I disturbed you." Shadow relished the cool, musky feeling of the den.

"No, not at all. Is something the matter?" Luna answered, shaking her head and padding closer to Shadow. "I smell blood." Luna glanced at Shadow from the corner of her eye.

"Not much blood. I was just marking the border with Scout and Miku when I spotted a mouse. I chased it, and it ran under some brambles. I followed it thinking I could fit, but…" Shadow spoke, embarrassed.

"It didn't work out, did it? Did you at least catch the mouse?" Luna asked, moving toward Shadow and motioning for her to sit down. Shadow sat, shaking her head with a bit of frustration. Luna scoffed. "Well, I guess it was for nothing, then. I'll get the rest of these thorns out. Some of them are wedged in pretty deeply," Luna said almost to herself. Shadow winced, gritting her teeth as Luna bit down on one of the thorns and pulled it out. Luna continued until all the thorns were removed, some more stubborn than others. She then cleaned Shadow's wounds and dressed her scratches with moss and tormentil. "Okay, Shadow, you're done. You can go now, but please tell me if these start to burn," Luna told her, sitting back.

Shadow dipped her head to the Healer before climbing up the slope to leave the den. It took her a few moments to get used to the sunshine as she emerged into the clearing. When her eyes had adjusted she trotted across the clearing to where Miku was sitting, talking with Breeze. She sat next to Miku, sighing as the sun shone brightly on her face. She ducked her head away from the sunlight, wincing as it blinded her momentarily.

"Hey, Shadow," Miku said. "Did you get the rest of those thorns out? I hope you weren't hurt too badly,"

"Yes. Thank you, Miku," Shadow replied, glancing at Breeze. "Hello Breeze," she added.

"Hey," he replied, giving a tiny smile. Shadow looked at him. Why did he look like that? He was staring down at his paws, ears flattened. Miku was sitting at her side, sniffing her wounds, cleaning the dried blood off her exposed fur. Shadow continued looking at Breeze, trying to figure out what was on his mind. With a shrug, she turned back to Miku.

"Let's go hunting," she said, standing up.

"Sure," he replied with a shrug, his tail wagging gently. Shadow began walking out of the clearing, casting a look over her shoulder back at Breeze. He looked angry now, and was staring hotly at Miku, his pelt bristling. Shadow hurried out, intent on talking to Miku.

"What's with Breeze? He looked angry," Shadow said when they were out of earshot of their packmates. Miku glanced at her, silent for a moment.

"Well, he thinks that you and I are, you know,… together," Miku replied, looking at her. Shadow blinked, her pelt prickling with fluster and surprise. Why did he think that?

"Why would he be mad about that?" Shadow asked, feeling her ears grow warm.

"I guess he…likes you? I- I'm not sure," Miku replied, looking away. Shadow glanced at him, flattered.

"Well, that doesn't make sense. Why would anyone like *me?"* Shadow asked, trying to hide her embarrassment.

"Well…You're smart, funny, and good at almost everything. You have a great personality," Miku spoke shyly with a glance at Shadow. Shadow looked at him with a heartfelt smile, ecstatic that he would think that way about her.

"Well…are we? Together?" Shadow asked softly, looking at him as they walked. He looked at her with warm, affectionate eyes.

"I guess it depends on what you mean by 'together'. If you mean 'friends,' then I would say no," Miku replied. Shadow felt her breath catch in her throat. *Maybe I was getting the wrong idea,* she thought. "If you meant 'best friends,' then I would say yes. Maybe even mates. Depending on what you think, of course," Miku added quickly, glancing up at her, hope shining in his eyes. Shadow looked at him, eyes wide.

"Of course!" She exclaimed, her tail wagging vigorously. Miku looked at her, smiling up to his ears. Shadow laughed and rubbed up against him. He wagged his tail happily, his paws shaking. Shadow's heart swelled with affection for him. "I love you, Miku," she whispered, her heart in her throat.

"I love you, Shadow," Miku replied with a smile. Shadow rested her head on his shoulder while he buried his nose in her fur.

"Should we go back and tell our packmates?" Shadow asked, pulling away. Miku nodded, and bounded off back toward the den site, his paws flying over the ground. Shadow followed, laughing, her eyes shining with love.

When they returned they told the pack of their decision. Every wolf was happy for them. Even Breeze pulled together his feelings and talked to his brother. Lynx and Storm were especially happy for Shadow, crowding around her and talking to her excitedly. Shadow returned their happiness, looking over to see Miku being showered in the same excitement, his eyes lit with joy. It was getting dark now, and Shadow was sitting next to Kele, talking with him. He always knew Shadow the best.

"So, you have a mate now, huh? You better still have time for me," Kele joked, and Shadow let out a laugh.

"When have I ever *not* had time for you?" Shadow asked, laughter filling her eyes.

"I don't know, maybe things will be different now. Besides, I probably won't ever have a mate. I still wonder why you chose Miku over Breeze. Breeze is a Hunter, like you. He would understand you better."

Shadow looked over at Miku, seeing his kind smile as he talked to Heather. She felt her heart swell with fondness for him. "I guess I never had feelings for Breeze. He's like a brother to me.

Miku is different," Shadow said, shrugging. Kele nodded to show his understanding.

"Well, anyway, I'm happy for you, Shadow. I truly am," Kele said, smiling affectionately at her. She returned the smile.

"Thanks, Kele. Are you sure you don't think it's too…early? I mean, we were only made full members a month ago. I've known him all my life, and I've always felt care towards him, but…I don't know," Shadow spoke in a hushed voice, wrapping her tail over her paws, crouching on the ground. Kele crouched beside her, hesitant for a moment.

"I believe that you know what's right, Shadow. It will all work out," Kele said, dipping his head. Shadow smiled in return.

"Thank you, Kele," she said, licking his shoulder affectionately.

"Any time!" he replied with a grin. He then glanced up at the setting sun, the dark amber glow reflecting in his deep orange eyes. The sky showed a soft dark blue mixed with edges of purple, and beautiful splotches of dark pink, with the dark amber sun shining from below a small, wispy cloud. The clearing around her was filled with the beautiful orange light, which was shining on the large ferns, causing them to nearly glow a soft emerald color mixed with dark green and with splotches of brown. Shadow then breathed the fresh evening air and stood up, dipping her head to her brother.

"I'm tired," she said with a twitch of her ears, "I'm going to get some sleep." Kele smiled and dipped his head in return, motioning for her to go with a move of his tail. Shadow turned and trotted off to her den, ducking under the maple roots to curl up in her sleeping hole. She laid down in her bed and closed her eyes, sighing happily. Life was finally beginning to lighten up for the pack. Lynx's pups would be born soon, bringing new life and joy, with the assurance that life will go on into future generations. Shadow fell asleep shortly after these last thoughts, thankful for the coolness of her den.

Shadow woke the next morning to the sound of paw steps outside of her den. Opening her eyes wearily, she looked around the den, her vision blurred with sleep. Heather and Breeze were still sleeping, while Sparrow was slipping out of the den, perhaps woken by the noise as well. Shadow stood and stretched before following him out, her eyes still dull with sleep. She emerged into the clearing to see Mako and Scout talking with horrified faces to Oak, their ears flattened and fur fluffed up. Shadow moved toward them, confusion and worry filling her blue gaze. Mako was talking as she approached.

"We were just out patrolling the field when we heard the loud bang of the humans' weapon! The human was running at us and using its weapon against us, even though we were in the forest. Amber told us to run, so we ran, and she fell behind. I think she wanted to distract it. Then we heard a loud bang and a yelp from Amber. We just turned around and saw that she was bleeding from an injury to her leg. She was unconscious when we ran to get her, so we don't know if it was a wound from the human or if she had just tripped and fell. There was a big bloody bump on her head, so we dragged her into the bushes, where the human couldn't see us. We waited until the human went back to its den then we carried her home," Mako said in a rush, stuttering occasionally.

Shadow gaped at him, listening intently. Sparrow was standing beside Shadow with the same surprised expression. Shadow then looked at Oak for his guidance, seeing that he looked worried, maybe even afraid. "Is Amber with Luna?" Oak asked, worry edging his voice. Mako and Scout nodded, both shifting nervously. Oak then regained a rigid face and dipped his head to the two males. "Thank you," he said before turning and jumping up onto the Alpha stone, his tail raised with power. "Aspen pack, gather before me!" he howled, loud enough to wake all of the wolves that were still sleeping. The light of morning sun shone dully around the clearing, lighting the trees that surrounded them and sending cold shadows stretching over half of the clearing.

Wolves began to emerge sleepily from their dens, yawning or grumbling about being woken so early. Some of them looked worried about what Oak could have called them about. As soon as all the wolves were in the clearing Oak raised his head for silence. "Something has happened," he began. "You all know I wouldn't have woken you unless it was important," he added, clearing his throat. "I sent out an early group this morning to check the human and its animals. Scout, Mako, and Amber were chosen for this. As they were marking our boundaries, a human attacked them. It used a weapon maniacally, injuring Amber. She is with Luna now. We do not know if she was wounded from the weapon, or if she had hurt herself running from the human, but it caused her to fall and injure her head." Oak was delivering this news with a low growl. The wolves stared up at him, afraid for their Beta. "I warn you all to stay away from the human den. I know in the past we planned to capture the prey it has penned up, but until we figure out more about how and where to do this we will have only one wolf at a time going near," he spoke, louder than before.

The wolves in the clearing gave their nods of agreement, each dipping their head to Oak, showing deep respect and understanding. He dipped his head in return, obviously glad they agreed with his decision. "Good," he said, then waved his tail for the announcement to be over. Shadow immediately stood and rushed over to the Healer's den, weaving around her packmates until she was at the front, right next to the entrance of the den. They were all talking anxiously, wondering if Amber would be okay. Suddenly, Luna's head popped out from the den and she looked up at them.

"Amber will be fine. It looks like her leg got caught in a root and was twisted. She wasn't harmed by the human. She fell, though, and cut her head. She should wake up soon, but until then, I can't have any wolves in my den. I'll have Max posted at the entrance until she wakes. If you need me send Max inside and I'll come to you," Luna said, a sense of urgency in her voice. The wolves nodded, including Oak, who had appeared at Shadow's side.

Shadow sighed in relief. "I'm so glad Amber will be okay! We can't lose any wolves to this human – not now, not ever," she said to herself as she backed away from the Healer's den. Other wolves around her broke up into smaller groups, talking nervously. Shadow and Oak then moved to speak with Storm. Oak looked at Shadow, his ears pinned. "Is there something wrong, Shadow?" he asked, tilting his head to the side. "You look like there is something on your mind."

Shadow shook her head, twitching an ear. "I would like to be the first to visit the humans' den. I want to find out more about it," Shadow said, dipping her head. She hoped that he agreed. Oak thought for a moment before giving a nod.

"Alright, Shadow, I trust you. You can visit the human den tonight when the sun has disappeared beneath the hills and the moon is rising over the treetops." Shadow smiled.

"Thanks, Oak. I won't let you down," she said, dipping her head politely. Shadow then turned and trotted over to Kele, who was sitting by the prey pile, eyeing a squirrel that sat to the side. "Hey, Kele," she said as she neared. He looked sharply at her, smiling.

"Hey, Shadow. What's up?" he answered, shifting to give her room to sit. She sat down beside him but not before she had grabbed the squirrel that he was looking at.

"Do you want to share?" she asked as she settled down beside him. He nodded vigorously, taking a hungry bite as she pushed it closer to him.

"Thanks," he added as he chewed. She nodded, grinning. She took a small bite, chewing slowly. Even though she was hungry, she would let Kele have most of the kill. It was a small morsel, anyway. She took another bite after he had taken one then sat back, satisfied. He ate the rest, licking his lips and beginning to clean his paws. She sat at his side, watching the trees shift in the slow, warm breeze. She then got to her paws and stretched, dipping her head to Kele.

"I'm going out," she said briskly before turning around and trotting out of the den site into the quickly warming forest. Shadow walked aimlessly for a while before stopping as she heard a quietly moving sound coming from in the bushes. Instantly lowering her head, she slowly stalked forward toward the noise until she could finally spot the creature. A small mouse, searching for food within the fallen leaves, its beady-black eyes shining. Shadow tensed before shooting forward. She crushed its spine before standing up, a look of satisfaction in her eyes. She tucked it under a shriveling fern before standing back up and moving off to look for more prey. She kept her nose on the ground as she sniffed vigorously for any prey scents. After a short walk, she caught the scent of a hare. She followed the scent trail until she found the animal sitting in the shade, nibbling on an acorn. Shadow squared herself to the hare's shoulders before swiftly and silently lunging out of the bushes. She bit down on its neck before it knew she was there, pleased at her kill. She again hid her prey under a fern and marked it before continuing along the hunting trail. After an hour of no luck, Shadow turned around and retrieved her prey. Back at the den site she dropped her prey on the prey pile and trotted over to Max, who was sitting outside of the Healer's den, eyes drooping with boredom.

"Hey, Max," Shadow greeted him casually, twitching an ear.

"Do you need something?" he asked, not moving.

"Yes. I need to talk to Luna," Shadow replied, nodding. He shook his head in return.

"Sorry, Shadow, Luna doesn't have time for small talk. She's taking care of Amber right now. She can't see you," he replied.

Shadow felt a spark of anger. "Oh, come on, Max. I just need a moment." Shadow spoke, attempting to push past him and into the den.

"I said no, Shadow. Now leave. She doesn't need any distractions keeping her from her work," Max growled, pushing her away. Shadow scowled at him before turning and trotting away, her worry for Amber gnawing away at her belly, dread sitting like a lump in her throat. *What If Amber isn't okay?* she couldn't help thinking, a frown forming on her face. She shook her head and sat in the shade near the edge of the clearing, her ears pinned to her head. She looked up as Oak approached her, his muscles rippling powerfully under his fur. He sat beside her, pelt blending with the shadows.

"Shadow," he said, drawing her gaze to his. "When you go to the humans' den tonight I don't want you to get too close. Don't be seen. I don't need anymore hurt wolves in the pack," he said harshly, but with concern in his eyes

"Don't worry, Oak, I won't be seen," Shadow replied with a dip of her head. He nodded thankfully and stood up with a wave of his tail.

"I should go join Sparrow and Mako border marking. Don't use too much energy today, Shadow. Try and get some rest. It may be a long night," Oak said before turning and trotting to catch up with Sparrow and Mako, who were already leaving. Shadow sat and watched him leave, her pelt prickling with unease. *What if the human catches me, or follows me home? What if something bad happens?* She couldn't help thinking these negative thoughts, her heart pounding in her throat. She shuddered at the thought of being in the hands of that creature, or not being able to return to her packmates. Although the sun was hot shining down on the forest, she still felt a chill run down her spine at the horrible thought.

Shadow trotted silently through the dark, cool forest, her paws pushing her forward as she made her way along the trail that led to the field that the human-inhabited. The day had passed slowly. Shadow talked with Miku for part of the day, spending the rest of her time helping with whatever she could around the den site. She had finally pushed off the negative thoughts, and she tried not to think about the bad things that could happen, for they scared her. Miku had helped to boost her confidence, but now that she was on her way, alone in the dark, cold forest, she had forgotten the things he had said.

Instead, thoughts about what could go wrong kept pushing their way into her head. She knew she shouldn't think about them, but she couldn't help herself. She quickened her pace, aware that the moon was already high in the sky, giving her limited time to reach her destination.

When she finally reached the humans' territory she was shocked by what she saw. In the short time that the pack had spent away from the humans' den a lot had changed. The hedge had been cleared and replaced by silver mesh that stretched far into their territory. The trees that had been inside the circle of mesh had been cut down, their bases chopped neatly. A thick, sour scent hung in the air around the chopped trees filling Shadow's nose and eyes. She barely stopped herself from retching at the horrible scent. Ears pinned and eyes narrowed, she made her way toward the tall, shiny mesh, her pelt bushed up. She peered through the holes, holding her breath. The trees had been chopped beyond that point and were lying dead on the ground. Some had been stripped of their branches and chopped into smaller pieces, which were now sitting in a large pile beside the large human den. The branches were piled between the two dens, the leaves beginning to fall from the branches.

Shadow saw that more mesh had been put up at the very edge of their territory and it stretched into the Cedar pack's land. It went as far as she could see into their territory, and although the trees hadn't been cleared from within she could tell that it stretched farther into Cedar pack land than Aspen pack land. Her eyes watered at the horrible scent that had begun stinging her throat. Horrified at everything she had seen she whirled around and began throwing herself through the forest, back toward safety. She needed to tell Oak about this right away. She veered along the trail, lungs burning as her paws pounded harshly against the ground and she propelled herself through the quiet forest.

When she reached the den site she burst through the entrance, not loud enough to wake any wolves but loud enough to startle Max, who was sitting watch. He eyed her wearily as she bolted across the clearing and skidded to a stop outside of Oak and Storm's den. "Oak?" She called softly into the den, her breath coming raspy in her throat. Oak appeared in front of her a few moments later, his eyes bleary with sleep, his face pulled back with confusion.

"Shadow? What happened? Why are you back so quickly?" Oak asked, ears twitching with worry.

"Oak," Shadow rasped, catching her breath. She was careful to be quiet, as she didn't want to wake any other wolves or alarm anyone else of the danger that they could be in. "I was checking on the human, just as you asked. Human mesh has been placed surrounding the field and into the forest. It stretched far across the border, and the trees that stood inside it have been cleared. The hedge is gone, too." Oak just stared at her, as if processing what she had just said.

"What do you mean by, the trees have been 'cleared?'" Oak asked, eyes wide.

"They were chopped down by the human!" Shadow replied burning with anger, disbelief still hanging in her voice. Oak stared at her, eyes wide.

"The trees are…gone?" He asked disbelievingly. Shadow nodded sadly. "How far in from where the hedge once was?" Oak asked, tilting his head down.

"Quite a way in. There is no way to get to the pond." Oak thought for a moment before turning to Shadow, indecision filling his gaze.

"Okay. Don't tell any wolf, not yet. There is no use starting a panic about something like this. Thank you, Shadow. I need to think now," Oak told her, dipping his head. Shadow dipped her head in return, slowly turning and walking back to her den, eyes wide with what she had seen. She slipped into the Hunters' den and curled up in her sleeping place, frowning. She knew that she wouldn't sleep, but she also didn't want to think. She would leave that to the Alpha of the pack. She just took a deep breath and shut her eyes tightly, hoping that if she did sleep no dreams would haunt her mind.

Chapter Ten

Shadow opened her eyes the next morning to see sunlight pouring in through the entrance of the den and wolves sitting around the clearing, all looking sleepy. Breeze, Sparrow, and Heather were already out, their holes empty. She stood up and blinked her eyes before stretching and slowly exiting the den. She yawned as she quietly made her way over to Oak, who was sitting beside the Alpha stone, his eyes wide as he gazed around the clearing. "Hello, Oak," Shadow greeted him quietly as she neared, dipping her head deeply. He glanced at her, his amber eyes shining in the morning sunlight. They seemed to glow like fire as he stared down at her wearily. It looked as if he hadn't slept at all last night.

"Hello, Shadow, and good morning. Did you sleep well?" he asked her with a twitch of his ear, suddenly parting his jaws to an enormous yawn.

"Yes," Shadow lied. "Did you sleep well, father?" Oak took a few seconds before answering.

"I did not, Shadow. Not at all. I'm…worried about the pack," Oak said quietly. He didn't know whether he should share his thoughts with her or not. Shadow looked at him, urging him to continue. When he didn't speak, she shifted her paws, eyes expectant. Finally, with a blink at her, he continued to speak. "I know it has been a hard summer, but… Well, what if the prey never comes back?" he asked, pausing to look at her. His eyes were worried. Tired. Duller than usual, she thought. He continued. "What If the stream is never drinkable again? What If the forest never recovers, or the human expands even farther onto our territory? There's barely enough food to go around now, and after that massive loss in territory…I'm afraid that our home will never return to its normal state," Oak confessed, dropping his eyes. He then glanced at her after a few moments of silence, as if wondering what she thought. Shadow took a second to process what he had said, and then come up with an answer.

"I…understand your worries, Oak. We are losing prey along with our territory. And you're right, the forest will never be the same as it once was. But, this is our home. We need to make the best of our situation, even if that means accepting change. We could expand out farther from the river. It might take a while to get used to, but…" Shadow said before Oak cut her off.

"That's exactly it, Shadow. We can't live here if there's no prey, or there's a danger of being killed by a human every time we venture into the territory! And I *know* pups," Oak spoke with a low growl. "They have good and bad qualities. They help the pack grow. They give us the promise of a future. But, they need food to survive, sometimes even more than fully grown wolves do. And we don't *have* that. If we don't have enough food to go around *now,* then imagine how much harder it will be to feed even more hungry mouths. Pups are also known to wander off. What if they decide to sneak out and have a drink from the stream? Then where would we be? This is not a safe place to raise our kin, Shadow, and I think you know it," Oak said sadly with a shake of his head. "We can't ignore the truth forever, Shadow. We, as a pack, cannot live here anymore," Oak spoke, glancing sideways at her. Shadow stared at him, her mouth hanging open.

"*Leave* the territory? Our home?" Shadow stared at him, unwilling to believe what he was saying. But a tiny voice in the back of her mind was telling her that this might be the best choice. She glanced at Oak. He was staring at her, his eyes dull.

"I fear this would be the best decision for the pack," Oak continued, "and I've thought on this for a long while. I've confided in Storm, and she agrees with me. So does Amber. That is why I sent Amber to check on the humans' territory, to make sure they weren't causing any trouble. And now here we are. She's injured because of it, and we've lost almost half our territory. We cannot stay here." Oak kept his voice low, aware that wolves were beginning to leave their dens and enter the clearing. Shadow stared at the ground.

"I…suppose that does seem like the best choice. To leave. Are you going to tell the rest of the pack?" Shadow asked looking at him through wide eyes. Oak dipped his head.

"Yes, but not now. Not today. Tell no wolf what I told you just now. I don't need any worried tension in the pack right now," Oak told her with a dismissive flick of his ears. Shadow dipped her head and slowly stood, making her way over to the prey pile, where Miku, Breeze, and Kele all sat, talking quietly. Shadow sat beside Miku, trying to look casual.

"Are you alright, Shadow?" Kele asked her before yawning. "You seem tense."

"I saw you talking to Oak. What did he say?" Miku added with a tilt of his head. Shadow blinked and flexed her paws, wondering what to say.

"Er, he just told me to go hunting with Sparrow and Heather," Shadow said with a twitch of her ears.

"Why aren't you hunting then?" Breeze asked, narrowing his eyes. Shadow blinked.

"Well, because he wanted you to come with me," Shadow lied again, the words sour as they rolled off her tongue.

"Alright," Breeze grumbled, standing up and stretching. Shadow sighed quietly with relief and turned, locating Sparrow and Heather on the other side of the clearing. They were sitting outside of the Hunters' den, talking and sharing a mouse. Shadow trotted over to them and waved to them with her tail.

"Greetings," she said, giving a nod of her head.

"Hello, Shadow," Sparrow replied with a brisk dip of his head.

"Oak wants you two to hunt with Breeze and me," Shadow spoke quickly as Breeze approached, his eyes still dull with sleep.

"Okay," Sparrow said as he stood. Heather got up more slowly, yawning. The remains of the mouse were set aside as Sparrow and Heather led them out the exit, talking politely to each other. Shadow hung back, leaving Breeze in the middle. She walked alone with her thoughts, her paws landing clumsily on the ground, her mind not focused on what she was doing. *Oak wants to leave?* she thought with a frown. *But this has been our home since the very beginning! Every other wolf, including me, has lived here all our lives. And, what about the Cedar pack? Would we leave them, or bring them with us? They will surely perish if they don't leave.*

Shadow snapped herself out of her thoughts and focused on hunting. It wouldn't be much help if she scared off all the prey in the area by walking so loudly. She quickened her pace, leaping nimbly over a holly bush and landing gracefully on the other side. She caught up to Breeze, who was sniffing a mouse den, his eyes narrowed. "I think there's a mouse in here," he said quietly, backing away from the hole and glancing at Shadow. Shadow stalked closer and stuck her nose in the hole, ears pinned. The scent was fresh, but not strong.

"Maybe we should find something that mice eat, to lure it out. What do mice eat?" Shadow asked with a twitch of her tail.

"Nuts, berries, seeds. Stuff like that," Breeze replied.

"Okay, try to find something like that, then," Shadow replied, moving off to try and find some food for the mouse. She wandered about the forest until she came across a holly bush. After plucking a few of the remaining berries she returned to Breeze to see that he was carrying some acorns. Then the two placed their trap beside the mouse hole and stepped back to wait. They sat in the shadows for a long while before they finally heard the faint sound of a squeak coming from the mouse's hole. A tiny nose suddenly poked out of the hole and Shadow felt her muscles tense. The mouse slowly emerged, letting out wary squeaks of hunger as it began to move toward the pile of food. Suddenly, another nose poked out from the hole, and a larger mouse emerged, its movements strong and confident. It raced up to the pile of food and began tearing hungrily at a berry, while the other, smaller mouse began nibbling at a small acorn. Shadow's eyes gleamed as she stared at the two scraps of prey. Like a flash, she shot out of the dark and closed her jaws on the smaller mouse. Breeze shot forward a heartbeat later and bit into the larger mouse's neck, killing it instantly. Shadow gave him a nod, still holding her mouse, and turned to hide their catch under a fern.

"Who knows how many mice could be under there. We only have all day," Shadow said, smiling after she had hidden her mouse under the plant. He hid his next to hers, nodding. Shadow then returned to her spot in the shadows, prepared to wait however long it took to catch at least one more mouse. It wasn't long before another mouse appeared, this one even smaller than the first, and began moving toward the pile of food left for it. It began nibbling on the berry that the large mouse had started. Shadow tensed her muscles, getting ready to attack, but Breeze was faster. He shot out of the bushes and broke the mouse's neck before it could even let out a squeak. He then gave a dip of his head to Shadow and hid it with the rest of the prey under the fern. Shadow gave a smile. Maybe they could cope with the loss of their territory after all. Breeze returned to his spot beside Shadow and they waited, ears pricked and eyes sharp, ready to catch even the smallest movements.

Shadow's gaze shifted to a movement in the branches of a small bush. Narrowing her eyes, she tensed her muscles, expecting some sort of prey to come out, but what emerged wasn't what she had expected at all. A large, brown and white muzzle poked out from the bushes, its large jaws parted to reveal sharp white teeth. Its pink nose twitched as it caught a scent, its lips drawing back to let out a hiss. Its head emerged from the underbrush, brown eyes glinting in the sunlight and its fur, brown mixed with a hint of gray and white, was shining. Its fur bristled as it took another step forward toward their mice. Its large, tufted ears swiveled around as it let out a low growl. Then, it emerged fully from the bushes, its large body rippling with its muscles as it looked around warily from where it stood. It had a small, stumpy tail. Its fur was groomed back neatly from ears to tail tip. Shadow stared at it, frightened by its large, muscular body and long, pointy teeth.

Letting out a low growl the creature began moving toward their mice, its eyes rounded with hunger. Shadow heard Breeze growl as the beast took his fresh mouse from the pile. The animal's eyes narrowed as Breeze emerged from the bushes with a snarl. Breeze stood tall, with his shoulders squared and fur bristling angrily. He let out a snarl as the animal took a step toward him. It looked undaunted by his growls of defiance. It let out a loud growl of its own as it dropped the mouse, its large, furry paws exposing long silver talons. Breeze's eyes widened but he didn't back down as the creature slowly began to advance, its eyes glinting menacingly. Shadow shot out of the bushes to help her friend, fear pulsing through her body and her heart thumping in her throat. The large animal looked shocked for a moment by her appearance but quickly regained its menacing look.

It let out a loud yowl and shot at Breeze, its paws flying as it swiped at his face. He backed away, eyes closed, as its claws tore through his fur and drew blood. He let out a whimper of pain followed by a savage growl as he fought back against the creature, rearing up and crashing down on its shoulders, paws outstretched. His claws sunk into its shoulder bones and his teeth met its cheek as he came down on it, his muscles rippling powerfully under his pelt. Shadow sprung into action to help him, shooting over to its flank and biting into its fur. It let out a hiss of pain and backed away, blood welling up at the wounds they had inflicted. The creature then lunged at Shadow, sinking its sharp teeth into her scruff. Shadow let out a yelp of surprise and twisted her head around, snapping at its face. She felt a pang of satisfaction as her teeth met flesh. Shadow hung on, tearing a chunk of its skin before it finally let go of her, yowling in pain. Breeze then came at it from the side, crashing into its chest and biting deeply into a soft spot under its leg. It let out a screech of agony as blood spurted from the wound, showering the ground and filling Shadow's nose with its sharp tang. The animal backed away, writhing in pain, and turned to disappear into the bushes, its ears pinned to its head in anger.

Shadow watched it go, panting, feeling a trickle of blood run down her back from the bite on her scruff. Glancing at Breeze, she realized that he was fine. There were only a couple of scratches on his face and a few places where fur was missing. "Breeze, are you okay?" Shadow asked after a moment of silence, taking a step toward him.

He nodded. "Yes, I'm fine," Breeze replied with a sigh. "We should get back to the den site, though, and tell Oak what had happened." Shadow nodded in agreement and shook out her pelt, sending droplets of blood flying around the clearing.

"One of us should tell Sparrow and Heather, though," Shadow said, and Breeze nodded. "I will," he answered. He then turned and slipped into the ferns, where Sparrow and Heather had disappeared. Shadow then licked the remaining blood out of her fur and grabbed their mice as she waited for him to return.

Within a few moments, Breeze returned and led them back to the den site. When they reached home, Shadow's paws throbbed and her breath came ragged in her throat. She pushed through the ferns and emerged into the clearing, heading straight for the Healer's den after dropping their mice on the prey pile. Breeze was already at the entrance of the den, talking to Max.

"I'll go get her," Max dipped his head and slipped into the den silently. Shadow watched him go, moving to sit beside Breeze and wait for Luna to appear. Luna emerged from the den carrying a mouthful of herbs in her jaws, her fur fluffed up.

"What happened to you two?" she asked as she moved quickly to Shadow's side and began working on the bite on her scruff.

"We were hunting, and were attacked by some sort of animal that I've never seen before," Shadow said to Luna.

"This is a deep bite. What did you say the creature looked like? These teeth marks are quite large," Luna asked Shadow, her head tipped to the side and her face creased with concentration as she dressed Shadow's wounds.

"I didn't. It was some sort of big cat, I think. It had a white-and-brown pelt, with lots of fur and big paws. It also had a small tail and big tufted ears," Shadow described the creature, sitting back down as Luna moved on to Breeze's scratches. By now, some wolves had gathered around and were listening quietly.

"That sounds like a lynx," Luna said, shuddering. "Those things only come this deep into our territory if they're looking for food. Vicious creatures."

"Shadow? Breeze? What's going on?" Oak called as he emerged from his den, ears pricked with confusion. He made his way across the clearing and to Breeze's side, his eyes wide. "I smell blood. What happened?" he repeated, this time quieter, directed at Shadow.

"Breeze, Sparrow, Heather, and I were hunting. Heather and Sparrow went off to hunt together, so Breeze and I stayed back to hunt by ourselves. Breeze found a mouse den, so we lured some out with some berries and nuts. We hid the prey that we killed under a bush, but the blood scent must have drawn the lynx to our location. It was going to eat our mice, so we chased it off," Shadow explained quickly, aware of the eyes and ears that were trained on her as she spoke.

Oak took in the information slowly. "Lynxes don't usually come near our territory unless they're starving. Did the lynx look healthy?" Oak asked her, twitching an ear.

"I- I don't know, I guess so," Shadow answered, ears pinned to her head. "It was healthy enough to put up a good fight."

"Okay, Shadow, thank you. You can rest now," Oak replied with a dip of his head. Shadow dipped her head in return and moved off toward an open spot in the clearing. She laid down in the shade and wrapped her tail around her forepaws, sighing. She then rested her head on her paws and watched the wolves around the clearing, her ears pinned back. Breeze was talking with Luna as she patched up his scratches, while Sparrow and Heather were entering through the ferns, Heather carrying a squirrel and Sparrow a small hare. The rest of the wolves in the clearing were all talking quietly in groups, or wandering around, carrying prey, or sharing gossip.

Shadow sat at the edge of the clearing listening to the sounds of the oak leaves shifting around her in the wind. Birds chirped overhead and the sun beat hotly down on the forest, filling the clearing and making the sand glow a warm yellow color. The maple trees surrounding the dens gave shade to about half the clearing, covering Shadow's fur and keeping her cool. It was still a hot day, but cooler than it had been the past few days. Maybe this meant that the heat was finally letting up? Shadow sighed with relief at that thought. The forest had been slowly shriveling under the intense heat of the sun. Shadow closed her eyes and drank in the musky, familiar scents of the forest around her. She was happy here, in their home. If she left, she would leave half of her heart here. This is where she grew up, endured the hardships of being a Learner, was made a *full member* of her pack. That would never leave her. Those memories would be kept here, where they were formed. She dug her paws into the dirt. This was her home. But, wherever she went it would always be with her. She knew that in her heart she would never leave. And that was all she needed.

Shadow padded alone through the forest, her paws landing softly on the ground as she made her way through the dense underbrush. Ferns and ivy leaves brushed against her pelt as she ducked under a tree trunk and continued along the thin trail that led to the lake. It was one of the few places that hadn't been tainted by the human's horrible scent. Her dark fur gleamed in the bright morning sun. The oak and maple trees shifted in the wind and sent their shadows moving throughout the forest, while the cool dew rested on the fronds of the ferns around her. The sun shining on the dew-covered plants sent crystal light sparkling throughout the clearing she passed through. She bent to lap up a few of the droplets of water that rested on the leaves. Then, turning back to the trail she continued forward, a gentle smile resting upon her face. When she finally made it to the lake, she went to sit at the shore. Listening to the waves lap at the sand below her paws she closed her eyes, feeling the breeze flow through her fur and smelling the fresh scent of the water.

Shadow opened her eyes to see a fish leap out of the water and then dive back in, its scales shining brightly as the light touched them. Shadow watched, smiling, her ears pinned. It had been only a few days since the encounter with the lynx, and nothing more had been spotted.

The human had continued its work clearing the trees and expanding its territory. No more mesh had been put up, but the humans seemed to grow more confident every day, venturing far into the territory, scouting out the land, and coming dangerously close to their dens. Her packmates were extremely frightened of the humans, and Shadow didn't blame them. Who knows what that human could do to them, or what it had in store for their territory? Shadow's dreams flashed back into her mind. *Fire? Is that what the human Is going to leash upon us?* Shadow shuddered. That was a horrible thought. Shadow sighed and stood up, moving toward the water. Pebbles shifted under her paws as she dipped her tongue into the cool crystal-clear water. She then placed her paw in the water, letting it cool her pads and soak into her fur. Shadow sat and lowered her head, her eyes searching for any movement coming from the water.

She figured she should fish since she was already here. Soon, a flash of light caught her eye. She turned her head toward the flash and spotted a minnow darting quickly through the water, unaware of her presence. As quick as a flash, she shot into the water and snapped her jaws down around something slimy and hard. Pulling her head from the water, she spat her catch out onto the ground. It was a twig that had been buried under the sand. The minnow darted away and disappeared behind a rock. Shadow huffed, frowning, and threw the stick back into the water, watching it sink.

Shadow returned to her position by the water, her eyes and ears more focused now. She blinked as a large water creature slipped out from under a rock, its movements slow and casual. *That must be a crayfish,* Shadow thought. Sparrow had told her about crayfish and how to catch them. Shadow slowly repositioned herself so that she was behind the crayfish, where it couldn't see her. Its tail curled slowly as it sat sifting through the sand. Shadow shot forward and bit into its pink flesh, ripping it out of the water. She quickly threw it onto a hard rock, killing it before it could clamp her with its tiny claws. After nipping its neck just to be sure it was dead she brought it back to where she had settled herself and hid it behind a rock, making sure no other animal could steal it from her. She then continued fishing, catching one big fish before returning home.

It was getting hot. When she returned to the den site the clearing was filled with wolves, all talking or lying in the shade. Shadow stepped into the clearing and dropped her prey on the prey pile, frowning as she saw that the only things that had been caught by the hunting group this morning were a mouse and a blackbird. That wasn't nearly enough to feed the whole pack. Shadow sat down with a sigh, her mind spinning. Maybe Oak was right and the best choice was to leave. She was distracted from her thoughts as Miku appeared next to her, his eyes warm.

"Hey, Shadow. Nice catch," he said, twitching an ear toward the carp she had caught.

"Thanks," She replied with a smile.

"Do you want to hunt with me later? I thought we might check on the humans, too," he added in a quiet voice, lowering his head so that his snout was next to her ear. Shadow glanced at him.

"We'll get in trouble if we're caught," she warned. Miku shrugged.

"Yeah, but what's life without a little risk? Plus, there can't be any harm in checking on what the humans have been doing," Miku replied with a grin.

"I don't know…I think Oak has enough to do without having to worry about us going behind his back," Shadow spoke, blinking.

"Oh, come on, Shadow. You know you want to," Miku replied with a twitch of his ear.

"Do I?" Shadow scoffed, glancing crossly at him. He shrugged.

Miku looked at her expectantly. Shadow hesitated. She *did* want to have a bit of fun… But she also didn't want Oak to have to worry. She gave a sly smile.

"You're right, Miku, I do want to. But, if we get caught, you'll regret it," Shadow said, scooting closer to him and butting him teasingly on the shoulder. He smiled, beaming.

"Great. Don't worry, you *won't* regret it," Miku said, licking her on the cheek.

"Yeah, okay. I'm going to go and check the border with the Cedar pack. Care to join me?" Shadow said, glancing at her mate.

"Sure," he replied, moving toward the entrance. Shadow chased after him, smiling.

They padded along the border stream, Shadow's nose wrinkled against the foul tang of the water. She wondered why this was happening and where it was coming from. She walked in front of Miku, his paws cracking against twigs and sticks under his feet as he walked. Shadow walked silently, placing her paws wherever she saw that they wouldn't make noise. "Do you think you could walk a little quieter?" she asked, her ears twitching with laughter.

He frowned. "I don't know if I can." He tried to place his paws where Shadow did but somehow this only made things louder. Shadow laughed.

"Didn't your Trainer teach you how to walk on a trail?" Shadow teased, chuckling.

"I was trained to be a Fighter, not a Hunter," he retorted lightly.

"Well, I guess I'll have to teach you, then," Shadow said, stopping to let him catch up to her. "Okay, listen. Place your paws down wherever you see fewer leaves or twigs. That way they won't crunch but will curve around your paws and make no sound. It's easy. Go ahead, try it." Miku started walking, slowly this time, placing his paws down thoughtfully.

He made much less noise, but still had some trouble finding places to place his paws. "Good! Now just keep practicing and you'll eventually make no sound, and be able to move effortlessly and silently along any trail," Shadow told him with a smile. She then ran up ahead of him and continued along the path, her paws moving silently over the forest floor.

"Thanks," Miku exclaimed, smiling, determined to make little or no noise as he walked behind her. They continued silently for the most part, with only the occasional crunch of Miku's paws as he stepped in the wrong place.

"Try to place your paws down lightly. To feel where you will land a step before you take it. Try to land on your toes, if you can," Shadow advised as he took another bad step. They continued on, and it was quiet except for the sounds of the forest around them and the light, soft sound of their breathing. They stayed beside the stream until they came to the edge of their territory, where the ground fell out from under the water and it crashed down to the pond below.

"Well, it's a good thing there weren't any Cedar pack wolves on our land. Oak would not be happy about that," Miku spoke with a sigh. Shadow nodded.

"Yes, Oak has been anxious lately, with all that is going on. The Cedar pack, the stream, the weather, the loss of prey, and now the human. Plus, Amber is out with a head injury. It all must be very stressful for him," Shadow said, her heart softening for her father. "It must be hard to cope with all of that." Miku nodded.

When they returned to the den site the sun was dipping low behind the treetops and the pack was settling down for the night. Oak was talking with Storm on the Alpha stone, while Luna was sitting outside her den, looking up at the stars that were beginning to show in the clear evening sky. Max was talking to Lynx, her belly swelling with pups, his eyes warm as he gazed at her. She spoke excitedly, his eyes bright and shining with the dying daylight. Sparrow and Scout were talking beside the prey pile, with Heather and Mako sitting nearby. Shadow turned to the Hunters' den, beckoning Miku with her tail. She called a "goodnight" to Oak before entering her den, her eyes sharp as they adjusted to the darkness of the den. Miku followed her inside, his eyes glowing amber in the fading light.

"Shall we leave at midnight?" Shadow asked quietly, aware that Breeze was sleeping in the back of the den, his eyes closed and his breath coming steadily as he lay still in his bed.

"Sure. Just make sure not to wake another wolf," Miku spoke with a grin. He then turned and slipped through the hole into his den, casting her one last glance before curling up in his sleeping place and facing away from her. Shadow smiled and laid down in her hole, her ears warm. Her eyelids suddenly became heavy and she fell asleep, hoping that she would wake up around midnight.

Shadow woke later that night to moonlight streaming in through the entrance of the den and glinting in her eyes. Blinking sleep from her body, she lifted her head and looked out the entrance, up at the sky. The moon was high, shining brightly although it was only half full. Shadow quietly stood and stretched, biting back a yawn. She twitched an ear and slipped quietly into the Fighters' den to see Miku sitting up in his hole, eyes blurry. "Hey," he said, breaking the silence. Shadow flattened her ears, eyes wide.

"Shush!" she whispered, flicking her ear. She padded toward him and beckoned him to his feet with her snout. He stood and slipped over to her silently, placing his paws lightly. Mako stirred but didn't open his eyes. Miku then turned to Shadow and slipped out of the den through the entrance, his tail tip pointed upwards. Shadow followed him tingling with excitement. They made their way toward the clearing's entrance, Shadow raising her head as Max stopped them at the front.

"What are you two doing?" he growled, his head raised high and tail wrapped around his paws. He glared down at Shadow, his fur bristling slightly. He acted like he still saw them as Learners, trying to sneak out at night. Shadow returned his glare defiantly, a sneer resting upon her face as she spoke.

"Moonlight hunting. Move out of the way," she growled, taking a step forward toward the entrance. Miku followed her as she shouldered past Max and slipped through the entrance and into the moonlit forest. A slight breeze ruffled her fur as they made their way through the territory toward the humans' boundaries. Shadow wasn't particularly in the mood for Max's bossy behavior. Making their way through the forest at a trot they soon reached the shiny mesh. The territory that surrounded the humans' filth seemed to grow thinner every day. Ferns and other ground plants beginning to shrivel with the poison that the humans inflicted on the land. Shadow peered sadly through the holes in the neatly woven shiny material. The trees had been cut short like blades of grass. The ground was covered in waste, with little life and a thick, sickly smell, like how the poison in the stream smelled, but stronger. Shadow watched a mouse scurry around within the ruin, its beady black eyes glazed and movements awkward. It began moving toward Shadow, as if unaware of her presence. It looked sick, filled with poison or rubbish from the humans' filthy ways.

Shadow watched it pitifully from behind the barrier. She then beckoned Miku onward with her tail, her eyes dull with sadness. If this was what her home would turn to, she didn't want to be anywhere near it. She made her way through the thin underbrush until she spotted the humans' den, the wood from the cut trees stacked even higher now. Shadow wondered suddenly why this human wanted so much chopped wood from their forest. Maybe it wanted to build another den with those materials? Shadow frowned, her eyes shining in the moonlight.

Suddenly, she felt the breeze blow from behind her, carrying their scent toward the human den. Shadow's eyes widened as she spotted a large, broad dog head poke up from the outer platform connected to the human den. Shadow guessed it had been sleeping, possibly guarding the den's entrance. The dog let out an angry bark, waking the second dog, which instantly turned to face Shadow and Miku.

The dogs suddenly shot off the stoop, barking madly, and sped off toward Miku and Shadow, their powerful muscles rippling furiously beneath their fur. They quickly ate up the ground before them as they tore away from the human den, froth flying from their mouths as they ran side by side, quicker than they looked. Shadow's eyes widened in alarm as one of the dogs, the bigger one, lunged at her flying fast through the air as it aimed its giant, bone-crunching teeth at her neck. Acting quickly, Shadow dove aside, feeling the wind from the dog's attack hard on her scruff. The dog yelped as it flew into the forest and landed awkwardly on a rock that jutted from the ground. It landed painfully on its back, letting out a yelp as an ear-splitting crack filled the air. Shadow stared helplessly as the dog slid lifelessly off the rock, leaving a trail of blood as it slid. It now lay motionless on the ground, blood pooling around its back and soaking into the ground. Its spine arched awkwardly, pale white bone jutting from one of the sides. Its beady black eyes stared furiously up at Shadow as the life began to leave its body, its tongue lolling out. Blood mixed with the drool as it pooled around its maw.

Shadow stared horrified at the giant dog, her ears flattening as she heard the loud, angry sounds of the human as it flung open the entrance of the den. Its eyes hardened with fury as it caught sight of Shadow and Miku. Miku was growling at the other dog, which had skidded to a halt and was staring at its partner's lifeless body, its eyes filled with confusion. "Run," Shadow whispered hoarsely to Miku, turning to him as the human began making its way toward them. "Run!" Shadow repeated, louder this time, as Miku still sat, growling at the second dog. She pushed him into the forest and began running, her legs bunching and stretching as she flew through the forest, the wind streaming through her fur. She felt Miku hard on her heels. When she thought they had reached a reasonable distance from the dogs she slowed to a walk, her eyes still wide and tongue lolling out. Miku came up next to her, ears pinned to his head as he caught his breath.

"What did you do to that dog?" Miku suddenly asked, glancing at her. Shadow closed her eyes, the vision of the dead dog, lying bloody on the ground, haunting her mind.

"I- I don't know," she stammered. "I just ducked aside, and it flew into that rock…" She trailed off, wincing as she sat down. Miku sat beside her, licking her nose.

"It's okay, Shadow. None of this was your fault. The good thing is, w…"

"There was *nothing* good about that!" Shadow cut him off with a snarl. "Now the human will be angrier than ever, driven by grief, determined to destroy us. I only made things worse." Instantly regretting her harsh words, she slumped down into a crouch, ears pinned to her head. "I'm sorry, Miku. It's just that whenever I try to help the pack, I end up making things worse for them," Shadow rasped sadly, glancing at him. Miku crouched beside her, unfazed by her words. He understood her, and how she could snap sometimes.

"That's not true, Shadow. At least you *try* to help the pack. Some wolves, like me, don't ever do anything important," Miku spoke, snapping his jaws shut. Shadow looked at him.

"You don't really think that, do you?" She asked softly. He shrugged, glancing at her. "Well, I, for one, find you very important," Shadow stated with a tiny smile. He shifted closer to her, smiling.

"Thanks," he said softly.

"No problem. Maybe we should start heading back. I'm sure Max is looking for a reason to get us into trouble. Let's not give him one." Shadow stood giving Miku a weary smile. Miku stood as well, glancing at her quickly.

"Good idea. And we can hunt on the way back," he added with a nod. Shadow dipped her head and followed him through the brush and ferns, her tail drooping at the memory of that farm dog, lying lifeless on the dirt, eyes wide and staring at her madly.

They returned with nothing to show from the hunt. Shadow almost caught a mouse, but she wasn't focused, and the prey scurried away to the safety of its home. They emerged into the dark clearing, the dying moonlight glowing softly. The night was still deliciously cool, although the sun was beginning to peek out from behind the horizon. It was beginning to get cooler at night, but the daytime heat hadn't let up. She wondered if this was how summers would be from now on. Shadow and Miku stalked silently through the clearing, looking as casual as possible, and sat down next to the prey pile.

Max watched them through narrowed eyes from the entrance. It looked as though he hadn't moved since they had left. Shadow wondered how he never got tired and admired his dedication to his rank. He may come across as rude or bossy sometimes, but he was an important member of the pack, Lynx's mate, and father to her pups. Shadow meant no disrespect to him. She knew he was only doing his job. Shadow frowned. *I should probably apologize,* she told herself, twitching an ear. "Later," she muttered quietly to herself.

"What?" Miku asked, twitching an ear in her direction. Shadow shook her head.

"Nothing," she told him, giving him a small smile.

Miku was silent for a moment before whispering, "Are you worried about the human? I mean, it looked pretty angry when he saw us." He glanced at Max to make sure he didn't hear. Max was staring at the ground, his ears angled toward the entrance of the clearing.

"Yes. I've had dreams before, about humans. They destroyed the den site and set fire to the forest. They killed…everything," Shadow finished with a shudder. Miku moved closer to her, wrapping his tail around her comfortingly.

"It's okay, Shadow. I'm sure they were just dreams." He tried to comfort her, but somehow it didn't help, especially since he didn't even seem confident in what he was telling her. Shadow just buried her snout in his fur and drank in his warm, familiar scent.

Shadow padded noiselessly through the forest, Kele at her heels. They decided to go on a walk together, to help Shadow clear her head. They were now walking quietly through the forest, the hot sun on their backs, their tongues lolling to keep cool. Shadow raised her head and sniffed the still afternoon air, flattening her ears at the humidity. She then licked her nose and continued walking, her paws landing gently on the ground as she stalked slowly along the narrow trail. Kele walked behind her, not quite as quietly. Shadow kicked a twig as she walked, sighing. She thought about the human, her eyes locked on the ground. She stopped as she heard a noise in the bracken – a loud shifting sound, followed by the loud noise of a rabbit chirping as it ate. The wind suddenly picked up and blew the scent directly into Shadow's face. Rabbit, she confirmed. Lowering her head, she squared her shoulders to the sound and crept forward, ears pinned. Peering through the bushes, she spotted a large furry shape sitting peacefully under a roof of brambles, its mouth moving quickly as it chewed. It was a nice plump rabbit with short stubby legs and a sleek coat. This rabbit obviously had not sensed any danger.

Shadow narrowed her eyes, her mouth-watering as she caught another whiff of its scent. She placed her hind paw down and didn't feel the twig until it was too late. The twig snapped, and the rabbit's ears perked up, now alert of the danger. It turned and fled into the bushes, letting out squeaks of alarm as Shadow charged after it. Luckily, this rabbit was fat and couldn't move as fast as some. She chased quickly after the creature, veering sharply along its trail as it tried frantically to lose her. Shadow put on a burst of speed and snapped her teeth shut around the rabbit's neck, biting down on its spine and crushing it between her jaws. The rabbit went limp, and Shadow stood up triumphantly, letting her muscles relax. She hadn't seen a rabbit this well-fed in a long while. This must mean that the forest was recovering! Smiling, she trotted back to where Kele waited, his legs folded neatly beneath him as he groomed his paws. His eyes instantly lightened when he saw the rabbit Shadow was carrying.

"That thing is huge! That rabbit could feed three wolves tonight!" he exclaimed, his tail wagging slightly.

"Yes. I'm so happy to see that the forest is finally coming back to life," Shadow said. Kele nodded, taking the rabbit from her.

"It's got some weight to it," he added, shaking the rabbit between his teeth. It dangled lifelessly from his jaw, its dark eyes glistening in the sunlight and its legs becoming stiff. Its neck was twisted awkwardly, and blood dripped from its wound. Its jaw was crooked with the tongue spilling out. Kele glanced down at it, grinning. "We should bring it back to the den site," he said, giving it back to Shadow. She gripped it in her teeth, its body now cold. She nodded and they began making their way back to the den site. Walking sure-footed, Shadow's head drooped from the weight of the prey.

Shadow dropped the rabbit on the prey pile, her neck aching from its weight. She nodded to Kele and he turned to walk toward Breeze who was sitting outside the Hunters' den, his eyes closed. Shadow glared up at the blazing sun, eyes narrowed. A wolf suddenly appeared beside her and she had to drag her eyes from the sky to see who it was. It was Lynx, she saw, her belly swelling with her unborn pups. Shadow smiled warmly. She cared deeply for Lynx and was glad to see the warmth in Lynx's gaze.

"Hello, Shadow. How are you? I saw that you put that rabbit on the prey pile. I haven't seen prey that big in a long while." Lynx said, sitting down. Shadow sat, too, smiling brightly.

"Greetings. I'm fine, thank you. How are you? And, yes, I was surprised to see this rabbit's size as well. I am proud to have caught it. I hope this means the prey will start coming back soon." Shadow replied, twitching an ear. Lynx nodded in agreement.

"I hope so, too. I…I'm worried for my pups. What if the prey doesn't replenish quickly enough, and they end up starving? I would never be able to forgive myself if that happened. I just don't know if this territory is…safe," Lynx spoke with a frown. Shadow gazed at the pretty she-wolf, her light blue eyes filled with understanding.

"Has Oak spoken to you?" Shadow asked quietly, wrapping her tail around her paws self-consciously.

"You mean about leaving to find a new territory?" Lynx asked, tilting her head to the side. Shadow nodded. "Yes, he has. I don't know that I completely agree with him, though. What if my pups are born while we don't have a home? We wouldn't survive," Lynx confessed, dipping her head in thought. Shadow frowned. She felt bad for Lynx. It must be hard deciding this matter, especially with pups on the way. At the same time, Shadow wondered why Oak had told Lynx his thoughts on leaving. She thought he didn't want to raise tension within the pack. *Maybe he just wants her to know so it's not a surprise when he announces it to the whole pack. He probably wants to give her a chance to decide what's best for her pups,* Shadow thought, stealing a look at Lynx. *She looks weary*, Shadow thought. Sad even.

"It will be okay, Lynx. Everything will work out, I promise. The pack will always protect you and your pups. We are family, and we will do anything to help you through this."

Lynx gave her a grateful smile. "Thank you, Shadow. You have a good way about you," Lynx spoke, licking Shadow's shoulder. Shadow felt her ears grow warm with the praise.

"You're welcome, and thank you, Lynx. You've always been a wonderful wolf and wonderful to me. I wouldn't be who I am now without you," Shadow said. Lynx stared at her warmly, her eyes filled with emotion. Shadow glanced away as Sparrow emerged into the clearing carrying two mice in his jaws. Heather and Storm came on his heels, one carrying a crow and the other a turkey. They added their prey to the prey pile as Miku walked over to Shadow, glancing fondly at her. She returned the look, smiling. Shadow then dipped her head to Lynx in goodbye and stood up, padding over to walk beside Miku as he made his way to the other side of the clearing where Breeze and Kele sat talking.

"Hey, Shadow. What's up?" Miku asked, licking her ear.

"Oh, nothing really. I was just talking to Lynx about the prey. Did you see the big rabbit on the prey pile? I was surprised to see prey that big. I caught it right in the middle of our territory!" Shadow exclaimed.

Miku's eyes brightened. "Yes, I saw it! I didn't know you caught it, though. I hope this means the prey is coming back."

"I hope so, too. Have you sensed any change in the amount of prey in the forest?" Shadow asked, tilting her head to the side. He shook his head.

"Not very much, no. I mean, we caught a few small animals, but that won't fill many bellies. I just wish that human would leave. It's ruining our land. I can smell its foul scent closer and closer to the den site every day," Miku said, shuddering. Shadow frowned at him, ears now pinned to her head as they reached Breeze and Kele. She sat down beside Kele and Miku sat at her other side. They continued talking.

"I'm worried about this human, Miku. It's powerful, and every day I feel its hold grow stronger and stronger on our forest. It's taking control, and there's nothing we can do to stop it," Shadow fretted, confessing her feelings. Kele and Breeze stopped talking and listened to what she and Miku were saying.

"I feel the same. But we can't let fear take control of us or that monster will truly devour us. We must stand strong and remember who we are and where we belong," Miku said. Shadow looked at him warmly.

"Yes, you're right. I'll remember those words," Shadow promised with smile as she tucked her snout under his chin and buried her nose in his fur.

Breeze and Kele had begun talking distractedly, paying no attention to either Shadow or Miku. "Let's go out for a walk," Shadow said. Miku glanced at her and then nodded, standing up.

They walked silently through the forest, with no noise except for the occasional rustle of the wind or the constant sound of birds communicating above their heads, flitting between branches or sitting on a perch. They walked until, in the distance, Shadow saw the line of mesh that surrounded the human den glinting in the sunlight. "We're almost there," Shadow told him, quickening her pace. Shadow didn't worry about her paw steps anymore. Instead, she hurried along the trail, veering nimbly around tree roots, rocks, or holes in the ground. Soon, they were closing in on the humans' den.

Shadow could see the tall human dens and spotted the two humans near the entrance of the small den, where she guessed they lived. They were communicating, speaking slowly, and...sadly? She wasn't able to read their emotions very well from so far away, but with the wind carrying their voices toward her, she thought she could detect a hint of sadness. The smaller human, which Shadow guessed was the female, was sitting hunched over, her face red. Fleshy paws covered her eyes as if she had been burned. Or maybe she was crying. Shadow had never seen a human cry before. Maybe they had emotions after all. She and Miku made their way closer, slowly and carefully. They peered out from the shadows and watched the two humans. The male human, or what she thought was the male, sat close to the female, speaking soothingly to her and patting her back with his paw. He looked sad, too, his eyes were dull and his other paw hung loosely below his knee. Shadow spotted one of the dogs sitting beside them, its eyes sad. It was whimpering softly.

Shadow watched, confused. Then the thought hit her. They must be grieving over the loss of the other dog, the one that had flung itself at Shadow and missed, instead throwing itself into a large boulder and breaking its spine. Shadow shuddered at the memory. Pity suddenly stabbed her heart as she thought of what it would be like to lose a sibling. She had guessed that the dogs were siblings. Friends, at least. Flattening her ears, her body tensed as the wind shifted and their scent was carried toward the dog. It almost instantly caught their scent, its muzzle drawing back into a snarl as it leaped off the platform and stared directly at where Shadow and Miku were hiding. *It has a good nose,* Shadow thought. They had no cover – hidden only by shadows. The dog lowered its head and let out a loud growl, its eyes burning with rage. It let out a series of blood-thirsty barks in their direction, but Shadow guessed that it knew better than to charge them after what had happened to its companion.

Shadow and Miku stayed absolutely still hoping the humans wouldn't see them. Almost instantly, the male human was on its feet following the dog's eyes until landing directly where Shadow and Miku hid. It began bellowing madly, bending to pick up a rock before throwing it directly at Shadow. It missed her, barely. She stayed where she was.

She felt her heart thrumming in her throat as she was frozen by fear, traumatized by what she had done to the other dog the last time she was here. The human stared at her, seemingly angrier now. Suddenly, the human let out a high-pitched whistle, like a loud bird. The dog charged toward Shadow barking madly, its eyes crazed with anger and revenge for its den mate. It hurled itself at Miku, jaws open. Miku tried to dodge the attack, but the dog was too fast. It grabbed ahold of Miku's flank and let out a savage growl as blood began seeping from the wound. Shadow let out a vicious snarl and threw herself on top of the dog, biting hard into the soft spot beneath its leg. She pulled. Flesh tore. Blood spilled onto the ground. The dog let out a panicked yelp and let go of Miku, flesh dangling painfully from the wound and blood pouring out from a vein that Shadow bit through.

Blood dripped from her chin as she backed away, staring at Miku. Blood was soaking into his fur from his bite wound. He had collapsed on his side, whimpering in pain. He bared his teeth at the dog as it tried to advance on him again, rage burning in its eyes. Shadow flung herself in front of Miku as the dog lunged at him. She felt teeth meet her shoulder. Yelping, she tried to shake the dog off, but its bite only went in deeper. She heard her flesh tear and felt the warm sticky blood drip down her shoulder as the dog's teeth scraped against bone. It hung on tightly. She tried biting its neck, but couldn't seem to get a good grip. She felt her energy begin to drain as the dog weighed her down, its long canines sinking deeper and deeper into her body. Its jaw was locked.

Shadow was so blinded by pain that she hadn't noticed the human drawing closer until the point of its weapon was aimed at her head. She stared blurry-eyed into the hole at the end of the weapon and heard it make a quick clicking sound. But before the human could use the weapon, Miku appeared behind it and bit into the back of its knee. As it fell forward a loud *bang* filled the air and Shadow heard the sickening sound of the weapon contacting flesh. A loud whimper rang in her ears, and her stomach dropped with the horrible thought that Miku had been hurt by the human. Shadow fell to the ground as the dog released its grip on her shoulder. Eyes closed, ears ringing she lay on the ground, whimpering softly. Pain throbbed in her shoulder and the bite wound burned horribly. The acrid scent of the weapon was mixed with the metallic scent of blood. After a few seconds, she mustered the courage to open her eyes. Ears still ringing, she couldn't hear anything around her.

Lifting her head and looking around she spotted Miku standing above her, eyes clouded with pain and worry. She felt unimaginable relief to see he was fine, aside from the dog's bite on his flank. He seemed to be speaking to her, though she couldn't hear him. His voice seemed very far away and she couldn't make out what he was telling her, but she could see he was agitated. Slowly, her hearing returned and she could make out his words. "…Come on, Shadow, get up! That human will be coming after us any minute!" he exclaimed, eyes wide with panic. Shadow raised her head and stared at what lay in front of her. The human was kneeling beside his dog as it lay on the ground, unmoving. Shadow followed his gaze and saw a hole about the size of an acorn in the dog's chest. Shadow realized what had happened. Miku had saved her life. When he pushed the human forward it had accidentally triggered the weapon and hit the dog instead of Shadow. The human stared unbelieving at the dog, his face twisted in pain and horror. Tears were streaming down its pink cheeks. The human was trembling, holding the dog in its arms, its neck stiff. Blood was slowly oozing from the wound that Shadow had inflicted, soaking into the human's pelt and staining it red. Shadow frantically got to her paws and shot off into the forest, Miku at her heels.

They ran as far as they could before the pain in Shadow's shoulder forced her to stop. She fell in exhaustion, her shoulder burning like fire.

Shadow let out a weak whimper and tried to catch her breath, which was coming ragged in her throat. Miku collapsed beside her and was licking the wound on his flank, cleaning away the blood. After catching her breath Shadow began doing the same while trying to comprehend what had just happened. They lapped at their fur for what seemed like hours until Miku finally broke the silence. "Are you okay Shadow?" he rasped, looking over at Shadow. Shadow winced. Her paws throbbed. Her head hurt. Her wound burned horribly.

"Yes, I'm fine," was all she managed to get out, her voice shaky. She was still trying to understand what had just happened. It was as if her brain didn't want to accept it. She groaned, closing her eyes against the setting sun shining on her face. She felt like she might vomit. Rolling onto her stomach, she tried to sit up. She held the injured paw off the ground as she slowly and shakily got to her paws. She looked around. They were at the edge of the territory, she realized. They were about a half-mile away from the clearing.

"Miku, get up. We have to get back and have Luna dress our..." She stopped short when she looked at Miku. He lay unconscious on the ground, blood seeping steadily from his wound as his breath came short and raspy. His tongue was sticking out and resting on the ground, and his body was unmoving except for the faint heave of his chest as he breathed. Shadow stared, horrified, before rushing to his side, ignoring the flaring pain in her shoulder. "Miku? Miku! Miku, wake up!" she howled, shaking his shoulder. He didn't stir.

Shadow looked around frantically for something to use to stop the bleeding. She saw a clump of moss growing on a tree trunk nearby. She rushed to it, wincing as her injured paw touched the ground. She tore as much moss as she could off the tree and carried it back to Miku. Shadow pushed moss into his wound to stop the bleeding, then packed moss all around his body to keep him comfortable. There was no way she could leave him, and it was already getting dark. She couldn't carry him, especially with her injured leg. So, she packed their wounds with moss and cuddled up beside him preparing herself for a long night.

Miku's skin felt hot beside hers. She wondered if his wound was infected. She had a feeling that she should go back to the den site and get Luna, but she couldn't bear the thought of leaving him all alone out here in the dark. What if he woke up and wandered off trying to find her? What if some predator found him? There were too many horrible things that could happen, she didn't want to think about it. She just closed her eyes and pressed her face into his fur, hoping, praying, that he would still be alive by tomorrow.

Chapter Eleven

Shadow didn't sleep much that night. She woke each time Miku stirred as he drifted in and out of consciousness. Their bleeding had stopped, but Miku burned with fever, and Shadow's pain threatened to pull her, too, into unconsciousness. She had to keep herself awake just to make sure that she didn't pass out. Her head drooped with the lack of sleep as the sun finally began to rise and light the forest. Suddenly, Miku's eyelids flitted open, and he stared straight at Shadow. "Miku," She rasped in a deep sigh of relief. She pressed her face into his fur as he lifted his head, his eyes blurry and glazed with pain.

"Shadow? What happened?" he asked, wincing as he moved his leg. "Was I out for long?"

"We ran away from that human, remember?" she said, "Then you passed out overnight. I stayed with you. Everything is fine. But you need to get back to the den site." Shadow stood painfully. "Come on, Miku, we need to get back as soon as possible. You need medical care."

"It looks like you do, too!" Miku exclaimed. He stared up at her looking as if he didn't want to get up. Shadow walked over to him and nudged him, telling him silently to stand up. Huffing, he put his paws under him and began to slowly stand up. Pain showed in his face as he stumbled, his injured leg giving way under his weight. Shadow hurried to his side and caught him as he was falling, helping to keep him up on his paws. She ignored her own pain as Miku leaned heavily on her.

He was weak. Together, they began making their way back, Shadow's wounds throbbing with every step.

By the time they reached home Shadow's energy was completely drained. Miku was still leaning on her, and now he felt a hundred times heavier. At the entrance of the clearing Shadow and Miku collapsed in a heap of mixed fur on the ground. His breath came quick and shallow and Shadow could feel his skin burning with fever as they lay huddled on the ground. Shadow's whole body stung. She wondered why she felt like this. Was the wound really that deep? Was that dog…sick? A powerful shudder wracked her body as she felt herself slowly slip into unconsciousness, her packmates' questioning voices fading around her as her mind went blank.

Shadow woke with a start, her eyes opening as she took in a fresh gulp of air. Her head shot straight up from where she lay on a pile of moss, her eyes wide and fur spiking up. She breathed heavily as she stared down at her paws, her mind whirling. Her wounds stung, but the pain was nothing compared to what she had felt earlier. She could also feel the gnawing feeling of hunger deep in her belly. She looked around. She was in the Healer's den, Miku sleeping next to her. His wounds were covered with herbs—she could smell them—and moss. She hesitantly reached forward with a paw and felt his body temperature. He felt almost normal, only a slight heat emitting from his skin. Shadow glanced at his face. His eyes were closed, and he was sleeping deeply. He seemed to be breathing normally and he was lying comfortably on a bed of fresh moss. *It looks like he's okay,* she thought with a smile. Luna wasn't in sight, so Shadow wondered if she was out collecting herbs. She also noticed that Amber wasn't in any of the beds that surrounded them. *Maybe the Beta returned to her duties while I was unconscious, she thought.* With a jolt, she wondered how long she had been asleep. She stared through the cracks in the roof, deciding that it was daytime from the light she saw shining from outside.

It was cool in the den. Shadow stretched out her paws one at a time, rolling the stiffness out of her shoulders. She placed her pads on the cool, smooth stone beneath her, and felt it pull the heat from her skin. She then heaved herself to her paws, amazed to find that the pain in her shoulder was almost gone. She gazed down at the wound and saw it had shrunk in size. The puncture wounds had grown smaller and were beginning to scab. The bite hadn't been as deep as she thought it was. Her fur had been groomed neatly, though she could see her ribs through her pelt. Smiling slightly with relief that her wounds were healing, she wiggled her haunches and began sliding through the narrow tunnel out into the main part of the den, then out the entrance and toward the smell of fresh air.

Shadow pushed herself out of the den and into the clearing, wincing as the bright sunlight shone in her eyes and blinded her. She stood rigid with her eyes narrowed until they finally adjusted to the sunlight and she began to relax. She looked around the clearing, her eyes resting on a couple of wolves sitting at the other end of the den site. It was Kele and Breeze, she saw. They had been sitting together but were now standing with their eyes fixed on Shadow. Kele looked strange. His fur was tangled and covered in dirt as if he hadn't bothered to clean it. His eyes were wide and rimmed with red and his ribs jutted sharply out from his skin as if he hadn't eaten in a long time. His tail was wagging but she could tell he was uncomfortable, possibly even in pain. He looked… starving. So did Breeze.

Shadow wondered what had happened when she had been unconscious in Luna's den. She snapped out of her daze and trotted towards Kele, her paws skidding across the flat-packed dirt as she made her way towards him. He had begun running to her, too, and they met in the middle, Shadow's mind whirling as she tried to figure out why he might look like that. "Kele!" she gasped as she came face-to-face with him. Now that she could see him more closely she could tell that he hadn't been taking care of himself. His eyes were round and red on the edges from lack of sleep and his shoulders sagged with exhaustion. His nose was completely dry from dehydration and his breath smelled like rotten meat. Shadow stared at him. "What…happened to you?" she asked after a moment of silence.

Kele stared at her blankly, anger rimming his eyes. "What happened to *me?* I think you mean what happened to *you!*" Kele exclaimed with a yelp and a lash of his tail. "How did you get hurt? Where did you go? Why didn't you come back that night? What happened?" Kele demanded hotly. He sounded upset, but his voice was edged with concern. He sighed. "I was worried. *We* were worried. Oak almost sent out a whole search party to look for you," he said, his voice wavering as Breeze came up to stand beside him. Breeze was staring at her, but she couldn't understand what his emotions were showing. His features were just as Kele's, tired and hungry.

"Where is Miku?" Breeze asked simply, concern filling his voice.

"He…he's still in the den. Still sleeping," Shadow told him with a nod. Breeze gave a dip of his head and then pushed past Shadow and towards the Healer's den, his muscles tense with worry. Shadow looked back at Kele and sighed. *I suppose I should tell him the truth… But, what will he think of me? I'll have to tell Oak, too.* Shadow thought. So many questions whirled around her mind she didn't know if they would have time in the daylight to talk about everything. "Okay, Kele. Let's sit down," She said. He nodded stiffly and Shadow led him to a quiet place where they could talk. The afternoon sunlight was burning down on them from the sky, no clouds in sight. "I'll tell you what you need to know if you'll tell me. I need to know what's been going on. First things first, how long was I in that den?" Shadow asked briskly.

Kele took a deep breath. "A week. Maybe more, maybe a little less," Kele spoke, shrugging sadly. Shadow stared at Kele like he was crazy. She scoffed nervously.

"A week?" she asked disbelievingly. He said nothing. Shadow took a shaky breath and stared at her paws. *What could have knocked me out for that long?* she questioned herself, eyes wide. *I...I'll figure this out later,* she told herself, shaking her head as if to clear her thoughts. After a few moments of silence, Shadow cleared her throat and looked back up at Kele. "Okay. Now, why do you look so tired and hungry? What's the news with the human? What's going on?" Shadow demanded, almost snappily. She hadn't meant it so harshly, but even if Kele had noticed her tone of voice he didn't seem to care.

"Things went from bad to worse since you came home injured. The human found our den site. It seems angry, I mean even angrier than before. It set traps in the forest. Huge shiny clamps that, if you step on them, snap around your paw like teeth and hold on. They don't let go. Oak and Amber watched the human set the traps, all around our clearing." When Shadow stared at him blankly at the mention of Amber, he added, "Oh yes, and Amber is better. She returned to her position as Beta just yesterday. Luna is keeping a close eye on her. She thinks that Amber may have suffered a concussion, but she doesn't know for sure," Kele explained, and Shadow nodded, her eyes wide as she waited for more.

"Anyway, ever since the human set those traps the prey has been disappearing. We think the human may be poisoning it because we found piles of dead animals near its den. We don't know why. Perhaps this human just wants us to suffer."

"What?" Shadow breathed, her stomach dropping like a stone in her belly. Kele glanced at her as if saying, "there's more."

"None of us have had a proper meal in days. We're starving. That's why Oak has sent out extra hunting groups, to watch out for the human as well as hunt. He sent *everyone.* Even the Fighters. Sometimes, we hunt all day and all night. We can never find anything. What's worse, the human expanded the mesh line. It's now stretched all the way around the lake. We can't even get to the water now. We think the human has lost its mind. I'm convinced it may even stretch its fence around the whole territory and trap us in. The only source of water we have now is the river. Oak tried sending out groups to bring water back, for Lynx and Luna and any injured wolves, but the water that they tried soaking into the moss evaporated before they could even get back. The heat hasn't gotten any better, either. In fact, I think it has gotten worse. I…I'm scared for the pack, Shadow." Kele spoke slowly, giving every detail.

Shadow stared at him, her mouth slightly ajar. "Oh my…this is horrible," she said, eyes glazed with fear. Suddenly, the ferns at the entrance of the clearing shivered and Oak walked purposefully into the clearing, his mouth empty of prey. Luna came behind him carrying a few shriveled herbs. Max and Storm followed, eyes dull with exhaustion. Oak's eyes widened as he caught sight of Shadow. He raced toward her, abandoning the group, who were all now gazing at Shadow. Their eyes widened in relief, but their look was questioning. They were obviously wondering what had happened to her.

"Shadow," Oak said, pressing his snout next to hers. Shadow pulled back.

"Oak," she sighed, standing and glancing apologetically at Kele. "We need to talk," Shadow said, motioning with her snout towards his den by the Alpha stone. Storm padded forward staring at Shadow, eyes narrowed as she heard what Shadow was saying. Oak nodded curtly and beckoned her with his tail towards his den. Shadow followed him, Storm on her tail. Max followed, Shadow guessed to position himself outside of the den and wait for the talks to finish. Shadow followed Oak into the den, pushing through the shriveling hazelnut bushes. Shadow sat down politely in front of her parents, waiting for them to ready themselves. They sat beside each other in front of her, ears pricked to listen to what she would say.

"When Miku and I left that night to hunt, we didn't only hunt. We walked all the way to the human territory." Shadow looked shamefully at Oak. She expected him to be angry and deliver a long speech about how stupid that was. But he just sat there staring at her, seething. That somehow made it even worse. Shadow continued. "We went into the human territory and the dog caught our scent. It attacked Miku, so I bit it behind the leg. It attacked me and bit me in the shoulder. It wouldn't let go, and I was so focused on trying to get it away that the human snuck right up to me. It was attacking me with its weapon when Miku pushed it forward to save my life. The human stumbled forward and…" Shadow faltered and looked up at Oak. Pain filled her eyes. "It killed the dog instead of me. And now I'm sure it blames me. It's angry and driven by revenge," Shadow choked, biting back tears. "It's my fault!" she blurted. "All those things Kele told me…They came to be because of me. I'm so sorry, Oak. I've made a horrible mistake. It's my fault…" She faltered, her voice cracking with horrible sadness and regret.

Shadow looked up at her father. He was standing, rage filling his eyes. Storm was staring down at her paws as if she couldn't believe what Shadow had just said. "You disobeyed *direct orders*, Shadow. If you had listened to me none of this would have happened! You put yourself, along with *your mate,* in danger!" He snarled with rage, fire burning in his eyes.

"I'm disappointed in you, Shadow. I could banish you for this," Oak spoke with cold, seething anger. He flattened his ears as if stopping himself from biting her ear. Shadow hung her head in shame, her stomach churning with a mixture of guilt and regret. Sadness twisted her heart, and a lump caught in her throat as she tried to swallow. She wished that she could just shrink down into the shadows and never come back. That would probably make things better for the pack, anyway. Shadow sat still and accepted what her father was telling her. Storm was looking at Shadow now, her deep amber eyes filled with a mixture of sadness and anger. Shadow stared helplessly at her parents. Guilt wormed beneath her fur. She wondered what her punishment would be. Oak was staring angrily at her, his eyes stone-cold and yet burning with rage. They waited there in silence for what seemed like hours until Storm finally spoke up.

"Oak," she said, half under her breath, her ears pinned to her head. Shadow averted her mother's gaze. Oak listened as Storm whispered something in his ear. He blinked, then gave a nod, though his eyes still burned with anger.

"Shadow, you have done something horrible that I cannot easily forgive. You could have been killed. I...I was worried about you. And Miku, of course, but...With so much going on I need all my wolves to follow me and listen to what I say. I am the highest-ranking wolf in this pack. Without that respect and understanding, we are nothing more than a pack of loners. I need you, of all wolves, to heed my advice and take what I say seriously. They respect you, Shadow. They know how skillful you are. They know you are a leader and have a kind heart. They admire how you always try to see the good in every outcome and try to solve things using peace instead of war. I, too, see that in you. But they also need to see that you can respect your rank and listen to what others have to say. You must *always* do what is best for the pack, and what you have done is the opposite."

Oak seemed to be cooling off as he continued, "For your punishment, you will be sent every morning to fetch water from the Winding River. You will give the water to Lynx and any other wolf that cannot make the trip on its own. You will be sent early so the heat does not evaporate the water before you can return. You will do this with Miku until I say you have done enough. Do you understand?" Oak spoke in a normal voice now, as if satisfied with her punishment. Shadow nodded quickly. "Good," Oak said and turned away as if telling her she was dismissed. Shadow crouched low and dipped her head to the ground in the highest level of respect. She flattened her ears and tucked her tail between her legs, making herself vulnerable to the Alpha. He gazed at her, hard as a stone, until he finally gave a jerk of his head for her to return to the clearing. "Thank you," Shadow said quietly as she stood and slipped out of the den, guilt weighing her paws down as if they were rocks. She stalked silently over to a dark corner and sat down with a small sigh. Would things ever go back to normal?

Shadow trotted silently through the earsplittingly silent air along a trail towards the Winding River. This was her second morning of fetching water and bringing it back to the pack. She trotted along the trail, ducking under a low branch and brushing past a few overgrown ferns. Miku woke up sometime last night, but Shadow hadn't been allowed to see him. Luna said that he needed to rest for more time. It was early morning, but already hot. Soon she could hear the faint sound of the rushing water in front of her. She continued until the river came into view. A large boulder sat on the near bank providing a small pool beside it to soak the moss.

Shadow trotted over to the creek and thankfully lapped up a few mouthfuls of the cool water, letting it soak into her tongue. She looked around, her ears pricked. She spotted a large oak tree with moss growing up its trunk. Shadow trotted over to the tree and tore off as much moss as she could carry. She carried it to the river and dropped it into the small pool. When the moss was thoroughly soaked she pulled the ball out of the water, huffing when she picked it up and realized that it was many times heavier now than when it was dry. She lifted it off the ground, but not quickly enough. Much of the water had already spilled out, and more continued to drain out, soaking into her fur. Shadow frowned and plopped it back into the pool. She looked around again and spotted a large ivy vine hanging down from a maple tree's thick branches. She trotted over to the vine and plucked off a mouthful of leaves before returning to her moss ball. Shadow wrapped the leaves around the moss figuring they would help keep the water inside. She lifted the moss out of the water, her neck aching as she held it. Her plan seemed to be working, Shadow realized happily. She bit a little farther into the moss and then began hauling it back to the den site, determination propelling her legs forward.

After delivering the water to Luna, Shadow was allowed to see Miku. She pushed into the Healer's den and slid down the cave towards the bedding area, eyes wide against the darkness. She spotted a light up ahead and, pushing herself forward, emerged into a sunlit cave with a small hole in the roof providing the light. Shadow looked around and spotted Miku lying in a bed at the other end of the cave. "Miku!" She exclaimed, running over to him and skidding to a stop at his side. Luna was arranging herbs in a different corner of the den, her paws moving expertly over the shelves as she sorted through the different types of leaves and berries.

"Shadow!" he heaved a sigh of relief, his eyes gleaming. "Thank you for the water, I was *dying* of thirst," Miku said, licking her cheek. She glanced around, spotting a small hole dug into the ground, providing a basin to hold the wet moss. The hole was filled to the rim. Shadow smiled, breathing in Miku's warm scent.

"How do you feel?" She asked, her eyes glinting in the sunlight. He looked good, with a freshly cleaned pelt and new bedding. He was skinny, though, just as skinny as the rest of the pack, with his ribs showing through his fur and skin hanging from his bones. Shadow frowned. She needed to talk to Oak again to tell him that he was right. This was no place for wolves to live. For now, she smiled at her mate and listened to him speak.

"I'm feeling fine. I honestly don't know why I can't leave until tomorrow. It seems like a waste of time if you ask me. I could be out there, helping the pack or something. But, no, I'm stuck in here, sitting on this bed and watching the Healer sort through her herbs," Miku spoke with a huff.

"I heard that," Luna growled, her tone brisk. Miku's eyes widened as he glanced apologetically at Luna.

"Um, I didn't mean it like that… Sorry," Miku said, his fur bristling slightly. Shadow glanced at Luna humorously. She had gone back to shuffling through her herbs, shaking her head and mumbling quietly to herself. Shadow stood up.

"I better go," she said. Shadow felt a sudden urge to be out of the den. She couldn't explain it. It was as if she could sense something outside that she needed to attend to. "I should go and hunt or something," she added quickly, flicking an ear towards the exit.

Miku looked at her, sadness showing in his eyes. "Alright. Just don't wear yourself out." Miku smiled at Shadow, who returned the smile before turning to leave the den. She felt a prick of guilt as she turned her back on her mate, but for some reason, she was drawn to the outdoors. She slipped outside and looked around the clearing. Wolves sat all around, talking or just sitting in the shade. Shadow spotted Kele with Max, Mako, Breeze, and Amber. Heather and Lynx were sitting under the shade of a birch tree that was balancing on a crumbling ledge of dirt. Sparrow spoke to Scout beside the entrance of the Tracker's den. Shadow sighed and went to sit underneath a low-hanging maple branch, her ears swiveling to catch the sounds around her.

She listened to the sounds of the leaves rustling against the ground in the slight breeze, the sound of her packmates' paws as they moved around the clearing. She took notice of the quiet talking around her. Catching the sound of paw steps behind her Shadow opened her eyes and whirled around. She heard Oak's voice mixed with those of Storm and Breeze coming from the other side of the buckthorn that surrounded the clearing. Shadow relaxed when she realized that it was only her packmates, but still, something seemed off. She slowly sat back down and closed her eyes. Her mind was drawn to the fact that Oak, Breeze, and Storm were behind the wall of bushes and she wondered what they were doing. Maybe they were simply making sure that there were no signs of predators around, or checking for new human traps. Shadow remembered the last time a fox had gotten into the clearing. It had nearly stolen some of their precious prey. Shadow listened as the three wolves' voices faded as they circled the clearing barriers.

Shadow was just drifting off when a noise jolted her awake. Almost immediately, she heard a howl coming behind the birch tree where Lynx and Heather were sitting. Shadow leaped to her paws and strained her ears to hear what was happening. She heard a snarl, but not a wolf's snarl. It was a snarl she had hoped never to hear again. The snarl of a fox, its horrible noise echoing throughout the clearing. Shadow heard a yelp and watched as the already leaning birch tree shook, the roots beginning to pull out of the ground as the extra weight of an animal pushed it down. Shadow watched in horror as the dry sand supporting the birch began to crumble and a giant rock fell to land on Lynx's tail, trapping her.

Everything seemed to move in slow motion as Lynx yelped in agonizing pain. Shadow heard the sickening sound of bones cracking in her tail. The tree was falling towards Lynx as she lay on the ground unable to move. Heather was digging frantically at the rock, trying to get

Lynx free. Shadow howled in horror and rushed forward with speed that she didn't know she had. She reached the opposite end of the clearing in seconds and began to push her back against the base of the birch, hoping to slow its fall enough to allow Lynx to get free. Her hope was quickly replaced by panic as she felt the tree pushing hard against her back with searing pain. She cried out in desperation but kept her back arched and legs locked against the still falling tree. Pain spread like fire through her body and she had to keep her mind focused, afraid that she might pass out. Sparrow and Max were helping Heather dig under the rock, while the rest of the wolves in the clearing had lined up beside Shadow and were now helping to keep the tree from falling on Lynx before she could be freed.

Shadow felt her mind darken as the pain grew even stronger. Her legs were shaking. She cried out as more weight pressed down on her spine. She was afraid that her bones might break. Pushing the thought away, she fought unconsciousness and screwed her eyes shut. "Get her out!" she screamed in desperation and pain, her voice cracking and body shaking with the effort. She could feel her mind whirling as the energy drained from her body. She could feel her packmates growing weaker as the weight pressed down on them, crushing them. In one last feeble attempt to keep the tree from crashing down on them she took a deep breath and screamed, "Push with all of your strength in one, two, three!" She howled with the exertion, somehow finding the energy to keep going. She pushed up with all her strength and heard her packmates grunts and howls as they pushed, too. She suddenly felt the weight of the tree lifting. They were lifting the tree!

"Push!" some wolf howled. Shadow couldn't tell whose voice it was. She was becoming weak. The sounds around her were beginning to grow more and more distant with each passing second. Fighting to stay awake, she pushed the tree away with all her remaining strength before collapsing. She lay panting on the ground, her eyes open, although she couldn't see anything. It was as if her mind had gone dark. Every bone in her body screamed in agony, the life drained from her muscles. Her paws throbbed and it felt as if her fur was burning with fire that was seeping into her blood and slowly killing her. Somehow she assembled the remaining bit of her strength and lifted her head. She slowly blinked her eyes, the color bleeding back into her vision. Shadow saw four blurry figures digging at the rock, and a bunch of wolves holding up the tree. Lynx was scrambling frantically to get away, screaming in horror at her mate, Max. She was crying. He was digging furiously, his eyes crazed with fear and determination to free Lynx.

Shadow, now filled with new determination to help her former Trainer, got to her paws, the world spinning around her. Her head throbbed, but she didn't care. She hurled herself at the boulder and began digging madly, dirt flying everywhere behind her as she ripped it from under the large, heavy rock. She soon felt the boulder begin to shift and watched it fall slowly down into the hole that they had dug into the sandy earth. Lynx was free. Shadow and Max rushed to her and pulled her from under the falling tree, while Mako and Sparrow ran to help the rest of their packmates push the birch away from them. Shadow crouched beside Lynx, trying not to look at her tail. Max was at her head, his nose pressed against hers. Lynx's eyes were glistening with tears and she was letting out weak whimpers of pain. Shadow could see her slowly fading into unconsciousness. *Maybe this is better,* Shadow thought. *At least she won't be able to feel the pain. It looks so painful...* Shadow winced.

Shadow couldn't help looking at Lynx's wounded tail. Most of the bone had been crushed and it was barely hanging on at the base by a few muscles that had not been severed by the rock. Much of the fur and skin had been torn off showing pure white bone, broken beyond repair. Blood ran from the gruesome injury. Almost instantly, Luna was at Lynx's other side, her eyes wide with horror. Miku followed her, carrying a mouthful of herbs. He dropped them at Luna's side, then rushed back to the den to get more. Luna got to work, feeding Lynx some small black seeds along with some daisy petals. Luna then turned to the she-wolf's tail and began her examination. Miku returned with more herbs and dropped them at Luna's side, his eyes wide with horror as he gazed down at Lynx's twisted body.

"Fetch the sharp rock that I showed you earlier," Luna snapped. Miku glanced at Luna with a sense of understanding before whirling around and racing back to the den. Shadow watched him go, panic flaring in her chest. Blood was still seeping from Lynx's wound and into the water-starved earth. By now, the wolves had moved the tree, and were huddling around, pressing in around Lynx. Shadow suddenly felt a sharp tang of anger. She leaped up and whirled around.

"Get back! Give her some room for crying out loud!" she snapped. Her packmates obeyed, standing back but watching and murmuring nervously to each other. Some were cleaning scratches they had received in the mayhem, others were simply resting to regain their energy. Shadow turned back to Lynx just as Miku returned, a sharp rock about the size of an oak leaf clamped between his jaws. He passed it on quickly to Luna, who gripped it firmly, then shifted to get a clear view of the injury.

"We're going to need to cut off the severed bone," she said, mostly to herself.

"Can't you do that in the den where it's more private?" Miku asked quietly, glancing at the wolves huddling around, trying to see what Luna was about to do. They all kept their distance, though, just as Shadow told them.

"No time. Too much blood. I need to do this quickly," Luna replied, her eyes flashing with determination. She then took a deep breath, and

Max tensed. It looked as if he wanted to object, but knew better than to argue with the Healer. "Max, hold her head. She should be asleep, but if I slip or she jumps it could be fatal," Luna said firmly. Max said nothing, but instead placed his paws on Lynx's shoulders and rested his chin on her head as he whispered softly into her ear. Luna gave a brisk nod then took a deep breath and moved towards Lynx's tail, fur bristling with concentration. Shadow winced with pain for Lynx as Luna began cutting through her flesh at the base of her tail. The process was slow, but eventually Luna turned and dropped the bloody rock from her mouth. It was a clean cut, right through the bone. Blood ran from the new wound. Luna quickly pressed on moss, then wrapped it with leaves covered with sap to hold it all together.

Luna sat back, panting, obviously happy with her work. "Okay, now we need to get her to my den. Miku, go prepare a bed as quickly as possible. Max, Sparrow, Scout, Mako, carry her into my den. Gently," Luna gave orders rapidly, gathering her remaining herbs and running back to her den. Just then, Oak emerged into the clearing, coated in scratches and patches of lost fur. Breeze and Storm emerged behind him, Breeze limping badly, leaning heavily on Storm's shoulder. Their faces were filled with pain. Oak ran over to Shadow and stared at the wreckage with a questioning stare.

"What happened?" he demanded, blood trickling from a wound on his forehead. The scent of fox emanated from his pelt, and she looked down to see his fur coated with blood.

"I…Uh…I will tell you in the den. First, you need to get cleaned up," Shadow spoke, her heart skipping a beat as she saw Breeze's wounds. His hind paw was twisted at an awkward angle and blood dripped from a deep scratch on his pad. Several of his claws had been torn out. A big red welt showed through the fur on the back of his head and he looked to be on the brink of unconsciousness. Storm was struggling with his weight as she helped him to the Healer's den. Shadow was about to jump in to help but Oak got there first, taking some of Breeze's weight on his shoulders as they squeezed him through the cave entrance. Wolves around the clearing were all dispersing, either splitting into groups to talk or going to examine the wreckage. Shadow huffed and followed the wolves into the den, her paws dragging wearily on the ground as she walked. She was exhausted. Slipping inside she relished the feeling of cold stone under her pads.

As Shadow entered Luna's den she was almost overcome by the heavy scent of blood that hung thick in the air. Luna was tending to Lynx who was still unconscious, her eyelids fluttering softly as she slept. Her tail was wrapped in moss, but the blood still scented the air. Holding her breath, Shadow made her way deeper into the den, watching as Oak and Storm rested Breeze down gently in a bed of his own. Luna quickly tucked bedding under Lynx's wound and rushed over to Breeze, applying moss and other herbs to stop the bleeding and clean the wounds. Shadow sat next to Lynx and watched patiently, ears pinned. She looked down at the sleeping she-wolf then leaned over and began to clean the dirt from her fur. Before she finished, Breeze's wounds had been dressed and Miku was now cleaning him, as Shadow had done with Lynx.

Sleep tugged at Shadow's mind and she felt exhaustion take over her muscles. She groaned and fought to stand up, her eyelids drooping. She managed to get to her paws and walked over to Oak, who Luna had just finished treating. "Hello, Oak," she said as she lay down next to him on the cold stone floor. Oak turned to her, his gaze dark from where he sat in his bed.

"Shadow. Now tell me what happened," he said. Shadow stared at him, gathering her thoughts, then taking a deep breath before answering.

"Well, I came out of the Healer's den after a visit to Miku. I sensed something was wrong. When I went to sit at the other end of the clearing

I heard you, Storm, and Breeze just outside the wall. I heard a howl and scented fox, and then I saw something like a heavy weight hitting that birch tree that fell. The dirt crumbled at its base and one of the big rocks on the hillside next to the tree fell on Lynx's tail and she was trapped. The tree was falling straight for her, so I ran over and tried to hold it up. Then the rest of the pack rushed in to help." Shadow spoke quickly. She was prickling with curiosity. "What happened outside of the wall?" she asked.

"You said that you *sensed* something was wrong?" Oak asked her, ignoring her question. Then, suddenly, Luna was at her side, staring at Oak, her eyes wide. It was as if some silent communication passed between them. Shadow looked at Oak, confusion clouding her gaze.

"Yes. Why?" she asked. Luna broke her stare and went to get some herbs from a crack in the wall. Oak gave a tiny shake of his head, his gaze thoughtful. They sat in silence for a while before Shadow spoke once more. "What happened on the other side of the wall?" she asked again, her ears pricked with curiosity.

Oak looked at her. "We were ambushed by a group of foxes. It was unusual to see a group of them, more than one or two. They are usually solitary hunters. We were ambushed by four or five of them. They were angry and thirsty for blood. They knocked Breeze into the birch tree that fell. That's how he hit his head and sprained his paw. Storm and I fought them off. We didn't know what had been happening here in the clearing. We eventually chased them off, but Breeze was badly hurt. I'm worried that…maybe I have been right," Oak answered slowly as if thinking out loud. Luna appeared at Shadow's side and began to dress her wounds, a long scratch on her back, and a rip in her pad. Luna put some herbs in front of Shadow and told her to lick them up. She said that they would help with shock and pain. Shadow obediently ate them up, then turned back to Oak. Luna hurried off to tend to the other wolves, her head low with exhaustion.

Oak had groomed his pelt as Luna was working on Shadow and now his fur was clean and shiny. It glowed amber in the dim light. Shadow stared at him in silence, her emotions mixed. Anger that foxes would have the audacity to attack her packmates so close to their den, worry for Breeze and Lynx, and fear for what would happen next. If foxes were ganging up to find food who knew what else could happen? Suddenly, Oak turned his head sharply towards Shadow, his eyes shining. "I'm worried that this place is no longer a livable habitat for us. I know I've told you this, but I've been thinking…What are your thoughts? I know you were hesitant about the idea before, but I don't know what you think of it now."

"I've been thinking, too, Oak and I agree with you. I now know we cannot remain here." Oak looked at her with approval, fear, and… something else, too. Shadow couldn't quite put her paw on what he was thinking.

"Good. Thank you, Shadow. I suppose I must announce this news to the pack," he said, his ears flattening at the thought. Shadow whined softly at her father's lack of confidence.

"They will understand. The hardships of living in this home are just as bad as leaving would be. You are their Alpha, their leader. You must show no fear and they will follow you without hesitation. I know they will," Shadow comforted him quietly. Oak glanced at her with warmth in his eyes.

"You would make a good leader, Shadow. Think about that," he said, then turned to Luna as she appeared at Shadow's side. Shadow craned her neck to look at the Healer, confusion stirring in her mind. *A good leader? What could he mean by that?* she wondered to herself.

"Come, Shadow. I must talk to Oak. Alone," Luna said with a stern voice. Shadow nodded obediently and got up from where she lay. Oak shot her a meaningful look before she turned and trotted out of the den.

Chapter Twelve

Pain shot through Shadow's tail and she was abruptly pulled from her nightmares about the boulder falling on Lynx. She jerked her head up with a yelp, sleep gone from her mind. "Sorry," Miku winced, lifting his paw off her tail. She sighed and looked at him, yawning.

"What are you doing?" she asked. She had been having nightmares about the boulder falling on Lynx's tail every night since the incident.

"Well, I just wanted to see if you were awake. It's kind of dark in here, so I didn't see your tail," he replied apologetically.

"Okay, it's fine," Shadow said, looking outside. It was still dark, the sun just barely peeking over the edge of the horizon. "It's still early," Shadow complained. Miku nodded.

"I know. I woke to a weird dream, so I decided to come and see if you wanted to go out hunting with me. The prey might be out, who knows?" Miku said, leaning closer to speak quieter. Sparrow stirred in the corner, growling in his sleep, his legs twitching. Shadow looked up at Miku, a soft smile spreading across her face.

"Sure, hunting sounds good. That's cute of you," Shadow spoke, standing up and stretching. Miku grinned.

"Yeah, well, the truth is I didn't want to go out alone," he answered, shrugging and licking her shoulder. Shadow smiled and followed him out of the den. The morning was fresh. Two days had passed since the boulder collapsed on Lynx. The giant rock still sat in the hole and the smell of blood still tainted the area. Breeze had largely recovered. Luna had tried to fix his paw, but after a few failed attempts she concluded that it would be forever crooked. Breeze was up on his feet already but still wasn't allowed to leave the den. Miku visited him every day.

Lynx was still in bad condition. She spent most of the days passed out. Her wound was healing, and Luna was keeping it clean and free of infection. She said it would heal nicely, but she was worried about Lynx's pups. She said the she-wolf was under a lot of stress, which wasn't good for pups, especially ones that are so close to being born. She said they could deliver early, which would be bad, especially considering the pack's food problem. Shadow was worried about the she-wolf. She had a strong affection for Lynx and thought Lynx was an important member of the pack. She was popular among all the wolves and they looked up to her. If she died Shadow would never feel the same. Oak still hadn't announced that the pack would be leaving, and he hadn't spoken to Shadow about it anymore since their conversation in the Healer's den.

Worry pricked at Shadow more and more every day and she could *feel* the tension within her packmates, even as they slept. They knew that something was wrong, and Shadow guessed they already knew Oak was planning to leave. Shadow looked up at the sky. It was empty of clouds but instead dotted with now-fading stars as the sun rose. Not a single leaf stirred. No wind blew. It was ear-splittingly quiet. Even the birds had gone silent. Shadow swiveled her ears around, trying to catch even the slightest noise. Nothing. She sighed and began padding out of the clearing, the gray-blue sky towering above her.

Shadow and Miku made their way through the forest silently, listening for any signs of prey as they walked. Suddenly, Shadow heard a squeak then what sounded like a snake in the bushes beside her. She immediately stopped, craning her neck and lowering her shoulders to see what was happening. A snake was coiled under a branch, a lump about the size of a small mouse sliding slowly down its scaly body.

214

Shadow guessed that it had just devoured the mouse. She immediately shot forward and clamped her jaws around the snake's skull, breaking it with one swift movement. She lifted it off the ground, relief washing over her. Maybe they would catch something this time. She gave a brief nod to Miku before continuing along the trail, ears straining to hear any other noises. The silence that thickened the air made it easier to catch any signs of movement.

They walked for what seemed like hours before Miku caught sight of something. He stopped and flicked an ear telling Shadow to stop, too. He pointed his nose at a blackbird sitting under a shriveled berry bush, pecking half-heartedly at what was left of the dried-up berries lying on the ground. Miku lowered his head and shot forward clumsily, snapping his jaws down on the bird's tail feathers. It let out a squawk of alarm and tried to fly away in a daze of pain. Instead, it flew straight into the branch above its head. Shadow dropped her snake and leaped over to the blackbird, snapping her jaws around its neck expertly. She then glanced at Miku with amusement. "Graceful," she commented, biting back a laugh. He glared at her, but he was smiling.

"Yeah? Well, at least I got its feathers. Those are the best part," he snorted, sneezing as a feather that was stuck in his teeth tickled his nose. Shadow laughed and picked up her snake to continue along the trail, Miku falling in behind. They soon reached the lake, which was also drying up. Shadow noticed the water was farther down the slope than it had been the last time she was here. She looked longingly through the human mesh, wishing she could take a drink.

Shadow and Miku switched to a different trail that led them to the river. They hid their prey near the beaver dam. They hoped to catch a beaver or possibly an otter. Shadow crouched with Miku in the ferns near the dam, watching sharply for signs of movement. After a while Shadow caught sight of a beaver, swimming through the slow-moving water. It was holding a bundle of sticks between its sharp teeth, possibly carrying them to add them to the dam. Shadow remembered learning about water hunting when she was a Learner. Lynx said to wait until it was close, then charge it, and hope to catch it. She also said there was a very slim chance of actually catching it. Shadow slowly and silently made her way through the darkness until she was close to the edge of the water. She ducked her head, trying to calm her racing heart.

Miku was watching her, eyes wide as he stared at the large animal. Shadow took a deep breath then shot into the water. She propelled herself forward, watching as it dropped the sticks it was carrying, hissed, and turned to dive into the water. Shadow swam with the current of the water, going as fast as she could, her muscles beginning to sore as she paddled. She reached the beaver just as it was about to disappear beneath the surface of the water. She plunged under and bit into its tail, tugging it back toward the surface, the metallic taste of blood bathing her tongue. Swimming with all her strength, she began to drag it back to the shore, growling as it attempted to get away. It ground its teeth in pain and scratched her with its hind legs, thrashing and writhing in the water. Just as the animal was about to wriggle out of her grip, Miku jumped into the water and grabbed its flank. Shadow got a better grip on its tail and together they dragged the squealing animal back to the edge of the river, where Shadow delivered the killing bite.

She then glanced thankfully at Miku. "Thank you. I thought for sure I wouldn't make it," she said, licking the blood off her lips, panting. He dipped his head, smiling, water dripping from his fur.

"Wow! This is great!" Miku said. "The pack will finally have a good meal for a night. Should we keep hunting?" he asked. Shadow nodded, wiping the blood from the scratches on her paw.

"Yes," she said. "Let's go."

Shadow helped Miku hide the beaver with the rest of the prey before turning and padding along the river, ears pricked for any more signs of life. When they found none, they ventured back into the forest. They came to a stop when they reached the human's mesh. Shadow sniffed the air and was surprised to catch the sweet scent of fresh meat. The smell made her mouth water. It didn't smell like rotting meat, but like a mouse that had been stripped of its fur and left out to dry. The scent was tainted with blood, but it was enough to lure her toward it. Miku caught the scent, too, because his eyes were wide and his tongue was hanging out.

"What is that amazing smell?" he asked, wagging his tail. Shadow began moving towards the scent, following the trail until she spotted it. A pile of seemingly untouched meat covered in leaves on the ground. "What's that?" Miku asked at her side. Shadow stared at the pile of meat suspiciously. It looked and smelled delicious, but was clearly placed by the human. Shadow moved towards it cautiously, sniffing lightly. She didn't smell any human on it, but she was still suspicious. Miku was at her side, smelling it, saliva coating his lips. Her stomach growled, and she couldn't help but feel drawn towards this suspicious pile of meat left out deep in the woods with no explanation.

Just as Miku reached forward to take a bite, the realization hit Shadow like a rock. "Wait!" she howled. Miku stopped instantly, jumping with the loud noise.

"What?" he demanded. "I'm hungry." Shadow searched the ground for something heavy to drop on the pile.

"Don't you see, Miku? It must be a trap, set by the humans," she said, picking up a small stick in her teeth.

"Yes, or it could be a pile of meat left in the woods for us," Miku said ruefully.

"Do you honestly think that the human would just leave food out for us?" Shadow asked, and Miku shook his head reluctantly. "Do you remember those traps we found around our den site? One of them is probably hidden beneath this pile. The human must have put the meat here to lure us in, then have the trap snap down on our legs or faces," Shadow said darkly. She then leaned cautiously over the pile and dropped the stick. Immediately after the stick hit the top of the meat, there was a loud *clank* of metal and the trap clamped shut. Two chunks of metal with large, sharp thorns weaved themselves perfectly together in a split second. The meat flew in every direction, splattering Shadow on the nose. Shadow and Miku both yelped so loud she was sure the wolves back at the den site could hear it. They both had horrified looks on their faces as they realized that Shadow had been right. If these dangerous things were all over the forest, the wolves who didn't know about them could be in serious trouble.

"Wow," Miku uttered, eyes wide with fear. Shadow stared at him, anger pulsing through her veins.

"The human did this!" she spat. "It's trying to kill us in our own *territory,*" Shadow growled with rage. Then, sighing, she stared at Miku with wide eyes. "We have to tell Oak about this," she said, trembling with rage. Miku nodded, and they went back to the lake to retrieve their prey. Shadow began trotting quickly back home, fur standing up with rage.

When they got back they put their prey on the prey pile and rushed straight to the Alpha stone where Oak sat talking to Storm. Oak turned towards Shadow as she approached. "Morning, Shadow. I see you've done some morning hunting. Good job. Nice catch, too." Oak stood and stretched, eyeing her beaver hungrily. Storm stayed where she was, staring at Shadow.

"What's wrong?" Storm asked. Oak looked down at Shadow with a mixture of curiosity and nervousness glinting in his eyes. Miku took a deep breath at her side. Shadow stared up at the Alphas, anger fizzing underneath her pelt. Oak jumped down from the rock, facing Shadow.

"What is it?" he demanded.

"The human has become bolder in its ways of trying to harm us," Shadow growled, fur bristling.

"How so?" Oak asked, his voice wavering.

"A new type of trap intended to cause us harm. It was baited with meat and hidden under a pile of leaves. A metal trap, like the ones the human placed around our dens, but bigger. As I applied the slightest amount of pressure it slammed shut. It could have taken my paw off. I fear that there may be others within the territory," Shadow told him.

"Well, how did you set it off without hurting yourself?" Oak asked. Storm slipped off the stone and was standing beside her mate, her moss-covered scratches shifting as she did so.

"I dropped a stick on the top," Shadow replied.

"Good. At least we know how to set it off. How did you know it was a trap?" Oak asked. Shadow looked at him, thinking.

"I don't really know. I just felt it in my gut. It just looked wrong, seeing a random pile of meat within our territory," Shadow confessed, shrugging. Oak studied her carefully before turning to Storm.

"We need to find the traps and make sure that no wolf is hurt by them. Send out four wolves to check the territory," Oak told the she-wolf, ears pinned. Storm gave a brief nod and turned to assign the wolves. "Shadow, Miku, you go and look for traps, too. Hunt along the way. The pack always needs more food." Oak nodded in dismissal before leaping back onto the Alpha stone and sitting down. Scout, Sparrow, Heather, and Amber accompanied Shadow and Miku with finding the traps. They all exited the clearing as a group, Amber leading the way.

In all, they found eight traps within the territory. Shadow seethed with rage each time she found a trap left by the human. When Shadow and her group returned to the den site they found the clearing filled with answer-hungry wolves. Oak asked them how many traps they had found. Shadow had found two, Sparrow three, Miku one, and Heather two. Scout and Amber hadn't found any, but they caught prey, surprisingly. When they were done talking and the pack had settled down, Mako, Amber, Scout, and Max were sent to mark the borders.

Shadow, relieved to have time to think, sat down at the edge of the clearing and began to go over all the things she had stored in the back of her mind. *When is Oak going to announce our leaving? The sooner the better, right? Maybe I should talk to him about it, we need to get out of here. It's only going to get worse. I know he talks a lot about leaving, but I don't think he actually wants to. He's going to do what's best for the pack even if he doesn't like it. I respect that. But, he should make the decision soon. The human is only getting angrier and growing bolder.* These and other thoughts swirled around her head.

As she sat thinking Oak suddenly appeared at her side. "What are you thinking?" he asked, tucking his tail under his paws. Shadow sighed and looked at him.

"When are we leaving?" she asked, getting straight to the point. Oak's face hardened.

"When I say we are. The pack needs time to heal, Shadow. I think we should wait until Lynx's pups are old enough to walk, and then we will go."

"Oak, you must understand. We don't have the time for that. The human gets angrier by the day. I've had terrible dreams. Dreams about fire, death, and destruction. I don't want that to happen," Shadow said quietly, ears pinned to her head.

Oak looked at her sadly. "You're right, Shadow. Of course, you're right. The thing is, I don't know if I can leave. I've lived here all my life."

"Oak, there is no choice. If we stay here, there may not even *be* an Aspen pack in the future. Who knows what that human is capable of? Who knows what it will do to us? We cannot take that chance. I'm scared, Oak. Do what you know is best and tell the pack we are leaving. Tonight. It must be done," Shadow said. She tried to keep her voice sounding strong, but her voice cracked in the end. Oak gazed at her, sadness clouding his eyes. Then he smiled wearily. "Oh, Shadow. You *will* make a good leader." Then he walked away.

Shadow sat at the entrance of the Hunters' den. Miku was at her side and he was slowly grooming her fur, the dark evening sun shining on her pelt. It felt warm. The group that had been sent to check the boundaries was casually reporting to Oak. Shadow guessed nothing had come up with the Cedar pack. She heard some words as the breeze carried them towards her. She heard snippets of Max's words, "…Another human den…Cedar pack territory…Loss of land…" and other small things. She didn't intend to eavesdrop, but she couldn't help overhearing. Maybe Oak would finally realize the danger that the pack is in and tell them his plans to leave. The day had been particularly hot, practically melting her skin if she wasn't in the shade. The stillness and humidity in the air hadn't helped either. It was now evening and the sun was setting, casting shadows over most of the clearing. Shadow was in one of the only sunny spots left, soaking in the last of the sun's rays before it began to disappear behind the horizon. Oak listened to Max give his report and then slowly made his way toward the Alpha stone. He held his head high with confidence. Storm was already at the side of the rock watching the pack carefully.

Oak jumped onto the Alpha stone and looked around the clearing before taking a deep breath and howling, "My pack, gather around me, for I have an announcement to make!" The wolves in the clearing stopped and quietly stood up, gathering in front of Oak. Shadow and

Miku stood up together and walked over to the gathering crowd slowly, ears low. They sat at the edge of the circle of wolves, Shadow's heart racing. Oak stood tall, his shadow stretching out across the wolves. She could tell he was trying to hide his fear.

"Wolves of the Aspen pack," he began, taking a deep breath. "I know all of you know the human has been slowly taking over our territory, one way or another. Now, something more has happened. The human has set traps to harm us inside of our territory. We have sent out wolves to disarm the traps, but we haven't the slightest idea of what the human might do next. Our wolves have been hurt because of this human, in ways that have angered me and, I know, all of you. So, I have been forced to make a decision. I have spoken with some of the wolves closest to me, heard their opinions, and worked out the best way to deal with this problem. I can only reach one conclusion. As your Alpha, as your leader, and as your packmate, I hope that you can understand why I must make this decision. We must leave the territory," Oak spoke loudly and clearly, his voice ringing around the clearing.

The wolves sat in stunned silence. Some looked up at him with understanding, like they knew this was coming. Others looked up in shock or anger. Shadow looked around hopefully, willing her packmates to agree with her father. *"Leave?"* Mako demanded, standing up. He looked angry, his fur bristling and eyes wide with shock. Shadow was surprised that Oak hadn't talked to him about this decision ahead of time. "Oak, this is nonsense! We cannot simply give up and leave our homes because of one lonely *human.* We are strong! We will retaliate!" he howled, looking around the clearing for backup. Sparrow nodded as if in agreement, but didn't stand up.

"I agree with Mako!" Max stated, standing up. "I want to raise my pups here, in the territory I grew up in. I wouldn't want them to be born without a home," he said loudly.

Oak was unfazed. "I knew there would be some disagreements, but believe me, this is the best way."

Mako let out a growl. "Well, you were right. I disagree! It has been too many times now, Oak, that you have made decisions without first involving the pack. It's getting on some of our nerves!" Some wolves nodded their heads in agreement, while some stared defiantly at Mako.

"Mako, you must see reason. Oak has stated truthfully that he confided with the wolves closest to him and they agreed with him. Oak is not doing this to be selfish. He doesn't want to leave our home anymore than you do," Shadow stood and growled at him.

Mako stared angrily at her, lips pulled back in a snarl. "Oak has grown old, and weak. He can no longer lead this pack. His mind has grown full of false judgment and selfish thoughts! He doesn't deserve to lead us anymore," Mako argued bitterly.

"Oak is not selfish! He has led this pack through thick and thin. He was *chosen* to lead, in case you've forgotten. He earned his place as the leader. It is in his power to command us, and we must listen to what he thinks is best," Shadow shot back. Mako let out a growl, baring his teeth. Shadow continued, "This place is no longer a livable home. It is dangerous. Who knows what this human could do to us! It has already harmed Amber, and now it's set traps to kill us once and for all. Is this really where you want to stay and live? To raise your pups? There's barely enough food to go around! Please, Mako, I beg you to see the sense in Oak's decision." Shadow pleaded, ears pinned. Mako stared defiantly up at Oak.

"Bah! If I were Alpha this pack would be thriving. That human would already be gone. Oak!" Mako growled, his fur sticking straight up. "I challenge you for power over the pack. A fight, if you may. When I win, you will be forced to step down as leader and I will be Alpha!" Mako howled. Shadow's heart caught in her throat. Mako? Leader? No.

"A challenge, you say?" Oak retorted, jumping down from the Alpha stone. "A challenge for rank hasn't been issued in years. I accept. If I win, I remain Alpha and you stay a Fighter. But, if you win, you take the place of Alpha and have full control over this pack. A fight until one wolf gives up, or is dead." At that, the wolves parted to form a circle in which they would fight. Shadow stared at Oak, horrified. What was he getting himself into? *Right now, we need our wolves to fighting alongside each other, not against each other!* Shadow thought. Storm watched with fearful eyes. Miku looked shocked. The air in the clearing tingled with tension.

The two large males circled each other, anger glinting in Oak's eyes. Mako's eyes were filled with power and triumph. Suddenly, Mako sprang forward, teeth aimed at Oak's neck. Oak jumped aside and butted Mako on the flank with his head. Mako then turned and lashed out, his teeth finding Oak's ear. Blood splattered on the ground as a portion of Oak's ear was torn off. Oak let out a yelp and lunged at Mako, biting down on his neck. Mako shook him off and flattened him to the ground, grabbing again at his neck. Oak whimpered as fur was torn from his neck, then kicked Mako off in a blur and sent him flying across the clearing. Mako landed heavily on the ground. Oak advanced on him quickly, hitting him with such force that the breath was knocked clean out of Mako's chest. He let out a strained howl as Oak tore flesh from his flank. Oak then dug his teeth into Mako's neck and applied pressure—not enough to crush his windpipe, but enough to tear through the skin and leave serious puncture wounds. Mako kicked Oak away and advanced, snarling. He ripped through Oak's flank then bit down on his tail. Oak let out a growl and grabbed Mako's snout in his jaw and held tight. He clamped Mako's mouth shut and pinned him to the ground. Mako fought hard, but Oak held strong. Finally, Mako went limp in defeat. Oak held him there for a few extra seconds before backing off, licking the blood from his snout.

"Are there any other wolves who would like to try and oppose me?" he demanded, turning towards the rest of the pack. Nobody moved. Oak snorted his contempt and went to Mako, biting his ear and snarling in his face. Mako slunk to the ground, his tail curled between his legs, fur flat, body pressed against the ground, showing the utmost respect. Oak gave a low growl then strode off to the Healer's den. Luna sat outside waiting as if she were watching two pups fighting over who gets the best place to sleep. Oak disappeared inside. Mako stood, seething with rage. Wolves growled at him as he passed to enter the Healer's den, his blood-stained fur glinting in the moonlight. Shadow watched him go, strong relief washing over her. Oak was safe. His rank was safe. The pack was safe… for now.

The challenge was over. Shadow stood with the rest of the pack. The wolves around her were in shock just trying to take in what had just happened. Storm rushed off to the Healer's den followed by Amber. Shadow was tempted to follow them but knew this was something they would want to talk about alone. At least now the pack knew of Oak's decision and they could prepare for it before it happened. Miku was at her side, a concerned look on his face.

"That wasn't good. We need the pack to come together. We can't have everyone fighting against each other," he said, worry darkening his face. Shadow gazed around the clearing, eyes darting from one wolf to another.

"You're right. We can't keep letting this happen. I don't know what to do…" Shadow murmured, frowning. Suddenly, a cold gust of wind made her shiver. She looked up. A few small withered leaves flew from the trees. A chilling breeze swept through the clearing. Miku looked up, as did the rest of the wolves in the pack. Clouds raced across the sky exposing the moon, allowing it to shine down on the clearing through a small opening. Then, as quickly as it started it stopped. The wind quieted, the clouds swirled together, and everything went still. The clearing was silent.

Miku broke the silence. "What just happened?" he murmured, eyes wide. Shadow glanced at him as the rest of the pack erupted into nervous chatter. "The first sign of fall," Heather sighed. Shadow couldn't tell if it was in relief, nervousness, or both. *Fall?* Shadow thought as she tucked her tail between her legs with fear. When the snow came it would be even harder to find a new home. Miku glanced at her, fear in his gaze. He knew, too. Shadow tried to shake the feeling of dread, padding silently off to her den, Miku at her tail. Sparrow was in the Hunters' den already, licking his paws. He looked unfazed but was still shaken about what had happened. Shadow curled up in her sleeping hole and closed her eyes, hoping for sleep that never came.

Chapter Thirteen

Shadow padded alone through the forest, her ears pinned to her head against the heat. It was the day after the fight between Oak and Mako and the pack had mostly recovered from the traumatic experience. Oak had slept in his den, while Mako had been forced to sleep in the Healer's den. His wounds were deep, but he would be let out today. Oak wasn't happy. Shadow could tell by the way he looked at Mako that he would never trust him again. It was stupid, what Mako had done. He created a tear in Oak's trust in his pack. The sign of fall wasn't a good sign for them, and Shadow could tell that there was more tension stirring in the air as she woke that morning. She trudged slowly through the shriveled underbrush; her eyes squinted against the bright sunlight. She could notice a slight drop in temperature.

She stepped on a branch of a fallen Hawthorne bush and a few tiny needles pricked her pad skin. Shadow yelped in pain and jumped back, dislodged from her thoughts. She growled in frustration as pinpricks of blood welled up on her paw. She gingerly licked the splinters out of her pad, glowering at the fallen bush. The bramble looked like it had shriveled up from the heat, but it also could have been pushed down to form some sort of shelter. Shadow investigated, looking around the large bush. She spotted a dark hole leading underneath and wondered what kind of animal would want to live in a patch of thorns. The entrance was too small for a fox den and too big for a rabbit hole. Shadow leaned towards it and took a few sniffs, finding with disappointment that the hole was empty, untouched.

Shadow caught a faint scent of a fox, mixed with blood. It was almost too faint to distinguish. The scent must have been left months ago, kept fresh by the heat and untouched without the rain. She sniffed deeper into the hole, wondering if maybe the animal was dead inside, but she caught no scent. It looked abandoned with no sign of a recent entry. The walls looked strong, protected from predators. A fox could have been living here for months and her pack wouldn't have known about it. It was well hidden and quite a long way from the nearest wolf trail. Shadow huffed and moved along, eyes now scanning the ground in front of her as she walked. She heard a faint shuffling sound and a mouse ran out almost tripping her. It ran right between her legs, catching her off guard, and then it disappeared into the bushes on her other side. She yelped with anger and plunged after it, biting blindly into a large piece of tree bark. She spit out chunks of wood and raced after the mouse's trail, anger causing her pelt to bristle. No mouse could just run out right in front of her and get away with it!

She followed its quick movements until she finally caught up with it, now going at a full sprint. She snapped her jaws around its tail just as it was about to run down a hole. She yanked it away from its home, growling. It let out a terrified, agonized squeak as she threw it into the air. She caught it mid-fall and killed it swiftly. It went limp, and she returned to the path she was following, head low. A short way down the trail she heard a strange sound. It sounded like the shuffling of leaves, but more amplified, swift, and coming toward her. A gust of wind picked up blowing out of a barrier of brambles and she caught the acrid scent of the human. As she looked up the human emerged from behind the trees, its strange weapon pointed at her head. The human's eyes were filled with hatred. A devilish smirk was plastered across its face, as if it were saying, 'I've finally got you.'

Terror racked Shadow's body from head to tail, and a chill ran down her spine. Her fur bristled and, without thinking, she lowered her head into an attacking position. Despite being terrified for her life, she felt obligated to drive this human off their land or die trying. She let out a savage snarl and dropped her mouse, baring her now bloody fangs. This startled the human and a wave of fear crossed its face. Still, the human knew it held the advantage. Shadow raised her tail and took a threatening step forward, eyes locked with the human's. Shadow flew forward with incredible speed, zigzagging side to side to avoid the human's deadly weapon. Shocked, the human began shooting wildly.

Pain shot up her leg as a bullet skimmed her flesh. Shadow kept running at the human, growling with satisfaction as she saw the look of terror in its eyes. The human quickly put more shiny rocks into its weapon and shot again. This time it missed entirely. Shadow launched herself at the human's ankle, biting down on its leathery paws and dragging its weight out from under it. The human fell with a *crash,* shaking the ground. Shadow then sunk her teeth into its meaty leg, the taste of its blood bathing her tongue. The human kicked her away with its other foot, and she yelped at its strength. Anger surged through her and she lunged again, this time biting down on its arm. She bit down deeply and shook her head back and forth, the human's yells of pain ringing throughout the trees. The human grabbed its weapon and tried to point it at Shadow, holding it awkwardly with only one arm. Shadow dug her teeth in harder and dodged one of the attacks, still shaking its arm back and forth, tearing flesh. The human grabbed a rock off the ground and hit her neck, still screaming. Shadow yelped in pain and let go before turning and darting into the bushes, the human's outraged bellows fading as she ran back toward the den site.

She realized that she had left her mouse but figured it was as good as gone by now. She had been running for a long while and was growing tired, the injury on her hind leg burning horribly. Just as she was about to slow to a trot she spotted the bushes surrounding her home. She found the entrance and entered, panting and shaking with exhaustion. She dragged herself to the Alpha stone where Oak was talking with Max. "Oak!" she called hoarsely, her tail drooping and her leg dripping with blood. Her body trembled.

"Shadow?" Oak answered, standing up, a look of confusion on his face. "What's going on?" he asked with concern.

"The human…was in our territory. It tried to get me with its weapons, so I attacked it to try and drive it off, and…"

Oak jumped down to her, cutting her off. "You did *what?*" He demanded, staring at her with awe and anger. Shadow stared at him, fear running through her body. Would Oak still trust her? "Shadow, that's suicidal. You could have died, attacking the human with its weapon!" Oak growled.

"It was hunting me! It wanted me dead!" Shadow retorted with a growl. By now wolves had begun to gather around them, listening in awe and shock. "Something is wrong with that human, Oak. It's crazy, driven by rage and uncontrollable want for us to be *dead*. It wants us dead, Oak! We can't stay here any longer!" Shadow snarled, looking around to see wolves nodding in agreement.

Oak was staring at her, grim determination shining in his eyes. "You're right, Shadow. We must leave. But not now. You must trust me. I feel that something is keeping us, wanting us to stay," he growled lowly, dipping his head. Shadow stared at him, frustration making her fur standing up on end. Then she bowed her head deeply to him and took a step back towards the Healer's den.

"Okay, Oak. I trust you, and I believe you," Shadow told him with respect, hiding her annoyance. Miku stepped aside to let her pass into the Healer's den. She was aware of her packmate's eyes on her back as she slipped into the cave.

Shadow padded with narrowed eyes through the darkness following the sound of Luna's voice deeper into the den. When she emerged into the cavern where Luna sat her eyes widened. Lynx was sitting up in her bed, her eyes weary but shining with life. She looked happy to be awake but was also clearly stressed about what had happened. Her stomach heaved with the pups that Shadow guessed would come any day now. Her tail was wrapped with fresh herbs and moss, only a stub of what it used to be. Shadow smiled at Lynx then leaped forward to rest her head on Lynx's shoulder, her sweet scent filling Shadow's nostrils. "Lynx! You're awake! How do you feel?" Shadow exclaimed, stepping back and smiling, her tail wagging despite all that had happened.

Lynx looked overjoyed. "I'm feeling fine, Shadow. A bit tired, but otherwise okay. How are you? What's happened while I was asleep? Luna has updated me on all she knows, but I thought I heard about some more commotion than usual with the human. Is that true?" Shadow took a deep breath and updated Lynx on everything that had been going on, including the human's traps. She also told Lynx how she had attacked the human and how she was injured in the process. Luna started working on Shadow's injuries, telling her, with relief, they would heal in only a few days.

"Well, Shadow, that was either very brave or very stupid of you," Luna told her.

"I think it may have been both," Shadow admitted with a slight smirk. Lynx nodded, pride glinting in her eyes.

"I taught you well, eh?" Lynx joked. Shadow smiled, letting her shoulders relax. She hadn't realized how tense she had been until she let herself relax.

"So, how are you feeling with the pups?" Shadow directed the question to Lynx, but twitched an ear at Luna as well, hoping to hear some news from her.

"Lynx has been under a lot of stress lately, with losing her tail…" Luna said. The light faded from Lynx's eyes and Shadow could tell that she was scarred by that experience, physically and mentally.

"I would probably be under the ground right now if it weren't for you, though, Shadow. You saved my life and my pups' lives. You held up that tree. You took that burden on your shoulders, and I couldn't be more grateful," Lynx said, licking her shoulder appreciatively. Shadow dipped her head.

"You're my family, Lynx. Of course, I would do that for you, or any wolf," Shadow said with a smile. Lynx returned the smile while Luna finished cleaning Shadow's leg. The wound was now well wrapped, and Shadow was sitting comfortably on the edge of Lynx's bed. "How long have you been awake?" Shadow asked her former Trainer.

"Since sunrise this morning, I think. I woke up to the sun, which felt good. Luna redressed my wounds and I've been sitting here since then, getting caught up with what's been going on. Luna says the pups will come any day now," Lynx said proudly, resting a paw on her swollen belly protectively. Shadow beamed.

"That's great! I can't wait to see them. I'll bet they'll be smart like you, and strong like Max," Shadow said with a smile. Lynx dipped her head with appreciation.

"Honestly, I'm not scared about being a mother anymore. The only thing that scares me is…" Lynx trailed off.

"The human," Shadow guessed, finishing her sentence. Lynx nodded, eyes low. Shadow stayed silent. "I'm sorry, Lynx." Shadow finally said, her ears flattening.

"What do you mean? What for?" Lynx asked, tipping her head to the side.

"I wish you didn't have to go through this. I mean, living in a place that you call your home, but still don't feel safe inside of it. And, knowing that your pups are going to be born into that world? That's even worse. I can't even imagine what you're going through. It must be a horrible feeling knowing there is nothing you can really do about such a dangerous threat." Lynx took in this information for a few seconds, then sighed in reply.

"It is hard, Shadow. You're right. But I have my pack to protect me and my pups. I'm not worried about safety, I'm worried about the loss of territory and lack of food," Lynx confessed. Shadow straightened, nodding. "Of course."

"Well, Shadow," Luna said, "you're all fixed up! You can leave now. Oh, and tell Breeze to come in here, would you? I need to check on him." Shadow nodded, dipping her head in gratitude as she stood to leave. She waved her tail to Lynx in goodbye then slipped out of the den and into the dimming sunlight. She had been so busy talking to Lynx she hadn't realized that it was already getting to be late afternoon. She and Lynx talked about the prey, the shortage of water, injuries within the pack, recent incidents involving the Cedar pack, and lots of other minor things that had happened while Lynx was unconscious. Wolves buzzed around her, talking quietly or eating their portions from the prey pile. Oak was talking with Max at the foot of the Alpha stone, Max's eyes glazed over with a lack of sleep. Oak dipped his head to Max who stood and made his way over to the Guard's den, probably to sleep.

Shadow made her way across the clearing to where Miku sat talking with Breeze. They were speaking quietly, heads low. Shadow stood in front of Breeze as she surveyed his condition. He looked skinny, like the rest of the pack. His ribs were jutting from his skin. His wounds looked to be healing. Some were still covered with dusty moss, while some were open. Shadow thought they should still be covered. "Luna wants to see you in her den," Shadow told him. He looked up at her, nodded, then stood and limped heavily over to the den. Shadow watched him go, sadness spreading like ice through her heart. Her pack was crumbling, and all because Oak refused to leave. They would either die of starvation or from some cruel trick by the human. Shadow sighed wearily and sat down beside Miku, her exhaustion returning.

"You don't look so great," he commented, scooting closer until their fur brushed together. She looked over at him noticing his glazed eyes, scrawny frame, and tight shoulders.

"Yes. You've seen better days, yourself," she replied, nudging him. He snickered, licking her nose. She smiled, the warm feeling returning to the tips of her ears.

"I don't know how Oak could be so hard-headed," Miku said at last. "I mean no offense, but we really, *really* can't stay here anymore. We're just withering away," Miku said, echoing her own thoughts. Shadow nodded in agreement.

"I know. I just feel so *cross* with him right now! I mean, come on! Can't you see the signs? Can't you see how much this human has impacted our lives?" Shadow growled. He nodded. "I just don't know what to do. Lynx will have her pups any day now, and..." Miku stopped her.

"Lynx is awake?" he asked, smiling a bit.

"Yes, she woke up this morning," Shadow said, sinking to the ground with a sigh. Miku glanced at her, his head tipped to the side.

"I don't understand," he said. "Won't pups be good for the pack?"

"Pups at a time like this?" Shadow replied. "It's good for the pack, sure, but is it good for the pups? So much stress, so much heartbreak. Leaving this home, the place they were born? That can't be good for them. We don't even know if they going to be *alive*. With the lack of food, water, and the stress of all that's been going on, they could very well be... Never mind. We can't let that happen. In fact, I'll bring some prey for Lynx right now." Shadow jumped to her feet. She glanced at

Miku, who was staring at the prey pile, a look of disappointment on his face.

"There's nothing there, as usual. The beaver is already gone. I wonder if Lynx got some of it? I hope so. Anyway, I think I'll go out to look around the buckthorn and make sure there aren't predator scents nearby. Like to come along?" Miku said, standing and stretching. Shadow shot a glance at the prey pile before shaking her head. "I'm going to hunt for Lynx. She needs food more than any other wolf," Shadow replied, and Miku nodded in agreement. "Sounds good," he replied and trotted out of the clearing, Shadow following him.

Shadow walked through the forest, thinking to herself. *I wish the deer herd would come back. Oak said that they are usually around during the summer, but they probably moved to a safer spot, out of the heat and away from the human. A good meal is just what the pack needs. Besides the beaver, I just haven't seen much big prey around. I wonder if there will be any near the river? It is a reliable source of water. I'll check there.* All this went through Shadow's head as she slid through the dried-up ferns.

When she reached the river, Shadow sat on the bank and lapped up a long drink of the sweet-tasting water, her ears swiveling around her as they searched for sounds of prey. When she heard nothing, she began making her way downstream, staying beside the water as she walked silently, her head low as she smelled and listened for prey. Shadow came to a stop after hearing the sound of movement in the bushes ahead of her. Angling her ears towards the sound she smelled the air and caught the scent of a strange animal. Shadow peeked through the leaves to see two large geese sitting in a pool beside the river. They had black heads, brown bodies, and white underbellies. They were cawing softly to one another, unaware of her presence, as she was downwind and hidden by the shadows.

Shadow watched them carefully, her ears pricked. She had never seen a goose so close before but was told by Sparrow what they look like. She almost felt bad, killing such peaceful-looking animals. But she had to put her pack first. Shadow shot from the bushes and leaped onto the fatter goose, breaking its neck before it even knew she was there. She then turned to the second one, which was beginning to flap its winds in an attempt to escape. It was letting out a loud honking noise, its voice strained with fear. Shadow quickly regained her footing on the bottom of the shallow pool and launched herself upward, biting into the goose's orange foot. It flapped its wings harder as it tried to get away, feathers hitting Shadow in the face. She growled and pulled it out of the air, cracking its head on a boulder. The animal went limp instantly, its calls of distress abruptly cut off. Shadow smiled at her catch and grabbed the birds by their necks, hauling them out of the water. *Lynx will be happy at this meal,* she thought with triumph.

Shadow sat at the edge of the den site listening to the crickets chirping in the distance and her packmates chattering around her. It was a calm, sweet-scented night. Shadow felt this was what life had been like before the humans. *No stress, no tension in the air. Full bellies, too,* she thought. They didn't have that now, but they did have each other and that was enough. For now, at least.

Shadow had delivered Lynx one of the geese and Lynx had been excited at the big meal. She shared it with Luna and Shadow put the other goose on the prey pile. Her packmates were happy to see they would have more than a single mouthful for their evening meal. When the pack finished eating the goose, along with a rabbit and two squirrels, they began talking pleasantly to each other under the setting sun. Shadow chatted with Miku. It felt good to laugh again. Miku always knew how to make her laugh, and she loved him for it. Now, as she sat with him under the paling sky she thought about how much she loved him, and how much she needed him. Without Miku, she would be lost, Shadow realized. She buried her nose in his neck fur and listened to his soft breathing, enjoyed his company, and allowed herself to feel protected for once.

Closing her eyes, she felt herself begin to drift off. "Whoa," Miku's voice jolted her back awake. She opened her eyes and lifted her head off his shoulder. He glanced at her with a soft smile. "You look tired," he said.

"Nice observation," Shadow replied, smiling. He chuckled, stood up, and helped her to her paws. "Let's go. I'm tired, too," he said as he led her off to her den. Shadow dragged herself into her sleeping place and curled up, almost instantly drifting off to sleep.

Shadow woke with a jolt. She jerked her head upward, looking frantically around the den. Sparrow and Heather were sleeping in the opposite corner of the den. Breeze slept closer to her, his injured leg jutting out awkwardly. The den was dark, just barely light enough for her to see. She could hear crickets chirping and frogs croaking from outside her den, but aside from that, the night was silent. Fully alert and suddenly filled with adrenaline she stood and slipped out of the den and into the moonlight. The crescent moon shone pale against the darkness of the sky. It gave a dim, eerie light to the clearing. She looked around. Not a wolf stirred. Max must be sleeping, Shadow thought, glancing at the Guard's den. He was curled up in his sleeping hole. Shadow guessed Oak was supposed to be awake, but he was sleeping on the Alpha stone. Shadow slipped silently out of the clearing, deciding she would go for a walk to calm her mind. She raised her head and sniffed the wind, surprised to smell the acrid stench of fire smoke. She recognized that smell anywhere. Shadow sighed. "I must be dreaming again," she muttered to herself, although this dream felt especially real to her. *How could there be a fire?*

She looked around as she walked along a dense hunting trail. Moonlight shone lightly through the tree branches, making splotches of light on the ground. Shadow followed the scent of smoke, wanting to get this dream over with. She followed the small path that led toward the human den, her pelt prickling as the scent grew thicker and even more unbearable. She coughed, lowered her head, and continued. Soon, the smoke became visible in the air around her. It seemed to be coming from behind a hawthorn thicket just ahead. When Shadow saw what was behind the hawthorn she stopped dead in her tracks, horror seizing her body. There, outlined by the moonlight, stood the human, holding fire in its hand. The fire was burning at the end of a stick. The human was lighting everything around it – shriveled ferns, grass, and dried-up oak and maple leaves that littered the ground. The fire was spreading fast, eating up the leaves quickly as they were touched. The human looked eerily evil, glowing red and orange with the flames. The bites she had inflicted earlier were bandaged. As Shadow stepped into the open the human looked at her and grinned. Its grin was sickening. Evil. Rearing back, it threw the burning stick directly at her. She yelped and turned, beginning to run.

She bolted as fast as her legs could carry her back to the den site. Her eyes stung from the smoke and her legs burned. She remembered her dreams. How could she have been so *stupid?* They were warnings. Omens. And now the human was burning down their forest. It was all her fault. Shadow burst into the den site, howling. "Wake up! Fire! Run! We must get out of here! It's coming!"

She ran from den to den frantically waking her packmates. Oak stood up and looked around, eyes bleary and confused. Above Shadow's head, he saw the smoke rising from the tops of the trees. Flames licked up everything in their path and the wind was carrying them right toward their clearing. Despite Shadow's best efforts, only a few wolves had woken. Miku was one of them. He was now running from den to den waking the rest of the pack. Oak stood in shock on the Alpha stone, eyes wide open with pure horror. Shadow ran up to him and howled, "Oak!" He didn't move. Storm appeared at Shadow's side, jumping up to Oak and beginning to talk into his ear.

Shadow turned and looked around the clearing. The flames had almost reached the buckthorn surrounding them. Without Oak, Shadow would have to lead. Storm had pulled Oak off the stone and he was now running frantically, gathering the wolves together and making sure that everyone was accounted for. Shadow jumped onto the Alpha stone and turned to the pack. "Aspen pack!" She howled, as loud as she could. The wolves turned to look at her, eyes wide with horror. "Get to the river! Away from the fire! Everybody stay together! Find a partner and don't leave them. Make sure everybody gets out!" Shadow jumped from the Alpha stone and turned to Oak. "Lead them to the river," she ordered. Oak nodded then he gathered the pack with a howl that split the air.

The pack gathered around him and he ran out of the clearing, away from the hungry flames. Smoke had now filled the air, making it almost impossible to breathe. The clearing was empty, except for Miku who was emerging from the Healers den, his eyes wide with fear. "Shadow! Lynx is still in here!" he howled to her.

Shadow stared at him with horror. *"What?* Where's Luna?" she asked, running towards him. Before he could answer she entered the den. Looking back quickly, she saw the flames had reached the den site and were eating at the ferns, spreading fast. "Hurry!" she exclaimed, coughing, slipping into the den. "Lynx? Lynx, where are you?" she called, going deeper into the den. She emerged into the moonlit cave and let out a howl of despair.

Pups would normally fill her with joy, especially Lynx's pups. Lynx was lying in a bed, her face twisted with terror as she stared at Shadow.

Four mewling puppies lay in the curve of her belly, each crying for milk. Lynx had her tail wrapped protectively around them. Luna was standing in shock by her herbs, her eyes wild with fear. "Oh, no, no, no! Lynx, why now?" Shadow cried, but of course, she knew that it wasn't Lynx's fault. This made everything even more complicated. With no help from the rest of the pack, they would never make it out alive.

"Could we just stay in here? I mean, the fire can't eat stone…" Lynx was saying frantically.

"No," Luna insisted. "The ceiling is partly made of soil and bush. It would collapse on us. If that didn't kill us, the smoke would. We have to get out of here."

Lynx whimpered. "It's impossible," Miku gasped, shaking his head helplessly. "Lynx can barely walk herself." Shadow thought for a split second before leaping towards Lynx's pups and scooping one up by the scruff. It was a she-pup. She had dark brown fur, just like the rest of them at this age. She was still wet from birth.

"Miku, you take two. We'll carry them. Luna, get Lynx out of here," Shadow directed.

"What? No! I'm not leaving my pups, not only for a moment!" Lynx exclaimed, attempting to stand, but failing and falling back into her bed, causing her pups to cry.

"Lynx, it's the only way. Trust me. We have to get to the river," Shadow spoke gently, yet firmly. She picked up a male who was the same weight as his sister. His eyes were closed.

Lynx looked up at her pleadingly. "Please, Shadow, keep them safe!" She then nodded to Miku as he scooped up the other two pups—a small female and a large male. Luna helped Lynx to her paws, her expression a mixture of fear and determination. Lynx was weak, leaning heavily on the Healer. Luna took the weight, helping her out of the den as quickly as possible. Shadow allowed Miku to leave next, then exited herself.

Smoke clogged their nostrils and Shadow resisted the urge to turn back. Coughing through the pup's fur, Shadow made her way outside. She was horrified by what she saw through the smoke. She stopped dead in her tracks. The fire had engulfed the entrance and most of the clearing's surrounding bushes. It was still spreading quickly, engulfing everything in its path. They were trapped. Lynx let out a yelp of alarm, coughing as a gust of smoke hit her in the face. Shadow squinted her eyes as much as possible while still being able to see. The smoke made her eyes water, blinding her. Embers flew through the air. She dodged a large, burning leaf as it floated toward her face. The pups wriggled and squeaked with the movement. Shadow searched frantically for a way out. Suddenly, it came to her. "Get to the Alpha stone!" she howled above the roar of the fire. "From there, we can jump over the flames."

Lynx and Luna turned towards her and limped slowly in her direction. Lynx looked thoroughly drained. The smoke sent her into fits of coughing. Shadow led them to the Alpha stone and climbed to the top, careful of the pups she was carrying. As gently as she could she set the pups down on the stone. "Lynx!" she barked, and Luna helped Lynx up onto the top. "Miku, help me get Lynx across. Luna, stay with the pups. Lynx," Shadow turned to the she-wolf, "We have to jump over the flames." Shadow pointed with her nose to an open area on the other side of a wall of flames that the fire had not touched. Lynx nodded. "We will go back for your pups, but first we need to get you out of here safely. Okay?" Shadow said quickly. She didn't know how this plan had come to her—or if it would work—but she went with it.

Lynx was paralyzed with fear. "Miku, get on her other side and press against her. We have to carry her in a jump to the other side. When you get across, jump right back. We don't have much time. This is the only chance we have. Ready?" Shadow asked. They both nodded. "Okay. To the count of three… One… Two… Three!" Shadow howled.

She put all her strength into her jump. Together, she and Miku pushed Lynx forward over the fire. She felt the flames singe her belly fur as she flew over them.

Lynx landed with a grunt and then limped off into the untouched bushes, her head and tail drooping with exhaustion. Shadow watched her go for a few seconds before getting a small running start and jumping back onto the Alpha stone. As she soared above the burning ferns, one of the flames licked at her hind paw. She yelped with pain, landing awkwardly on the stone and turning to lick her hind paw. The fur had been burned, but her skin was fine. Shadow scooped up a male in her mouth and handed it to Luna. "Go," she ordered. Luna obliged, bunching her muscles and leaping messily, but safely, to the other side. Luna and the pup squeezed through the bushes and disappeared. Shadow scooped up a female, the smoke in the air choking her as fire surrounded the clearing.

Standing on the Alpha stone, Shadow felt the heat on her back. Miku gave her a frightened look and then jumped to the other side, one of the pups in his mouth. He shot Shadow a glance over his shoulder before following Luna through the brush, the pup in his mouth swaying as he trotted away. Shadow coughed, attempting to shield the pups from the smoke with her fur. She realized that there were two left, and she was the only one to carry them. She picked up the last pup by the scruff and bunched her muscles to leap. As she was about to jump the flames roared skyward and a maple tree crashed to the ground blocking her route of escape. She was filled with horror from ears to paws. Not only was she failing Lynx by not saving her pups, but she was also failing the whole pack by dying. She curled up into a ball around the pups, coughing, and hoped that maybe they would survive. Maybe, if she shielded them well enough...

"Shadow!" A loud howl jolted her from her thoughts. She lifted her head from the mewling pups, her eyes blurry and stinging from the smoke. Her body burned. Looking around, she spotted a dark figure below her, blended in amongst the smoke. "Shadow!" The voice howled again. This time she recognized who it was. Max. He was running up to her, eyes wide with horror. "My pups? Where are my pups?" he demanded. She coughed and gently lifted her paws to reveal the two pups. They were sitting in the curve of her belly, squirming against the heat and mewling pitifully in discomfort. They probably had no idea what was going on, she mused inwardly. Max scooped up a pup in his teeth and howled, "Follow me!"

Against the roar of the fire, Shadow found strength. She picked up the last pup and jumped down from the Alpha stone. Max led her to the Fighters' den. Shadow noticed now that Max's front paws were seeping blood and realized he must have dug through the rocks and dirt of the Fighters' den to get under the flames. Max pushed into the den with Shadow following. She was right. Max had dug a hole from the outside of the Fighters' den, under the flames. When Shadow emerged on the other side she gasped with relief. The air refreshed her lungs and gave her new strength. She pushed the pain in her hind paw to the back of her mind and moved on.

Max led her at a sprint through the forest, all the way to the river, where the rest of the pack was gathered. Miku, Lynx, and Luna were already there, Lynx crying into her pups' fur. They were alive but their fur was covered in dirt and soot. Max rushed to her side and set down the pup he was carrying. Shadow limped after him, leaving Lynx and Max to clean the pups and nurse them. She saw that Luna had fear and sadness in her eyes. She looked unbelievably weary, like she could collapse at any moment. Shadow looked around. Her packmates were sitting in a group, crying and howling at the loss of their home. Sadness suddenly overwhelmed her, and she broke down, burying her head in her paws. Miku appeared at her side and began comforting her. She wept into his fur. They had lost their home. Anger shook her so hard she couldn't speak. The human had done this. The human had finally driven them from their home. Sadness dragged at her heart, but she forced herself to sit up. She leaned on Miku for a few seconds, then got to her feet. She looked around, taking in everything around them.

They were gathered right next to the river. It ran slowly, probably slowly enough for them to be able to swim across. The trees above them had not yet caught fire, but she saw that the smoke was thick up there. The air around them was mostly clean and Shadow guessed they were far enough away to not have to worry too much. They could cross the river to get to safety if they had to. Shadow saw Oak giving orders at the side of the river. His eyes were weary and sad but filled with determination. Some of her packmates were drinking from the river and washing their paws. Shadow watched them, glancing at Miku as he trotted forward and found an open place to start drinking. Shadow then turned to watch their den site burn. Sadness overwhelmed her once more and she felt her eyes well up with tears.

She turned away from the flames as Miku appeared back at her side. He pressed himself against her in silent grief, his head hung low. It pained Shadow to see him so sad. She pressed her body against him and breathed in his scent, mixed with smoke. They sat in silence for a while until Miku finally got up and licked her cheek. "Come and have a drink. I promise you, it'll be the best thing you'll ever taste," he said, helping her to her paws. Shadow obliged, letting him lead her to the water. She bent down and began taking mouthfuls of water, drinking until her belly was full. She sat back, satisfaction spreading through her body. She felt better. "Thank you," she said. Miku nodded, then stood up. He looked over to the rest of the pack, many of whom had started digging holes to sleep.

Oak sat on a fallen tree trunk, watching. Storm was at his side, her eyes red and fur matted. Shadow laid down next to Lynx and

Max. Miku dug a hole beside her. Lynx was lying in a well-made bed of moss, her pups shiny clean and suckling from their mother's belly. Lynx was sleeping, Shadow noticed, her head wrapped around her pups protectively. Max was lying at her side, his head resting on her flank. He was looking at his pups, admiration and love shining in his eyes. Shadow thought she saw regret, too. Maybe he was mad at himself for not being there to help from the beginning. "How are your paws?" Shadow asked him quietly. He shrugged lightly, glancing up at her, his head not moving from Lynx's flank.

"They're fine. Luna wrapped them with moss. I'll be okay." Shadow nodded and looked back at the fire. It was dying down, the flames flickering softly as if their hunger had been satisfied. Another pang of longing hit Shadow's heart. She had talked and thought about leaving, but she had never known that it would feel this excruciating. She looked up at the sky, at the quarter-moon.

The sky was beginning to grow lighter as morning approached. The sun had just barely peeked its head over the rims of the hilltops, its light shining upon the land and giving the sky a sweet pink color. Smoke still filled the sky, though the wind had started pushing it away so they could now breathe without difficulty. Oak had made a sleeping hole beside Storm and they were now talking quietly to one another, no doubt discussing what would happen next. Shadow made a mental note to talk with Oak later about what she thought would be best. Around her, some of her packmates slept, while others lay restlessly in their holes, talking or crying. Heather and Sparrow were talking with Mako and Scout, their eyes weary and filled with sadness. Mako looked shameful. He had probably been talking about how stupid he had been to challenge Oak's decisions. Breeze and Kele were both sleeping, and Shadow realized that Max had fallen asleep, too. Amber was talking to Luna, who was working furiously scraping moss off an oak tree. Amber looked to be soothing her, probably telling her to sleep, or at least rest. Finally, Luna gave in and, with her moss, went to lie in a bed that Amber had built for her next to Lynx.

As Luna laid down Shadow walked over to her and licked her ear. "Thanks, Luna, for helping Lynx back there. It meant a lot," she said with a dip of her head. Luna nodded.

"Of course. It's what any wolf would have done," she said simply, yawning. Then she motioned towards the moss that she had collected. "Take some. For your wounds," she said, beginning to clean her paws, her eyes drooping. Shadow dipped her head and obediently took the moss. All of the moss. Luna either didn't notice or if she did, she didn't care. Shadow took them back to her sleeping place and put some on her hind paw. She then helped Miku dress his before helping the wolves that were sleeping. Most of them hadn't been treated yet, so she told them things that Luna would have told them: "Clean the wound with your tongue, then put some moss on it. Make sure to get enough water." When she ran out of moss, she went and found more. When the whole pack had been cleaned and treated with moss Shadow returned to her sleeping place. She collapsed. Almost instantly, she fell asleep.

Shadow padded through the charred, black forest, her tail drooping and head hung low with sadness. She was leading a group back to the clearing to see if she could find anything to scavenge and bring back. Luna had requested herbs and bedding. Shadow's group was made up of Amber, Mako, Scout, and Sparrow. The rest of the pack had stayed back, hunting or starting to build a sheltered place to sleep. They walked in a single file line, Shadow in the lead, then Amber, then Sparrow, and so on. It had been two days since the fire. They traveled in the evening. They made sure to let the flames go out completely, to be safe. Oak had sent out hunting groups to venture farther beyond the river and help Luna collect herbs. Lynx's pups were still coughing from the smoke inhalation but were otherwise doing okay. The pack was doing its best to feed Lynx and help her to feed her pups, and Max hardly left her side. The pack had tracked down a deer on the other side of the river, and though it was skinny, it was a good meal for the pack. That raised the pack's hopes that maybe somehow everything would be okay.

Oak, Amber, and Storm had done their best to take charge of the chaos, but they sometimes looked confused or had trouble making decisions. Shadow did her best to lead her packmates, but they were all pretty shaken up. Lynx and Max had begun thinking of names for the pups. For when it was time – when they were older. Shadow's group had almost reached the dens and Shadow could tell her packmates were getting a little nervous. Shadow was nervous, too, to see the carnage. She was itching to run to the human's den and tear its throat out, but that wasn't going to happen. Her packmates needed her now to help lead them. Shadow ducked under the trunk of a charred birch tree that was still smoldering, following no particular path back towards their den site, yet knowing exactly where to go. She passed a heap of pure black coal and smoldering branches, which she could only assume had once been a clump of bushes.

Pushing forward, she tried to ignore the pain in her heart at seeing the forest she had grown up in burn to ashes. She sensed her packmates felt the same way but were trying to hide it. The alternative was too depressing. Her paws throbbed from running so much in the past few days and her eyes and throat felt like they were on fire from enduring so much smoke. She thought that she would probably never lose the scent of fire in her nostrils and the lingering scent of destruction in her fur. The memories would be forever vivid in her mind. This tragedy would haunt them all for years on end. Shadow pushed these sad thoughts aside and sped up to a trot. The rest followed her lead, not questioning why they were speeding up. They either didn't notice or didn't care.

Shadow swerved around a charred pine tree, wincing as the remaining branches raked through her fur as she got too close. A towering oak tree lay on its side in the middle of the path that she was using, so she leaped nimbly over it, not breaking stride. Soon, they reached what was once the barrier wall of their den site. Shadow stopped and stared at the sight that lay in front of her. The rest of the group filed in beside her, taking in the damage that their former home had endured.

The bushes that had once surrounded their home were burned to the ground, their gray and black ashes swirling as the breeze kicked them into the air. The bushes and ferns were all burned to nothing. The dens that her packmates had once slept in were all now just heaps of burning memories. The roofs had caved in on all, except for the Alphas' den and the Healer's den, which were dug into the side of a rock wall. Everything else was gone, never to be seen again. The flames had killed *everything.* Shadow couldn't help but let out a whimper. She stopped herself from turning and running away, to hide from her life and the misery that came with it. No wolf said a word. They just stood silently and mourned. Shadow looked around. The forest was nothing but a graveyard of lost homes, lost memories, and lost hopes. A chilling wind swept down from above. She looked at her packmates. Their faces were rigid with emotion. Shock, sadness, loss, anger, pain. Shadow felt it within all of them. Loss of hope. Shadow just couldn't believe this was happening. *Maybe this is just a dream… Maybe I'll wake up in my sleeping hole, and everything will be normal.* But she knew her hopes were too good to be true.

She turned to her packmates, her ears pinned back to her head. "We were sent here to gather any remaining herbs and bedding, and to collect information about what our home had endured. Amber and Mako, go through the dens and collect anything that could be of use for building our temporary shelter. Scout and Sparrow, come with me to collect herbs from Luna's den. Meet in the middle of the clearing when you're done," she said. They each gave solid nods and trotted off toward the wreckage, tails drooping. Shadow followed wearily, sadness creeping into her heart as she looked around her. She jumped over a pile of ashes and slipped down the steep drop that had formed the edge of their den site.

It was about a foot-long drop from the edge of the forest to the main ground level of the clearing. Tall, thick walls of buckthorn had once surrounded the edge, making it hard to see through from the outside. Shadow pushed past this memory and walked through the barren clearing toward the Healer's den. She passed the Alphas' den, glancing at the Alpha stone, where she, Lynx, Luna, Miku, and the pups had all stood a few nights before trying frantically to escape. She passed the pile of rubble that had once been the Newborns' den, where she had been born and raised as a pup. She looked across the clearing and spotted a collapsed hole in the ground that had once been the Learners' den and memories flooded over her – when she had been made a Learner, training with Lynx, finding out that Sparrow would be her Advanced Trainer, falling in love with Miku, and then being named a Hunter.

Tears welled up in her eyes as she moved towards the Healer's den. Surprisingly, it was largely still held together. Since it was mostly made of stone, only the bushes and lichen that shielded the mouth of the cave from the weather were destroyed. Shadow braced herself and followed her packmates into the den as she had done so many times before. When she came to the main chamber of the den she stopped, taking in what she saw. The ceiling of the den had collapsed, just as Luna said it would. Large chunks of dirt and rock were on the ground around her. *If we stayed here, we would've been crushed,* Shadow thought. The herbs in the holes looked almost as they had left them, aside from the dirt that fell in some of them. Others had been scattered when the winds blew in from the holes in the roof. Scout and Sparrow were both creating piles of herbs that they thought were important. Shadow moved over to Luna's moss stash and pulled out giant mouthfuls. She made a pile with the rest of Scout and Sparrow's herbs, then moved on to another hole. She spotted what looked like pine needles. She wracked her brain to figure out what they were called and what they were used for, but she couldn't remember. She just grabbed a few and threw them on the pile.

She continued gathering herbs until she was sure that she wouldn't be unable to carry any more. Sparrow helped her balance herb bundles on her back and moss between her shoulder blades. Scout helped to load the remaining herbs onto Sparrow's pelt. They carried some in their teeth, too. When they finished, they went outside to see Max and Amber standing in the middle of the clearing, moss coating their pelts and held between their canines. They were carrying as much as they could, but it would still only make good beds for about three or four wolves. Shadow padded up to them, gave them a nod, and began waddling back towards the clearing entrance, herbs tucked under her chin and supported against her neck. Shadow led them at a steady walk back to their makeshift shelter, leaving their destroyed home behind. Shadow knew it would be the last time she ever saw it.

Chapter Fourteen

Shadow trotted along the riverbank, ears alert and fur standing on end. Miku was at her flank and Storm was at her other side. The group trotted along together, Oak in the lead, Amber in the back. The group was made up of Oak, Storm, Amber, Scout, Luna, Shadow, and Miku. They were on their way to the Cedar pack's home. Oak had gathered the pack that morning and told them they needed to join forces with the Cedar pack if they were to survive. Some wolves disagreed, but all wolves went along with it. Some had even volunteered to be on the patrol, like Shadow and Miku. The rest of the wolves had stayed back, hunting or protecting the weak. Shadow padded along in the middle of the group right behind Scout.

They crossed the border into Cedar pack territory. Oak leaped over the stream, then Scout, then Storm. Shadow went next. She readied her muscles and leaped over the small three-foot-wide stream, the ferns brushing against her belly fur as she landed on the other side. The rest followed and then, in formation, they began to trot again. Shadow couldn't help but fear what Slate would say about them entering their territory unannounced. The Cedar pack land had also been scarred by the fire. Almost as badly as the Aspen pack territory had been. Trees had been burned to the ground. The ferns and bushes were nothing but ash. Shadow guessed that the fire had traveled through the air and caught on to the trees here, lighting them up. Shadow gave a silent prayer that none of their wolves had died.

No wolf said a word as Oak led them deeper and deeper into the Cedar packs' land. Shadow grew nervous as they reached a burned clearing that looked to have been home to wolves. She surveyed the large clearing, frowning as she saw that everything was burned to the ground. "The Cedar pack's den site has been destroyed, too," Oak said, almost under his breath. The wolves nodded.

"Follow the scent," Scout said, sniffing the ground and beginning to trot in a different direction, towards the river. Shadow followed, then Oak, then the rest of the wolves. They trotted behind Scout for a while, listening to him murmur things to himself until suddenly he stopped. "They're behind this hazel brush," he said to them, turning to Shadow. She sniffed the air and angled her ears in front of her. She caught the scent of many Cedar pack wolves and heard them talking quietly. Some of the sounds were blocked by the noise of the river, but Shadow was sure that some of the Cedar pack wolves were behind the towering hazel thicket, but probably not all.

"Okay," Oak said, taking charge once more and trotting up to Scout. The Tracker dipped his head and turned back to join the rest of the group. Oak then turned to the thicket and veered around until he was facing the far side. "Greetings," he called. His greeting was followed by snarls and lots of voices.

"Oak?" a booming voice echoed from the other side of the wall. Shadow stepped forward and stood beside her father, looking in at what he saw. The Cedar pack wolves were staring at them wearily, snarls echoing from their throats and fur standing on end. Some of them were extremely scrawny, just skin and bone. Others were built more sturdily, but still extremely underweight. They looked in no shape to be fighting but still held their ground. A large female with long silver fur and grayish-green eyes was snarling at them, her head low. Shadow guessed she was the Guard because she was the only one sitting on this side of the clearing, guarding the entrance. Shadow looked around trying to locate the Alpha and spotted him standing on a fallen tree trunk. His lips were pulled back in a snarl and his fur was standing on end.

"Hello, Slate," Oak said, stepping forward and dipping his head slowly, showing deep respect. Shadow followed his movements then stood up to face the leader. Slate was a large, well-built, well-muscled male wolf with long silver fur and scars covering his body. He had savaged ears and one milky blue eye, which Shadow guessed was blind. A long, pink scar ran down his face. His other eye was a warm golden color. He looked to be about five or six years old but was still in good shape. He was hungry-looking, like the rest of his pack, but still looked like he could take down a deer with a single swipe of his paw. Shadow felt like she should be frightened by his appearance, but she only felt defiant toward him. He was almost two times Oak's size, and yet Shadow's father stood up to him confidently. "We come in peace, Slate. My packmates have no intention of invasion," Oak said calmly, waving his tail. Amber, Luna, Scout, and Miku emerged from behind the brambles, all dipping their heads slowly.

"Silver, back off," Slate said, twitching his ears. The she-wolf with the grayish-green eyes stopped snarling, though she was still glaring at Shadow and her packmates. Slate jumped down from the tree trunk, eyes weary, muscles rippling under his fur. "What do you want, Oak?" he snarled, unfazed by the Aspen pack wolves' arrival and walking toward them with power.

"I would like to speak with you, in private," Oak said evenly, twitching an ear. Storm opened her mouth to object, but Oak hushed her with a twitch of his ears. Slate thought for a moment, staring at Oak, expressionless. Eventually, he gave a reluctant nod.

"Very well, Oak. But, I do not have all day, and you had best not be wasting my time," he growled. *Was that a threat?* Shadow's ears flattened and she let out a quiet growl as Slate led Oak toward the oak tree trunk he was standing earlier, his tail raised in the air.

The Cedar pack wolves were sitting uneasily, staring warily at the Aspen pack wolves or talking to each other under their breath. Shadow recognized Aria, Slate's mate, and the Alpha female. She was a light gray, sleek-furred she-wolf with a long scar running down her shoulder. She also had a single light blue eye on her right side and a golden-brown eye on her left. She looked almost like Slate. She was the same build, maybe a little smaller, and had scars covering her pelt. She had a long bushy tail and a light brown stripe running down her spine from her ears to her tail tip. Shadow also recognized Venus, the Healer, a small, dark brown she-wolf with white flecks of fur surrounding her eyes and a white tail tip. She also had one white paw and white ear tips, with blue eyes and large ears. She was sitting beside a male wolf that Shadow recognized as Birch, the Beta. He was a tall, white-furred male with brown spots dotting his flank and tail. He also had brown paws and ears and amber eyes. His fur looked sleek. He didn't have as many scars as the two Alphas, but he had some.

None of the wolves looked to be injured from the fire but they were all skittish and wary, with ears pinned to their heads and fur standing on end, muscles tensed. Shadow and her group sat huddled together at the edge of their makeshift shelter, eyes darting from side to side or watching Oak talk to Slate. They were deep in conversation, sitting on the oak trunk, heads low and close together. Aria had joined them and was listening, putting in a comment every so often. They looked like their talk was ending and Slate looked cooperative. Oak looked confident as he jumped down from the tree trunk and trotted over to join Shadow and the rest of the group. He turned and whispered something to Storm before turning and looking up at Slate and Aria, eyes hopeful. They were standing side-by-side, faces intense, foreheads creased with concentration.

"Cedar pack," Slate howled, and the pack turned to him, ears perked. "In two days we will meet with the Aspen pack and travel with them to find a new home together, as one pack. Once we find a suitable home we will split apart once more and return to normal life. Oak and I have reached this agreement. If there are any complaints, keep them to yourselves. This is the only way to survive." His words were loud and clear. The Cedar pack broke into murmurs, shooting glances at the Aspen pack wolves and at Slate. The Cedar pack Alpha was staring at Oak as if silently telling him to leave. Oak dipped his head and turned away, leaving from the way they had come. Shadow and the rest of the patrol followed, hope flaring in her chest. Maybe they would succeed in finding a new home after all.

Shadow jumped from rock to rock to cross the river, her paws sliding on the wet stone as she made her way across. Miku was following her. They had been tasked with hunting far away from the river, where the prey would be untouched by fire or cruel humans. Sparrow and Heather would be coming after they finished helping Max build up a shelter for Lynx's pups. Shadow bunched her muscles and jumped to the next rock, enjoying the feeling of the mist from the water as it stuck to her underbelly. When she reached the other side, she turned to see Miku land beside her. "Maybe we can fish later. I saw some big fish earlier," he said as he padded up to her, shaking water from a paw. She nodded, glancing at the shiny water as it slid past the rocks they had used to jump across.

"Good idea," she nodded, turning and slipping through the ferns and into the underbrush. Miku followed quietly. The scents of the forest calmed her, and she enjoyed the feeling of wet leaves under her paws as she walked along a thin path that her packmates were using. She was so used to stepping on charcoal and ashes that she had almost forgotten what it had felt like to have her fur brush against ferns and her feet stir up leaves. This was the first time that she had been across the river, and it felt good to relive memories of walking through the forest with Miku, not a care in the world. Now, they had many things to worry about, however, and were on a mission to hunt and bring back as much prey as they could. The pack needed strength before they left the territory for good.

Oak told the rest of the pack about what had happened with the Cedar pack almost as soon as they returned. Shadow's packmates were relieved to hear they had a better chance of finding a good home. It gave them hope, and that was exactly what they needed. *Hope.* There had been so much pain and destruction, but now there was finally something to look forward to. Shadow veered along the path, relishing the sounds of the forest around her. Birds chirping overhead, the faraway sound of the river, and the singing of leaves in the breeze. It was just about evening, the sun beginning to set over the treetops, and a slight breeze was picking up. She looked up at the sky just as a roll of thunder rumbled in the distance. Only now did she notice the dark clouds that were building in the sky. The breeze ruffled her fur, sending a chill down her spine.

"Come on, Miku, let's hurry up," she said, craning her neck to look back at him. He gave a nod and Shadow quickened the pace to a steady trot. Soon, they reached a thick patch of ferns and began hunting. Shadow lowered her head and turned to Miku. "Spread out. We can cover more ground that way," she said quietly. She swiveled her ears listening for any signs of prey. Nothing. Miku gave a nod and rushed off away from the fern patch, his tail tip disappearing in the bushes as he did so. Shadow took a deep breath and closed her eyes, taking in her surroundings. She blended with the forest. She let her feet merge with the ground. Let her ears stretch up to the sky. She went completely motionless and listened.

Shadow sensed something off to her right. She snapped her eyes open as she turned her body in that direction, her gut tugging her forward. She moved ahead slowly until she heard a soft chewing noise that only one animal could make. She slipped silently forward and angled her ears to the front. There, in the clearing, sat a huge rabbit, nibbling on some raspberries from a nearby raspberry bush. It was facing away from her, its white bushy tail bobbing up and down as it moved carefully, eating swiftly. Shadow instantly shot forward with the speed and stealth of a Hunter, biting into its neck and snapping its spine. She felt a rush of satisfaction at her kill. This animal would feed two, if not, three wolves tonight. She then carefully hid it under a fern bush and masked its scent with leaves and dirt to keep it safe from other predators. Shadow then returned to hunting, venturing deeper into the forest, ears strained to hear the slightest noises.

Shadow continued for some way before hearing a clucking noise coming from behind a hazelnut bush. She tilted her head to the side, her ears strained forward, trying to catch the noise again. She heard the shuffling of leaves and what sounded like a bird pecking at the ground. Shadow lowered her head and slowly crept forward, peeking from behind the bush. She spotted three, no four, big birds moving slowly across a small clearing and pecking at the dirt. They were speaking to each other in gobbles and chirps. They had dark brown feathers with beady black eyes and red necks, and they seemed not to sense her presence. She remembered something that Sparrow had told her. Something about big birds like this that fit all the physical traits. He called them turkeys, she thought. She racked her brain trying to remember how he had told her to kill them. *Did he say to bite their throats first?* She thought with frustration.

Suddenly, one of the birds let out a series of loud calls and began flapping its wings towards Shadow. She panicked, lunging from where she hid and sinking her teeth into its neck. She bit down hard, cracking the bones and crushing its windpipe. Its cries died as it went limp in her jaws. She dropped it and lunged at the next turkey, cutting its cries off as she bit into its feathery neck. It pecked frantically at her eyes before eventually going limp, dead. Shadow turned to kill another but was instead met with an empty clearing. She went completely still and swiveled her ears around, trying to catch the sounds of the other two birds. She heard nothing but the sound of the wind blowing through the treetops. They must have escaped.

Miku's scent washed over her as he appeared carrying a small vole. "Hey, Shadow, I heard some…" he stopped as he saw her two kills. "Holy…Wow! Shadow, these birds are the biggest prey I've seen in weeks! What are they?" he asked, dropping his vole and moving closer to the bird closest to him. He sniffed it cautiously.

"They are turkeys. Miku, stay here and guard these two. I have to go catch the other two," Shadow said quickly. Turning, she pushed through the ferns without waiting for an answer. Shadow pressed her nose to the ground and almost instantly caught scent of the birds. She followed the scent until she heard chirping. The birds were together, eyes darting from side to side as they checked their surroundings, still unaware of her presence. Shadow lunged forward, pinning one to the ground while closing her teeth around the other's neck. They let out cries of pain and fear as Shadow quickly killed the one she was holding in her teeth before turning to drive her bloodied fangs into the other's spine. She cracked the bone, feeling the bird go limp under her paws. Shadow sat back with satisfaction, licking the blood from her lips and staring at the two dead birds. She then dipped her head to the birds and gave thanks that their lives had ended to save others.

After sitting in silence for a few moments Shadow stood and collected her prey. This was a good day for the Aspen pack. They would eat well tonight. She turned and trotted back to Miku, tail raised and ears perked with triumph. Miku was accompanied by Sparrow and Heather, Shadow's rabbit at their paws, the two turkeys were set to the side and were closely guarded by Miku. Shadow guessed Heather or Sparrow had found her rabbit and grabbed it. Sparrow was the first catch sight of her, his eyes lighting up as he saw the birds she was carrying. "Shadow! The pack will eat well tonight thanks to you." Heather and Miku both stood, smiling, tails wagging.

"This is the biggest meal the pack has had in months!" Heather said brightly, picking a turkey off the ground. Miku picked up another turkey while Sparrow took a turkey from Shadow and collected the rabbit. Miku also took up his vole, grinning sheepishly as if comparing it to the turkey he was already carrying.

"It's a gift. A miracle, if you will, that I found these. The pack really needs this," Shadow said, smiling as she fell into line with Miku. He nodded, giving her a sideways glance, a grin plastered on his face. They walked in comfortable silence until they came to the river where Shadow stopped. Sparrow and Heather emerged from the bracken behind her, their expressions light. Shadow was first to cross, bunching her muscles and leaping onto the first slippery stone. The weight of the turkey threw her off balance and she clamped her jaws tighter to keep from letting go. "Careful with the turkeys!" she called over her shoulder.

With five more of these slippery wet stones to go, she took a deep breath, bunched her muscles once more, and jumped. Her paws slipped as they hit the slick, wet rock. One of her paws slid over the edge of the rock where it was tugged at by the rushing water. Her eyes widened with fear as she scrambled backward, grappling for a hold on the rock. Her claws found a paw-hold and she stopped herself from falling, swallowing back the bile in her throat. She clamped her jaws firmly on the turkey as Miku called from behind her, "Be careful!" Shadow took another deep breath and jumped to the next stone, trying not to let the weight of the turkey throw her off balance again. Three more stones. Wolves on the other side of the river began to gather, watching as Shadow jumped to the next stone. Oak was there, standing at the edge of the riverbank and watching with wide eyes as Shadow grappled for a foothold on the stone. She let out a growl and hauled herself upright, determination filling her and giving her strength. Wolves had begun calling out to her, giving her confidence. She could sense that Miku was on the stone behind her. She leaped to the next stone, and then to the next one. Almost there. One more jump. She bunched her muscles for the last time and jumped, landing on the sandy beach and spraying sand around her.

She nearly dropped the turkey but forced herself to keep it in her mouth. Exhaustion nearly overwhelmed her as Breeze and Kele appeared in front of her, Kele taking the turkey out of her mouth. "Wow, Shadow! You caught a bird? Nice job!" Kele congratulated her, and the rest of the pack surrounded her, smiling as Miku, Heather, and then Sparrow landed on the riverbank. Sparrow looked to be having a bit of trouble carrying both the rabbit and the turkey. He staggered when he got to the sand, panting as Oak took the bird from him. The bird's feathers were wet with the water spray, but the meat would be good. Mako took the rabbit, weighing it, and then smiled.

"This will make good meat! We will eat well tonight," he said, looking from Shadow, to Sparrow, to Heather, to Miku. "Who caught this?" he asked, ears pointed upward.

"Shadow caught all of it, except for my vole. I caught that by myself," Miku said proudly, smiling at Shadow. She smiled back, still recovering her strength. The wolves went silent, looking at Shadow.

"She caught *all* of it?" Max asked, grinning, breaking the silence. Shadow's face warmed, and she smiled shyly, nodding.

"Shadow, that's wonderful! You fed the whole pack in one hunt!" Storm said, pushing through the crowd and smiling warmly at Shadow. Shadow couldn't keep her tail from wagging at her mother's praise. Just then a loud boom of thunder rumbled across the forest and lightning exploded in the sky. Rain began pouring down from above.

"Keep the prey dry!" Oak commanded, grabbing one of the turkeys and running towards the shelter of a large willow growing on the bank of the river. Other wolves followed, putting the rest of the prey under the tree to keep it dry. Shadow trotted over to the shelter of a maple tree and laid down below it, eyes drooping from weariness. Miku, Breeze, and Kele followed her. They lay together without a word watching the rain fall on the thirsty ground. The four wolves huddled together as another rumble of thunder shook the ground. Shadow rested her head on Miku's flank and closed her eyes, falling asleep to the calming sounds around her.

Shadow woke to sunlight shining through the branches overhead hitting her eyes. She groaned and opened her eyes, lifting her head to look around. Miku, Breeze, and Kele were still sleeping, their eyes closed, and heads buried under their paws. Shadow smiled, licking Miku's shoulder. He stirred but didn't open his eyes. Shadow looked up. The maple was dripping with last night's rain, but the leaves and branches had kept them mostly dry. The soft bed of leaves under her paws had given her comfort throughout the night. The sky was light blue with white, wispy clouds drifting by slowly. Shadow didn't feel any breeze, and the sun shining down from above the treetops felt good as it warmed the air.

The ground outside the shelter of the tree was soggy. Shadow guessed that it had rained hard for most of the night. Her packmates were all sleeping or talking quietly under trees or willow thickets. It was peaceful. Shadow could hear birds chirping in the nearby trees.

She looked over to where the food had been hidden, smiling to see that it was dry and untouched by other animals. Shadow stood and silently stretched, yawning. She stepped out into the sunlight, smiling as it warmed her pelt. She shivered as a raindrop dripped from the trees above her and landed on her nose. She shook out her pelt and trotted over to the prey, dragging out a turkey. Shadow laid the turkey in the center of the clearing under a patch of sunlight then went back to collect the rest of their meal.

She took the vole for herself and returned to where she had slept, spinning around and curling up next to Miku. She slowly ate the vole as she watched wolves wake up around her, eyeing the prey. Miku suddenly shuddered and yawned, stretching. "Good morning, sleepyhead," Shadow teased. Kele's eyes fluttered open and he sighed, raising his head. Breeze woke, too, yawning. Miku got up, stretched his back, and yawned again.

"Morning," he said sleepily, shaking out his pelt. He then looked up at the sun before looking at the prey. Oak and Storm were beginning to eat, Amber and Luna walking over to them. Sparrow, Heather, Mako, and Scout were walking in a group towards the prey, their spirits high. Shadow stood, followed by Breeze, and finally Kele. "Come on, slowpokes, everyone is going to eat," Miku said, already walking towards the center of the clearing.

Shadow chuckled and followed him, her tail raised light-heartedly. Breeze trotted after them, his limp now barely noticeable. He called Kele, who was trying to go back to sleep. Shadow stopped and ran over to Kele, grinning, grabbing his scruff. Kele was taller than her, but she could still drag him to his feet.

"Ugh, Shadow!" he complained, but she could see he was smiling. She let go of his scruff as he walked with her over to the prey pile, his fur ruffled. Shadow and Kele sat beside Miku and Breeze, their mouths watering.

"Good morning," Storm said. She was holding a half-eaten turkey in her mouth. She dropped it in front of them and sat down, her eyes shining in the morning light. Shadow dipped her head to her mother and smiled, thanking her quietly as Miku, Breeze, and Kele dug into the food. "Shadow, you should eat," Storm told her with a flick of her tail.

"I already had a vole," Shadow said, but her stomach rumbled indignantly. Storm looked at her from the corner of her eye, eyes narrowed.

"A tiny vole won't be enough to satisfy your hunger," Storm said.

"Yes, I know, but I have to put the pack before myself," Shadow replied, glancing at her mother. Storm shook her head.

"You will need your strength to help this pack. Eat," Storm said.

Miku walked over to Shadow carrying a piece of turkey. He dropped it at her feet. "Thanks, Miku," Shadow said, craning her neck to eat the meat. It was tough to chew but tasted like heaven on her tongue. When she finished, she looked around her at her packmates. They had all finished eating and were sitting back with satisfied looks on their faces. Shadow smiled. She was glad she killed those turkeys. They had given her pack strength and a renewed sense of hope.

"Well, we are leaving today. We should hunt more," Oak said as he stood up, surveying the wolves around him with narrowed eyes. "Sparrow, Heather, Scout, Amber, and Breeze, I would like you to go across the river and hunt. After we eat, we will leave. Luna, I would like you to wrap your most important herbs. We will bring them with us." Oak's voice carried across the clearing. Shadow gave a small sigh of relief that she wasn't chosen for hunting. She was still weary from yesterday. She decided she would help Luna with her herbs. Breeze, Sparrow, Heather, Amber, and Scout gathered and Oak sent them off. Shadow then turned to Miku, twitching her ears.

"We should help Luna with her herbs," she said, and he nodded.

"Hey, Luna. May we help?" Shadow asked trotting to where Luna had begun sorting herbs into piles.

"Yes, and I'm glad you asked. Would you start wrapping these piles in ivy leaves? Stick the leaves together with tree sap to hold them together. Here, watch," Luna said, wrapping two leaves around a pile of seeds and sticking them together with a dab of sap on the tip of her paw. "Then just set them to the side."

"Okay," Shadow and Miku said simultaneously, sitting down next to Luna and beginning to put the bundles together. Shadow gently collected ivy leaves with her teeth, then swept a pile of small dark green herbs into the center. She dabbed her paw in a small puddle of sap and closed the leaves together, making sure they closed all the way so no herbs would escape. She pushed the new bundle to the side, then started over. She continued doing this until there were no herb piles left.

"Okay, now we need to figure out a way to carry all of these," Luna said, frowning. Shadow frowned, twitching an ear, thinking.

"I have an idea," Miku said, standing up. "We can put the herbs in a hollow log then drag it with an ivy vine," Miku smiled, obliviously proud of his idea.

"Where will we find a hollow log?" Shadow asked, tilting her head to the side. "I mean, the forest was just burned to the ground."

"I'm sure we can find something," Luna said in support of the idea.

"Ok, Miku and I will go look," Shadow said. Luna nodded. Miku and Shadow raced from the clearing, hopes high. Shadow looked at the fallen trees – some burned, some not – until she finally found something. "Miku, over here!" she called to him over her shoulder. He was looking at some charred trees a short way away. Shadow stared at the log she found. It was about the length of Shadow's body and the width of her flank. It looked like an oak, but it could have been an ash. Half of it was charred, falling apart, while the other half was still strong. The middle was hollowed inward, shaped like a crescent moon, the insides burned away by fire. It would work just fine.

Miku stared at the log before turning to Shadow, grinning. "This is perfect, Shadow!" he exclaimed, moving forwards to sniff it. "I'll go find an ivy vine." Miku raced away toward what was left of the forest. Shadow turned back to the tree trunk, frowning. *How are we going to drag this with an ivy vine?* Then, an idea hit her. If they could somehow put a hole or two in the front of the trunk they could push an ivy vine through and drag the log by pulling the vine. She looked around for something to use to make a hole in the wood. She found a small, sharp rock on the ground and picked it up. Holding it in her mouth, she began carving through the soft side of the wood. Eventually, she created a hole and she went to the other side of the log to make another. She winced as the rock ground on her teeth.

When the holes were completed she smiled. She tasted blood on her tongue and realized that she had cut her gums while she was carving through the wood. Spitting blood, she put a paw on the wood and pressed down, testing its strength. It was strong. Shadow smiled at her creation. Miku returned dragging a long, thick brown vine.

"I couldn't find an ivy vine, but I found this! It's twice as strong. I pulled it off an oak tree," he said proudly, dropping it at her feet.

"Perfect!" Shadow exclaimed, grabbing the end of the vine and pushing it through one of the holes. Then she pushed it through the other hole and pulled it tight. Taking both ends of the vine in her teeth she pulled, surprised at how light it was.

"Perfect!" Miku said, jumping up. Shadow grinned, handing one end of the vine to Miku.

"Just be careful not to bite through the vine," Shadow said. Miku and Shadow pulled together and soon were making their way back to the makeshift shelter at a fast pace. They returned to see the hunters had returned. They were holding two crows, a large raccoon, and a plump squirrel. Breeze was holding the squirrel proudly and she guessed that he had caught it. Shadow smiled as she dragged the log into the clearing and brought it over to Luna, who was looking at the log in astonishment.

"That's brilliant!" Luna exclaimed, walking over to the log. "This will hold the herbs perfectly! I wrapped the bundles in leaves and moss so we know none will fall out," Luna said, eyes wide as she looked at the log.

"Great!" Shadow said as she started loading the web-covered herb bundles into the log. Miku helped load the bundles, and Luna began to arrange them so that they would be sure to not fall out. When they were all loaded they stood by to admire their work before moving off to eat with the rest of the pack. Shadow took a bird to share with Miku and they sat down to eat. Shadow ate her fill, then she sat back in satisfaction.

"How did you make that log?" Kele asked as he appeared at her side, his mouth full of rabbit.

"Well, Miku and I found the log in the burned-out part of the forest. Then, Miku found a vine and I carved a couple of holes in the front. Then, we simply wove the vine through the holes and dragged it along," Shadow said proudly. Miku nodded, his mouth stuffed with bird.

"That's excellent, Shadow! Very creative," Kele exclaimed, grinning, butting her on the shoulder playfully with his snout. She smiled, content with what was happening now. Shadow wished that this moment could last forever, but knew that wasn't possible. She stood up and shook out her pelt, looking up at the sky. It was mid-afternoon, with the sun shining bright, high in the sky. If they were going to leave, it should be now.

"Excuse me," she said to Kele and Miku, turning and trotting toward Oak. "We should leave soon," she said, dipping her head as she approached. He dipped his head to her, licking his lips after he had finished chewing the bird he was eating with Storm.

"We will leave when I say. I was just talking to Storm," he said. Shadow felt a stab of guilt for trying to tell her father, the Alpha, what to do.

"Oh. Okay, sorry," Shadow apologized, flattening her ears with shame. She then turned and looked around for some wolf to talk to. She spotted Lynx talking to Max on the other side of the clearing, so she trotted over to the she-wolf, smiling. "Hey, Lynx," she said as she approached, smiling at the four puppies that squirmed in the curve of their mother's belly, their quiet mewls filling Shadow's heart with love.

"Hello, Shadow," Lynx spoke warmly, smiling, her eyes shining. Shadow sat down beside Lynx, smiling down at her pups. One of them, a small male, squirmed towards her, his little pink nose twitching as he sniffed at her. She lowered her head to look closely at the pup, her heart swelling. The little pup leaned forward and licked her nose.

"Aww!" Shadow exclaimed, eyes warm. She licked the little pup's forehead, smiling with the warmth she would have shown her own pups. "Have you thought of names for them yet?" Shadow asked Lynx, looking up at the she-wolf. Lynx was smiling lovingly, sweeping the little gray pup back towards her belly with her tail.

"We are thinking, but haven't come up with anything yet. They will have names when it is time," Max answered happily, licking Lynx's cheek. Lynx nodded, glancing at her pups.

"They're adorable," Shadow said before tilting her head to the side and looking around. Her eyes landed on Oak, who was standing on a rock about half the size of the Alpha stone, his narrowed eyes surveying the clearing coldly. Shadow walked over to him and sat at the base of the rock. The rest of the pack began doing the same. All, that is, except for Lynx and Max, who stayed where they were, watching from afar.

"We must leave now," Oak declared. "This forest is not meant for us any longer. It has become a place of loss and destruction. We will unite with the Cedar pack and travel with them to a new home. Gather what you need, and I will lead us out." Oak's voice traveled across the clearing, reaching Lynx and Max clearly on the other side. The wolves began chatting with a mixture of excitement and nervousness. Shadow looked around for Miku, her heart racing and mind spinning. When their eyes met she ran over to him, tucking her tail between her legs.

"I'm scared," she whispered. He met her eyes tenderly.

"Me too. But, we're going to make it through this. Together," he said. Shadow smiled.

"Together," she repeated, and they walked off to where Oak was gathering the rest of the pack.

Oak led the pack through the forest toward Cedar pack territory. He held his tail high as they emerged into a large clearing. The Cedar pack was waiting on the other side of the stream, still on their own territory. Slate and Aria were sitting beside the water, watching the Aspen pack with narrowed eyes as they entered the clearing. "Greetings," Oak called. He and Storm walked forward to meet the Cedar pack Alphas. Shadow and the rest of the pack sat uneasily in the clearing, paws itching to leave. Oak, Storm, Slate, and Aria talked for a while before they dipped their heads to one another and returned to tell the rest of their packs the plan.

"We will walk along the stream until we reach the edge of the territory. Then, we will cross the river and head north. We do not know what we will find there, but it is our best chance at finding a better, safer home." Oak said all this to his pack after gathering them together with a wave of his tail. The wolves nodded their heads in agreement. Shadow also nodded and twitched an ear. *This is our best hope,* she thought. She looked over at Lynx, who was carrying one of her pups. Max,

Scout, and Heather were carrying the other three. Shadow reminded herself to offer Lynx help later if she noticed any of them getting tired. Luna was dragging the tree trunk filled with herbs, her eyes showing excitement mixed with nervousness. Oak began walking along the edge of the streambed, Storm at his side, Amber right behind. Slate, Aria, and Birch began walking, too, and the rest of the pack followed. Shadow fell in between Miku and Kele. Oak was setting a quick pace—almost a trotting speed—but no wolf complained. They were leaving the territory. Shadow passed a giant half-charred oak tree and a pile of ashes that must have once been a bush of some kind. She looked out at the vast destruction from the fire. Sadness pricked her heart once more as she realized that she would never see her beloved home again.

Chapter Fifteen

Shadow walked in the middle of a group of wolves, the scent of the Cedar pack surrounding her. It was now two days since they started their journey. Soon after leaving the clearing the Cedar pack was using as a temporary home, they reached the edge of the territory and were forced to cross the river. They found a birch tree that had fallen over the water and crossed that way without any casualties. The packs had joined, and they walked until their feet turned raw, finally stopping for the night when it was too dark to go on and the winds chilled their pelts. They sheltered from the weather by hiding behind a pile of large boulders.

Shadow hadn't slept well. Her slumber was disturbed by a midnight chill, and her paws ached from the long walk. In the morning, the packs woke early and hunted. Shadow, Sparrow, Heather, and Scout were chosen from the Aspen pack, while Echo, Fog, and Reed joined them from the Cedar pack. They hunted for a long time before returning with two big hares, a trio of cottontail rabbits, and three birds. The packs ate and were now on the move again, Oak, Slate, Aria, and Storm in the lead. Shadow found it strange traveling with so many wolves. Miku was at her side, with Kele on her other side, and countless other wolves surrounding them. Walking quickly, talking quietly. The Cedar pack had merged with the Aspen pack, and now some wolves were interacting, warming up to each other, or growing to dislike each other even more.

Shadow was forced to break up an argument between Kele and a Cedar pack wolf, Bone, over the fair share of prey. Bone was a mean-looking wolf with several scars and pale white fur. He was now walking at the back of the pack, making sure no wolves were falling behind. Amber, Mako, and another Cedar pack wolf named Creek were also in the back. Silver from the Cedar pack was always picking fights. She got into a tussle with Max about prey as well. She was arguing that Lynx was getting all of the prey, and Max had retaliated angrily. The Cedar pack wolves had elders within their pack named Cinder and Mallow. Cinder was almost completely blind, and Mallow was blind in his left eye. They walked together in the front, urged along by their packmates as they complained about their paws being sore. Lynx seemed to be doing fine. She was flanked by Max, Breeze, and Heather, who were each carrying one of her pups. The pups grew hungry quickly, so the pack had to stop frequently and let her feed them. Max was constantly running to find more food for his mate, with the help of any other wolves he could gather. Shadow stayed busy helping Luna drag her bundles of herbs. They switched frequently. It was a heavy load, and Luna grew tired easily.

As the sun was setting the combined pack finally stopped. Oak and Slate ordered out two hunting groups, one from each pack. Shadow was not chosen to join the hunt. She gave a silent sigh of relief and collapsed on a pile of ferns, sighing. Her paws throbbed and her head hurt from the long, grueling walk. Dragging that herb-filled log had sapped her energy. Luna was sitting beside Lynx, feeding her some herbs. Lynx was nursing her pups with Max looking on and licking her gently in between her ears. The rest of the wolves found places to rest under rocks and trees, or on top of ferns and shrubs. None of them took the time to dig out sleeping holes, knowing they would be back on the move in the morning. Shadow watched as Max cleaned his pup's fur. Her attitude toward him had changed, she realized. She now saw him as more of a friend than an authority figure. She thought of him as an equal, and no longer held any resentment towards him.

Shadow turned to Miku, sighing. "The days are getting shorter, and colder," she said. He nodded as if he had been thinking the same thing.

"Yes. I just hope we can find a home before the first snowfall. After that, it will be hard to find anywhere livable."

Shadow nodded thoughtfully. "That's a good point," she said. Shadow looked around. Two unfamiliar Cedar pack wolves were sitting close by, talking and smiling. They looked to be siblings. They had the same body shape and eye color and spoke to each other as littermates would. One of them was a male, with long gray fur and amber eyes. He also had a short, stubby tail. The other was a short she-wolf with creamy gray fur and amber eyes, with a dark gray chest and tail tip. They both looked to be about her age. "Miku," Shadow asked, still looking at the two Cedar pack wolves.

"What?" He replied.

"Should we go talk to them?" she asked, pointing her snout towards the two Cedar pack wolves.

He glanced at them. "What for?" he asked, tilting his head to the side, eyes narrowed.

"I don't know. To get to know the other pack, I guess. We're going to be walking with them for a long time. So, why not make some friends?" Shadow got to her paws and motioned for Miku to do the same. He shot a wary glance at the two wolves before reluctantly standing up.

"They look nice enough…" he said. Shadow trotted over to the siblings.

"Greetings," She said, smiling and wagging her tail friendlily. "Is this spot taken?" she asked, motioning towards an empty spot beside the she-wolf.

The siblings glanced warily at each other before the she-wolf answered, "No." Shadow dipped her head and sat down. Miku approached, smiling.

"May I sit, too?" he asked, and the dark gray male nodded, motioning to a spot beside him. Miku sat down.

"I'm Shadow, and this is Miku," Shadow introduced them formally, dipping her head.

"I am Sage," the she-wolf answered, "and this is Gray, my brother." Gray smiled and twitched an ear in her direction.

"Nice to meet you both!" Shadow said. Gray and Sage both dipped their heads, smiling, shoulders relaxing.

"Why have you come to sit with us? Have you something to tell us?" Gray asked Shadow.

"No. We just thought we should be friendly and sit with you," Shadow said. "Maybe share a little gossip. Make some friends, you know?"

"Yeah," Miku chimed in, smiling.

"Well," Sage replied, glancing at her brother, smiling, "that's a relief. For most of our lives, we've been ignored and cast aside. It's nice to know that some wolves still care."

"What do you mean?" Shadow asked, tilting her head to the side.

"We weren't born into this pack. You see, we were abandoned by our mother beside the river. The Cedar pack found us and took us in. They brought us up but never treated us as equals. Since the fire, things have been changing a little and they have been slowly warming up to us. We saved the elders," Gray said.

"We've earned our way into the pack," Sage explained, smiling.

"I'm sorry to hear of your past," Shadow said, shuffling her paws at the she-wolf's history.

"Thank you, but it's fine! It's all in the past now. What matters now is the future," Gray said optimistically. Shadow smiled.

"So, are you siblings?" Sage asked Shadow.

"No, Miku is my mate," Shadow replied. Sage and Gray nodded.

"I wonder when the hunting groups will return?" Gray asked. "I'm starving!"

"I'm sure they'll be back soon," Sage replied, looking up at the sky. "They've been gone for quite a long time. I hope nothing happened to them." Just as she finished speaking the hunting groups returned. Their mouths were full of prey. Hares, mice, rabbits, birds, voles, you name it, they had it.

"Wow!" Gray exclaimed at the sight of the prey, jumping to his feet. "I've never seen that much food in my life!" Gray raced over to where the hunters were piling their prey. *In his life?* Shadow wondered, twitching an ear with a frown. She thought the Cedar pack had a deer herd within their territory, or at least around their territory. Miku, Sage, and Shadow all stood and walked over to the food pile, waiting with the rest of the wolves as the Alphas took the first pick. The Betas were next, then the Elders and the wolves nursing pups. Lynx took a big rabbit. The Healers, Trackers, and Hunters went next. There was still plenty when Shadow got to pick her share. She picked out three mice and a vole. It turned out that Sage was a Hunter, too, so they picked out their prey together and waited for the rest of the wolves to get their own. After the Fighters and Guards took their share there were only a few scrappy morsels left. They would need to hunt again in the morning.

Shadow sat with Miku, Kele, Sage, Gray, and Breeze in a circle, talking happily and eating their prey. Shadow sat between Gray and Breeze, smiling as Breeze told them about the hunt. "We found a *huge* field that was filled with prey! We caught so much we didn't think we could carry it all back. Tomorrow morning, everyone should go out and catch some! The prey was *plump,* too! It was the best hunting I've had for a long time," he said as he chewed on a rabbit leg.

"Nice job, Breeze! You fed the pack," Miku said.

"Thanks!" Breeze replied. "The Cedar pack wolves are good hunters. Echo is *excellent*. She caught that big rabbit that Lynx is eating." Shadow grinned, along with the rest of the wolves around her.

"Yes, Echo is an outstanding hunter. She was our foster mother, along with Fog, her mate," Sage said, smiling.

"What does Fog look like? I've seen Echo before, but I don't know who Fog is," Shadow said, looking around the clearing. Sage looked around, too, then pointed with her nose toward a tall male wolf with long black fur and dark amber eyes.

"That's him. He's a Hunter, like Echo," she explained. Shadow looked at him, her head tilted to the side.

"He looks cunning," Shadow commented before taking another bite of her vole. Suddenly, a chilly wind picked up and the sun disappeared behind the hills. The moonrise shone brightly in the sky and the stars were starting to peek through the wispy clouds. The sky was painted rich colors of pink and dark blue, and the trees rattled with the wind as leaves from the surrounding aspen trees blew down into the clearing.

"The sky is pretty," Kele said, looking up with wide, shining eyes. All the wolves in the clearing were looking up. It was a beautiful sight. Shadow blinked as a chilly wind cut through her fur and chilled her skin.

"I guess the fall season has begun," Sage muttered, just loud enough for Shadow to hear. Shadow nodded. She took another bite of her vole and looked at the wolves around her. They were continuing to eat, smiling. They looked happy for the first time in a long, long while.

They had been walking for almost a week. Shadow's feet had grown used to the constant pain. So far, there had been no casualties aside from a few minor fights over prey. Oak and Slate worked surprisingly well together. They led the pack easily, Aria and Storm helping them as needed. The Cedar pack and the Aspen pack were close now. They talked to one another with ease. For the most part, at least. Mako and

Bone still hadn't gotten used to each other and remained wary. They would often fight over the littlest things and either Oak or Slate would have to break them up and send them away. "They're acting like pups," Shadow said once to Miku. He agreed with her and they spoke to Gray and Sage about it. They were now close friends. They traveled easily together and talked often about their adventures as Learners. It turned out that Sage and Gray were both accomplished at fighting and hunting, as their mother had taught them at a young age before their mother was killed and they were abandoned.

Shadow continued to help Luna drag her log full of herb bundles, and although it was hard work she enjoyed just being alone and doing a task by herself once in a while. Luna had started taking longer shifts as she was growing stronger by the day. Lynx's pups were thriving. They had just opened their eyes and were now running around playing every time the group stopped to rest. The wolves took turns playing with them, and by the end of the day, the puppies were exhausted. It was fun playing with them. Shadow would roll an acorn and watch the pups chase it, tumbling over one another. Or, she would dangle leaves in the air and see who could reach them first. Shadow was always first in line to be playing with the pups. They were learning to speak, and they could already say Shadow's name. Her heart swelled every time she saw them.

She was now dragging the herb log across the leaves that littered the trail, her muscles burning and her paws throbbing. The vine was in her mouth and she was pulling hard. Every bone in her body ached. Heat pulsed across her skin in waves. Luna was walking in front of her, and Kele was walking at her side. None of them said a word. Shadow had been pulling for quite a while, but she didn't want to give the vine to either Kele or Luna. Luna was limping from stepping on a thorn earlier, and Kele had been complaining a lot about a pain in his legs. It was mid-afternoon, the sun still high in the sky with not a cloud in sight.

The sky was a light blue today, putting every wolf in a good mood. As good as their moods could get, anyway. They were all very tired from walking, and no wolf was exactly 'happy' to not have a home. But they kept walking. No wolf complained, except for maybe the Elders and some pups.

"Why do we have to keep on walking?" one of the pups asked Shadow that morning as she was playing with them.

"Well, because we don't have a home. We have to go and find one," she explained.

"But why? Have we been walking forever?" another of the pups asked.

"No. We had a home once. Before you were born. But...it became unsafe and we had to leave," Shadow said.

"How was it unsafe?"

"Well, there was a human who set fire to our territory, so we had to leave," Shadow replied.

"What's a human?"

"A tall, evil creature that walks on two legs and doesn't have any fur covering its body. If you ever see one, run away from it," Shadow told them.

"Ugh! it sounds ugly," one of the pups said, sticking his tongue out. Shadow laughed and continued playing.

Luna stopped and turned around. "Okay, my turn," she said, stopping Shadow. Shadow obediently gave up the vine and nodded to Luna, who began pulling it forward.

"Come on, Kele, let's go join Miku and Breeze," Shadow said, trotting off toward the two brothers who were walking next to each other. Gray and Sage were with them and they were talking quietly together. Shadow and Kele joined them and jumped into the conversation. Oak branches were spread overhead as they continued walking. Though there were still some oak and maple trees around the area, Shadow was noticing more and more pine and spruce trees as they continued north. Bird calls and the quiet voices of wolves filled the air.

Suddenly, Shadow raised her head and stopped. She smelled a strange, unpleasant smell, mixed with the scent of blood. Deer blood. Her ears were pricked with interest. Maybe there was an injured deer nearby. She looked around and saw the wolves around her could smell it, too. Oak, who was in the front, raised his tail, signaling for the wolves to stop. He was staring straight through the bushes at something. His eyes were wide with surprise. Shadow suddenly heard a few loud barks of a... Dog. The scent grew stronger. She smelled the gross, thick scent of dog breath, and heard the growls coming from behind a thick wall of gray dogwood bushes. Slate had his head lowered and was growling a warning at the dogs behind the bushes.

The wolves around Shadow were tense, slowly beginning to understand what was going on. Shadow, eyes wide, rushed over to Oak and looked at what he was seeing. Other wolves did the same, standing behind the Alphas. There, in a very large clearing, was a group of eight to twelve dogs, all with black and brown fur. Their hackles were standing on end and their lips were drawn back in snarls. They were standing around a dead, half-eaten deer. Behind the dogs was a litter of six puppies that were casually eating the meat from the deer. The dogs were forming a protective line around the deer, their fur on end, mouths dripping with saliva. Wolves around Shadow were growling defensively, while Oak was trying to back away, looking down at the ground, trying not to look like a threat. Slate stared at the dogs, then lunged forward, snarling, as if trying to scare them away. The dogs held their ground. Their beady black eyes shone furiously as Bone from the Cedar pack took a step forward, growling. Shadow lunged at him and pulled him back before he could move again. He snapped at her loudly, startling the dogs, who attacked in defense.

The biggest dog lunged at Slate. It sunk its teeth into his shoulder and pinned him to the ground. Oak jumped in to help, but the other dogs attacked as well, defending their food and their offspring. Shadow watched with wide eyes as one big dog lunged at her, snarling ferociously. She sidestepped, but not quickly enough. The dog got a grip on her tail and was pulling her down, sneering. She yelped in pain and snapped at its ear, just missing. It reared back and tried to hit her in the head with its paws, but she ducked under its blows and bit into its soft underbelly. The dog howled in pain and kicked at her, clawing at her face. She let go, panting, as the dog lunged again, ramming into her shoulder and pinning her to the ground. She kicked with her hind legs, scratching deep into its belly. It stumbled back, whimpering, blood dripping onto the ground. She took its weakness as an advantage, lunging forward and biting into its neck. She pinned it down, holding it by the neck until it nearly went limp. She let go and the dog scrambled away yelping. Shadow turned in a circle to see what was going on around her.

Oak and Slate were driving the Alpha dog back together, while Storm and Aria were fighting back-to-back against two huge dogs. The rest of the pack seemed to be doing fine until, suddenly, Shadow heard a loud howl coming from a wolf on the other side of the clearing. She spun around to see a Cedar pack wolf, Creek, pinned to the ground by two large dogs that each had her by the throat. Shadow put on a burst of speed and reached the dogs in seconds. She let out a savage snarl and plowed straight into one of them, her canines automatically connecting with its neck. She snapped her jaws shut and heard a loud *crack*. The dog instantly went limp. Shadow then turned to the remaining dog. Its teeth were buried in Creek's neck and her blood was pooling on the ground. Shadow let out a howl and lunged at the dog, biting through its ear and tearing most of it away. The dog howled in pain and let go of Creek's neck, falling backward. Shadow bit into its paw and snapped it backward, anger surging through her body. The dog howled in agony and lay on the ground, bleeding, its paw bent back awkwardly.

Shadow turned to Creek, horror shaking her body when she saw the she-wolf wasn't moving. Shadow pressed on Creek's neck, trying to hold in the blood that ran through her paws. Creek's eyes were wide open and staring blankly up at the sky. Shadow was unable to move, overwhelmed by shock. Suddenly, a wolf appeared at her side and her ears were filled with a heart-shattering wail. Reed, Creek's only brother, crumpled next to his sister, sobbing into her fur.

"Creek, no! No, no, no, how could this happen?" he sobbed, his body shaking as he cried. Shadow sat beside him and let out a whimper.

"I'm so sorry, I couldn't save her in time," she said, her voice shaking, eyes screwed shut. Reed whirled on her, teeth bared and cheeks stained with tears.

"Get away, Aspen pack scum! You killed my sister!" he snarled, his face contorted into a mixture of anguish and hate. Miku appeared at Shadow's side and glared at Reed, but the male was already back whimpering into his sister's fur.

"Shadow, let Reed mourn with his pack," he said after a moment. He then led her slowly toward Kele and Breeze, who were watching with wide eyes. The rest of the Cedar pack began to form a circle around Creek, tears in their eyes. Some of them were shooting angry or sympathetic looks at Shadow. Cinder and Mallow, Creek's parents, were crying next to their son. *I was only trying to help! I didn't kill her!* was what Shadow wanted to say, but she knew Reed wasn't thinking straight. The battle was over. The dogs were gone from the clearing. They had taken the deer. They must have dragged it away, for there was a trail of blood leading into the bushes. Shadow sat sadly in a group of her packmates as the Cedar pack mourned, howling to show their sadness. Luna and Venus were treating wounds, while some Aspen pack wolves were dragging away the bodies of the dogs who had died. Aspen pack wolves that had been friends with Creek were sitting with the circle of Cedar pack wolves, mourning silently. Regret filled Shadow's mind. If only she had been quicker, maybe she could have saved her. She hung her head in shame while Miku sat beside her, embracing her silently. She breathed into his pelt, despair hanging in the air around them.

The next morning the wolves were awake and getting ready to leave. Shadow was sitting with Lynx's pups, trying to force a smile. Creek's death troubled her mind. The she-wolf's blank stare and the way Reed had cried into her lifeless pelt tugged at her heart. She shuddered at the memory, half-heartedly kicking an acorn for the pups to fetch. The Cedar pack wolves had buried Creek during the night and the packs had howled for her spirit, helping it to pass on to the stars. Shadow hadn't slept. The Cedar pack was still mourning her death and none of the wolves were in a very good mood. The Aspen pack gave them support and urged them to keep going.

"All right, let's get going," Oak called loudly from the fallen oak tree trunk he was standing on. The wolves around Shadow stood up. Luna took the hollow log that was filled with herbs and others took charge of Lynx's pups. They began walking, following Slate and Oak as they led the pack away. Shadow was one of the last to leave, making sure that all the wolves had exited the clearing before she followed. Miku was waiting for her at the rear of the group. She joined him and they began walking.

"Ugh, we've been walking for hours," Miku complained quietly to Shadow as they walked side by side through the undergrowth. Shadow sighed in agreement and silently kept walking, listening to her packmates' voices around her. Every wolf was grumbling about being tired, yet Oak and Slate just kept on pushing forward, ignoring the complaints of the wolves. They had crossed streams and rivers; passed human dens; gone through valleys and fields of corn; crossed the black paths that humans used to move from one place to another; and walked through forests during the days that they had been walking. They only stopped to hunt in the evenings and sleep during the nights. The packs were exhausted. The Cedar pack elders collapsed a couple of times during the journey and other wolves were forced to carry them. They had gone hungry for many nights now. Prey was scrawny and hard to come by, as they were usually forced to hunt in places with very little shelter for animals or areas infested with humans.

They hadn't yet had any trouble with humans, or any other animals for that matter, other than the dogs that had killed Creek. The she-wolf's death still hung in the air like a storm, and the Cedar pack wolves were still mourning her. Shadow had tried to speak with Reed a few times to give her condolences, but Reed was avoiding her. Still, they were forced to move on. Slate and Oak woke the packs early for the past days and they had walked until the moon was rising. Now, it was evening and the sun was hidden behind dark gray clouds that blanketed the sky. Shadow could hear thunder in the distance. She sniffed the air and smelled rain coming their way. She kept on walking, frowning at the ground. She hoped they would stop soon. The packs needed sleep and her paws felt like were about to fall off.

Glaring at the sky as a drop of rain fell on her nose, Shadow sighed. She shook her head and kept walking. She was aware of the sound of thunder that was getting closer by the second. Suddenly, there was a downpour. Rain pounded them from the sky, shaking the ground as the clouds released all the water they had been holding. Shadow listened to the grumbles and whines of the wolves around her as the rain soaked them to their skin. They walked on without a word from Oak or Slate.

Lynx's pups were complaining about being wet and Luna was fretting about her herbs getting soaked. Still, they kept marching on.

In an instant, the world around her lit up with a sharp bolt of lightning just as a horrific crack of thunder shook the ground. Wolves cried out in fear as multiple lashes of thunder and lightning exploded around them. Shadow's ears rung painfully as an enormous boom of thunder rattled her bones. She heard the sizzle of lightning before a bright flash of light blinded her and a crack of thunder seemed to burst in her head. She looked around to see wolves cowering under trees, huddled together in fear.

Shadow pressed against Miku and they splashed through the mud to a thick pine tree, hiding together under its overhanging boughs. Kele and Sparrow joined them, and they huddled together in fear. Rumbling thunder shook the ground, and sizzling lightning lit the sky. Shadow spotted Lynx and Max, covered in mud, as they shielded their pups from the lashing winds and pelting rain. Luna was with them, her herbs stashed away under a thick elderberry bush. A huge crash of thunder, louder than those before it, exploded around them. Shadow watched as a zigzag of pure white light streaked from the sky to hit the base of a giant aspen tree. Fire instantly burst from the touch of the lightning and the tree began to fall. Shadow screamed as the huge aspen fell heavily towards them, the wood creaking painfully as it fell.

Shadow scrambled with Miku, Sparrow, and Kele to get out of the way, sliding on mud as they ran. Running clear, they stood panting as the tree crashed to the ground, its branches shaking with the impact. There were howls of fear and horror from the wolves as more thunderous explosions shook the air. Shadow scrambled over to Luna, Lynx, and Max, and hid with them, shaking uncontrollably. "Are you all right?" Lynx asked, her eyes wide and body shaking with fear. Shadow forced herself to nod, even though she really wasn't. She sat pressed against

Max. Miku was at her other side, shaking as badly as she was. She was drenched to the bone, shaking weakly. Her eyes were wide open with fear as lightning continued to streak across the clearing.

The rest of the night was awful. The storm continued right up until dawn when it finally began to clear. Every time Shadow found herself drifting off into sleep, a crack of thunder would shake her right back into consciousness. Finally, it was morning and the sun was beginning to poke out from behind the still dark-gray storm clouds. There was mist in the air and droplets of water were showering from the trees with every gust of wind. Shadow, who was soaked even hiding under the pine tree, sat huddled against Miku. He was looking out wearily. The ground outside was as muddy as a swamp. Shadow could see the wolves around her cowering under trees and rocks. The only noises she could hear were the breathing of her packmates and the faint tweeting of birds in the distance. Shadow stood hesitantly and crawled from under the pine tree, looking at the sky and sniffing the air. The scent of rain and mud hung thick in the air, but there was no more thunder. The clouds were finally rolling away and the shadows slowly fading.

Shadow gave a deep sigh of relief and then shook the rain from her pelt until she was dry enough to be satisfied. She looked back at Miku. "It's good to come out now," she said, loudly enough for every wolf to hear. Wolves slowly began coming out of their hiding places, looking warily at the sky. Shadow looked down at herself and saw that she was covered in mud. She growled and began cleaning herself with her tongue, filling her mouth with a bitter, sandy taste. As wolves began to talk about hunting, she found a not-so-soaked place to sit and groom her fur, pulling out leaves and bits of twigs. When she was done, she looked up to see a nearly cloudless sky. Her packmates were milling about, beginning to sort out hunting groups. Shadow volunteered, of course, and went out to hunt with Sparrow, Sage, and Breeze.

They returned with two rabbits and a vole. As she watched the pack eat Shadow became unbearably weary. She ate a mouse that Heather brought back with the other hunting group and nearly fell asleep propped up against a fir tree. But, paws had shaken her awake and Luna told her that the packs were moving again. Shadow got up sadly and helped Luna drag her herbs.

It was afternoon and they had been walking since early morning. Shadow's paws were scabbed and red and her legs were screaming at her to stop. She could tell that other wolves were feeling the same. She shook her head vigorously to keep herself from collapsing as she dragged Luna's herbs across the weeds and grass. The log seemed to be getting heavier by the minute. When it was finally Luna's turn to take over, Shadow went sorely over to Miku to walk beside him. She was practically blinded by exhaustion when Oak finally stopped them for the evening. Shadow collapsed on a pile of leaves and pine needles and fell asleep almost instantly.

Shadow woke to a paw shaking her shoulder urgently. She drowsily opened her eyes to see Sparrow looking down at her, his eyes shining. "Shadow, wake up, wake up," he was saying.

"Wh…What?" Shadow asked sleepily, her words sluggish.

"Shadow, we need you. I'll explain once you get up. Miku, you too." Shadow noticed Miku sleeping next to her. He was lying on his back, paws in the air, tongue lolling out of his mouth. Sparrow shook him awake. Miku let out a yelp, rolling onto his side to face the male wolf.

"Sparrow, what is it? I was just sleeping – it's the middle of the night," Miku growled.

"Get up," Sparrow said sharply. Shadow forced herself to her paws. She felt better after that deep sleep and her legs felt refreshed. She stretched her sore muscles, yawned, and shook the pine needles from her pelt. She looked up to see a half-moon in the sky, the moonlight shining brightly down through the clear night sky and filling the clearing with light. Shadow observed a group of wolves standing impatiently, waiting for Sparrow to wake Shadow and Miku. The group included Oak, Slate, Storm, Aria, Breeze, Heather, Sage, Scout, Fog, and Reed. Most of the others were asleep, though Amber, Birch, Silver, and Max were sitting together quietly at the other side of the clearing, watching with shining eyes.

Shadow turned to Sparrow. "Okay, we're up, now what's going on?" Miku stood up beside her, yawning deeply. Sparrow began walking quickly over to the group of wolves, beckoning Shadow and Miku to follow with his tail.

"Oak and Slate sent out a small group to look for predators or prey in the area. Oak's group came back with a report of a small herd of deer roaming the woods. The Alphas ordered that we find the herd and bring down a deer or two for the pack. It will be the biggest meal we've had in many, many days!" Sparrow exclaimed, glancing over his shoulder at Shadow and Miku as he spoke. Excitement coursed through Shadow's veins at this news. They were going to bring down a deer! It's been a long time since they have had the taste of deer meat.

"Great! Let's go then," Shadow replied. She gave a nod to Oak, who was watching her. He gave a nod in return and led the group into the forest.

They walked in the moonlight for a long time until Oak finally gave the signal that he had found the deer. He waved his tail in a downward movement and at once all the wolves behind him dropped into a stalking position. They advanced swiftly and silently, ears instinctively strained to hear any sounds of the animals. Shadow was one of the last to catch sight of the deer. Three does and one buck deer were standing together in a large moonlit clearing, grazing quietly on grass and berries. The wolves instinctively formed a circle around the deer, eyes wide at the sight of so much prey in one spot. Shadow's mouth watered at the thought of fresh deer meat.

The clearing was silent. The only sound Shadow could hear was the beating of her own heart. Not a breath of wind rustled a single leaf on a tree above their heads. The deer had no idea that they were about to be attacked. Oak and Slate's collective growls broke the silence and they shot from the bushes side-by-side, targeting the big buck deer. The animal, caught by surprise, reared in defense, swinging its giant hooves at the Alphas' heads. They both ducked, the deer missing Oak by an inch. Shadow, along with the rest of the wolves, shot out of the shadows with snarls of fury and attacked the group of deer. Aria, Storm, Heather, Breeze, Sage, and Sparrow attacked one of the does, while Scout, Reed, Shadow, Miku, and Fog helped Oak and Slate bring down the buck.

They surrounded the buck and attacked from behind while keeping it busy from the front. While its back was turned to her, Shadow lunged forward and bit into its warm flank, the metallic taste of blood filling her mouth. She hung on as the buck reared, snorting angrily. It stomped its feet and Shadow let go just quickly enough to keep from being kicked in the stomach by its hooves. She fell back, letting out a yelp as it turned on her, antlers aimed at her flank. Just as it charged forward, Miku rammed into its shoulder, throwing it off course. The buck stumbled and tripped, going down on one knee. Oak lunged at its neck but was thrown aside as it swung its antlers at him. Oak let out a yelp of pain as he was thrown to the ground. Reed and Fog lunged from behind and bit into opposite sides of the flank. The deer snorted and tried to shake them off, his attempts in vain. Slate lunged forward and dug his canines into its shoulder, while Shadow and Miku each grabbed a front leg. The buck kicked with the leg that Shadow was holding, and she felt her head connect painfully with the ground. She held on, dazed, her head spinning. Scout lunged forward, gripped a leg, and pulled. The deer fell as it struggled to run.

Shadow, still dazed and in pain, bit into its neck and clamped her jaws down, waiting for it to stop moving. As it let out its last strangled breath Shadow squeezed harder, her head spinning. The buck finally went limp and Shadow let go, groaning, blood dripping from her muzzle and pooling around the dead deer's neck. She looked around to see her packmates staring at the deer triumphantly. Shadow looked across the clearing to see the other group of wolves dragging a doe to the ground. Shadow sat down, her head spinning and her vision slowly blurring into darkness.

The next thing Shadow knew, she was lying on the ground, her headache worse than ever. Wolves were circled around her, looking at her with worry in their eyes. She looked around, confused. "Ugh…" was all she managed to get out as her vision began to blur again. Fighting to stay awake she raised her head, wincing as a horrible pain filled her head.

"Shadow, lie down. We just sent Sage to get Luna. Are you all right? You passed out," Miku said worriedly as he gently nudged her. Shadow rested her head on the grass and groaned, the pain in her head not fading at all.

"I hit my head," she groaned, the scent of blood filling her nose. She opened her eyes again to see blood pooled on the ground around her. She was lying in the deer's blood. Had she simply just fallen asleep while she was standing? She almost gagged at the strong scent.

Suddenly, she felt herself wake up again. Wolves were talking anxiously around her. She identified Miku, Oak, Luna, and quite a few more. Had she passed out again? She let out a low groan and opened her eyes, a nauseating pain churning in her stomach. She resisted the urge to vomit, her paws twitching. She whined in pain and looked up, seeing Luna staring down at her, puzzled.

"…Can't seem to find what's wrong with her… hit her head… put some herbs on it… get her back to the rest of the pack…" was all that Shadow heard as she slowly slipped back into unconsciousness.

Shadow woke to the sound of wolves talking beside her. She opened her eyes, wincing as a light blinded her momentarily. It was the sun, and it was already high in the sky. She could hear wolves talking around her and realized she must be back where the pack had been sleeping during the night. She scented Miku and Lynx beside her. She opened her eyes a little wider to see Luna rearranging her herbs in the log and Lynx sitting with Miku at her side. Lynx's pups were nowhere in sight. Well, at least from what Shadow could see. Both Lynx and Miku had worried looks on their faces, and they both smiled when they saw Shadow's eyes open.

"Oh, Shadow, thank goodness you're all right," Lynx said softly as she pressed her snout into Shadow's neck fur. Her scent was of milk and pups and Shadow found herself breathing deeply into the beautiful she-wolf's fur. A warm feeling washed over her as she smelled the familiar scent of milk. She was brought back to when she was a pup and she was safe in the Newborns' den with her mother and Kele. As Lynx pulled away Shadow couldn't help but smile. Miku came over to her and curled up alongside her, licking her cheek.

"The deer kicked me," Shadow croaked, clearing her throat at the sound of her raspy voice.

"Yes. You passed in and out of consciousness on the way back here. We had to carry you. I was so worried," Miku said gravely.

"Hm. I don't remember that," Shadow said slowly, thinking hard. Then she shook her head, realizing with relief that the headache was nearly gone. Luna must have given her some herbs. "Did they get the deer get back okay?" Shadow asked, glancing at Lynx. The she-wolf nodded, smiling slightly.

"Oak said that you killed the buck deer. I wish I could have been there to see it. It's too bad that I had to stay here with the pups," Lynx said, glancing humorously at Max, who was trying to control the four pups but was instead being controlled by *them*. Shadow smiled light-heartedly when she saw one of the pups jump on Max's tail, pretending it was a juicy mouse. One of the other pups clambered up onto his shoulders and flattened him to the ground.

"Ey, get off... What are you... Wait, don't bite my tail! *Hey, get back here!"* Max exclaimed, spinning around in a circle trying to get the pups off him. Shadow bit back her laugh and then glanced at Lynx, who was looking lovingly at her mate and pups. Luna limped over carrying a leaf wrap of herbs in her jaws.

"Here, eat these. They'll help you recover," she said, putting the bundle down in front of Shadow and then sitting down to make sure that she ate them. Shadow obediently licked up the bitter-tasting leaves and swallowed them appreciatively.

"Thank you, Luna," She spoke, dipping her head and trying to stand. Luna watched her cautiously as she slowly got to her paws. Shadow stretched out her sore muscles and then looked around the clearing they had been staying in. What was left of the two deer was pushed up against a big boulder where they were shielded from any rain or wind. Both were almost stripped of their meat, and Shadow noticed the wolves in the clearing had full bellies. Wolves were sitting around talking casually in groups or pairs. Oak and Storm were sitting together on the boulder next to the deer, while Slate and Aria were lying down beside some dogwood brush. Kele and Breeze were talking to Gray and Sage in the shade of a pine tree, while most of the other Cedar pack wolves were talking in a group in the center of the clearing. They were all smiling and laughing, a good mood spreading throughout the clearing. Bright sunlight was shining down from above the treetops, while birds called happily in the branches above their heads.

Shadow listened quietly to the chilly wind rattling the branches of the trees that surrounded them. She also caught the noise of a creek or river close by, recognizing the familiar sound of water moving across the pebbles. Shadow took a few shaky steps forward, heaving a sigh of relief when she felt that she could stand on her own. Tail waving in goodbye to her packmates, she walked over to the deer, her stomach rumbling hungrily. She licked her lips at the sight of the deer meat waiting to be eaten. Shadow didn't hesitate as she bit into the soft flesh and tore off a piece. She chewed happily and then continued eating until she couldn't eat any more. She sat back happily, satisfaction washing over her. Shadow licked the blood off her lips and laid back in the sun, letting its warm rays soak through her fur right down to the skin. She dozed off, listening to the sound of her packmates around her.

Shadow woke later on her own, opening her eyes slowly and glancing groggily around the clearing. The sun was lower in the sky, but not yet behind the trees. Bright white clouds were traveling lazily across the soft blue sky, while birds flew overhead. Shadow, who was lying on her back, rolled onto her side and looked around slowly. She noticed that most of the Fighters from both packs were gone. So were the Trackers and Betas. The rest of the wolves were sitting around lazily, talking or beginning to build up walls around the clearing, so it couldn't be seen from the outside. Shadow sat up, stretched, and opened her jaws in a massive yawn. She then stood and shook the dust from her pelt. She spotted Oak sitting alone beside a cedar tree and trotted over to him.

"Greetings, Oak," She said, sitting beside him after dipping her head respectfully.

"Hello, Shadow," he said, dipping his head in return.

"Where are the Fighters, Trackers, and Betas?" Shadow asked, twitching an ear at him.

"Slate and I sent out groups to check the territory. They haven't yet returned. I've noticed you have been sleeping most of the day. Are you feeling all right? It isn't like you to sleep instead of work. I did see that you hit your head pretty hard when we attacked that deer. I hope it wasn't too bad." Oak spoke slowly as if he had been thinking a lot about it.

Shadow felt the tips of her ears burning with shame when he spoke about her sleeping. "The reason that I've been sleeping is that I have just been exhausted lately. I'm sorry," Shadow replied. "And yes, I did hit my head pretty hard." Shadow looked at Oak wondering if she would see any anger in his eyes at her sleeping for so long. Instead, all she saw was compassion and worry.

"Well, I hope you're feeling better," was all he said. They sat in silence for a few moments before Oak spoke again. "I think that we may have found a good place to live. Right here in this clearing. It has everything we need. Plenty of big trees for making dens, thick underbrush that surely hides prey, a stream that provides water. When the groups come back they will tell us if it is a suitable territory. I'm hoping the deer we saw are a sign that many deer may live here. We need a reliable source of food. I also hope that there are no humans nearby, or any other predators, for that matter," Oak spoke slowly as if thinking about every word.

Shadow nodded as he spoke, agreeing silently with what he was saying. "How are you feeling, Oak? I've noticed that you've been staying in the clearing more than usual. Have you been hurt?" Shadow asked with a slight frown. Oak heaved a deep sigh, then lowered himself down into a more comfortable position.

"No, Shadow, I haven't been injured. My bones are getting old, that's all. It gets harder and harder to walk every day. I'm afraid that I'm not as young as I used to be," Oak confessed, flattening his ears to his head. Shadow stared at him, confused.

"You? Old? No, no. I'm sure it is just the strain of walking so much," Shadow said confidently, though deep down she knew he might be right. Oak just grunted in response.

As if on a signal wolves stood up around the clearing and a large group of Cedar and Aspen pack wolves emerged from behind a patch of spruce trees. They all had smiles on their faces and seemed to be in a laid-back mood. They made their way quickly into the clearing and then broke apart, going to talk to the other wolves that were sitting around. Amber and Birch made their way across the clearing to where Oak and Shadow were sitting. They stopped and waited for Slate, who was emerging from a patch of underbrush that looked like some sort of a den. He made his way over groggily to hear what the Betas had to say, his eyes cloudy from sleep.

"What's the news?" Slate asked, going over to Oak and sitting down, wrapping his tail neatly over his paws. Storm and Aria walked over from where they sat at the edge of the clearing. They sat beside Shadow, ears angled at their Betas, and Shadow suddenly realized they were all accepting her as one of them. None of the Alphas treated her as a lower-ranking wolf – they sat beside her as if she were equal to them. She felt awkward sitting with the high ranks, but she also felt accepted. It felt right to be sitting with them. Looking at their faces, she believed they had all accepted her into their group.

Amber cleared her throat and Shadow's attention was drawn back to the moment. "We traveled through the whole territory," she said. "There is a stream near this clearing that gives a plentiful supply of water. The stream leads to a large fish-filled lake. We also found a meadow that was filled with deer sign. I can assume these will make a very reliable source of food. There is also plenty of prey hidden under the bushes. We found a few fox and badger dens, but nothing too close to this clearing. There are no signs of big cats, humans, bears, or any other predators that could be a danger to us."

Shadow listened calmly, excitement tingling in her paws when Amber finished. *The territory is perfect!* She thought excitedly. Oak looked just as happy as Shadow felt. "Thank you, Amber. Birch, is there anything you would like to add?" As Oak spoke his amber eyes were shining in the dying sunlight.

"Well, there is one thing," Birch began, clearing his throat. "While we were checking the east border, the Trackers caught the scent of what could be a rival pack. They scented wolves on the wind, and stale border marks. We decided to ignore this, but I think that there might be a bordering pack that wants a share of this land."

Oak's gaze hardened as Birch spoke of this rival pack. "That may be something we need to watch carefully," Oak said.

Aria looked doubtfully at the Aspen pack Alpha. "We don't need to bother them If they don't bother us," the she-wolf spoke up, glancing from Slate to Oak, to Shadow, and then to Storm.

"What if they decide to attack without warning? We should find out how many wolves are in their group, where they are set up, and where they hunt," Storm said, looking at the wolves. Shadow sat with her tail wrapped around her paws, listening quietly. She didn't quite know if she should state her opinion, or even if she *had* an opinion.

"I think that we should at least send a group of wolves to check and see what's going on over there," Oak agreed.

"No, that's a *bad* idea. What if they assume we are scouting for an attack and drive us out?" Aria argued, eyes shining defensively.

"Well, obliviously we are going to need to know sooner or later *something* about this pack. We can't exactly just live right next to them and not communicate with them," Oak shot back, his fur beginning to bristle.

"Why would we need to do that? The only thing we need to know is that we are strong. It doesn't matter if they have *a hundred* wolves!" Slate growled, ears twitching.

"We don't even know that it is a *pack*. It could very well just be a group of loners hoping to gain some territory. That's why we need to check," Storm spoke, shifting closer to Oak. Shadow sat between the two arguing sides, glancing at the two Betas as they sat beside each other, watching the Alphas quietly.

Suddenly, Oak turned to Shadow and asked, "Shadow, what do you think that we should do?"

Shadow thought for a moment, glancing at her father before speaking. "I think that we should indeed send, if not a group, at least one wolf to gather some information about the other wolves. It is true that we do not know anything about them, which is why we should check and see if they will be a threat in the future or not. If it is a small group, we should get them away from our land. But, if it is a large group, then we should try to make peace with them. It would be good to have more wolves on our side. If they refuse to make peace, then we should ignore them and hope for them to move on." Shadow spoke slowly, thinking carefully about every word making sure to not offend any wolf. Oak was nodding, the edges of his mouth twitching in a proud look. Storm looked as if she agreed as well, and so did Aria. Slate looked somewhat unfazed, though his hackles were lowering slowly.

"Those are good points, Shadow, but I think that since they are causing no harm, we should leave them be," Slate growled stubbornly.

"If that is what you think, Slate, then you don't have to send any wolves. The Aspen pack will send three wolves to gather information about this other pack," Oak decided, standing up and staring squarely at the Cedar pack leader. Slate gave a reluctant nod of agreement, and then trotted away from the group of Alphas and Betas. Aria followed him, giving a nod to Oak and Storm. Storm spoke a few quiet words to Oak before smiling at Shadow and trotting over to Kele and Breeze, who were talking casually.

"Those were good words, Shadow," Oak praised her, and then turned to the large clearing of wolves. "Aspen pack, gather before me," he barked, and the Aspen pack wolves all made their way over to stand around Oak, their ears pricked. "Tomorrow morning, before the sun has risen, three wolves will go to gather information about the wolves near the east border of this territory. Shadow, Scout, and Amber will make this journey. Amber will lead. Do not confront the wolves – stay under cover. We only wish to know more about them, not to make trouble." Amber and Scout nodded at Oak as he finished speaking. Shadow dipped her head, honored to be chosen for the mission. Oak flicked his tail in dismissal, and the wolves around him broke into groups. Shadow let out a yawn and made her way over to Miku, who was curling up in a hole that he must have dug. She gave a nod of greeting and then laid down next to him, sighing happily.

"I hope we really found our home this time," Miku stated, glancing at Shadow. She nodded in agreement. "I hope so, too. This would be a good place to raise pups," Shadow spoke softly, closing her eyes and burying her nose in her mate's fur. He smiled and rested his head on her shoulder. Shadow soon fell asleep, listening to the quiet sounds of her packmates around her, and the soft noises of the forest around her.

Chapter Sixteen

Shadow trotted silently behind Amber as the small group of three made their way overland toward the rival pack's territory. Scout trotted behind. Shadow felt butterflies fluttering in her stomach as she thought about what they would find across the border. She wondered if it would be a large group or just a few loners. Hopefully, whoever was there didn't plan on staying near the territory the Cedar and Aspen packs chose as their own. The Aspen pack needed as much space that they could get, with Lynx's pups growing so fast and the hope of more pups in the future. Shadow wondered if they would have to drive the rivals away. She hoped not. She didn't want any wolf to be hurt.

Shadow's ears were pricked as she trotted behind Amber and listened to the forest sounds around her. She heard birds chirping overhead, wind rattling the tree branches, and the sounds of her packmates. She looked up, noticing how the lingering oak trees' once-green leaves were now beginning to turn yellow, red, and brown. The beautiful mixture of colors, combined with the light warm sunlight, made Shadow smile. She glanced up as a gust of cool breeze swept through the trees, knocking down a cloud of leaves that were ready to fall. She shivered against the cool morning air, tasting the wind. She smelled the sweet syrupy scent of maple trees, and sap from the pines. It was now autumn, and soon it would be winter. *We will have a new home by then*, she thought.

They crossed the border, heads now low and muscles tense, eyes wide, smelling and listening for signs of the rival pack. Almost instantly, Shadow smelled the marks of another wolf. The smell was coming strongly from a clump of ferns, and Shadow realized that the rival wolves had marked their territory. Their scent was strong. It was definitely a pack. Amber flicked her tail, signaling for Shadow and Scout to be quiet, and they continued at a walk. Soon, they began to hear wolves up ahead. They kept on walking until Amber whisked her tail to the sides signaling that Shadow and Scout should fan out so they could walk three abreast.

Heads low, going upwind, they walked quietly until they reached the wolves' den site. Shadow peeked her head through the bushes, careful to not let her fur get snagged on any branches. It was a large clearing, surrounded by ferns, brambles, hazelnut and dogwood brush, and a few pine trees. There were den holes dug under the roots of the larger trees, and a small creek trailed through the center of the clearing. The pines provided shade to the clearing below. Prey was piled between two of the dens.

Shadow looked at the wolves closely. At first, she thought that they were all wolves, but then she realized that some of them were large dogs. Shadow noticed that all of the wolves had pitch-black fur. The dogs all looked to be the same breed, too, with large shoulders, vicious canines, and massive paws. They had the same fur pattern, a mixture of brown and black colors. The wolves were unbelievably large, with huge muscles and sleek pelts. They were well-fed and in good shape. It would be an even fight if the packs had to drive them out. Shadow backed out of the bushes. She had seen enough.

"Let's go," she said in a hushed whisper to Amber, who nodded in agreement. Just as Shadow spoke, however, the wind shifted, carrying her voice, and her scent, into the rival pack's clearing. Almost instantly, she heard growls from behind the bushes and paw steps getting closer. As Shadow turned to leap away, two large wolves poked through the brambles, their lips pulled back in loud snarls, muscles tense, heads and ears lowered, fur fluffed up to maximum size.

Amber, Scout, and Shadow let out yelps and turned to run at full speed back towards their territory. Shadow heard howls behind them as the rival wolves and dogs left their clearing to give chase. Fear coursed through Shadow's veins, screaming at her to keep going, to run faster. Shadow's group covered ground quickly, not slowing even as they reached their side of the border. Shadow could hear the howls and snarls of the wolves as they chased the three into their territory. They were still following!

"Lead them away!" Amber barked to Scout and Shadow as she skidded to a quick stop. "Keep them away from the den site. I'll go and bring a group to drive them away. Quickly!" Amber growled and disappeared into the brush. Shadow nodded gravely to Scout, and the two squared their shoulders at the rival pack as they approached.

"Keep their eyes on us," Shadow panted, and gave a snarl at the wolves as they broke out of the undergrowth. Shadow and Scout raced off, leading their rivals away from their unsuspecting packmates. Shadow swerved around trees and clumps of brambles as she ran. She could still hear the wolves gaining on them, their jaws snapping with anticipation to hurt, or maybe even kill, the wolves who had intruded on their land. Shadow had never seen this much aggression before in wolves. In the Aspen and Cedar packs, they would only chase rivals off their territory. They wouldn't chase other wolves on their own land.

Shadow's muscles screamed at her to stop, and her lungs felt as though they were ready to burst, but the adrenaline kept her going. She gasped for air, feeling Scout start to slow beside her. Her paws ached. It was now either life or death. If they stopped now, they would surely be torn to pieces. "Keep going!" Shadow coughed, bunching and stretching her legs as they covered more and more ground. Shadow heard the barks and snarls of the wolves gaining ground behind her. She forced herself to keep going. As she ran, she gave a desperate howl for her pack.

Scout abruptly let out a yelp and crumpled to the ground. Shadow looked back to see he had tripped on a root and was lying on the ground, writhing in pain. Her vision blurred and was dimming around the edges. She hoped her pack was near. Shadow leaped to his side and stood over him, protecting him from the rivals as they emerged from the undergrowth, their lips dripping with saliva. She gave a snarl of fury, bushing up her fur to maximum size. The rivals looked undaunted by her stance. Two wolves pushed their way to the front, both of them bigger and meaner-looking than the rest. *The Alphas*, Shadow thought as she snarled at them. They waved their tails for their pack to stay back and then lunged forward.

The female bit into Scout's scruff. Shadow tried to drive her away from him, but the male was already attacking, lunging for her neck. *He is early twice my size!* Shadow thought as she side-stepped, using her agility against his size. She bit into his tail as he flew past her, pulling him to the ground. She jumped on his shoulders and, using her weight, attempted to pin him down. He quickly threw her off and advanced on her, teeth bared as he snarled. Shadow quickly got to her paws as the male butted his head into her ribs, knocking the wind out of her. She wheezed for breath, but didn't back down, staring him in the eyes, challenging him.

Shadow showed no fear. He lunged, as quick as a snake, and his teeth connected with her throat as she tried to dodge him. Her eyes widened, as she knew that he could kill her like this. She let out a whimper and scrambled to get out of his jaws, but he was strong, and his teeth only dug deeper as she struggled. She snapped at his eyes, kicked at his belly, and tried to wriggle out. He held fast. Shadow felt her blood soak into her fur as her attempts grew weaker. She looked over at Scout and saw that he was pinned to the ground, the female's jaws in his neck. She was making him watch as the male killed her. She could see he was bleeding and wished she could help him. Finally, as a last attempt, she went limp, but the male did not let go. He must have still felt her heart beating. As her vision began to go dark, she heard a savage growl from the bushes beside her.

Miku hurled himself at the wolf that was pinning Shadow. Miku had a firm grip on the Alpha's throat, forcing him to release his hold on Shadow. Shadow collapsed to the ground, her blood pooling around her. She blinked away unconsciousness and took a series of gasping breaths. All around her, Aspen and Cedar pack wolves filed through the bushes and attacked the rival pack, their snarls and howls filling the clearing. Although outnumbered, the rivals were larger and stronger than most of Shadow's packmates. Shadow forced herself to her throbbing paws and looked around. Miku and Breeze were taking on the Alpha, while Scout and Mako took on the female.

Shadow spotted Kele through the chaos. He was fighting a female that was almost twice his size. Shadow raced to help him, letting out a howl and lunging at the female, who turned to her with surprise. Shadow bit into the wolf's ear and tore half of it away. The she-wolf let out a cry of agony and lunged at Shadow, teeth just brushing Shadow's neck as she stepped to the side and dodged the attack. Kele hurled himself at the dark-furred rival and dug his teeth into her scruff, planting his paws on the ground and throwing her to the side. The rival turned tail and fled, wailing, into the bushes, back toward her own territory.

Shadow looked at Kele, panting. Warm, sticky blood coated her fur. Kele gave a nod of thanks and then lunged back into the battle, eyes wild. Shadow watched as two more rival wolves fled with their tails between their legs. Shadow spotted Gray and Sage battling a large male dog and looked over to see Slate pinning a she-wolf to the ground.

Aria and Storm were working together against a large male, while Reed and Ebony fought skillfully against one of the larger dogs. Echo, Fog, Silver, and Bone dueled against three massive males. Max and Mako were each fighting a wolf, their fiery eyes shining. Another rival wolf ran off into the bushes.

Shadow jumped in to help Max and Mako, throwing aside a black she-wolf and biting into the flank of a male. The rival turned on her, snarling, blood-tinged saliva dripping from his fangs, and snapped at her ear. She dodged it quickly and bit at his paw. She clamped her jaws and pulled, sending him crashing to the ground, his leg bleeding heavily. He let out a howl of pain and limped away, his tail tucked between his hind legs. Shadow watched him go, panting heavily, exhaustion pulling her down. She felt as though she had just run around the territory five times with no breaks. She was dripping with blood from her neck and the wounds on her flank.

Shadow watched as more rivals turned and ran until finally the last of them began to retreat. Oak led Amber, Mako, Max, and Sparrow to chase them to the border, while Slate led Gray, Bone, Ebony, and Reed. The rest of the wolves in the clearing stood panting, eyes dull with exhaustion. Shadow sat down wearily, breathing heavily, her muscles throbbing. Miku came to her side and helped her up. Storm and Aria gathered the remainder of the wolves and led them back to their den site. Shadow limped beside Miku, glancing back at the bloodied clearing they had made.

Back at the den site, Luna and Venus got to work, using their herbs and other remedies to tend to the wounded wolves. Luna came straight to Shadow after seeing the blood on her neck. "Shadow, I want you to start cleaning that wound the best you can. Clean out the dirt and dried blood and then start cleaning the fur around it so that I can put herbs on it." Shadow collapsed on a bed of leaves and moss and began to clean out her wound, wincing with every lick. When Luna returned with the herbs she took over, making sure it was clean before applying willow root poultice. She then covered it with a finishing layer of moss to hold the poultice in place and keep the bleeding from starting again. "Where else are you hurt?" Luna asked, and Shadow pointed at a series of bites and scratches on her flank. Luna cleaned and dressed them, moving on to the next wolf after telling Shadow to clean her fur. Shadow began to clean obediently. When her fur was thoroughly run through, she let herself rest and relaxed her muscles.

Across the clearing, Oak and Slate emerged from the bushes and led the rest of the wolves into the clearing. Luna and Venus got to work treating the wounds of the new arrivals. Meanwhile, Lynx, the pups, and the Elders from the Cedar pack were making beds for the injured wolves. Shadow looked around. They would need to start making dens soon. She wondered if the two packs would combine to create one large pack. She shook her head. *Slate would never let that happen – he is too controlling. Neither of the Alphas would allow the other to have control over their wolves. I wonder if one of the packs will have to leave this clearing. If so, which one? This is a perfect environment for a pack. Neither of the Alphas will want to give up this clearing and settle into a new territory. They are both too stubborn.* Shadow's eyes widened at the thought. *Will there be a fight?*

No, she answered herself. *Oak wouldn't let that happen. He would rather move than be forced to fight.* But was that true? Oak was stubborn. If he wouldn't back down to a rival pack, he wouldn't back down to Slate, either.

Shadow was so involved in her thoughts she didn't notice Miku approaching until he was at her side. "Shadow, are you alright?" he said as he laid down next to her. She relished his warmth and breathed in his scent as she buried her nose into his neck fur.

"Yes, I'm fine, my love. Thank you for saving me," Shadow replied, her heart beating quickly, like it always did when she was this close to Miku.

"It was no problem. I'm glad you're okay." Shadow looked up as Oak approached, his wounds covered with moss and eyes shining in the afternoon light.

"It was brave of you and Scout to lead the rival wolves away from our den site. If you led them to us, our clearing may have been destroyed and they would know where we were living."

Shadow dipped her head. "Thank you, Oak." Her father nodded and turned to walk over and share prey with Storm, who was lying in a spot of sunlight with her eyes half-closed. Wolves sat all around the clearing, sharing prey or talking in small groups. Luna and Venus were just finishing dressing wounds and were taking stock of what herbs they had left. Shadow relaxed into Miku's warm fur and closed her eyes as he began to lick her face. Soon, she fell asleep.

Shadow woke up later that day to Oak and Slate organizing hunting groups. "Sparrow, Breeze, Heather, Amber, and Scout will go from the Aspen pack," Oak said, glancing at Slate. "Birch, Fog, Reed, and Sage will accompany your wolves," Slate replied, and the gathered wolves nodded. Shadow got to her feet, glancing at Miku who was sleeping beside her and trotted over to Oak.

"I can hunt, too, Oak," she said. Oak shook his head.

"Your wounds need to heal first. The wolves I chose for the hunt were barely injured in the battle," Oak answered, twitching an ear. Shadow's fur bristled slightly with annoyance.

"Please, Oak, I'm fine. I want to help the pack," Shadow replied. Oak stared at her through narrowed eyes before finally giving a weary sigh.

"Fine. But check with Luna first," he said before walking to join Storm, who was grooming her paws in the shade of a birch tree. Shadow looked around the clearing for Luna, spotting her at the opposite end of the clearing sorting through some freshly gathered herbs. Shadow trotted over to her.

"Luna, Oak told me to check in with you before I left to hunt with the rest of the group," Shadow said, dipping her head as she greeted the Healer. Luna glanced at her wound, sniffed it, and then went back to sorting herbs.

"Go ahead. Just don't stretch your wound too much," Luna warned over her shoulder, not looking up from her paws.

"Thanks." Shadow turned and joined the rest of the hunting group just as they exited the clearing. She trotted up to Sage and walked beside her.

"Hey, Shadow," Sage said. "Have you had a chance to explore the territory yet?" Shadow shook her head. "Well, now's your chance. It's beautiful. There's a high waterfall that goes into the lake. We'll hunt in that direction and explore it as we go."

Shadow and Sage walked side-by-side, listening, and smelling the air for prey. Shadow noticed how many thick, tall spruce and pine trees there were in this forest. In their old territory, there had been mostly oaks, birches, and maples, with very few pines or spruces. The forest floor was thick with hazel brush and dogwood in the openings and ferns and berry bramble along the edges. All seemed to be good homes for prey. The ground was damp, which kept it cool under the trees. Wet leaves and pine needles stuck to Shadow's paws. The musky forest scents filled her nose, and she couldn't help but feel happy that they had found their new home. They just had to drive those rival wolves away and the land would be theirs. The Cedar pack—or the Aspen pack—could take the rival wolves' territory and den site, and then everything would be sorted out. Shadow sighed with content and continued walking beside her friend, listening to the birds chirp overhead, and the squelching of their paw-steps on the soggy ground.

To her right, Shadow heard a squeaking sound coming from the bushes and two squirrels shot out from the undergrowth. They were chasing each other, as if unaware that the wolves were even there. Shadow leaped towards them, catching one by the tail. Sage, who had a slightly slower reaction, gave chase to the second squirrel. The squirrel squealed as Sage bit down first into its tail and then its throat. Shadow killed the squirrel that she caught and was carrying it by its tail. "Great! Now we can explore," Sage said, carrying the squirrel by the scruff back to where Shadow was sitting. Shadow gave a nod of agreement and then continued along beside Sage, walking towards the waterfall.

"Maybe we can catch some fish, too," Shadow said with the rumbling of the waterfall heard in the distance.

"Come on!" Sage exclaimed, running forward. Shadow followed, breaking into a run as they emerged into the clearing by the lake. This lake was about twice as large as the lake at their old territory, with shining clear water. Ferns and sedges grew thickly along the edge. The lake was too large to easily swim across but small enough that Shadow could see the other side clearly. No cattails or reeds were growing from the water, making it very clear and reflective. They were standing near a waterfall that fell from a high, rocky cliff, the water flowing effortlessly over the edge of the rocks before crashing into the pool below and sending up a veil of mist. The loud rumbling of the waterfall shook the ground.

Shadow stared in awe for a few seconds before Sage trotted over to the water and began to drink. Shadow followed, laying her squirrel beside the water before filling her stomach with the icy liquid. Looking into the water she spotted a group of minnows darting around the rocks, their bellies flashing in the sunlight as they turned from side to side. She spotted a larger fish swimming lazily through the sun-filled water, its rainbow-colored scales glinting in the light. Shadow also noticed a rabbit drinking from the water farther up the shoreline and she thought about giving chase.

"Should we explore?" Sage asked, breaking into her thoughts. "Sure," Shadow replied, and trotted along the shore toward the waterfall. Sage began investigating the sedge along the shoreline while Shadow was watching the waterfall crash into the pool below. She was thinking about going to try and fish when she felt teeth dig into her neck, and the scent of fox washed over her. She let out a yelp of surprise and pain as a fox bit into the flesh of her scruff. Shadow thrashed to get away, kicking the fox's underbelly and sending it crashing to the ground. A second fox let out a snarl and lunged at her, biting her shoulder and shaking its head back and forth, creating a bigger wound. Shadow howled in pain before clamping her jaws on its nose and throwing it away from her.

The first fox was now standing, growling savagely. Its blood-coated teeth bared. Saliva was frothing from its mouth. The fox was a big male, almost as big as Shadow, with large shoulders and rippling muscles. Shadow glanced over its shoulder and noticed now, for the first time, there was a den in the bushes, with three little fox-pups inside. *That must be why they are attacking*, Shadow thought. The male lunged at Shadow again, but this time she was ready. She stepped to the side and used the fox's weight for her advantage, tripping it with her hind leg and sending it crashing to the ground. The female attacked from behind, biting into Shadow's scruff and trying to pin her down. Shadow easily threw the smaller fox off and advanced on it, giving the female's neck a warning bite. The fox yelped in submission and then scurried away back to her pups. The male attacked Shadow again, though now he was limping from his hind paw. He must have sprained it, she thought. The fox snapped at Shadow's tail but missed, and Shadow retaliated by grabbing his flank and throwing him to the ground. The fox whimpered in pain and limped quickly back to his den, crouching beside the entrance, growling quietly.

Shadow limped over to Sage, who was running toward her from the sedges she was exploring, her eyes wide with alarm. "What happened? I didn't even hear you over the sound of the waterfall! Were you attacked? Are you okay?" Sage asked quickly, staring at Shadow's new wounds.

"Two foxes attacked me. We have to get back to the den site," Shadow grunted, limping over to the squirrel she caught earlier and scooping it up painfully. She looked down at her wounds. The bleeding from her neck was concerning. Blood was seeping from the bites from the earlier fight to mix with that from the new wounds inflicted by the foxes. Her shoulder wound was bleeding, too, but not as heavily.

"Shadow, wait. You need to rest. Where did the foxes go? Are there more? We need to stop that bleeding." Sage trotted over to Shadow, her eyes wide with concern, and took the squirrel from her.

"The foxes are gone. I chased them off. I don't think that there are any more," Shadow said, not wanting to tell Sage about the fox pups. Shadow laid down on the ground as Sage began to lick the dirt and blood out of the wound on her shoulder. Shadow licked the blood out of the fur on her neck, frowning when the bleeding refused to slow.

"Moss! We need moss. I'll find some," Sage said before racing to the nearest birch tree, where she began looking for fallen trees where moss may have grown. Shadow limped over to the lake and lapped at the water, letting it calm her down and cool her burning throat. Sage soon returned with a ball of moss in her teeth. There were only enough to cover one wound, and she applied them messily to Shadow's neck before racing back to the trees to collect more. She dressed Shadow's shoulder with what she found. Sage then helped Shadow to her feet, grabbed the squirrels they had caught, and they began walking back to the den site. Shadow looked at the sky, noticing how late it was getting.

The sun would be setting soon, and Oak would be wondering where they were. Shadow limped alongside Sage.

It was dark by the time they got back to the den site and the moon was slowly rising from behind the treetops. They were greeted at the entrance by Max, who was guarding the clearing.

"Shadow! What happened?" he yelped in surprise when he saw Shadow's wounds.

"There was a fox attack near the waterfall," Shadow explained. There were only a few wolves still awake. Oak and Storm were sitting together in the moonlight, while Miku sat anxiously beside Oak, his paws shuffling nervously. When he saw Shadow, she watched the worry turn to relief, and then to a mixture of confusion and shock. He raced across the clearing to her and surveyed her wounds with round eyes.

"Shadow, what happened to you?" he asked, rushing to her side and beginning to lead her towards Luna, who was sleeping beside her herbs, ears twitching vigorously as she slept.

"There was a fox attack," Shadow replied, wincing at the wound on her neck as she spoke.

"Luna, Shadow is hurt," Max woke the Healer as he rushed over to her. Luna's eyes shot open, her breath catching in her throat as if she had been woken from a bad dream. She looked around wildly, relaxing as her eyes rested on Lynx and her pups, who were sleeping peacefully in a large bed. "What's wrong, Luna?" Max asked gently as Shadow and Miku made their way over, Shadow leaning against him. Sage returned from putting the squirrels on the kill pile and stood beside Max, staring at Luna with wide eyes.

"I had a dream. Nothing to worry about." The Healer shook her head, as if clearing a bad thought, and turned to Shadow. "What happened?" She asked, her eyes widening as she noticed Shadow's new wounds.

"I was attacked by two foxes while Sage and I were exploring the territory," Shadow said, sitting down in front of the Healer.

"Sage, are you injured as well?" Luna asked, sniffing the she-wolf's pelt.

"No, Luna. I didn't notice the attack until the foxes were already gone," Sage replied, dipping her head shamefully, as if she felt responsible for Shadow being attacked while she had no idea the attack was even occurring.

Luna nodded. "Fetch Oak. We need to tell him about these foxes," Luna ordered, and Sage obediently raced over to inform Oak. Luna then turned to Max, who was standing silently, watching. "Go and check on Lynx and the pups. I want to make sure that my dream didn't mean anything bad," she told him, and he immediately trotted over to his mate and woke her quietly. Luna turned next to Shadow and motioned for her to lie down in a bed that had been made earlier for injured wolves.

Shadow obediently sat as Luna began sniffing her pelt, checking to see how serious her wounds were. Oak trotted up to them while Luna was applying the herbs, and Shadow turned to him.

"We need to make sure that those foxes are chased off. I'll send a group of wolves right away in the morning..." Oak started, but was cut off as Max and Lynx came running up to them, their eyes wide and fur bristling with fear.

"One of the she-pups is missing!" Lynx exclaimed when she was close enough for Oak to hear. Shadow felt her eyes widen with surprise.

"We have to go look for her," Max exclaimed to Oak, his eyes pleading. Oak nodded.

"Wake Scout and take him with you. If you don't find her by morning, the pack will search," Oak promised, and the two wolves raced off to Scout.

"Let me go with them!" Shadow exclaimed, trying to stand up, but falling back down at the pain in her shoulder.

"Shadow, no," Luna growled firmly. "You are staying here until these wounds are in check. The one on your neck might get infected if you don't allow me to treat it." Shadow reluctantly backed down, her ears flattened.

"I should go with them. I'm not much use sticking around here, anyway," Sage offered, and Oak gave a nod of gratitude. Sage raced after Lynx, Max, and Scout as they slipped through the ferns and out of the clearing. Luna finished dressing Shadow's wounds quickly, and Shadow looked over to see Lynx's three other pups sleeping quietly in the nest where Lynx had left them.

"Storm, perhaps you could give the other pups company until Lynx gets back," Shadow said to Storm as she trotted over to join them. Storm looked quizzically at Oak, and he motioned for her to go with his tail.

"I'll tell you what's happening later," Oak promised as Storm went to watch over Lynx's three sleeping pups. Miku cuddled into Shadow's nest and began to clean her fur, his tongue lapping rhythmically over her blood-stained pelt. She pressed her snout into his neck fur thankfully, trying to get over the worry churning in her belly as she thought about Lynx's lost pup.

"I hope that they find the she-pup," Shadow spoke quietly to Miku. Before he could reply, she turned to Luna. "What did you dream about?" Shadow asked, eyes questioning. "What happened to Lynx and her pups in your dream?" Shadow stared at Luna intently, aware that she did not want to talk about it. But Shadow needed to know.

"I dreamed that Lynx's pups were in a dark forest, all alone. They were scared, and…a she-wolf was killed by a fox," Luna admitted after a moment's silence. Shadow's eyes widened with horror as she turned to look at Oak, who was staring at Luna with bristling fur. He suddenly looked old and weary, as if his fur were heavy as stone.

"We have to trust that Lynx, Max, Sage, and Scout will find the pup," Oak said and turned to trot over to Storm, who was curled up with Lynx's puppies, her eyes closed. Shadow watched him go, her ears twitching with anxiety.

"I want you to stay near the clearing for the next few days. Your wounds need to heal. I shouldn't have let you go hunting so soon," Luna told Shadow as she sorted through what was left of her herbs. Shadow let out a low growl of frustration and rested her head on Miku's flank as he finished cleaning her fur.

"It's okay, Shadow. I know you hate being confined to the clearing, but there are things to do here. I can stay with you and we can start building the dens, if you like," Miku offered, his tail curling around Shadow's flank. Shadow smiled fondly at him, but then shook her head.

"No, Miku, the pack needs you to hunt and provide food for us, since you're strong. I'll probably build the dens with the elders and the wolves who are too injured to hunt, but healthy enough to work."

Miku nodded in agreement, his eyes beginning to droop as he let out a yawn. "I've been waiting for you to get back since dusk," he said.

Shadow smiled softly. "Get some sleep," she told him, and he obediently rested his head on her shoulder and dozed off. Shadow rested her head on his flank but did not sleep. She knew that too much had happened that night for her to be able to doze off so easily. She looked around the clearing, thinking.

Oak sat on guard beside the entrance, his eyes shining protectively in the moonlight. Storm slept beside Lynx's pups, her flank rising and falling rhythmically. Luna was sleeping lightly beside Venus, while Heather, Ebony, Fog, Breeze, and Echo slept in beds nearby. Aside from Shadow, these were the most injured wolves. Cinder and Mallow, the two Cedar pack Elders, were sleeping side-by-side in a sheltered corner of the clearing, while Silver, the Cedar pack Guard, and Birch, the Beta, slept beside them, protecting them. Slate and Aria were under a fallen tree, while Kele slept beside Storm, his ears twitching as he was dreaming.

Shadow was just about to close her eyes and sleep when Max burst through the entrance, his fur ruffled and eyes wide. He had blood trickling slowly from a couple of scratches on his flank, and Shadow's nose was immediately filled with the scent of fox. Shadow watched him race over to Luna and shake her awake as Lynx and Scout entered the clearing. Lynx was carrying something heavy in her jaws. The scent of blood filled the air as Shadow realized that Lynx was carrying her lost pup. Shadow could hear the faint whimpers of the puppy as Lynx and Scout drew near. Venus was also awakened by the commotion, and the two Healers rushed to meet Lynx as they realized what was happening.

Ignoring the pain in her shoulder, Shadow stood and trotted over to watch, her eyes wide with horror. Lynx's eyes were shining with tears as she gently laid her pup down in a fresh bed, the pup's whimpers of pain shattering Shadow's heart.

"Tell me what happened," Luna demanded as she immediately began looking at the pup's wounds. The pup reeked of fox and blood, her fur matted with the crimson liquid. The pup's eyes were closed, and Shadow thought she must have passed out from blood loss. Deep bite wounds covered her pelt and blood flowed steadily from the pup's small body.

"We found her in the forest, cornered by foxes against a boulder. We killed the foxes and got her back here as quickly as possible," Scout said, aware that Lynx and Max were too grief-stricken to answer sensibly. The poor she-wolf was sobbing into her mate's fur, and Max's eyes were sodden with tears. Shadow rushed to comfort them, telling them that everything would be okay and that the she-pup was strong, and would recover quickly. As she gave comforting words, she watched as Luna and Venus worked together to stop the bleeding, pressing moss onto the bites and gently feeding the pup honey to help with the shock and pain.

When the bleeding stopped the Healers cleaned the wounds and applied herbs to the deep punctures. They finished by applying moss to make sure that the bleeding didn't start again. Sometime during this operation, Oak and Storm appeared, asking what had happened. Scout explained the situation to them, and they trotted off to talk alone. At the Healer's orders, Scout had lifted the pup out of its blood-soaked bed and put her into Luna's bed, which was clean. Lynx and Max were then allowed to comfort the pup, cleaning her fur and keeping her company, though she was still unconscious. Storm returned to Lynx's other pups, who were now awake, wondering where their mother had gone.

Daylight was approaching and some wolves were wakening, wondering why the scent of blood was in the air. Oak did his best to keep them at bay, telling them only the bare minimum to keep the panic levels low. Shadow was working with Scout to build Luna a new bed, using moss and ferns to build a comfortable spot. Venus was talking to Slate and Aria, who were questioning the Healer about the night's activities. Luna was sitting wearily beside Venus, watching Lynx and Max care for the sleeping pup, and answering questions coming from Slate and Aria. Seeing the tiredness in the Healer's eyes, Shadow quickly finished building her bed and told her to get some sleep.

"Thank you," Luna said to Shadow and Scout as she passed by them, going to her bed and quickly falling asleep. Shadow dipped her head to Scout and wordlessly made her way over to her shared bed with

Miku, who was still sleeping despite all the noise of the stirring pack around him. Shadow curled up beside him and tucked her nose under her tail before closing her eyes and letting her mind rest.

Shadow woke sometime in the afternoon to the sun shining directly in her eyes. She groaned and lifted her head, blinking away the darkness and looking around her. Miku was gone, she noticed – probably hunting. Shadow yawned and sat up, her stomach growling at her with the movement. She winced, looking around the clearing to see what was going on. Luna and Venus were checking wounds, their fur ruffled and their eyes blurry as if they had just woken as well. Lynx was back with her pups, but her eyes kept drawing back to her injured pup as if she would rather be giving her comfort. The clearing was empty aside from the injured wolves, Lynx, her pups, and the Elders. Shadow wondered if Oak was leading a group to chase off the foxes that Shadow had quarreled with the day before. Oak would want the territory checked thoroughly for any more danger, too. If there were foxes around, no pups were safe.

Shadow stood and stretched her sore muscles, wincing as she stretched her neck and her wounds pulled. She flicked her tail and looked towards the prey pile, noticing there wasn't much to eat. All that was left were two squirrels and a rabbit. Shadow picked out a squirrel and the rabbit, guessing that Luna and Venus hadn't eaten yet. She offered them the rabbit, and they took it gratefully, their mouths watering at the sight of it. Shadow then settled down in the sunlight to eat her squirrel, glad that she finally had some time to relax. She ate slowly, enjoying the sounds, scents, and sights of fall. The leaves on the few leafy trees were painted beautiful shades of orange, red, and yellow, and as the cold breeze blew through them, the leaves fluttered gently down to the ground. Birds flitted around, their feathers glinting in the sunlight as they raced to fatten up for winter. Shadow closed her eyes and enjoyed this time by herself, trying to push away any worry or anxiety that she had about Lynx's pup or the foxes in the territory.

When she finished her squirrel, Shadow went to join Ebony, Heather, Echo, Breeze, and Fog, who were sitting together having their wounds checked by Luna and Venus. "Shadow, let me check your wounds, too," Luna said as Shadow approached. Shadow obediently sat to let Luna look over her neck, shoulder, and flank. Luna finished quickly and sat back, looking at Shadow thoughtfully. "Remember, no leaving the clearing. Your wounds are healing, but they need more time." Shadow dipped her head respectfully.

"Of course, Luna," she said. Shadow then watched as Luna walked back to her bed and curled up, closing her eyes to doze in the sun. Shadow turned and moved to sit between Breeze and Heather, facing the others. "Did the Healers tell you to stay in the clearing today, too?" Shadow asked, and they all nodded. "I think we should begin building the dens for the pack. Once it starts getting cold, we will need places to sleep," Shadow said, looking at the wolves to read their expressions. Fog looked confused.

"The *pack?* What do you mean by that? There are two packs. Surely Oak and Slate haven't said anything about merging them together?" Fog said, twitching his ears.

"Yes, there is only space in this territory for one pack. The Cedar and Aspen packs have been separate since the beginning," Echo added.

"Does this mean one pack has to leave?" Breeze asked, his eyes narrowing.

"The Cedar pack won't leave. Why should we? We deserve to be here just as much as the Aspen pack does," Ebony growled, staring at Breeze.

"We aren't fighting about this right now," Shadow raised her voice, standing up. "This is for the Alphas and Betas to decide. I can talk to

Oak about this, and we can sort it out as a group. But for now, we should start building. Breeze and Heather, let's go," Shadow said, turning and walking away from the Cedar pack wolves. "Which den should we start with first?" Shadow asked them when they were a reasonable distance away.

"I think we should start with the Newborns' den. Lynx and her pups will need shelter from the fall weather," Heather said, and Shadow nodded in agreement.

"Good idea," Breeze added.

"Okay, now we have to decide where it should be built," Shadow said, looking around.

"I was thinking we could dig under the roots of that large pine tree over there as a base," Heather replied, pointing with her tail towards a large, tall pine tree with roots spreading in all directions.

"Good idea. It's sheltered, and big enough for wolves to sleep under," Shadow said with a nod. Breeze nodded, and the three wolves went to work. Shadow grunted as she scooped dirt from under the pine roots, her muscles rippling under her pelt as she worked. Miku, Heather, Breeze, and Max now all worked beside her, helping to dig the hole or distribute the dirt around the clearing as it was scooped out. The wolves had been working on the den for hours, making sure the walls were as strong and sheltered as possible. They were now joined by the wolves returning from hunting or marking borders and were making the finishing touches. Other Aspen pack wolves were working on either the Alphas den or the Healer's den. Slate had taken the Cedar pack wolves to explore the forest.

When the Newborns' den was finished, Shadow led Miku and Kele to fetch moss and ferns for making a large bed for Lynx and her pups. Since the pups were growing bigger, they would need more bedding. They quickly made the bed and made sure all was completed. Shadow trotted over to Lynx, who was sitting with her pups, and told her that the den was ready.

"Thank you so much, Shadow. It's good to have a place to sleep again," Lynx said, dipping her head and giving Shadow a lick on the cheek.

"No problem, Lynx," Shadow said warmly as the she-wolf gathered her pups and walked over to the new den. Shadow then looked at the progress of the other dens, wondering if she should help. Oak, Storm, Amber, and Kele were working on the Alphas' den, while Luna, Sparrow, Miku, and Mako were working on the Healer's den. For the Alphas' den, the wolves were using an old fallen oak tree as the base and building outward using branches, brambles, and ivy vines to hold it all together. The den would be smaller than the one in the old territory, but big enough to fit two, maybe three wolves. For the Healer's den, the base was a large fallen maple tree. There weren't many maples in their territory, but this one was *huge.* It had large, thick branches and a big, sturdy trunk. Shadow wondered how the tree had fallen. *Perhaps during a big storm?* She thought, watching as Luna, Sparrow, Miku, and Mako dug a hole under the fallen tree roots that stuck out of the ground. Shadow decided to help them, noticing how hard it looked to dig so far underground.

Shadow trotted over to Luna and offered to help. "Sure. We could always use some extra paws. We need a big hole to fit all of the injured wolves," Luna said, motioning towards Mako and Sparrow, who were digging strongly, dirt flying out from under their legs. Miku sat down next to Shadow, and when Mako and Sparrow were tired of digging, Miku and Shadow switched places with them.

Shadow and Miku dug powerfully, Shadow ignoring the sharp pain in her shoulder. Now they were making progress, digging deep under the fallen tree. Shadow realized the den would be bigger than she first imagined. When Shadow and Miku grew tired of digging, Mako and

Sparrow took over again. The four wolves continued this cycle until the hole was dug out deep enough for a wolf to stand up straight without touching the roof above. Six wolves could easily fit inside, and though it would be crowded, more could fit. Sparrow, Miku, Mako, and Shadow were standing inside, looking around to admire their work, when Luna came in to thank them, telling them to go and rest.

"You're welcome, Luna," Shadow replied, and slipped out of the newly made den behind Miku. The Alphas' den was also nearly finished, and the wolves in the clearing were beginning to unwind. The sun was setting, the sky was getting darker, and the winds were growing colder. Shadow noticed that the Cedar pack, who had returned earlier in the evening, was staying away from the Aspen pack, their eyes somewhat hostile towards the Aspen pack wolves. Shadow wondered why this sudden change – usually they would be relaxing together as a group. Shadow shrugged and looked at the prey pile, her mood lightening when she thought about satisfying her hungry belly. She noticed that wolves were already eating. She grabbed a large grouse and limped sorely over to Kele and Miku, who were eating near the Alphas' den.

"Hello," Shadow said as she sat in between them, settling down to eat and beginning to pluck the feathers from her bird.

"Hello, Shadow. I'm so sore after digging out that den," Miku said with a little laugh. Shadow nodded in agreement.

"That was hard work," Shadow agreed through a mouthful of bird.

"I'm glad the pack is finally settled enough to begin working on dens," Kele said.

"Me, too. I thought we would never get settled in," Miku agreed. Shadow nodded, chewing thoughtfully. They sat in silence, watching the wolves around them. When Shadow finished eating, she began cleaning the dirt out of her paws drowsily, watching as the sun set slowly behind the distant horizon.

Chapter Seventeen

Shadow walked slowly along a hunting trail, her head low, eyes wide open, ears pricked. She had been searching for prey for quite a while now, but couldn't seem to find anything. Oak was sending out a hunting group tomorrow morning to track deer for the pack to eat, and Shadow wanted to stretch her legs before going on the long journey. It had been nearly a week since Lynx's pup had been attacked by the fox, and the pup was regaining her strength quickly. Shadow's wounds were nearly fully healed as well, and the packs were finally strong again. The rival pack had not crossed the border since the last attack, but still showed no sign of moving. Oak and Slate gathered the wolves together just the other night to talk about the issue of which pack was to leave the den site, and the packs agreed the problem would be looked at again when the rivals were driven away. Oak said the packs would be stronger together, and it would be hard to communicate easily if the Alphas were separated. The packs agreed and the issue was postponed.

The dens were finished with no help from the Cedar pack. Despite this fact, Slate had the nerve to tell his wolves they were allowed to sleep in the dens the Aspen pack built. Oak disagreed, and the Alphas argued until they decided that only Aspen pack wolves were allowed to sleep in the dens. Shadow thought it to be fair but still felt bad for the Cedar pack wolves, who were forced to sleep outside in the cold.

Shadow continued along the trail, then stopped to listen carefully. She pricked her ears and listened to the sounds around her, breathing deeply, trying to detect signs of life. Prey had become harder to find as they moved deeper into fall, but the packs were managing fine so far. Shadow pricked her ears as she heard the scuffling of prey in the bushes nearby. She lowered her head and advanced towards the noise, eyes wide. The scent of squirrel bathed her nose, and her stomach growled in anticipation. She hadn't eaten yet today, and she was hungry. She nudged a branch out of her way and locked her eyes on the squirrel that she scented. It was seemingly staring right at her, but since she was hidden by shadows it didn't know she was there. Before it could realize what was going on, Shadow shot forward and closed her jaws around its neck, killing it swiftly.

Before she had time to admire her work a huge black bird dropped down from a branch above her and landed in the clearing. Shadow left her squirrel and quickly shifted her attention to the bird, who was sitting beside a berry bush eating the red berries that had fallen on the ground. It was a raven, she noticed. Shadow tensed her muscles, then launched herself forward, attacking from above to cut off its escape. The bird squawked in anger as Shadow grabbed the back of its neck. It flapped its wings several times before going limp, staring lifelessly up at the sky. She blinked her thanks for the bird's life and returned to her squirrel, picking it up by its tail and trotting back to the den site.

Shadow sat with the rest of the group that had been chosen for the deer hunt, her tail wrapped neatly around her paws. Oak and Slate were talking quietly beside the entrance of the clearing. Shadow sat with Amber, Sparrow, Scout, Birch, Echo, Sage, and Reed. Sage sat beside Shadow, waiting anxiously.

"I wish Oak and Slate would hurry up. It seems like they've been talking for ages," Sage said under her breath to Shadow, who nodded in agreement. They were all anxious to hunt. Finally, Oak and Slate trotted over to the group and beckoned for them to leave. Shadow was the first to get up, following her father out of the clearing and into the forest. She walked behind him, the others catching up quickly. Soon, they were all trotting through the undergrowth in a single-file line, eyes open and ears pricked. They were heading towards the field where the deer herd had been spotted.

Slate was in the lead and he stopped them occasionally to check the area for signs of deer. They had no luck until they reached the field. There, Slate told the wolves to spread out. Shortly after, Reed caught the scent of a deer and he signaled for the wolves to follow him through the tall, dry grass.

Suddenly, Reed stopped, raised his head, and peered through a patch of the light brown grass. He flicked his tail and looked at Oak, letting the wolves know he had found a deer. Oak crept closer to see for himself, then waved his tail telling the wolves to get down. Shadow lowered her head and slowly crept forward, her heart racing in her chest. The other wolves followed her lead and began to circle the deer, being careful to stay downwind. Shadow peeked through the brush and saw a large doe standing gracefully in a small clearing. Shadow tensed her muscles, waiting for Oak's signal.

As Oak's snarl filled the air Shadow lunged forward, sinking her teeth into the doe's shoulder and pulling downward. The deer, caught off guard, stumbled as Shadow threw her weight onto it. Wolves appeared all around her. Oak let out another snarl and held the doe by the haunch. Echo had it by the neck. The deer attempted to run but was dragged down by the weight of the three wolves. It crumpled to the ground, eyes wide with fear. Echo snapped her jaws around its throat once more and the deer went still, its eyes still open. Shadow let go of the shoulder and sat back, licking the blood off her lips.

"Let's get this deer back to the other wolves," Oak said, his eyes shining. The wolves around him spoke excitedly to each other as they

322

grabbed the deer and began to drag it back towards their den site. Shadow grabbed a leg and began dragging with the rest of the wolves, her stomach rumbling at the taste of blood.

Shadow sat with the rest of the pack surrounding the deer. She sat between Miku and Sage and was listening to the wolves talking around her. The deer was nearly gone. Shadow took another bite, trying to savor the flavors before it was gone. She filled her stomach and then laid on her back, looking up at the darkening sky, her ears pricked, listening to the sounds around her.

She was speaking with Miku when a fearful howl abruptly filled the air. Shadow lifted her head to see what was happening, her eyes wide with confusion. Max, who had been guarding the entrance, was pinned to the ground by a large black wolf. Rival pack scent filled Shadow's nose, and she immediately got to her paws. Lynx rushed to get her pups inside the Healer's den since it was closest to where she was sitting. Oak and Slate barked orders while Luna and Venus got the Elders to safety. Shadow watched as the Alpha of the Rival pack strode forward from his wolves and stood face-to-face with Shadow. Since the last time he and Shadow had fought he hadn't gotten any smaller. Instead, it seemed like he had grown. His muscles rippled powerfully under his sleek black fur, and his piercing blue eyes seemed to stare right into Shadow's soul.

He bared his gleaming white fangs and lunged forward, aiming for Shadow's neck. Shadow, thinking quickly, ducked and snapped her jaws upward, feeling her teeth contact *his* neck. The giant male shook her off easily and advanced on her, grabbing her by the leg. He then threw her aside into a wall of bracken. She yelped in pain as he lunged for the killing bite, targeting her exposed neck. Shadow heard a distant howl of agony as she looked over and saw that the rest of the rivals were attacking her packmates.

Time seemed to slow down as Shadow saw Miku pinned to the ground by a large female, her jaws closed around his neck. Her packmates were matched in numbers but heavily outmatched in strength and size. This was a battle that they could not win. Shadow watched the Alpha draw closer, his bloody teeth aimed straight at her neck. Shadow felt a surge of anger and threw herself upright, turning on him, teeth bared, and fur fluffed up to make herself look bigger. The Alpha kept coming, grabbing at her ear and biting part of it off. Shadow howled in pain as blood trickled down her face and blocked the sight in her left eye. She blinked away the blood and lunged at the Alpha, snapping her jaws repeatedly. He was quick, dodging her blows and sometimes landing his own when she got too close. Shadow felt her strength slipping away as she continued the offense, attempting to bite at his neck or face.

But the big Alpha was quick, and thirsty for revenge since he had been beaten last time. Shadow threw herself forward, landing on the Alpha's back, and biting down hard into his scruff. He attempted to throw her off, but she held on, digging her teeth deeper into the back of his neck. He rolled on the ground, crushing her with his weight. The wind was knocked out of her and she let go, gasping for breath. He stood up and pinned her down, lips pulled back in a sneer. "Pathetic. I expected more from a wolf of our kind," the Alpha snarled in her ear.

"I'm nothing like you," Shadow growled back, not flinching as the Alpha grabbed her neck and shoved her against the ground.

"You're right. You're just a pathetic excuse for a wolf," he snarled as he sunk his teeth deeper into her throat. She coughed, blood trickling from her lips. As her vision began to blur, she heard an outraged howl come from beside her. Kele flung himself at the Alpha, digging his fangs into the black wolf's throat and bringing him to the ground. The Alpha was caught off guard and pinned, but not for long. He quickly regained strength and threw Kele aside, turning on him and biting into Kele's throat. Kele wriggled hopelessly for a few seconds before going limp, his eyes closing. Shadow got to her feet, her breath coming in ragged gasps as she wobbled towards Kele, who lay still. The Alpha kept his teeth fastened on Kele's throat until Shadow reached him. He then whirled around and lunged for her, seeking to finish the job.

Finding the last of her strength, Shadow stepped to the side and dug her fangs deeply into his flank. He yelped with surprise as she kicked his hind legs out from under him and pinned him down, eyes filled with anger. She bit hard into his neck hoping to kill him once and for all. But the Alpha was strong. Stronger than she was. He jerked his head back and hit her right in between the eyes with his snout, making her dizzy. He then threw his weight into her and she collapsed beside Kele, tears streaming subconsciously from her eyes at the impact on her face. The Alpha advanced on her, obviously not planning to stop until she was dead.

Shadow tried to stand but collapsed back to the ground with exhaustion. She looked around and saw that her packmates were losing as well. Oak and Slate were both pinned to the ground, their eyes filled with hatred. Shadow noticed that many wolves were outnumbered, and realized that some had abandoned the clearing, either having been chased off or hiding in the dens. They wouldn't win. Shadow knew what she had to do. She stood up and glared at the Alpha, ears flattened to her head. "Leave us alone. We will leave the territory, but you don't need to kill us," Shadow pleaded, forcefully tucking her tail in between her legs.

"But I want to kill you. It's fun to kill. It makes me feel powerful," the Alpha replied with a sneer.

"Your wolves will die, too," Shadow tried to reason, her voice hoarse and uneven. The Alpha hesitated, looking around the clearing. His gaze rested on a black female, who was lying sprawled on the ground, not breathing. His breath caught in his throat, but he turned to look back at Shadow, his expression unreadable.

"Yes, death comes with a price. But it will all be worth it in the end," he growled, waving his tail dismissively. *He is stubborn,* Shadow thought.

"You would kill a pack that you have no connection to just because you are *powerful?*" Shadow demanded, fur bristling.

"Of course," he responded casually. "You can't reason with me, wolf. Now I kill you," the Alpha growled, and suddenly lunged forward, teeth bared. Shadow stepped away, growling, letting him fly past her.

"You can kill me, but leave my pack alone!" Shadow snarled, her voice ringing throughout the clearing, her body shaking with rage. The Alpha turned on her, laughing evilly. "You have no reason to kill me or my pack! Leave us alone!" Shadow howled at him, her voice shaking. The Alpha lunged at her, and she met him head-on. They clashed, snarling, biting, and clawing bloodily at each other. Shadow threw her weight into her paws and slammed down as hard as she could onto the Alpha's face, feeling her claws rake down his eyes, nose, and neck. He fell backward, blood seeping into his fur. Shadow sunk her teeth into his neck with crushing strength, feeling his flesh tear inside of her mouth. If she were to die, she would take him with her.

He clawed at her underbelly, and pain flared in her stomach. She growled and bit deeper into his neck. He let out a strange gurgling noise, still fighting frantically. "You will leave this territory, or I will kill you," Shadow growled, tightening her grip threateningly.

The Alpha reluctantly went limp, growling in defeat. "We will be back, and next time, I'll finish the job," the Alpha said, and Shadow let go, her legs shaking with exhaustion. The Alpha stalked backward and glared at Shadow before calling his wolves away. The blood-covered wolves retreated from their den site, most of them heavily injured.

Shadow sat down and looked at the broken clearing around her. There were two dead rival pack wolves lying on opposite ends of the clearing. The scent of blood was so strong it made Shadow gag as she blinked it out of her eyes. The dens were all destroyed, aside from the Healer's den that had been protected at all costs. Oak, Slate, Storm, and Aria were helping Luna and Venus get the most severely injured wolves to the Healers den, where the elders, along with Lynx and her pups, were making more beds for them. Shadow remembered Kele, and turned to him, seeing that he was blinking his eyes open, his breath coming in ragged gasps. Shadow raced over to him and saw that blood was still oozing slowly from the bite. "Kele, I'm going to get you to the Healer's den, okay? Luna will help you," Shadow said, gently grabbing his scruff to help him to his paws. Aria trotted over to Shadow and looked at her, and then at Kele.

"I will help him. You need to rest," Aria said, her eyes round with anxiety. Shadow reluctantly backed away from her brother, letting the she-wolf nudge him to his paws and then help him towards the Healer's den. Shadow limped after them, her tail tucked between her legs. She peered through the entrance of the Healer's den saw that it was filled with wolves. Lynx and the Elders were quickly building moss beds out in the clearing for the injured wolves, where Luna and Venus could see to them more easily. Shadow carefully sat down in a bed just outside of the Healer's den and began to clean her wounds, knowing that Luna or Venus would tell her to do that anyway. When her wounds were clean she looked around, her eyes beginning to droop. She forced them to stay open and looked at Amber and Birch, who were helping the Elders move beds for the more injured wolves. Luna and Venus were skillfully covering wolves' wounds using what was left of their herbs. Thankfully, they had stocked up recently, so they had what they would need, but Shadow could see the stress in their eyes as they quickly grew thin on moss.

Shadow busied herself with cleaning the stench of blood out of her fur, though the clearing was still coated in a layer of crimson liquid. Shadow wondered if any Aspen or Cedar pack wolves had died in the battle. *Surely Oak or Slate would have announced if any wolf had died.* Shadow shook her head, as if clearing the thought, and looked up as Luna emerged from her den, her paws smelling of blood. "I'll get some herbs for you, Shadow," Luna said before scrambling back into her den. Shadow nodded and looked at the other wolves in the clearing. Miku and Breeze were sitting beside Sparrow and Heather, looking as though their wounds weren't too bad. Sparrow had a large gash on his flank, but it was clean and was no longer bleeding. Miku also had some deep puncture wounds on his neck, but it looked like he had cleaned them. Shadow hoped that they would both be all right. Fog, Reed, and Gray were all sitting together, cleaning each other's wounds, and talking quietly in a group near Shadow. She was close enough to hear what they were saying, but she was too tired to care. She blinked the sleepiness out of her eyes and looked up at the moon, which now sat calmly above the treetops, shining down on the clearing. Shadow hoped that she would be able to sleep tonight, but knew it would be hard.

Luna emerged from the entrance of the Healer's den carrying a mouthful of herbs. She sat down beside Shadow. "Where are you hurting the most?" Luna asked her calmly, though her eyes betrayed her weariness and fear. Shadow pointed to her leg, her neck, and her flank, and Luna began covering the bites and scratches with herb juices and moss. "Okay, where else?" Luna asked, and Shadow told Luna about the rest of her injuries. The Healer dressed her bites and scratches, and then moved on to Sparrow, Heather, Miku, and Breeze, asking them about their wounds and then going to retrieve more herbs. Shadow laid down in the bed, trying not to stretch any of her bandages, and rested her head on her paws. She closed her eyes and quickly fell asleep.

Shadow was jolted from her slumber the next morning to howls of sadness coming from the Healer's den. Shadow opened her eyes wearily, blinking the sleepiness away and looking up at the sky. It was very early, the sun was barely showing above the horizon. Shadow pricked her ears curiously as she heard another howl of sadness coming from the Healer's den. Wolves were beginning to wake all around Shadow, their eyes wide with confusion and concern. Shadow heaved herself to her paws and peeked inside the den, worry making her heart race. Venus and Bone were comforting Echo as she cried into Ebony's fur, the she-wolf's eyes pale and lifeless. Shadow's eyes widened with sadness as she realized that Ebony was dead. Luna was watching them sadly, her shoulders slumped. Shadow continued watching for a few moments before turning and leaving the den, deciding to give the Cedar pack wolves some privacy.

"Ebony is dead," she announced gravely as she faced the group of three Cedar pack wolves lying near the entrance of the den. All three stood with their eyes wide and unbelieving.

"She can't be dead," Reed uttered, shaking his head slowly. Just as he finished, Venus and Bone pushed through the entrance to the Healer's den, carrying Ebony between them. They laid her down in the middle of the clearing, letting the packs mourn her. The Cedar pack wolves gathered around their fallen packmate, each letting out sobs and howls of grievance. The Aspen pack wolves took their places in a circle surrounding the Cedar pack wolves, sitting quietly, heads down. Shadow howled at the sky showing her grief, then sat silently beside Miku, listening to the Cedar pack mourn.

Shadow sat in the middle of the clearing beside Miku, looking up at Oak and Slate as they stood together on top of a fallen oak tree. They had called the wolves together with a howl, and the packs were now gathering in front of them, their eyes lit with curiosity. It had been a day since Ebony's death, and the packs were now on edge, and still grieving. Their wounds were healing, but slowly. If there was another attack, the packs would surely be driven off, if not killed. "I wonder what this is about," Miku whispered in Shadow's ear as wolves made their way out of the Healer's den and into the clearing.

"Me, too. I hope it's nothing bad," Shadow replied. As she finished, Oak raised his tail for silence, and Slate stepped up.

"After the death of our packmate, Ebony, I have made a decision. The Cedar pack will leave this territory. The Rival pack is far too dangerous for us to stay any longer." Some wolves gasped in unbelief, while others nodded their heads. Shadow had known that they would leave since the moment she first saw how strong the Rival pack was.

"The Aspen pack will leave as well," Oak announced. "This is an unsafe place to raise a pack. Slate and I have agreed to leave the morning of the full moon, which is three days from now. We will give each other some time to heal before we leave. Are there any questions or complaints?" Oak's commanding voice silenced the wolves. No wolf said a word. At that, Oak flicked his tail to dismiss the wolves. Shadow sighed and walked over to her bed of moss, her wounds aching. It was midday, and she wanted to hunt. She decided that she would ask Luna. Shadow looked around the clearing for the Healer, finally spotting her ushering injured wolves back into the Healer's den. Shadow limped quickly over to her and stopped her before she could disappear into her den.

"Luna, I am asking your permission to hunt. I swear I'll be careful," Shadow asked as she approached. Luna thought for a moment before shaking her head.

"I don't want you to get hurt more, like last time."

Shadow searched for a reply. "I will bring a few others. I'll be safe and stay with them. It would be good to stretch my legs," Shadow assured. Luna thought for a moment before reluctantly sighing in defeat.

"Fine. Just don't hurt yourself, and send the wolves that you choose over to me so I can check their wounds before you leave," she said before waving her tail and slipping into her den. Shadow grinned and turned to look for Oak, spotting him talking to Storm near his destroyed den.

"Oak," Shadow greeted as she approached him and her mother.

"Yes, Shadow?" Oak replied, looking up from his mate.

"I would like to take a few wolves to hunt. The pack is hungry and needs to be fed," Shadow said.

"Did you check in with Luna?" Oak asked after thinking for a few seconds. Shadow nodded. "All right, but don't run into any more foxes," Oak told her, and she dipped her head in gratitude.

Shadow turned and trotted over to Miku, Breeze, and Heather, who were talking together under the shade of a pine tree. "Anyone up for hunting?" she said, dipping her head. "Oak said I could bring a few wolves to re-stock the prey pile."

Heather and Breeze stood up, their eyes shining. "We'll hunt," Heather said. Shadow nodded to them, then turned to Miku.

"Do you want to hunt?" she asked.

"I don't think I should. This would on my neck hurts when I walk too much. Have fun, though," Miku replied, licking Shadow's nose.

Shadow frowned. "I hope you feel better soon. We're going to be walking quite a lot when Oak decides to leave."

Miku nodded. "I'll check in with Luna later today." Shadow nodded and licked his ear before turning back to Heather and Breeze.

"Luna told me to send you to her before we leave so that she can make sure you are fit to hunt," Shadow told them, and they nodded, turning and trotting over to the Healer's den. Shadow watched them go, pricking her ears as she heard Sage's voice behind her.

"Are you going hunting?" she asked. Shadow turned to her and nodded. "Do you mind if I come?" Sage asked.

"Not at all," Shadow replied. "You better check in with Venus first, though." Sage nodded before hurrying off to check in with her pack's Healer. Shadow walked to the entrance to the clearing and sat to wait for Heather, Breeze, and Sage to return.

Later that day, Shadow pushed through the battered entrance of their clearing with Heather, Breeze, and Sage following, each carrying their catch. Shadow had a rabbit and a groundhog, and she carried them now, trotting over to drop them on the prey pile. She took a pheasant from the pile and carried it to Miku, who was sleeping in a patch of sunlight. She curled up next to him, plucked the feathers, and began to eat. When she finished, she rested her head on Miku's shoulder and closed her eyes, breathing in his scent. Just as Shadow was about to sleep, the sun disappeared behind a large, dark gray cloud, and a cold wind blew through the clearing. A drop of rain fell on Shadow's nose, and she looked up, frowning. Gray storm clouds rolled in quickly and began to drop their rain. Large drops fell on the ground around her, turning the dirt into mud. Shadow sighed and woke Miku with a nudge. He opened his eyes slowly, then shut them abruptly as a drop of rain fell on his forehead. He let out a low growl and sat up, shaking his head. "I was trying to sleep," he growled grumpily, and Shadow smiled.

"Okay, sleepyhead. You can sleep once we get under a pine tree. Now let's go." Shadow stood and walked to the nearest pine tree, where Echo and Fog were already sitting, talking casually as if they did not mind the rain. Shadow sat beside Fog, while Miku flanked her other side, yawning as he laid down. Just as the wolves were sheltering under the pine boughs the skies opened and the rain came pouring down, soaking anything it could get its grip on. Shadow watched as the rain fell while Miku rested his head on her paws, his eyes already closed. Shadow laid her head on his neck and quickly fell asleep listening to the rain as it hit the ground around her.

Chapter Eighteen

Shadow walked slowly along the trail that her packmates had forged, her paws as heavy as stone. The packs had been on the move for days, slowly getting farther from their old home and deeper into unknown territory. The forest grew thicker and richer as they continued along, and the scent of humans grew fainter every day. The packs had been keeping an eye out for possible places to build their den site, checking the territory around them each night as they hunted. No place had been suitable yet, so they continued walking, searching for the right home.

Shadow walked behind Sparrow, half-heartedly listening to him speak with Heather. It had been rainy for the past few days, so now Shadow was wary of the dark gray clouds as they towered overhead, ready to start pouring or sleeting at a moment's notice. Shadow guessed that it was about midday, though with the clouds hiding the sun, it seemed more like evening or early morning. She sighed and trekked onward, hoping for the day the packs never had to move again.

"Oak, we need to find shelter!" Shadow called loudly to her father as he faced the sky indecisively. Winds whipped the trees and bushes loudly from side to side, threatening to tear the wolves from the ground. Sleet pelted them from above, soaking their pelts and everything around them. Lightning lit up the dark gray sky as thunder shook the ground and rang in their ears. The packs had tried to push through it, but they now needed shelter. The storm was more than they could handle.

"I see a cave!" a wolf suddenly called above the howling wind, and the wolves all turned to look. Shadow spotted a large rocky cave not too far away, standing strong against the wind and rain. Oak spotted the cave, then called loudly, "Follow me!" The wolves followed Oak and Slate, huddled together against the freezing sleet. The wolves entered the cave, shaking out their pelts and gathering close to keep warm. Shadow huddled with Miku, bushing out her fur and pressing against him as she shivered. The scents of her wet packmates filled her nose. She frowned. If any other animals were already in the cave, the wolves wouldn't know.

A loud roar suddenly shook the cave, and Shadow realized it was a noise she had never heard before. A shiver ran up her spine as a huge creature emerged from the shadows, glaring at the wolves menacingly. It was flanked by a smaller one of the creatures, its giant teeth bared and small, round ears flattened to its head.

Wolves let out yelps and growls of surprise as the giant creatures lumbered forward, their matted fur standing up in anger. The larger one gave an ear-splitting roar and heaved itself up on its two hind legs, somewhat like a human. Wolves scrambled away quickly, yelping in surprise and fear. It was at least three times larger than a wolf, and probably a hundred times scarier. "Bear!" some wolf howled in panic, and Shadow scrambled to her paws, eyes wide, tail tucked between her legs with fear. The bear gave another roar and swiped one giant paw at a group of petrified wolves in front of it. Its claws tore through some poor wolf's flesh with a sickening sound, and the scent of blood filled the air. Wolves screamed and howled with fear and began to run out of the cave. Mako and Sparrow lunged forward side-by-side and attacked the bears, snarling and growling. The smaller bear backed away, and Shadow realized that it must be the big bear's cub. Shadow's eyes widened with fear. She remembered Sparrow telling her that bears would fight to the death to protect their cubs.

"Run! Get out of here!" Shadow howled when she found her voice. She lunged toward Mako, who was cornered by the grizzly animal, his fur bushed out and teeth bared. "Mako, run!" Shadow snarled, and threw her weight into the bear, attempting to set it off balance. It turned on her, growling. Mako obediently ran for the entrance. "Sparrow, get out of here! You'll die if you fight!" Shadow barked at him, and he backed away from the bear, eyes wide and indecisive. "Run!" Shadow snarled and shoved him with her shoulder. She whirled around and ran beside him, leaving the bear behind. When she got outside, she looked around for the rest of the pack, blinking rain out of her eyes. She spotted a large group of her packmates huddled around something under the shelter of a pine tree. Shadow raced over to them with Sparrow beside her, their pelts fluffed out against the rain.

"What's happened?" Sparrow asked, loudly above the sound of the rain and wind. Shadow pushed through the crowd of wolves to see what was the matter, and her breath caught in her throat as she saw what was on the ground. Amber was lying on a pile of leaves, her pelt soaked with blood and rain. Her eyes were half-closed as blood oozed from a huge gash on her flank. Luna was rushing to cover her wound with moss, but the blood refused to slow.

"It won't stop. Why won't it stop?" Luna whimpered frantically, trying again to press moss onto the wound. Amber breathed painfully, her breath ragged and labored. Shadow watched with wide, wet eyes as the blood-soaked she-wolf took her last breath. She lay still as blood flowed a moment longer from the wound, and then stopped. Sadness engulfed Shadow, and she closed her eyes, allowing tears to stream down her face, along with the rain. Wolves around her let out wails of sadness as they faced the death of their Beta. Grief filled the air as the Aspen pack wolves surrounded their dead packmate, crying softly or sitting still with disbelief. Storm was crying into Oak's fur as Shadow's father looked sadly down at his lost Beta. Grief filled his eyes. Miku appeared at Shadow's side, his eyes wet and ears laid back with sadness. Shadow lifted her head and howled in sorrow, letting her voice be heard above the sound of the storm. Then, she sat back, tears streaming down her face.

"My pack, gather around me, for I have an announcement to make," Oak called into the quiet morning air, his eyes still blurry with sadness. He stood on the broken stump of a fallen tree, his tail raised in the air. The Aspen pack had just finished burying Amber, and now they were silently mourning her death. The rain stopped sometime during the night, but raindrops were still falling lazily from the trees above. The sky was painted blue, pink, and orange, and there were only a few wispy white clouds left from the storm. The sun was rising slowly, beginning to warm the cold morning air. Shadow looked up from where she sat next to Miku, her eyes droopy from lack of sleep and the tears that she had cried. Miku gave her a nudge and she stood to follow him over to where Oak was calling the pack.

The Aspen pack gathered around their Alpha, the Cedar pack hanging back, watching with tired eyes. Shadow sat down on a wet pile of leaves, waiting patiently for the rest of the Aspen pack to gather around. When every wolf was seated, Oak took a deep breath and began. "As you all know, Amber was killed by a fatal wound inflicted by a bear, a creature I have never seen before. We have been told stories of the beasts, but never knew how powerful they were. Amber was the Aspen pack's Beta for a very long time. She led well and was a wolf that I could always count on and trust." The Aspen pack wolves gave nods of agreement, some of them giving sniffs and whines of sadness. "Now that Amber is gone, I must appoint a new Beta. I have talked with Storm, and we agree the wolf we have chosen is fit to be the Aspen pack's second-in-command. This wolf has led well, and has always been loyal to the pack." Oak's gaze bounced from wolf to wolf, his eyes finally resting on Shadow's. "Shadow, please step forward," Oak said, and a ripple of shock coursed through Shadow's body.

Her eyes widened with disbelief as she looked around at the faces of her packmates. She slowly stood and walked through the crowd of wolves as they parted to let her through. Her packmates gave her encouraging smiles and looks of pride. Lynx dipped her head as Shadow passed, the she-wolf's eyes filled with praise. Shadow smiled. Her stomach felt as though it was stuffed with butterflies as she walked toward Oak, who had jumped from the tree trunk and was now watching Shadow with proud eyes. Shadow stood before her father, eyes wide. "Shadow, ever since you were a pup, you were a leader. I knew that someday you would do great things. You've always done what was best for your pack, even if it might cost you your life. You have never been afraid to step up and help your packmates through their troubles. I believe that you will succeed me someday and that you deserve to be a leader of this pack. Do you accept the role of Beta?" Oak asked.

Shadow's breath caught in her throat as thoughts raced through her head. *Me? Beta?* Shadow met her father's gaze, determination shining in her eyes. "I do." Oak smiled softly.

"Then you must know what challenges will lie ahead of you as Beta," her father said.

"I do," Shadow spoke again, and Oak dipped his head.

"Good. From this moment forward, you are the Beta of the Aspen pack. I trust that you will take good care of your packmates," Oak said, and then lifted his head to the sky to lead a howl. Shadow tipped her head back and let out a long howl, listening to her packmates' yips and howls behind her. When they finished, Shadow dipped her head to Oak, and he dipped his in return. Shadow then turned and sat down beside Miku, where he whispered congratulations and covered her face with licks. She laughed quietly, thanking the wolves around her as they congratulated her, too. Oak raised his tail for silence after a few seconds, then looked at Lynx and her pups, who were all sitting together. Lynx was straightening her pups' fur with her tongue. "Lynx, it is time to name your pups," Oak announced as he walked over to the she-wolf and sat in front of her. The rest of the Aspen pack wolves formed a circle around them, excitement filling the air and chasing away the sadness. Max sat beside Lynx, his tail curled around hers. Shadow remembered when she was a pup, and she had been named. It was very exciting. "Lynx, have you talked to your mate and pups about names?" Oak asked.

"I have," Lynx replied.

"What are your thoughts?" Oak asked. Lynx turned to her pups, smiling.

"Tell Oak what you want your names to be," she told them, and all four of them stood, eyes wide with fear of speaking in front of the entire pack. The first one who spoke was a small, light gray male with dark gray ears. "I want my name to be Fern," the pup said, his eyes shining. "I want my name to be Flame," said a female with the same fur patterns as her mother. "My name is Night," said a large male pup with short, black fur. "And I am Laika," said the final pup, a small she-wolf with dark brown fur.

"Those are beautiful names," Oak said, and Storm nodded in agreement.

"Thank you," Lynx spoke, nudging her pups to say the same. "Th-thank you," Laika said, and the rest of the pups mumbled their thank-yous as well. Oak smiled.

"Does the rest of the pack agree with these names?" Oak called into the crowd, and every wolf nodded, giving smiles of encouragement to the pups. Oak smiled down at the four puppies, his eyes shining. "Well, then. It looks like everyone likes your names," Oak said, and the pups smiled happily. "From now on, until the end of your lives, you will be known as Fern, Flame, Night, and Laika. You will be known by your packmates by those names, and you can never change them," Oak said, and the pups' tails wagged with excitement.

"Thank you, Oak," all four of them spoke at once, and they took turns rubbing their snouts on Oak's. Oak then waved his tail to signal the end of the meeting. The wolves broke into groups, the sadness of Amber's death forgotten for the moment, replaced by happiness for the pups. Some wolves were congratulating Lynx and Max, while others sat around the clearing, their paws probably itching for something to do.

Shadow decided she would send out a couple of hunting groups to stock up on prey. First, she went to the Cedar pack Beta, Birch, who was sitting by himself under the sun, his eyes half-closed as he silently watched the Aspen pack. "Greetings, Birch," Shadow called as she seated herself beside him to talk.

"Shadow," he said with a smile. "Congratulations."

"Thank you," Shadow replied. "I was going to send out a couple of hunting groups to fill the pack's bellies before we move on again, and was wondering if you would like to send out a few Cedar pack wolves as well."

"Yes, good idea. Just let me check in with Slate. I want to make sure we aren't going to leave any time soon," he said with a nod. Shadow dipped her head.

"I'll check with Oak as well." She then turned to trot over to Oak, who was sitting on the log again, watching his pack silently. "Oak," Shadow greeted him as she approached. "I am going to send out a few wolves to hunt. We want to be strong for when we leave again." Oak nodded his approval, then returned to watching the pack, his eyes weary. Shadow dipped her head, then looked around for wolves to send out. "Sparrow, Heather," Shadow called to them as she spotted them sitting together beside Lynx, Max, and the pups. The two wolves ended their conversations and trotted over to Shadow, ears pricked.

"What is it, Shadow?" Sparrow spoke as they stopped in front of her.

"I need you to come hunting. I would like to take Scout and Breeze as well. The pack should have full bellies before we start traveling again."

"Alright," Heather replied, and Sparrow nodded.

"Thanks. Would you go and tell Scout and Breeze? We will leave soon." Sparrow and Heather nodded, then turned to find Breeze and Scout. Shadow looked over at Birch, who was gathering his Hunters with his tail. She greeted him with a twitch of her ears as he approached. "We should split up, to find as much prey as we can," Shadow suggested, and Birch nodded.

Shadow turned to Heather as the she-wolf led the rest of the group to Shadow. "Let's go," Birch said and led his wolves out of the clearing first. Shadow followed with a twitch of her ears.

Shadow lowered her head slowly, her eyes set on a rabbit. The plump creature sat a few yards away, chewing on some berries from a wilting berry bush. Its large ears swiveled around as it listened for signs of danger. Shadow stayed very still, glad that she was downwind. She was in the rabbit's blind spot just as a gust of wind picked up. Shadow tensed, then shot forward, letting out a growl. The rabbit let out a squeal of fear and scrambled away, its white bushy tail bobbing up and down as it disappeared into the bushes, dodging Shadow's jaws. She snarled and raced after it, her ears down. She put on a burst of speed and caught up to the animal, lunging forward and grabbing it by the flank. The rabbit called out in pain and fear, its black eyes shining. Shadow pressed her paws on the rabbit's legs, holding it down while she bit down on its throat. It gave a few weak cries of protest before going limp. Shadow stood, holding the rabbit by its scruff, and trotted back to where she had left Breeze with his catch. She dropped the rabbit at his paws, grinning.

"That's a good rabbit," Breeze commented, sniffing it.

"Thanks," Shadow replied, sitting down to wait for Sparrow, Heather, and Scout to return.

"Should we go back out? This might not be enough," Breeze said, motioning towards his squirrel and bird.

"Sure. I'll go. Stay here with the prey," Shadow replied. Breeze nodded as Shadow turned to slip back into the undergrowth, sniffing to catch the faintest scents of prey. When she was far enough away from Breeze, she planted her feet into the ground and closed her eyes, breathing slowly. She listened to the wind above her, felt the ground beneath her, and felt the presence of the trees around her. She strained her ears to hear every sound, every paw step, and every breath of the forest and creatures within. She faintly heard paw-steps off to her right, and she opened her eyes, smelling raccoon. She lowered her head and crept toward the sound, eyes narrowed. She spotted the animal gnawing on the bones of a mouse beneath a spruce tree. Its grayish-brown fur was shining in the sunlight. Shadow lunged forward and bit down on its throat before it even knew what was happening. Scout, Sparrow, and Heather had already returned when she got back.

"That was quick," Breeze commented before standing up with his prey held between his teeth. Sparrow had caught two groundhogs, while Heather and Scout each held a plump pheasant. It was a successful hunt. They returned to the pack with their prey and made a pile. Shadow took the squirrel for herself and sat down to eat under a pine tree. She took a bite, looking up as Storm approached and sat beside her.

"Would you like some?" Shadow offered, and Storm politely shook her head.

"No, thanks. I shared a rabbit with Oak," her mother replied, and Shadow couldn't help but smile. She probably ate the rabbit that Shadow had caught. "I'm proud of you, Shadow. I always knew you were gifted, ever since you were a pup. I knew that you would be the leader of this pack one day, and I'm counting on it," Storm said, lying down, her fur brushing against Shadow's. Shadow looked at her mother with love filling her heart.

"Thank you, Storm. That means a lot to me," Shadow said softly and buried her nose in her mother's warm fur. Storm's scent reminded her of when she was a pup, living in the Newborns' den. Her ears flattened with sadness as she thought of their old territory. Shadow then took a bite of her squirrel and looked around, her eyes resting on Miku, who was sitting with Breeze, watching Lynx play with her pups. His eyes looked somewhat… longing. *Does Miku want pups?* The question made Shadow's breath catch in her throat. Storm followed Shadow's gaze and seemed to realize what she was thinking.

"Ah, pups. They're worth it, you know. You and Kele were the light of my life. I just wish I had more." Shadow looked at her mother, her ears twitching. Storm locked eyes with Shadow, and warmth spread throughout Shadow's body as her mother smiled. "Miku is a good wolf. He is a good wolf to raise pups with. I know that you will make the right decision when the time comes," her mother said licking Shadow's nose. Then, she stood up and trotted over to Kele, who was eating beside Oak next to a birch tree. Shadow watched her mother go, her heart beating faster than usual. She looked up as Miku trotted over to her, a smile on his face.

"Hello, Shadow," he said.

"Hi," she replied as she buried her face in his fur when he sat down beside her.

"Is something wrong?" he asked. "You seem quiet."

"No," Shadow replied, breathing in his warm, familiar scent. She loved him so much that she felt tears begin to blur her eyes. He sat with her, tails curled around each other, eyes closed. "I don't know if I want to be Beta yet, Miku. What if I'm not ready?" Shadow eventually said to him, when she was sure that her tears wouldn't come. Miku looked her in the eye, his eyes filled with love and understanding.

"You *are* ready, Shadow. You are smart, brave, and willing to help your packmates in any way possible. That's why Oak chose you, and that's why I love you. That and a million other reasons, too. Oak is your father. He would never choose you for something if he wasn't sure you were ready for it. He believes in you, and so do I." Miku's voice was filled with confidence. Shadow pressed herself against him and rubbed her snout against his chest.

"Thank you, Miku. I love you." Miku rested his head on her neck. "I love you, too, Shadow." They sat together, listening to the wind blow through the trees.

Chapter Nineteen

Shadow walked beside Miku at the head of the pack, her ears laid back casually. It was a little after midday and the packs had been walking since early morning. Before the sun had risen Shadow had led a group of Aspen and Cedar pack wolves hunting, and they had come back with a lot of prey. Shadow wondered if the packs would settle down in a good territory soon. It was now or never. Shadow couldn't smell any humans, but she figured if they kept on walking, sooner or later she would. Shadow walked behind Oak and Slate, Storm and Aria flanking them. Miku was walking between Venus and Shadow, while Birch walked in the rear to make sure that no wolf was left behind. Luna was taking turns dragging the herb-filled log with Max and Mako, while Lynx herded her pups near the back. The Elders were walking in the middle of the group, with the Cedar pack making sure they kept up and weren't getting too tired. The rest of the wolves walked in a large group, heads usually down, enduring the long, draining walk. Shadow looked at the sky, wishing that the sun would set soon so that they could rest again. Her paws throbbed, and her legs were sore. She sighed and continued onward, willing this nightmare to end.

"Let's stop here for now," Oak said loudly so that all the wolves huddled around him could hear. The packs stopped in a large clearing surrounded by tall, thick bushes and towering spruce trees that gave shelter from the wind. The wolves gave collective sighs of relief and broke off into groups to find a sheltered place to spend the night.

344

Shadow walked beside Miku over to a huge boulder and sat down, resting her aching paws. Miku sat beside her and began to lick her shoulders soothingly. She blinked gratefully at him, shivering as a cold wind chilled her skin. She noticed her fur was growing thicker with the coming of winter, but that didn't mean that the cold didn't still get to her.

"We should find a more sheltered place to sleep," Miku suggested as he began looking around for any trees that could give more shelter. Shadow looked down and saw a hole beneath the large boulder. She sniffed it cautiously, making sure no other animals were hiding inside. When she found it was empty, she crouched down and squeezed herself through, surprised at how easy it was to get inside. She looked around, letting her eyes adjust to the darkness before slowly crawling forward. There wasn't much room from the floor to the ceiling, but the hole was plenty wide, and with the right digging, it could be a good den. Shadow turned back around and squeezed herself out to see Miku standing in front of her, his head tilted to the side.

"I didn't notice that before," he said, sniffing the hole as Shadow crawled out. Shadow shook the dirt out of her pelt before telling Miku that it could be a possible den.

"Good. Should we tell Oak? Maybe this could be a good place to mark our new territory," Miku suggested, and Shadow nodded eagerly. They trotted over to Oak, who was talking with Storm, Slate, and Aria.

"Oak," Shadow said as she approached, giving a small dip of her head. "I found a possible den under that large boulder over there. It was wide enough to be a den, but not quite high enough. With the right digging, I think that we could make a good den out of it." Shadow sat down and motioned for Miku to do the same. Oak exchanged glances with Storm.

"We should explore the territory more before we start finding dens. If this is a good place to live, we can devote our time to making dens, but we haven't gotten that far yet," Oak said, twitching his ears.

"Okay," Shadow spoke, hiding her disappointment, and dipped her head to leave. Oak flicked his tail in response. Shadow turned with Miku and went to sit beside the boulder again, wondering if she should order hunting groups yet. The wolves hadn't had much time yet to relax, but it was getting dark fast. Shadow decided she would lead a hunting party before it was too dark. "Miku, will you come hunting with me?" she asked as they sat down.

"Sure," he replied. Shadow nodded her thanks, then turned and looked around at the wolves in the clearing. She spotted Sparrow and Heather talking together under a pine tree and trotted over to them, Miku at her tail. "Are you both well enough to come hunting with Miku and me? I want to get some prey back here before the sun goes down," Shadow said, and they both nodded. Shadow then turned to Scout, who was sitting beside Reed. "Scout, we need you for a hunt," Shadow called to him, and he looked up, nodding. He spoke his goodbyes to Reed before trotting over to Shadow and her group. Shadow nodded to him, then led the wolves away into the unknown forest.

Hunting was good and they returned as the sun was setting below the horizon. In all, they brought back three rabbits, two pheasants, and two squirrels. The wind had grown cold and bitter as they hunted – so cold that Shadow's breath had puffed out in a cloud in front of her. The forest was filled with fat prey, even though it was near the end of autumn. The Cedar pack had sent out a hunting group as well, so hopefully, they had caught their own food. While they were hunting, Shadow led her group around the territory and explored. They found no signs of predators and had discovered a good stream not far from where they had set up camp for the night. These facts excited Shadow. Maybe they had finally found their new home! Shadow led the wolves to drop their prey in a pile under a birch tree, her eyes scanning the clearing for Oak. She spotted him sitting alone beside a large aspen tree, his eyes half-closed with sleep. She trotted over to him and dipped her head as he looked up at her.

"I just got back from exploring the territory, and I thought I should talk to you about it." Shadow sat down beside her father, her breath clouding out in front of her. She hoped they had dens before the real cold set in during winter. Oak looked at her with mild interest, yawning before twitching an ear, signaling for her to continue. "This territory is rich with prey and vegetation. There is a steady stream not far from where we are now, which can provide water. And, as you know, if we do decide to make our dens here, we already have a good den made for us," she said, motioning with her tail toward the large boulder and the hole underneath it. "There are no signs of major predators around, at least from what we saw on our hunt." Oak looked hopeful, yet doubtful at the same time. He didn't trust it. She could see it in his eyes. When he didn't say anything, Shadow twitched an ear. "Look, I know it was hard to leave our only home, especially one our pack has lived in for generations. Then, to be chased off again by a rival pack just as we settled into a new territory was even harder. But we must keep trying. We can't just go on walking forever. Lynx's pups need a place to grow up. This might be our best chance at a new home, Oak." Shadow's heart was beating fast now. "We can't throw that chance away." Oak held her gaze, his eyes betraying his indecisiveness. She could tell he wanted to give it a chance and willed him to believe her when she said they needed a home. Finally, Oak heaved a sigh and dropped his gaze.

"You're right, Shadow. I just cannot stand to lose another home. We need to make sure the territory is safe before we make any commitments. You can lead a group tomorrow at sunrise to look at the whole territory, and mark the borders. If you are satisfied the land is safe, I will talk to Slate about it." Shadow dipped her head, feeling as though a weight had been lifted from her chest.

"Thank you, Oak," Shadow said, her head buzzing with relief. He looked up at the sky silently, and Shadow turned to trot over to Miku, who was lying under the fronds of a large fern. She sat down beside him and sighed with satisfaction. A moment later, he stood and trotted over to the pile of prey, grabbed a rabbit, then carried it back to where he left Shadow. He sat down beside her, letting her take the first bite. She thanked him, and they ate together. When they were finished, Shadow gnawed on a leg bone while Miku took the bones to bury them. It only took the edge off of her hunger, but it was still better than nothing. Tomorrow, when they had more time to hunt, they would catch more, and the pack would have full bellies when they went to sleep. Shadow cuddled up beside Miku when he returned, sharing his warmth and enjoying his company.

"I told Oak I think this is a good place to make our new home, and he believed me. He told me to lead a group of wolves tomorrow at sunrise to explore the territory, set the marks, and make sure there are no threats anywhere near the land. Will you come with me?" She spoke softly, her eyes beginning to droop as she finished.

"Of course I will. I hope we finally found a safe home," Miku replied before yawning. Shadow nodded. "Me, too," she said softly as she drifted off into a deep sleep.

Shadow woke the next morning, standing and stretching before waking Miku with a shake of his shoulders. "Ug," he groaned, blinking one eye open and looking up at Shadow.

"Time to get up," she said softly, and he moaned, sitting up slowly. "Who should we bring with us?" she asked in a whisper, looking around at the sleeping wolves around them. Her breath puffed out in a cloud in front of her, but she hardly noticed, the adrenaline warming her body.

Miku thought for a moment before concluding, "Mako, Scout, and Sparrow." Shadow nodded. Those were her picks, too. She left Miku to wake up fully and trotted over to Sparrow, who was sleeping between Breeze and Heather. She woke him with a nudge.

"What is it?" he muttered, opening his bleary eyes and looking up at Shadow.

"I need you for a patrol. Don't wake Heather or Breeze," Shadow said, and then turned and trotted over to Scout, who was sleeping alone. "Scout," she whispered his name, not wanting to wake any other wolves. He looked up as though he had been sleeping, but she suspected he had already been awake.

"Yes?" he replied, and she told him about the patrol. He nodded and stood up, stretching. Shadow looked over at Miku as he approached, a sleepy Mako trailing behind him, his eyes grumpy. "Sorry to wake you on such short notice. Oak asked me last night to lead a patrol and I didn't have time to tell you. We're going to look through the territory and make sure there are no threats nearby. Oak also asked that we mark territory lines, so we will do that, too." The wolves nodded, now awake and ready to explore the territory. Shadow nodded, then led them away.

The sun was nearly at its highest point in the sky when Shadow returned to the den site with the rest of her group. They had finished exploring and marking the territory and found the land was covered in dense forest with the occasional low, swampy ground and open meadows. They found two fox dens and a coyote den within their borders, and Shadow had caught the scent of a lynx just outside of their territory. Shadow told her group to leave the dens alone, deciding that she would talk with Oak to see what they would do about it.

The stream that Shadow found the day before led to a pond that was filled with fish and crawling with life. And, while the wolves were marking the farthest border from their den site, they spotted a rather large herd of deer grazing in a forest meadow. Mako noticed them first and pointed them out to the rest of the group, and they stood for a while to watch the graceful creatures. Eventually, Shadow broke the silence by saying, "let's leave them be," and they had moved on, marking any bushes or trees that would keep their scent strong.

They also discovered a tall cliff at the edge of their territory. Shadow agreed with the rest of the group that if you fell, you would be seriously injured, maybe even killed. They moved on, careful to stay far away from the edge. When they returned, Shadow told all of this to Oak, his eyes growing brighter and brighter at every good thing Shadow told him. When she finished, he was staring hopefully into Shadow's eyes, a smile rested upon his face.

"This is great news, Shadow. Thank you. We will give the territory a try. I will talk to your mother, then with Slate. We will see how they take it." Shadow smiled with relief, then dipped her head.

"Thank you, Oak. I think this may be a good—if not the best—place for a pack to live," she said. Shadow then turned to look at Miku, who was sitting under a birch tree, his paws shuffling anxiously as he waited for Shadow to return. When he saw her trotting towards him, he stood up, eyes wide.

"What did he say?" he asked, his tail wagging.

"He said he will talk to Storm and Slate about it," Shadow said, smiling with excitement.

"Great! I hope Slate agrees. We need a home before winter hits," Miku replied. Shadow nodded, sitting beside him, watching as Oak spoke quietly to Storm, his eyes shining. When he finished, she was nodding excitedly, talking quickly back to him. He nodded after a few moments and then trotted over to Slate and Aria, who were talking together. Storm accompanied him, and the four Alphas faced each other, talking in low voices, Oak and Storm keeping their composure, but still looking happy. Shadow's heart soared when she saw that Slate was nodding slowly in agreement, as though he had been thinking the same thing. Aria looked a little more hesitant, but after a few moments of Slate's reasoning with her, she began to nod in agreement, too. The four Alphas talked for a while, unaware that Shadow and Miku were watching them closely, eyes wide, waiting for something to happen.

Finally, Oak and Slate broke off from the two females and trotted over to a large boulder, Slate jumping up first. Oak jumped but didn't quite make it. He fell back to the ground with a grunt, his paws scraping on the rock as he slid down. He tried again, bunching his muscles, jumping, and this time making it to the top with Slate's help. The two Alphas stood side by side, Oak panting as if it had been very hard for him to get to the top. Shadow saw this very keenly – her eyes fixed on Oak as Slate's voice called out.

"Wolves, gather around us, for we have an announcement to make." Shadow was the first one seated in front of them, looking up excitedly, her heart racing in her chest. The rest of the wolves gathered around quickly, interested in what Oak and Slate had to say. Oak began after finally catching his breath.

"As most of you know, this morning I allowed my Beta to take a group of wolves to check out the territory and mark the borders. She has reported to me that the land is full of prey, including a large deer herd." There was a chorus of gasps of excitement as Oak said that. He hushed them with a wave of his tail.

"Oak and I believe that this territory is the one for us. There is a stream that will provide water, little signs of danger throughout the land. I say that we have been traveling long enough," Slate spoke loudly and confidently, his tail raised in excitement. The wolves around Shadow gave yips and howls of agreement, their eyes shining in the daylight. Shadow joined in with them, showing her relief and agreement with Slate and Oak.

"It's settled then," Oak's voice, loud and clear, overpowered the rest of the wolves, and they gradually fell silent. "Now, the only thing left to do is to decide which pack will leave this territory," Oak spoke, glancing at Slate.

"The Cedar pack will go," Slate spoke willingly, and Shadow's eyes widened with surprise. She hadn't expected either of the Alphas to give up the known territory so easily. The Cedar pack gave some murmurs of disagreement, but no wolf spoke out. "The Cedar pack will find their own place for a den site in a territory somewhere near the Aspen pack. We will keep in touch." Slate looked at Oak, his eyes warm. "It was a pleasure traveling with you," he said, then dipped his head and jumped down from the rock, gathering the Cedar pack around him with a wave of his tail.

Oak watched him, his face echoing Shadow's feelings of surprise and relief. Slate stood next to Aria, giving goodbyes to Aspen pack wolves. Shadow pushed through the crowd to get to Gray and Sage. Kele and Breeze were already with them, their eyes shining with sadness, as well as excitement for what was to come. Shadow smiled sadly, her eyes meeting with Sage's. She embraced her friend, resting her chin on the she-wolf's shoulder and breathing in her scent. "I suppose this is goodbye," Sage said softly, and Shadow pulled back, sadness stabbing her heart.

"We'll see each other again sometime – even if it is from different territories," Gray said, then embraced Shadow. She rested her chin on his shoulder, her heart aching at the thought of seeing her friends go. She had come to love them like they were her own pack. She had come to love *all* of the Cedar pack wolves. But, now they were leaving, and the packs would be rivals once more.

"That's right. We will still be friends, even from different packs," Kele piped in as Miku approached, his eyes filled with sadness.

"Goodbye," he said, and they shared looks of sadness. As they finished their goodbyes, Slate called his pack together with a few barks, and then led them one by one out of the clearing. Sage went last, giving Shadow a sad look over her shoulder as she left, her tail hanging low. Shadow watched her friend go, sighing as she disappeared. "We'll see them again. I promise," Miku said, shifting closer to Shadow, and she pressed against him. After a few moments of silence, Oak scrambled painfully slowly back onto the boulder, his eyes shining even as he fought to catch his breath. "The Aspen pack has found its new home. I want to get working on the dens immediately – we have no time to waste before winter breaks." Oak spoke loudly, gathering the scattered wolves back into a group in front of him. Oak then walked over to Shadow, flicking his tail.

"Split the wolves that can work into three groups for now. One for the Learners' den, one for the Healer's den, and one for the Newborns' den. I think that it's nearly time to make Lynx's pups Learners, so we'll need a den for them. I'm taking Storm and Luna out to get a look at the territory, so I might not be back until later this evening. If you finish all, or any, of the dens, go hunting," Oak spoke, and Shadow dipped her head when he finished.

"Okay," she replied as he trotted over to Storm, who was already sitting with Luna as if waiting for him. Shadow turned to the rest of the Aspen pack and began giving orders. She decided that the safest place for the Newborns' den would be beneath the big boulder that Shadow had found, so she told Mako and Max to begin making the hole bigger. She advised them to be careful not to make the dirt shift too much, or the rock could crush them. Shadow then looked for places to start building the other dens, finding a spot under an uprooted aspen tree that would be good for the Learners' den. Scout and Kele began digging out a hole in the softened dirt. After searching for another place to put a den, the rest of the wolves finally found a place to start making the Healer's den beneath a huge spruce tree. The roots of the tree had grown over and around a big boulder, creating a large, deep cave-like space underneath. With a bit of digging, it could become a large den. Sparrow, Heather, and Breeze began working on that, while Shadow went to help with the Newborns' den and Miku went to help with the Learners' den.

Shadow greeted Mako and Max as she approached, and they stopped digging to acknowledge her greeting. She took her place between the two and began digging, scooping pawful after pawful of dirt out from under the wide rock. When they finished, Shadow's paws throbbed from scraping them on rocks or hard dirt while digging. The entrance was small but would be good for keeping pups inside when they needed to be. Farther into the den it was now deep enough to stand without ears touching the large rock above. It took a lot of digging, but Shadow was happy with the outcome. When they were satisfied the rock was sturdy overhead and that all of the holes in the sides were patched with dirt or rocks, they collected moss from nearby spruce trees to use as bedding. Shadow arranged beds for Lynx and the pups, then gave them the 'ok' to go inside and get settled in.

"Thank you, all of you," Lynx said to Shadow, Mako, and Max as she passed. She pressed her face into Max's fur as she reached him, and he stood up, following her into the den. Shadow watched them go, smiling. She turned to Mako, who was watching Miku, Scout, and Kele finish digging out the Learners' den, which was now deeper than Shadow would have thought possible. Shadow exchanged glances with Mako before trotting over to the three who were still digging, eyes wide with astonishment.

"Nice digging, you three!" Shadow exclaimed, peering into the den. The entrance was wide open, exposing the depth of the den. It stretched far under the uprooted tree, with a flat floor at the bottom. It looked like it could hold at least four wolves with plenty of space.

"Lynx's pups should like it," Kele commented, standing beside Shadow to admire his work.

"You bet your tail they will," Scout huffed, panting as he finished digging a bit more dirt from one of the walls. He scooped the upturned dirt out of the den and into the clearing, spreading it out over the ground.

"This is perfect. It's sheltered, yet open enough that we can see if they're getting into any trouble," Shadow spoke humorously, watching as Miku scrambled out of the hole.

"Yes, I hope that Oak makes those four Learners soon. They're almost as big as foxes!" Miku added, shaking the dirt from his paws. Shadow turned to Sparrow, Heather, and Breeze as they approached Shadow, their pelts covered in dirt.

"We dug out a large space for the Healer's den. It's all clean, and safe for Luna to move her herbs into," Sparrow reported to Shadow, and Shadow nodded.

"Great. Can I look?" she asked, and Sparrow nodded, leading her over to the den. It was farther away from the rest but was still close enough to be seen. Shadow crawled into the hole and peered inside, seeing that it, too, was much deeper than it appeared. There were plenty of crevices and rocks in the walls to store herbs, and there was even a small crack in the roof deeper into the cave to let in some light. The tree was strong overhead, and the roots held the dirt in the walls surrounding the space inside. "Great job! This looks great. I'm sure Luna will appreciate it," Shadow said as she pushed herself out of the den. After shaking the dirt out of her pelt, she turned to the wolves in the clearing, eyes shining. "Great work, all of you, on the dens. We will work on the Hunters', Fighters', Alphas', Guard's, Tracker's, and Beta's dens tomorrow. For now, we need to hunt. Sparrow, Heather, Breeze, and Scout, you will come with me to hunt. The rest of you, stay here and rest. Oak should return soon," Shadow said, looking up at the sky, which was painted dark colors of orange, purple, and blue. Heather, Sparrow, Breeze, and Scout gathered behind Shadow as she led them out of their new den site and into their territory.

Shadow returned with her group to find Oak giving instructions on building a den. They were using a fallen tree as a base, building up brambles and sticks around it to make a small den. It looked cozy. Shadow guessed that it was probably the Alphas' den since Oak could use the fallen tree to stand on when he wanted to gather the pack. Shadow dragged a deer into the clearing, smiling. Scout had picked up the deer's scent and they had found the animal standing injured in a small clearing. Shadow guessed it had strayed away from the herd. Shadow, Heather, and Sparrow were dragging the animal now and left it in the center of the clearing. Shadow trotted over to Oak, who was helping Mako and Max weave the brambles together, forming thick, sheltered walls. Oak's eyes widened with joy when he saw the deer they had brought back.

"That is a beautiful deer, Shadow. We will eat well tonight," Oak said with a smile. He waved his tail at Mako and Max, signaling for them to rest and come to eat.

"Thank you, Oak. We found it near the center of our territory. It was injured, and must have wandered away from its herd." Oak dipped his head at this news, his ears laid back with relaxation and happiness. At the scent of deer blood, the pack was stirring, mouths watering as they waited for the Alphas to eat first. Storm and Oak each began to eat, taking the most delicious meat in the belly. When the Alphas had their fill, Shadow ate alongside Luna. *It feels weird eating so soon after the Alphas.* She filled her belly quickly so that the other wolves could eat. When Shadow finished, she trotted over to a corner of the clearing and watched her packmates. After Shadow came Heather, Sparrow, Breeze, and Scout. Up next were Lynx and her pups, and lastly came Max, Miku, Kele, and Mako. When the deer was gone, Shadow went with Breeze,

Miku, Kele, Sparrow, and Heather to sleep in the Learners' den. She curled up next to Miku, content with their new home and a full belly. She felt warm, happy, and *safe*.

Shadow woke early the next morning, looking around the den to see all the wolves were still asleep. The sun had hardly risen above the horizon and was just starting to warm the forest. The trees stood still – there was no sign of wind or rain. The sky was clear aside from a few wispy clouds, and even though it looked warm and bright, the morning air was wintry and bitter. Shadow resented the thought of getting out of the warm den, but she knew that wolves would be waking up soon, searching for ways to keep warm, and Shadow thought there was no better way than to go hunting or mark the borders of the territory. It was usually the Beta's job to send out these patrols.

Deciding to get it over with, Shadow pushed herself out of the Learners den and into the cold morning air. Bushing out her fur against the cold, she trotted over to the Alphas' den where Oak was sitting peacefully awake, watching the clearing from inside. Storm was beside him, still sleeping soundly. "Good morning," Shadow said, shaking out her pelt before sitting beside the den, where Oak could still see her.

"I wouldn't call it *good*. More like, *cold* morning," Mako growled, his fur also bushed up to maintain the warmth. He was coming from the Healer's den, where Shadow guessed he had been sleeping. Shadow flicked her ears in agreement.

"A bit cold for my old bones, as well," Oak added, twitching an ear. Storm woke at the sound of their voices, yawning as she lifted her head. She looked at the sky, tasted the cold air, then let out a low growl of pain. Her stomach tensed, and now Shadow noticed that her stomach was swelling abnormally. Shadow's eyes widened with surprise.

"Storm, is something wrong?" Shadow asked. *Is Storm pregnant?* Storm grimaced, curling into a ball.

"My stomach isn't feeling well. I think I might see Luna. It's been bothering me for quite a while now. Plus, I have these strange bumps on my skin, and I don't think that my winter coat is growing in yet," Storm confessed, though she looked reluctant to admit to her pain.

"Can I get you something to eat?" Oak asked. He looked worried as Storm stood and began to limp over to the Healer's den.

"No, thanks. I'm not hungry," Storm replied before disappearing into the den. Shadow watched her with worry churning in her belly when she saw how skinny her mother was and how distended her stomach looked. Her fur was also dirty and unkempt, as If she hadn't bothered to clean it in a while. Oak stood up to follow her, his eyes glazed with worry.

"I'll talk to Luna," he said and trotted over to the Healer's den. Seconds later, Scout and Max slipped out of the Healer's den, yawning, and flinching at the bitter cold. Breeze emerged from the Learners' den a moment later, shaking out his pelt.

"You would think it would be a little warmer from the way the sky looks today," Scout muttered, and Breeze nodded in agreement as he approached. Max was making his way across the clearing to the Newborns' den to check on Lynx.

"Will you go wake the rest of the wolves that are in the Learners' den?" Shadow asked Mako. "I need to organize some groups before we can get working on the dens," Mako grunted, then trotted over to the Learners' den to wake Kele, Miku, Sparrow, and Heather. He returned with the four sleepy wolves trailing behind him, grumbling about the cold and being woken up so abruptly. "I know that you all want to rest, but before we rest, we need to work. Sparrow, Heather, Scout, and Breeze, you will come with me hunting." Shadow said. "Mako, Miku, and Kele, you will mark the borders and make sure that there are no predators around. You could Bring Max with you.

When we return, we will work on the rest of the dens." The wolves nodded in agreement. "Let's give the sun a few more minutes to warm up before we leave. You should get something to eat, too," Shadow continued.

Shadow watched as Max took a squirrel and a rabbit to share with Lynx and the pups, and she decided to take something to Luna, Storm, and Oak. Shadow took two squirrels from the pile and trotted over to the Healer's den, where she was met by a horrible smell. Shadow wrinkled her nose and pushed inside, seeing that Storm had been sick on the floor, her thin body shaking. Oak was sitting next to her, comforting her, while Luna got a mouthful of herbs from one of the crevices in the wall and laid them out in front of her.

"Eat these, Storm. They will help you," Luna said. Shadow could hear a hint of doubt in Luna's voice. Storm shook her head quickly.

"No. They will just come back up again. I don't think my stomach can take it," Storm replied, her ears flattened in pain. Shadow pushed her way farther into the den, her eyes wide with fear and worry.

"What's wrong with my mother?" she demanded to Luna, setting the squirrels down beside Storm.

"I...I don't know. I've never seen anything like this before," Luna replied, a look of pure bewilderment on her face.

"Well, what are her symptoms? I'm sure you can relate them to something," Shadow said, and Luna began to list them off.

"Abdominal swelling along with pain, fever, loss of hair, loss of appetite, nausea, discharge from the eyes and ears, and...bumps on the skin. I don't understand what those could mean!" Luna exclaimed, eyes wide with fear. "Storm, please, I need you to eat these herbs. There are lily petals for the fever and stomachache, and daisy leaves for the rest of your pain. I don't know what to do for the bumps on your skin, hair loss, or discharge... But, the petals should help with your vomiting, and maybe your abdominal swelling. I also think that you should eat something... You look like you haven't eaten in weeks!" Luna's voice was becoming frantic.

Storm looked pleading—sad even—as she took Luna's herbs. "Will you share a squirrel with me?" Oak asked gently, but Storm shook her head. Luna took a shaky breath.

"Just wait for the herbs to start working, then you might get your appetite back," Luna said, and Storm nodded, resting her head on her paws. Shadow gave a squirrel to Luna, then took the Healer aside.

"Will she be okay, Luna?" Shadow asked quietly, making sure that Storm and Oak couldn't hear her.

"I...I don't know, Shadow," The Healer whispered. "I've never seen anything like a sickness this bad. If it gets any worse..." Luna looked up into her eyes, but Shadow didn't need to hear anymore. She turned and slipped out of the den, breathing in the fresh air. She watched the wolves around her as they finished eating and sorted themselves into the groups that Shadow had assigned. Giving a deep sigh, Shadow lead the Hunters out of the clearing after sending the border markers out ahead of them.

Shadow could not seem to focus on what she was doing during the hunt. Her worry for Storm took up all the space in her mind, and as a result, she lost two birds by trying to rush at them instead of attacking from above. "Shadow! What are you thinking? That's not how I taught you to catch birds!" Sparrow instinctively growled, but then remembered that Shadow was Beta now, and he probably should not talk to her like that. Shadow sat down miserably, her head down and her tail tucked between her legs.

"Sorry, Sparrow," she mumbled, heaving a deep sigh. Sparrow's expression softened when he saw that Shadow was bothered by something so badly.

"What's wrong, Shadow?" he asked, sitting beside her. Shadow sighed before telling Sparrow about Storm, and how she was sick, and how Luna didn't know what to do. Sparrow looked horrified before eventually gaining his composure and softening his expression.

"That sounds bad. It's understandable for you to be worried. I'm sure Oak wouldn't mind if you went to take a walk instead of hunting. You should have some time alone with your thoughts," Sparrow said.

Shadow nodded. "Thank you, Sparrow," she said, and he dipped his head. Shadow began to walk, not entirely knowing where she was going. She let her paws lead her to wherever they wanted. Eventually, she got to the cliff and wondered if her mind had led her there on purpose. She laid down at the edge and looked ahead, scanning the wide field of ferns and grass in front of her. She spotted a buck deer emerge from the trees and wander through the clearing, his large brown eyes shining. When he saw it was all clear, he craned his neck over his shoulders and snorted towards the woods behind him. Seconds later, a doe appeared, leading a half-grown fawn behind her. The two cantered gracefully over to the buck before he continued onward, his head and tail raised high to show his dominance. Shadow watched them silently, noticing how the sun shone on their brown fur, and how the buck's antlers pointed skyward. As they disappeared into the dense undergrowth on the opposite side of the clearing, Shadow stood and looked at the sun. It was rising slowly toward the top of the sky. Shadow guessed that by the time she got back to the den site it would nearly be sunhigh already. She began trotting back toward their new home, glad to have had some time alone to clear her mind.

Chapter Twenty

Shadow dug her front paws into the soft dirt and flung it behind her. Along with Miku, Scout, and Heather, she had been digging out a hole for the Hunters' den under a large pine tree. The tree's roots stretched outward strongly, making it easy to dig a hole under them. The four wolves had been working on the den since Shadow returned from her walk. Her paws were sore from digging, but now that it was done, she was glad she had helped.

Shadow told the Hunters to make their sleeping holes before helping Miku, Kele, Mako, and Max work on the Fighters' den. The four males had already done most of the work, clearing the dirt from the inside of a huge hollowed-out pine tree, but Shadow helped by patching the holes in the roof with moss, leaves, and pine sap to hold it all together.

It was a very old and very big tree, the inside hollowed out by bugs, and whatever other critters had dug into it to make a home for themselves. There was a wide space inside – Shadow's only worry was the roof caving in during bad weather. If a heavy wolf decided to jump on the top of the log, it might break. "Are you sure you want this to be your den?" Shadow asked.

"Well, do you have any better idea?" Mako replied. That had been the end of it. Now, the sun was getting low in the sky, although a bit of daylight remained. Shadow went over to the wolves who were working on the Elders' den, keeping her mind off Storm, who had not improved.

Sparrow and Breeze were working on the den, digging diagonally underground to make a cave.

"The dirt is dry and easy to take out," Breeze explained to her over his shoulder as he dug. Shadow watched them for a while before going off to find a place for her own den, the Beta's den. After looking for quite some time, she found a hole in the roots of a large, tall spruce tree. The roots parted to make a small entrance. Shadow pushed her head inside, seeing that there was space for a one- or maybe two-wolf den under the roots of the tree. Shadow began to dig, trying to make the entrance bigger, dirt flying out behind her as she dug. When the entrance was big enough for her to push through, she crawled inside, noticing that space inside was smaller than she had thought. She began digging again, making the space large enough for her sleeping hole. She scooped the dirt out of the den, then dug her sleeping place.

When she finished making her den Shadow pushed herself out and stood at the front of the clearing, watching the Fighters finish their den. Nearly all of the dens were now complete. The only dens that still needed to be built were the Guard's den and the Tracker's den. Their den site was made. "Now, we can enjoy the prey that we caught earlier and settle into our new home," Shadow said loudly, making sure that every wolf could hear. Lynx sat with Max, watching her pups play with a pine cone, while the Hunters and Fighters sat outside their dens talking and sharing prey. Shadow, not catching sight of Oak, Storm, or Luna, turned and pushed into the Healer's den, glad the earlier smell was gone.

When her eyes adjusted, she saw Storm sleeping on the same bed of moss that she had been on that morning. Oak was sitting next to her, his tail wrapped around her, eyes closed. If it was possible, Shadow thought that Storm looked even worse. Her breath was coming in short, raspy gasps, her ribs were showing through her pelt, and her stomach was rounded as if it was filled with pups. Shadow feared for Storm. She looked at Luna, who was sitting in her bed, watching Storm as well. The Healer's eyes met Shadow's, and Shadow crept forward careful not to wake her parents. Shadow sat beside the Healer, her belly filled with butterflies as she thought of what Luna would say.

"She hasn't gotten better. In fact, I think she has gotten worse. Her fever keeps climbing, and she still refuses to eat. Those bumps on her skin are worrying me, too. That's not normal." Shadow looked at the Healer, eyes wide.

"Did you give her herbs for her fever? Why won't it go down?" Shadow asked. Luna just shook her head, dismayed.

"I've done everything I can. Plus, no matter how much water I send Oak to fetch for her, she remains dehydrated. I don't know what else to do," Luna admitted, defeated. The Healer hung her head with shame, and Shadow could tell that she felt useless. Shadow rested her tail on Luna's flank.

"It's okay, Luna. I know that you're doing your best," Shadow said, though she only half meant it. *What use is the Healer if they don't know how to help the sick?*

"I'll try more herbs once she wakes up," Luna spoke, then buried her face in her paws, dismissing Shadow. Shadow stood and slipped out of the den. She hoped that Oak would come out soon. The last thing the pack needed right now was to worry about them both. Shadow trotted over to the prey pile, though she wasn't hungry. Sighing, she took a bird and walked over to her den, lying outside of it, watching the wolves around her. She forced herself to eat, bushing out her fur once more against the cold as a breeze blew through the clearing.

Dark gray clouds rolled in overhead and it began to snow. Shadow gazed up in wonder as thick snowflakes fell, lightly at first, but soon more thickly until they began to coat the ground. The wolves around her gave gasps and groans as the snow came down, signaling the start of winter. Shadow watched as one of the snowflakes landed on her nose, melting quickly. It began to coat her pelt. Not wanting to get wet, Shadow slipped into her den, thankful for its warmth. She sat alone for a while before she heard a noise outside.

Miku poked his head in. "Room for me?" he asked. Shadow nodded and moved over to make a spot. Miku crawled inside and curled up next to Shadow. "I didn't want you to be alone, especially given Storm's condition," Miku said.

Shadow's eyes widened. "How do you know?" she asked.

He sniffed. "Every wolf knows. Oak announced it earlier. I hope it isn't too bad. He didn't really give details," Miku said, a troubled look in his eyes as he leaned his head on Shadow's shoulder. Shadow took a shaky breath before telling him about Storm's symptoms, and Luna's confusion.

"All we can do is pray that she gets better. Er…I mean, she will get better, but, you know, just in case," Miku said. Shadow silenced him by burying her nose in his fur and letting out a sad whimper.

"I'm scared," Shadow whispered, listening to the wind whip outside her den.

"It's okay, Shadow. Everything will be okay," Miku promised, and Shadow closed her eyes, hoping, praying, that he was right.

Shadow was walking between Sparrow and Miku, her head low, ears pinned to her head. They were hunting. Shadow's breath puffed out in front of her like a cloud, then disappeared, to be replaced with another breath. It had been nearly three days since Storm had been confined to the Healer's den, too weak to move. She was slowly getting worse, her fever never breaking, her fur coming off in clumps, and anything she ate coming right back up again. Shadow was worried sick about her, barely even able to hunt without being distracted. Luna was giving Storm the best treatment possible – changing her bedding every day, constantly fetching her water from the stream, and trying, again and again, to get the she-wolf to keep the herbs down. Oak spent almost all his time with her, keeping what was left of her fur clean, and trying to get her to eat. Shadow and Kele visited as much as they could, but most of the time they were either hunting, marking borders, or strengthening the dens. Shadow hadn't slept well at all, her thoughts always drifting back to Storm, who was lying in the Healer's den, sleeping most of the time, but constantly in pain. Now, Shadow walked distractedly between the two males, her thoughts wandering, eyes locked on the ground.

Suddenly, Sparrow's tail shot up in the air, and Miku and Shadow stopped, watching as he lowered himself to the ground and shot into the bushes, a loud squeal of prey following. Sparrow returned with a large hare in his jaws, his eyes shining. "Nice catch," Miku congratulated, while Shadow simply nodded her head in agreement. Sparrow dipped his head and they pushed on, walking quietly through the wet leaves. Even though it snowed overnight, the snow had melted quickly and now the ground was damp and cold. They continued onward for a while before the scent of blood bathed Shadow's tongue, and she looked up. Miku and Sparrow also looked up, confused. Shadow raised her tail for them to stay put and lowered her head, stalking forward quietly.

She peeked through the underbrush to see a large cat, probably half her size, gnawing on a rabbit carcass, its white paws and muzzle covered in crimson blood. The cat was looking around wildly as if it knew that it was on wolf territory but didn't want to leave. Shadow let out a low growl and barked, letting the cat know that she was there and that it didn't belong here. The cat whirled on her, hissing, baring its large teeth. It was brown with spots of black covering its pelt, its eyes a dark brown. It also had a short, bobbed tail and a white underbelly. Shadow pushed through the brush, growling, baring her teeth and raising her tail, showing that she wasn't afraid. The cat sized her up before turning tail and fleeing, its long legs bunching and stretching as it ran.

"Let's make sure that it leaves the territory," Shadow barked to Miku and Sparrow as they chased after it, letting out snarls of anger. Shadow followed them, chasing after the cat until it got to the edge of their territory. Shadow then stopped and watched it run off before turning to Miku and Sparrow to tell them to spread out and hunt before returning home. They agreed and slipped into the bushes, heads low. Shadow tipped her head up and sniffed the air, scenting a rabbit upwind. She lowered her head and trotted towards the scent, poking her head through the ferns. There she spotted two rabbits eating next to each other, their ears pricked, listening for signs of predators. Shadow decided that she would kill the closest one quickly, then chase the other one if it began to run.

Shadow bunched her muscles, held her breath, and burst silently from the bushes. She broke the neck on the first one, killing it, and watched as the second rabbit began to run, squealing, into the bushes. She snarled and gave chase, catching it quickly and grabbing it by the foot, jerking it backward. It squeaked with pain and fear before Shadow dug her teeth into its neck and crushed its windpipe, blood soaking her muzzle and dripping onto her paws. When she was sure the animal was dead, she carried it back to collect her earlier kill and returned to where she had left Miku and Sparrow. Her mother was momentarily forgotten.

They returned to the den site with their jaws were full of food and their eyes bright. They dropped their prey on the pile and then Sparrow left Miku and Shadow, going to talk with Heather. Shadow sat with Miku under a bramble bush, thankful for the sun shining on her pelt. Miku brought over a fat squirrel and they ate, talking. "I wonder what this winter will be like. I hope it isn't too cold," Miku said, glancing up at the sky.

"Yes," she agreed.

"At least the prey is still fat," Miku said, nodding at the squirrel that they were eating.

"True. These squirrels are so big, they could nearly feed a whole wolf!" Shadow exclaimed, and they began to laugh. It felt good to laugh again.

"Hopefully, Lynx's pups will be old enough soon to become Learners. They're almost as big as her! The Newborns' den must be crowded," Miku said, glancing at Lynx, who was resting next to her pups as they played. "I wonder if I will become a Trainer. I would like that, but maybe Oak would want to choose the more experienced wolves, like you," Miku continued, glancing at Shadow.

"If you wanted to train a pup, I'm sure Oak would let you," Shadow said kindly.

"I suppose. I wonder when some wolf is going to bring new pups into the pack," Miku said after a few moments of chewing. Shadow blinked at him.

"Pups in the winter? That probably wouldn't be best," Shadow pointed out. Miku nodded in agreement.

"You're right. It would probably be best to wait until spring…Don't you think?" Miku asked, and Shadow's face warmed self-consciously.

"Yes. That would probably be best," She agreed, staring down at her prey.

"Shadow, are you okay?" Miku asked, and Shadow looked at him, smiling.

"Yes, I'm fine," Shadow started, but was cut off as Max came running from the Healer's den, his eyes wide with fear.

"Shadow, come quickly. Storm is…not well," Max exclaimed as he approached. Shadow was on her paws in an instant, Miku beside her.

"Thank you, Max," Shadow said, her breath catching in her throat. A stone dropped in her belly with fear at what she would find in the Healer's den. Max raced off to find Kele, who was eating beside Breeze at the other end of the clearing. Shadow raced to the Healer's den, turning to Miku as he raced beside her. "Stay out here," she said and slipped inside without waiting for an answer. In the dim light, she saw Storm lying in her bed, her eyes half-open and glazed over. Oak was beside her, a forlorn look in his eyes, ears laid back with sorrow. Luna was sitting on the other side of Storm, trying frantically to ease some herbs into her mouth. Storm wasn't moving except for the faint rise and fall of her chest, as if she couldn't hear or see Luna. Shadow raced to her mother's side, sitting beside Oak, her eyes wide and cloudy with tears.

"Storm… Please, no… You have to survive!" Shadow pleaded, her body beginning to shake. Storm's eyes rolled to lock with Shadow's, and Shadow could see the pain in the depths of her mother's eyes.

"I love you, Shadow," her mother croaked, and she took one last raspy breath before going still.

"Storm… No! No, no, please, mom… You can't die! I love you. I love you so much," Shadow whimpered. She looked into Storm's lifeless eyes. Shadow had never felt so helpless in her life. "Come back!" She wailed, then broke down, blubbering into her mother's fur. Oak was crying silently beside her, his face also buried in his mate's fur. His body was shaking, his shoulders rising and falling as he silently sobbed.

Shadow wept, tears rolling down her face as she thought of all the times she and her mother had together. Shadow let out her tears, not caring that Luna was watching. Kele appeared a moment later and crumpled beside Shadow at the sight of their mother's lifeless body. Shadow looked at him through blurry eyes and saw his face was twisted with anguish and denial.

"No… No, she can't be dead…" Kele choked as he began to sob. Storm's fur was soon wet with tears as Shadow curled up with grief shattering her heart. Luna began to ease Shadow away from Storm. Shadow's voice was hoarse and her eyes were red.

"Eat this, Shadow. It will help you with your pain," Luna said sadly, motioning towards a cupped leaf that was filled with a thick liquid that smelled like honey. Shadow reluctantly licked up the herb, the honey soothing her throat as it went down. Almost instantly, she began to feel sleepy, and Luna laid her down in a bed that was already made. Shadow cried softly to herself before falling into a light, troubled sleep. Later that night, after the pack had mourned, Storm's body was buried by Kele and Oak. Luna gave Shadow more of the sleeping herb, and she slept with Miku at her side.

Shadow sat outside her den, a fresh squirrel laying by her paws. She hadn't eaten for more than a day, but she didn't feel hungry. It had been two days since Storm's death, and Shadow was still in denial. The pack was mourning. Oak sat in his den most of the time, complaining to Luna about aching bones or splitting headaches. Shadow did her best to run the pack, though her heart was still shattered by the loss of her mother. Luna was still confused about what the sickness could have been. Shadow now sat silently beside Miku, picking at the vole that lay in front of her. *If only I had noticed her pain sooner, maybe I could have saved her,* Shadow thought. *Why didn't you tell us sooner, Storm?* She thought angrily, scraping her claws along the ground. She winced, feeling tears begin to well up in her eyes once more. *Maybe this is all a dream, and I will wake up sooner or later. Maybe Storm is still alive…*

"Shadow, eat," Miku urged, knocking her out of her thoughts. Shadow ignored him, laid down on her belly and rested her head on her paws, trying to hide her anger and pain. It was a cold day, and the chilly wind buffeted her fur as she sat, drearily watching the birds fly overhead. The sky was blanketed with a thick layer of dark gray clouds, hiding the sun and casting shadows down on the forest. Miku sighed and moved closer to Shadow, pressing against her and licking her shoulder soothingly. "Please, Shadow, I need you to eat. I know that it's hard to lose your mother..." Miku said, glancing at Heather, who was sitting with Sparrow under a birch tree. "But you are the Beta of your pack, and right now they need you to stay strong. If I could take your place, you know I would. But I can't. You are the only one who can do it. I have said before that I will stand with you through thick and thin, and I'm standing with you now, to help you get through this." Miku's voice was firm and confident. Shadow looked at him with tears welling up in her eyes.

"I can't do it, Miku," she cried softly, pressing her face into his fur. They sat in silence for a few moments, Miku comforting her, even though no words were spoken.

"Yes, you can," he said softly. Shadow pulled away, sighing. She didn't want to be angry at him, but right now, it seemed like she was angry at the world. She ate her squirrel in a few bites, forcing herself to swallow, even though her stomach felt full.

"I'm going on a walk," Shadow said. She stood and walked slowly away from Miku, her head down and tail trailing in the dirt. She slipped out of the clearing and into the open forest, her fur bushed as a cold gust of wind blew against her face. She walked aimlessly before finding that her paws had led her to her mother's burial place beside a birch tree. Ferns grew peacefully around the gravesite. Shadow felt herself shaking, then she sat down and began to cry. Tears flowed down her face and dripped off her nose, changing the color of the dirt that they splattered on the ground. "Oh, mom...I miss you," Shadow said softly, sniffing, tail tucked between her legs. "I can't do this without you." Crying silently, Shadow sat beside her mother's grave, the cold wind chilling her to the bone.

As Shadow was preparing to return to her packmates, Oak emerged from the bushes. His eyes were glazed from heartbreak and lack of sleep. He limped over to Shadow as if his joints were stiff, and sat beside her. His head was bowed. Shadow sat in silence with her father for a long while, mourning their loss. Finally, Oak straightened and turned to Shadow, his eyes tired. Old.

"Shadow," Oak began, and Shadow noticed that his voice was raspy as if he had aged two years in the past two days. "It is time for me to leave the pack." Shadow looked up at him, head tilted to the side, distraction clouded in her mind. *What does he mean by "leave the pack?"* She thought. "I have grown old and lame. I cannot hunt, fight, or lead anymore. I'm holding the pack down," Oak spoke calmly, and Shadow's eyes widened.

"Oak, no! What do you mean? You are still strong. As strong as you always were. I know that Storm is gone, but—" Oak cut her off, his tail silencing her.

"It is important to do what is best for the pack. Always," Oak insisted. Shadow stared at him, not able to bear the thought of the loss of her father.

"But… You could retire and become an Elder! That way, you won't have to leave me or Kele…" Shadow was pleading now, tears filling her eyes. Oak looked sad, his face showing his pain.

"No, Shadow. I cannot live any longer with the loss of my mate. I would only be taking precious prey from the wolves who really need it." Shadow shook her head slowly, trying to swallow the fear creeping up inside of her. *If you leave, that means* I *will become Alpha… I'm not ready for that!* But no matter how hard she tried Shadow knew that she would not be able to change his mind. His gaze softened and he nudged her gently. Shadow knew it would be the last time she ever felt his touch. "You are strong and capable, Shadow. More than any member of this pack. You have a sense of the future and can lead this pack to a better life. If I didn't know that you could do this, I would not be saying it." Oak stood up slowly, grimacing with pain. "I will always be with you, even if you cannot see me," he said and smiled sadly. "I love you, Shadow, and I trust that you will lead this pack well." Oak rested his chin on her head, and she breathed in his scent, a tear sliding down her cheek.

"I love you, Oak," she breathed as Oak turned and walked away. He faded from sight into the falling snow, his scent already beginning to abate. Shadow stared after him, the feeling dawning on her that she would never see her father again. Her head drooped at the loss of both of her parents and she was filled with overwhelming sadness. She turned to Storm's grave and whispered, "What do I do, mom?" When she got no answer, she stood and took a deep breath. A sudden assurance filled her. She felt a determination to lead her pack well, in honor of her father, who left his pack to die to ensure its future. She wiped her tears away with a paw, looking up into the falling snow. She then took a deep breath and let out a long, low, sorrowful howl, followed by a brighter, more hopeful howl. Her spirit raised, she lifted her tail with determination and strode back to her pack.

Acknowledgments

My deepest thanks go to my grandpa, who gave so much of his time editing and helping me keep this book moving along. He was constantly pushing me to continue writing, and I wouldn't have been able to finish, let alone publish, this book without him. He is the backbone of this book and I am forever grateful for what he has done to help me fulfill my dream of becoming a writer.

Thank you to my parents, who helped fashion ideas to make the book interesting and never stopped believing in me. They were always supportive and helped give me the courage to share my story with the world. It would take a lifetime to repay everything they have done for me. Thank you.

I would like to thank my little sister for all the help she gave me in coming up with the characters' names and for cheerleading along the way. She always spoke her mind about what I wrote and was quick to point out what I should change. She liked to look over my shoulder while I typed, which I found somewhat annoying at the time, but in the end, I appreciate it.

Thank you to Morgen Butts, Kassea Boche, and Nick Miller for taking the time to review *Shadow* and provide valuable insights. Their opinions are greatly appreciated, and their advice was heeded.

About the Author

E.M. Lynch has used her lifelong fascination for wolves as a basis to fulfill her passion for writing. She began work on *Shadow* at age 12 and published it a year later. Ms. Lynch lives in rural Minnesota with her parents, siblings, a golden retriever, and two cats. In addition to writing, she plays soccer for her high school varsity team (she plays defense) and enjoys spending time with her family, especially in the outdoors and at the lake.